QUEEN OF KINGS

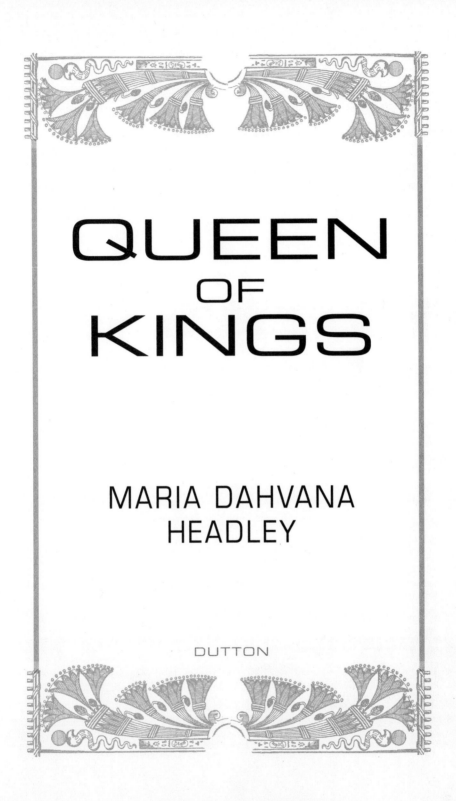

QUEEN
OF
KINGS

MARIA DAHVANA HEADLEY

DUTTON

DUTTON
Published by Penguin Group (USA) Inc.
375 Hudson Street, New York, New York 10014, U.S.A.
Penguin Group (Canada), 90 Eglinton Avenue East, Suite 700, Toronto, Ontario M4P 2Y3, Canada
(a division of Pearson Penguin Canada Inc.); Penguin Books Ltd, 80 Strand, London WC2R 0RL,
England; Penguin Ireland, 25 St Stephen's Green, Dublin 2, Ireland (a division of Penguin Books Ltd);
Penguin Group (Australia), 250 Camberwell Road, Camberwell, Victoria 3124, Australia (a division of
Pearson Australia Group Pty Ltd); Penguin Books India Pvt Ltd, 11 Community Centre, Panchsheel
Park, New Delhi—110 017, India; Penguin Group (NZ), 67 Apollo Drive, Rosedale, North Shore 0632,
New Zealand (a division of Pearson New Zealand Ltd); Penguin Books (South Africa) (Pty) Ltd,
24 Sturdee Avenue, Rosebank, Johannesburg 2196, South Africa

Penguin Books Ltd, Registered Offices: 80 Strand, London WC2R 0RL, England

Published by Dutton, a member of Penguin Group (USA) Inc.

First printing, May 2011
10 9 8 7 6 5 4 3 2 1

 REGISTERED TRADEMARK—MARCA REGISTRADA

LIBRARY OF CONGRESS CATALOGING-IN-PUBLICATION DATA

Headley, Maria Dahvana, 1977–
Queen of kings / Maria Dahvana Headley.
p. cm.
ISBN 978-0-525-95217-6
1. Cleopatra, Queen of Egypt, d. 30 B.C.—Fiction.   2. Queens—Egypt—Fiction.
3. Egypt—History—332–30 B.C.—Fiction.   I. Title.
PS3608.E233Q44   2011
813'.6—dc22
2011004281

Printed in the United States of America
Set in JansonTextLTStd
Designed by Leonard Telesca

PUBLISHER'S NOTE
This book is a work of fiction. Names, characters, places, and incidents either are the product of the
author's imagination or are used fictitiously, and any resemblance to actual persons, living or dead, business establishments, events, or locales is entirely coincidental.

For Robert Schenkkan
Chief Wonder of My World,
On whose behalf I'd gladly negotiate with any Gods,
And battle any monsters.

QUEEN OF KINGS

Prologue

I, Nicolaus the Damascene, once philosopher to a king, once tutor to the children of a queen, once biographer to an emperor, now live in exile. I move toward the tomb, whether to journey into Hades or to wander as a spirit lamenting on the shores of Acheron. I cannot say which gods will claim me, for I left behind Damascus and her gods long ago for those of Egypt and of Rome. My body will end its days here at Avernus, unmourned.

The one thing I know with certainty is that she will come for me.

By virtue of position, I have been witness to more than any other man. I have seen rooms filled with gold, and streets stacked with bones. I have seen lakes turn to blood. I have watched the moon dance on the fingertips of witches, and stars extinguishing their lights at the behest of immortals. I have seen the beasts of the wilderness commanded into war by a woman. I have seen a lioness become a queen, and a queen become a monster.

I have seen things I cannot say aloud, though I am bound to write them here.

I will recount the story the emperor forbade me to tell. I will write the truth as far as I know it, in desperate hope that this may be enough. I cannot fight alone. All I have are words.

May these words be enough to save you.

The old scholar paused in his writing, tracing his fingers over the twisting branch of scar that ran from his palm to his shoulder and down across his back. It had been there so long that it seemed an original part of him, but it gave him pain still, particularly when the thunder came. Outside the sibyl's cave, the air smelled of storms, and Nicolaus's scar lit with knowledge of the weather. There was a tremor in his hand that nearly obliterated his writing, and when he drew breath, it was with difficulty. He'd delayed almost too long. She walked the earth, and there was nothing he could do to stop her now, nothing but this.

He willed his thoughts back to the Egypt of his youth. The pale, marble-paved passageways of Alexandria, the flashing-eyed women, the feel of his sandaled feet against the road. The gilded barges and shining faces. He'd come to the center of the world. All these things, in memory, held a sweetness, a tenderness that he knew would flee him as he wrote. That far-off past was a clear pool, and his subsequent history was a measure of dark ink fouling the waters. Or blood, perhaps. His memories were stained with red.

He'd been an innocent back then, convinced of immortality, if not of the flesh, then of the words. He'd thought himself a writer of great truths, imagining his histories held in the hands of young scholars, his name inscribed on monuments, his tomb garlanded.

Those dreams were long gone. Nicolaus had seen the future, and it was not a place for poets.

He thought of the Museion, where he'd studied with his friends, working, so arrogantly, on what he believed would be the first and only true history of the universe. He'd finished it, a hundred and forty-four books of it, only to watch them burn. He'd written too much of the truth, where he ought to have written lies. He'd imagined himself a friend of the emperor and therefore untouchable, and he had been wrong.

Nicolaus was lucky. The Romans had never found his real work, and for this he was thankful. It was this work he held in his hands now, as he tried to summon the courage to finish writing what was necessary.

He thought of her, of the graceful beckoning of her jeweled hand, when she'd set him the task that would ruin his life as well as her own.

"Find me a spell," she whispered, as alive in his memory as though she stood before him. He smelled the spicy perfume of her skin, the honey on her breath. "A spell for a summoning."

It was not even a question that he would help her. She smiled at him, and he looked into her beautiful, dark eyes, seeing her hope, seeing her need.

The last time he'd seen her, her eyes had been changed into something quite different.

He promised then to do her bidding, and he did it willingly. How could he not? Nicolaus hadn't been the first man to sacrifice his own life for hers, but he had also sacrificed the lives of countless others. For more than fifty years now, he'd watched helplessly as the prophecies came to pass, knowing she'd scarcely begun.

He'd seen the future in his emperor's eyes. The ruler, in delirium, sleepless and haunted, had confided his visions to Nicolaus, swearing him to secrecy, but there was no point in it now. The emperor Augustus, he who had controlled the world, or thought he had, was dead, and Nicolaus was soon to follow.

The scholar shuddered, feeling frost skittering over his bones. His scar throbbed. *Fatale monstrum*, the Romans had called her. "Fatal omen." Or, if one were to think of the double meaning of the word, and this had certainly been the intention, "fatal monster."

Mistress of the end of the world.

And yet he knew her. Her heart had not always been dark. Perhaps it was not wholly dark even now.

Nicolaus wished that he'd died years before, knowing nothing of the things he was bound to tell today. His life had been long, and his memory remained perfect. This was his particular punishment.

Now he was the only one left who knew the truth. The only one, save her. Though it was sacrilege, though it was foolhardy to set down the words, he had to give warning to the world to come. To leave this life without doing so would be an irredeemable act, and his soul was already weighted with sins. They'd know more in the future. They'd learn. Perhaps they would learn enough to save themselves from the monster that Nicolaus, in his idiotic youth, had helped release into the world.

He looked into the sky above Avernus for a moment. The sun hung at the horizon, a fiery orb, and above it, the gathering clouds glowed copper and violet. Lightning slashed through one of them. The moon rose, yellow and ominous, even as the sun fell, struggling against the night and thunder.

Everything was at stake.

The people of the future would not know what was coming for them, not unless Nicolaus told this story. They'd have no defense. He thought for a moment of that world, the world he'd never see. It was a future so distant that almost nothing would remain of the things he had loved. Augustus had told him of his visions: buildings crumbling, cities disappearing beneath the waves, wars and bloodshed. Strange and shining machines, and untongued masses, all speaking the languages of barbarians.

The emperor had seen the future, and she was in it.

Fatale monstrum, Nicolaus repeated silently. Her name and her destiny. He would be gone by the time it came to pass, and yet he had a part still to play.

The scholar lit his lamp and picked up the stylus and tablet. He drew in a deep breath. This would be his last work. He must get it right.

> *Let this be the true and accurate history of the falsified death of Cleopatra, queen of Egypt, in the first year of the reign of the emperor Gaius Julius Caesar Augustus, and of the wondrous and terrible acts which followed thereafter.*
>
> *Let this be the story of the rising of a queen and the falling of a world.*

BOOK OF RITUALS

For they report also, that she had hidden poyson in a hollow raser which she carried in the heare of her head: and yet there was no marke seen of her bodie, or any signe discerned that she was poisoned, neither also did they finde this serpent in her tombe . . . Some say also, that they found two litle pretie bytings in her arme, scant to be discerned . . . And thus goeth the report of her death.

—Plutarch, translation by Sir Thomas North
Lives of the Noble Grecians and Romans

1

The boy sprinted down the cobbled streets, leaping and dodging, trying to make up for the delay the chaos in the city had caused him. Alexandria was filled with the bruised and bloodied soldiers of Mark Antony's infantry, and the boy flung himself between their bodies, here slipping alongside the flat of a sword, here ducking to avoid a flailing fist. This was his own city, and he knew the secret pathways to his destination. He flung open a street-side door and bolted through the household within, hoisting himself out a window in the back and shouting his apologies to the old mother he'd disturbed. He somersaulted over the sill, landing on his feet and bouncing as he resumed his run, imagining himself at the head of a rushing army, a raider storming the gates of some exotic city.

No one pursued the boy, but he was employed today, a salaried messenger, and the man who hired him had emphasized that speed was necessary.

His heart swelled with pride as he felt the small purse clenched in his fist. He'd receive the other half of his fee when the message he carried was delivered. The assignment had been pure luck. They'd grabbed him by the shoulder as he was returning from the countryside, where he'd been visiting a friend without his mother's knowledge.

Outside the city walls near the hippodrome, the Romans waited in their tents, and inside the city, the soldiers who still served Antony milled about, drunk with defeat, crowding themselves against all of the other civilians.

It was all the boy could do to keep from being trampled as he made his rushing way through the Jewish quarter near Cleopatra's Palaces and into the Greek portion of Alexandria. He flew past the Museion, where the scholars could be seen bending over scrolls, still at their work despite the fall of the city. There was the scholar who tutored the queen's children, standing in the middle of the courtyard, arguing with one of his cohorts, both of them red-faced and waving their hands in the air. The boy wondered if the physicians were still working in the Museion's buildings. He'd heard glorious stories of dissections, corpses smuggled in through hidden doorways, blood pooling in the stones of the streets. It was a thrilling thought.

The boy made his way through the center of Alexandria, where the markets were transacting business, as though this were not a city under siege. There was money to be made on warfare, and soldiers, even in defeat, thirsted. The boy dashed past the tempting stalls, the soothsayers and the makers of toys, the sellers of toasted nuts and the dancers stamping their feet and flinging colored scarves in the air.

He gazed longingly into a brothel, pushing his chin into the doorway and inhaling the scent of perfume.

"You're bad for business, boy," said a scowling courtesan, and smacked him smartly on the ear, escorting him back out into the street.

The lighthouse still shone on Pharos island just offshore, and the boy grinned up at the glowing white limestone facade of Alexandria's marvel. It was said that the light harnessed the power of the sun, that it could be directed to shine onto enemy vessels far out on the water, causing them to burst spontaneously into flame. The boy wondered why the lighthouse had not been directed to destroy the Roman ships that way. Perhaps there had been too many of them.

At last, the boy arrived at the alley in the Old City that would lead him to his destination. It was easily recognized, guarded as it was by armed legionaries, the only soldiers in the city who were not drunk, and the only people in the area who were not Egyptian.

A legionary appeared in front of the boy, his arms crossed over his chest. The boy looked up to meet the man's eyes.

"I have an urgent message," he said.

"What message?" the soldier asked.

"I cannot speak with anyone but the general, Mark Antony," the boy said.

"Who sent you?" another soldier asked.

"I come on behalf of the queen," the boy replied, reciting the words exactly as he'd been instructed. "I serve Cleopatra."

⇒ 2 ⇐

Twelve hours earlier, Mark Antony poured wine for all his servants and soldiers, toasting their bravery and bidding them good fortune if they chose to leave him, and a good fight if they chose to stay for the final battle.

As the whores arrived to comfort those who had wartime wages, Antony walked the streets of Alexandria, making his way back to the palace, past the guards and slaves, past the sad-faced statues of former rulers, kings and queens, princes and conquerors. Past the bedchambers where his children slept, innocent of the coming fall. Antony looked in at their faces, those of the twins and of his youngest son. The two eldest children, one his and one his wife's, had already been sent from the city. What would become of them? He dared not think of it. It was not the Roman way, to kill royal children, or at least it had not been thus far. He did not wish to think that things had changed since his departure from Rome's service. Still, this was war. He'd been the conqueror in the past. It was strange to suddenly be the conquered.

Cleopatra awaited him in the doorway of their bedchamber.

"It is not over," she said, breaking his trance. He shook off his thoughts and took her in his arms, relishing, even in these dark times, her shape against him.

"It is," he told her. "It will be."

He ran his hands down her back and over the roundness of her hips, pulling her tightly to his chest. Grief nearly overtook him then. If he did not win the next morning, the Romans—his own Romans—would tear her from him, and there would be nothing he could do to stop them.

Antony had been married three times before and had even thought he loved before, but he had been wrong. This woman was all he wanted. She was his general, his queen. The gods had willed it.

Antony put out a hand to run his fingers along Cleopatra's throat and over her collarbone, and she tilted her head, watching him as he touched her. Her body had borne three children for him, another for Julius Caesar, and still, at thirty-eight, she looked like a young girl, with her smooth, bronze skin, her humorous mouth, her dark, long-lashed eyes. He could see the beginnings of lines around those eyes. The passage of time became her. Her curves had gotten softer, though she was still slender. She'd never looked more beautiful, even in her simple nightdress, her face without its customary paints, her fingers and arms stripped of their jewels. He untied the knots at her shoulders and let the gown fall.

She walked to the window and drew back the curtains to let the full moon shine in on them.

"A good omen," Cleopatra whispered, smiling at him. "We will win this war."

He looked at her as she stood naked in the moonlight. Her straight spine, her golden skin, her black hair still twisted up with glittering pins.

"We *will* win this war," she repeated, her tone suddenly fierce.

"I fear we've already lost it," he said.

"Perhaps I know something you do not," Cleopatra replied.

"Is there a legion hidden in the palace cellars?" he asked, and laughed bitterly. He didn't have enough men. He had known it from the beginning, and he'd fought anyway.

"The gods are on our side. I can feel it," she said, her jaw tensing with determination. She suddenly leaned out the window, looking at something passing on the street below, her brow furrowed.

Antony rose to see what she was looking at, but she whirled, guiding him away from the window and pushing him back onto the bed.

"Don't look out there," she said. "Nothing is wrong. The city sleeps. Look at me."

Antony wondered for a moment what it was she kept him from seeing, but she stroked him, kissed him, swore to him that together they would prevail.

As ever, he was unable to resist her. In truth, he did not wish to. If this was the end, then let it be spent with his beloved, his hands memorizing the smooth hollow at the top of her thigh, his lips singing the silken folds of her. Antony marveled at the miracle of it, feeling her take a breath in even as he cried out, her fingers clenching his shoulders and her muscles tightening around him.

"Again," she whispered, and he saw that her eyes were full of tears. He kissed her face until they were gone.

They made love for hours, even as the sounds outside the window grew louder and louder, music and laughing, screaming and shouting.

"I am yours," she swore again and again, and he believed her, took strength from her.

"As I am yours," he told her. "Until we both are dead."

"And thereafter?" she asked.

"And thereafter," he answered, holding her tightly, feeling his heart beating, and feeling hers as well.

At dawn, he kissed Cleopatra good-bye and marched his remaining troops through the Canopic Gate and toward the hippodrome, resolved to meet his death with honor.

He watched from a hillside as his fleet, rowing in galleys from the harbor, threw themselves courageously against Octavian's force. Maybe Cleopatra was right. They might win yet.

He drove his fist into the air, preparing a battle cry, when, out on the water, his men suddenly raised their oars to salute the enemy. A moment later, his Egyptian legion hoisted the Roman flag and joined with Caesar's fleet. The two armies rowed back toward Alexandria, attacking the city together.

Antony spun to consult with the head of his Egyptian cavalry, and the man finished the war with a single sentence.

"Cleopatra belongs to Rome now," the man said. "Egypt's armies go where Cleopatra goes."

"What do you mean?" Antony asked. The words did not make sense. Egypt's armies served Antony, and Cleopatra's only goal was to defend her city.

The man looked at Antony with a pitying expression for a moment. "Your queen has betrayed you, sir. We no longer serve you."

"Liar!" Antony shouted, tearing his sword from its scabbard to strike the man for his impudence, but he was already galloping away with his company, leaving Antony and his last loyal soldiers hopelessly outnumbered by enemy Romans and by his own former men. Still, they did not take him prisoner. They did not kill him. Why not? Whose orders did they follow?

Surely not hers. She would never do such a thing. Never.

With the remainder of his infantry, Antony attacked Octavian's forces near the hippodrome, but he was forced back into the city in retreat, even as the ghastly understanding sank into him. Antony staggered as he made his way into Alexandria, scarcely noticing the enemy forces pushing their way through the gates behind him.

Betrayed. The knowledge boiled inside him.

"*I am yours,*" she'd sworn, but she had lied.

There was no other explanation for what had happened.

Cleopatra had directed the Egyptian legions to leave him, commanded his own men to abandon him. She'd sold him to save herself.

What would she receive in return?

Had she done with Octavian as she had done with Julius Caesar when he'd marched into Alexandria? Smuggled herself into his camp and wooed him? Caesar had given her the throne. Octavian might let her keep it, given the right bribe. This was a personal war more than a political one. Octavian wanted Antony's shame, and what better way than to take his wife and all of his loyal soldiers? To laugh as Antony stood alone and beaten?

His men surrounded him, drawing him into the warrens of the Old City and hiding his recognizable figure behind their shields.

"What have you done?" he screamed, again and again, and his guards, pressing him into a decrepit building, surrounding the building with their swords, could not tell whether he referred to his queen or to himself.

→ 3 ←

The queen of Egypt willed herself to press the point of the knife deeper into her palm. Slowly, blood rose to the wound, and with it, a strange and terrible feeling. For an instant, she felt as though everything she loved was sealed away from her, forever trapped on the other side of the mausoleum walls. She stopped, her heart pounding.

No. They were only fears, and she was running out of time. Determined, Cleopatra cut more quickly until blood trickled over her fingers and into the goblet she held to catch it.

She glanced down at the incision from life line to heart line, trying not to tremble. She was doing the right thing.

There was no other choice. Her enemy was camped just outside the Gate of the Sun, his forces overwhelming the remaining resistance of Egypt.

Cleopatra must perform this spell or lose the kingdom. Her country had once been a place of magicians and gods. It would be again. She would not surrender.

She stood, her hair unbound, her feet bare and painted, her eyes rimmed in thick kohl, in the center of an intricate, faceted symbol incorporating countless glyphs etched in pigments. At each locus, priceless pyramids of fine-ground ebony, cinnamon, and lapis balanced, ready to be dispersed with a breath. Here, a scarab drawn in dust of malachite, and here, a sun disc poured in saffron. Polished metal bowls placed at intervals around the room smoked with clouds of incense, a perfume both sweet and biting. Her crown, with its three golden cobras, shone in the lamplight.

Cleopatra shivered, noticing the chill of the marble beneath her feet. The blood welling over her fingertips was the warmest thing in the room. She was alone in the mausoleum she'd built with Antony, the safest and most secure location in the city, or so she hoped. Cleopatra's two handmaidens kept watch over the stairs that led to the second floor of the structure, though there was little need for that. The crypt, designed not just for burial but as a fortress, was two stories high, and the lower floor had no windows or doors, just thick, smooth stone walls. The top floor had only one entrance, a barred window some forty lengths above a man's head, accessible only from the interior. The place was unfinished—Cleopatra and Antony had not expected to need it so soon—but it was complete enough to be formidable.

All the treasures of Alexandria were piled around her, the entirety of Egypt's war chest, along with firepots, papyrus, and wood, stacked from end to end of the chamber, the better to kindle the flames should things not go as Cleopatra planned.

Everything was ready. Everything but Antony, who was somewhere outside the city walls, stubbornly fighting a last, hopeless battle against the invaders. He belonged here, beside her, but time had run out. Two hours before, she'd sent a messenger running across the city to tell her husband that all was not lost, to bid him join her, but Antony had not come.

She could not let herself think about what that might mean.

She'd woken up beside him that morning, and for a moment, looking at the lines in his sleeping face, at the gray in his beard, at the scars and bruises on his body, she felt more woman than queen. The past year had aged Antony, and where Cleopatra had always seen his courage and strength, she now saw his mortality. The time for hesitation was past, and yet, as she thought of the day ahead, of the power she planned to invoke, her heart raced with uncertainty.

Cleopatra had not told Antony what she planned to do. She knew he would not approve, and there was no time to argue with him. She was the queen. The decisions were hers alone. This was her home country, not his.

Looking at him beside her in the bed, however, she'd suddenly felt very foolish, wondering if this would be the last day she held her children, the last day she kissed her husband. She sought to summon powers unseen in thousands of years. What if she did not succeed?

Cleopatra nearly shook Antony awake with a plan to flee and take their children with them. As she put her hand on his chest to wake him, though, he opened his eyes.

"We will win this war," he told her, and smiled.

His resolve brought her duties back to her, her responsibilities to the kingdom, to her people, to her crown. Of course she could not flee. She was the queen. She must save the kingdom.

She helped Antony don his armor, kissed him good-bye, and went to her throne room to meet with her advisors as though this were a day like any other, instead of a day on which she might lose everything.

The advisors urged her to send her ancestral crown out to the conqueror, but she refused. Instead, she made a public sacrifice to assure Octavian that she was on the verge of giving Alexandria over to him. Goat. Her nostrils curled at the smell of its blood. There was no question of surrender, but it was in her interest to suggest that there was.

Now Cleopatra felt like vomiting, whether from fear or anticipation, she did not know. She'd be the first in thousands of years to perform this spell, such as it was. There were pieces missing from it, and Nicolaus, the scholar who'd translated the spell, had guessed at them. She only hoped he was right.

The scholar had refused to accompany her to the mausoleum, insisting nervously that there was no role in the spell for him. He was not wrong, she reminded herself. No one but she could perform this sacrifice. She was the ruler, the pharaoh. It was hers to do, reserved for royalty, and if it ended badly—

She must not lose courage now.

In the darkness of the siege, Cleopatra had remembered the stories of the time before Alexander. The old gods of Egypt had intervened frequently in the lives of men, savage instead of beautiful, bloodthirsty instead of thoughtful. They'd been born out of the waters of Chaos, and their natures—lust, rage, hunger—were undiluted by the rules of civilization. Cleopatra's patron goddess was Isis, but Isis was not the right deity for this task. She'd evolved over the centuries into something too much a part of the new world, too much a part of Rome.

Sekhmet, Nicolaus suggested. An older goddess, and a darker one.

The Scarlet Lady some called her. That, or the Lady of Slaughter. Sekhmet's breath was the desert wind, and her purpose was warfare. The lion-headed deity was a protector in battle, stalking over the land and destroying the enemies of the pharaoh. Death and destruction were her nectar. She was the goddess of the end of the world, the Mistress of Dread, and she drank the blood of her foes. Sekhmet would as easily drink the blood of the Romans. They would have no idea what had come for them. If Octavian thought to conquer Cleopatra, he could die trying.

Cleopatra surveyed her preparations. The goddess, in the form of an icon encrusted with coral, lapis, malachite, carnelian, bloodstone, and opal, occupied a new place of honor, enshrined near the tombs. The icon was older than anything else in the room, dating from a time long before Cleopatra's family had reigned. As for the rest, Cleopatra had spent a lifetime acquiring these treasures. More than a lifetime. The portions she hadn't obtained herself as offerings and gifts had come down from her father, and his father before him, from her queenly grandmothers and from Alexander himself. They had accrued over three hundred years, from all of Africa and Macedonia, from Italy, from India, from the waters and the deserts, from the sky and caves and stars, from the edges of the world.

All that time, Egypt had been ruled over by her family, beautiful, ferocious descendants of the gods.

It was fitting that it would be she who saved Egypt, using her own wits and talents. Her father had been a weak-willed ruler. The men before him were the same, fattening on the luxuries afforded them as kings. Cleopatra and her grandmother, on the other hand, warred and gained lands. They'd made alliances and brokered compromises. This was the culmination of Cleopatra's work.

Why, then, was she so afraid? A droplet of blood flew out from her shaking hand, spattering on the icon. She quickly pulled her hand back.

"Find me a spell," she'd ordered the scholars days before, when it had become clear that Octavian would not give up his claim on Egypt. "A spell for a summoning."

Nicolaus the Damascene, tutor to Cleopatra's twins, found this one deep in the collection, although he complained that it was not entirely complete. A part of the scroll had been lost in the fires at the Great Library of Alexandria, and what remained was unclear.

Cleopatra called upon another scholar, this one Egyptian, to assist in the translation. He startled when he saw the scroll.

"Where was this found? It should not exist. The spell is not to be used lightly," he informed her indignantly.

"Lightly?" Cleopatra asked. "I do nothing lightly. Do you believe that Egypt is governed lightly?"

"It is forbidden," he insisted.

"I am a queen. Nothing is forbidden. It is not a spell for commoners. I will do it myself."

"Then you are a fool," the Egyptian said, looking her in the eyes.

She was shocked. How dare he speak so? She was still the ruler, though she did not know how much longer that would be true.

"The lost portion of the text would contain spells to protect the pharaoh who summoned the goddess. Do not think that your station will force Sekhmet to obey your wishes. She destroys. That is her nature. Such a one will not be easily controlled."

"I thought you were a man of letters," she said. "Not a common villager. Translate the spell. What I do with it is none of your concern."

"I will not," he replied, his voice shaking. "I cannot."

"Then you will die," she warned him. How dare he delay Alexandria's defense?

"I would rather die by the hand of a queen than by the hand of this goddess."

She stared at him a moment, impressed by his bravado but disgusted by his resistance. She had him beheaded, and Nicolaus nervously translated the remainder of the scroll himself.

Now, as her blood filled the goblet, Cleopatra felt the dread she'd banished that morning rising again. She placed the goblet beside the icon and lit a pyramid of incense, breathing in deeply. *The scent of death*, she thought, and instantly corrected herself. No. It was the scent of victory.

A year had passed since the Battle of Actium, and Octavian, the man Cleopatra still thought of as the child general, had spent it mocking Egypt, while gathering his forces to invade it. The slight boy with the pale gray eyes was a child no longer.

It was sixteen years since she'd seen him last, during a visit to her then lover, Julius Caesar. She was twenty-one and the new mother of Caesarion, Caesar's first and only son. Octavian was stretched across a sickbed, a reedy, fevered skeleton by the time Caesar and Cleopatra arrived at his mother's house.

How she wished that she'd known then what she knew now: that the frail great-nephew of Rome's imperator would one day besiege her city. She might have killed him and saved herself years of pain.

Instead, she sat beside him on the bed and smoothed his fine, curly hair from off his brow. Octavian had just turned seventeen, but he looked twelve. He opened his eyes to survey Cleopatra.

"Am I dying?" the boy asked her. "They will not tell me."

"Certainly not. You will live a long life," she promised, though she could see his heart racing beneath nearly translucent skin, and the edges of his bones protruding, birdlike, all over his body.

Poor little thing, she actually thought, tucking his coverlet more tightly around him before leaving the room.

Now that poor little thing wielded more power than anyone else in the world.

Cleopatra had spent every moment of the past year at his mercy, fruitlessly bribing and extracting promises of protection from her neighboring rulers, all the while comforting her husband. Antony was guilt-ridden, blaming himself for the defeat at Actium. Cleopatra did not blame her husband. *She* was the queen. She should have known better than to do what she'd done in that battle. Funds for the continuing war had seemed the most important thing, and so, when Actium began to look like a defeat, she fled for Alexandria with her gold. Her husband followed her, his ships shielding hers, and this armed Octavian with damning propaganda, painting Antony as loyal to a foreign queen instead of to his home country.

Antony's Roman troops, some fifty thousand men betrayed by his departure, deserted him, leaving Egypt with a fraction of the legions it had previously commanded, and Octavian declared victory, shouting his triumph from end to end of the world.

Now he came nearly unopposed to the shores of Alexandria, held off only by Antony and his small remaining forces. He thought he'd already won the country.

He had not.

The ritual knife had been sharpened enough to kill without the victim noticing the wound. If the spell failed, however, it would not be Octavian who was killed. Cleopatra would never get close enough to him.

No. If the summoning failed, it would be she who died, and by her own hand. She could not let the Romans take her as their captive, a trophy to parade in the streets of Italy. She and Antony had long since agreed that if the city were taken, they'd both commit suicide. It would be the only honorable course of action left to them.

Where is he? Another jolt of panic ran through Cleopatra. It had been hours since the messenger was sent, hours since Antony should have returned.

She shook herself back to focus. She could not stop to worry. There was no time. Brilliant crimson filled the agate goblet, and Sekhmet would accept it.

She must, or Egypt would fall, and Cleopatra and Antony with her. The queen of Egypt was not ready to die.

Thus far, this war had been fought entirely between mortals.

Things were about to change.

Cleopatra threw her hands into the air as she'd practiced, spinning like the desert winds, calling up the forces that lay stored in the sand. The guttural syllables of the spell twisted, clicking and melting from her mouth, her tongue tasting the bitter words and then flinging them out into the heavens.

The door shook with a frantic pounding. Cleopatra stopped mid-phrase, the goblet poised over the bared teeth of the icon. Who was brave enough to interrupt the queen? She could think of only one person who would dare, and only one person who also knew how to access the secret passageway that led from the palaces to the mausoleum.

"Antony?" she called, relief flooding her body. She stepped out of the sacred circle and ran to the door.

It was not Antony but Cleopatra's maid, Charmian, her eyes wild. She looked at Cleopatra's bleeding hand and made a sound of dismay.

"Where is Antony?" the queen asked her, and when the maid did not answer, she shook the girl by her shoulders. "Where is he? Why has he not responded to my messenger?"

"They say he's retreated into the Old City." The girl paused. "Perhaps your message did not reach him."

"And?" Cleopatra prompted, her skin prickling with fear. Something had happened.

"They say he came through the gates mad with rage. His men joined with Rome and abandoned him in the battle. He swears that you betrayed him."

Cleopatra felt the air in the room humming, the spell half complete.

Why was this happening? What had she done wrong? She was a goddess. *The New Isis.* And Antony was her Osiris and Dionysus. Yet here she was, barricaded in her own half-finished mausoleum, caged with her treasure. Everything would be worthless without his love, everything broken.

She looked down at the knife in her hand, at her blood already staining the blade. She felt the power in the room crackling in the air. She had not yet finished the spell, but it was begun.

There was no turning back.

→ 4 ←

Mark Antony sat with his head in his hands, alternately raging and despairing. His mind flashed to the night before, to Cleopatra's body in his arms, to her lips on his, and he shook his head, trying to rid it of the image. They'd pledged to die rather than surrender, and now—

If she'd gone over to the side of Octavian, there was nothing left for Antony in heaven or on earth.

In the days since the beginning of the invasion, he'd watched four legions of soldiers, once his loyal forces, assaulting Alexandria from the west. The enemy's trumpets (and oh, what pain to call Rome his enemy, the place that had birthed him, the city that had been his mother and his love) drowned his speeches, and the men had no desire to listen.

They hated him for Actium, and they were right to do so.

He'd chosen Cleopatra over them, over everything.

"Cleopatra belongs to Rome," the head of the cavalry had said. To Rome, and not to Antony. How could he have been so stupid? She had never belonged to him.

When he'd first met her, twelve years before, she'd only recently ceased belonging to Julius Caesar. Antony had summoned the queen to Tarsus to answer charges that she had financially assisted Cassius, the enemy of Rome who'd conspired in Caesar's assassination.

At the time, Rome was poor in the wake of several years of civil war. Egypt and her queen, the scion of generations of Ptolemaic royalty, were wealthy, not just in treasure but in grain. Antony needed her support, and if he had to prod her with allegations in order to get it, he was more than willing to do so.

She sailed to him in a gilded barge with purple sails, beneath a canopy made of cloth of gold. Antony, apparently the only person in Tarsus who had not received knowledge of Cleopatra's arrival, was left alone just as he was readying himself to address a crowd. He was bewildered by the sudden exodus of merchants and customers, but as he departed the marketplace, he caught the scent of eastern perfumes on the air and found himself drawn toward the water.

Squinting into the sun, he finally detected a glittering presence, costumed as Venus, attended by servants dressed as cupids and nymphs. He sent a messenger to invite the queen to dinner. With her typical disregard for hierarchy, she instructed Antony to dine as her guest instead.

They sat together after the feast, on the deck of her barge, the lamps above them sparkling like constellations. Her voice was low and musical, and she spoke to her various servants, and to the people of Tarsus as well, each in their own tongue. She flattered him with the comment that she'd been following his military career for years. Most seductively of all, she laughed, throwing her head back in pure delight, joking with him and teasing him, as though neither of them were persons of consequence, as though they were two children who'd met in the marketplace and were playing a game of riddles.

Antony's then wife, Fulvia, had no sense of humor. He had never heard her laugh.

The evening ended in Cleopatra's bedchamber. He had no shame; any man in his senses would have done the same.

As he made his way to the queen's rooms, already stiff with anticipation, Antony gloated, thinking himself tremendously clever. He would gain power over Cleopatra, and she would gain tenderness toward him, both of which would smooth their business dealings. He fumbled into her bedroom, peering into the dark, but she wasn't there. He was running his hands over her pillows to be sure, when she leapt on him, a knife in her hands. He was so startled, he didn't make a sound as he fell to the floor.

"Rome wants to use me," she said. "Is that true?"

"Not Rome," he said, grinning. "A Roman. And only for my own purposes."

"Surrender," she said in his ear, kneeling atop him. He inhaled her scent, felt the soft skin of her thighs against his chest. Naked and shameless.

"Surrender to me," she repeated, and he nearly laughed. Did she not realize how small she was? He could span her waist with one hand. Did she not know she was a woman?

His smile faded as he felt her lashing ropes around his wrists and tying him to the bed. He could not tell if she was playing with him or warring against him. The knife was sharp, that was certain. It pressed against his jugular.

"I surrender," Antony agreed, already plotting his next move. He would flip her onto her back and disarm her, and then there would be a conversation. What did she think she was doing? He was a general. He'd summoned *her*.

"Then you are mine, Roman," she said, and he heard the smile in her voice. She slipped forward, and he tasted her wetness. He forgot the knife.

She did not untie him until morning, and when she did, she laughed at his sore wrists.

He was lost.

Years passed. Fulvia died, and he married again, forced into a political alignment with Octavian's sister, Octavia, but Cleopatra remained his true wife. Two years ago, he'd divorced Octavia and married Cleopatra in a formal ceremony. Even as Octavian declared himself an enemy, even as Antony was vilified in the streets of Rome, Cleopatra stood beside him, his equal.

Twelve years had passed since their first meeting, and it was still as glorious as it had ever been. He glanced bitterly at his arm now and could still see the white marks her teeth had left on him that first night, the scar like a tattoo commemorating a victory. As the sun rose, he'd heard the words coming from his mouth, unplanned.

"I love you," he swore.

It shocked him, but he knew it to be true, truer than anything else in his life. He held her face in his hands and looked into her eyes.

"I am yours," she told him. "You are mine, and I am yours."

Had she been lying even then?

Of course he'd chosen her over his troops. She was his wife. There was no other option, but fifty thousand men, his dearest friends, his own soldiers, had become with that one decision his enemies. They'd gone back to Rome.

Two days before, Antony, weary of sacrificing soldiers, had sent a letter challenging Caesar to man-to-man combat, the results of which would settle the war, but Octavian sent back a terse if cowardly reply: that the sort of combat Antony proposed, that of the common gladiator, was beneath the standards of Rome's first citizen and that Antony had many other options if he wished to die. Antony had not expected better. The new Caesar had no reason to fight in such a contest. He had the city surrounded already, and Octavian's army wanted Antony's blood.

"Traitor!" the men had sneered at Antony on the battlefield in the previous days. *Traitor.*

Antony's thoughts were disturbed by the sounds coming from the adjoining room.

"I come on behalf of the queen," a high, determined voice insisted. "I serve Cleopatra."

Antony swore. What was he doing here, at the mercy of her messages?

His servant Eros entered the room and widened the door to admit a young boy who reminded Antony of his own small son, Alexander Helios. Had she chosen this messenger purposefully? He would not see his children again, whatever happened here.

He imagined his wife on Octavian's arm, her purple robes, her crown. Why wouldn't she follow this new Caesar? He was to be the ruler of the world. Octavian would give her everything Antony had not. That prim boy, that self-righteous child, was to be emperor and she would rise with him. *Empress Cleopatra.*

The messenger bowed his head in respect.

"Say it," barked Antony. "You waste my time."

"The queen is dead," said the messenger.

Antony thought he'd misheard. He leaned closer to the boy, looking him in the eye.

"What did you say?"

The boy spoke slowly, as though the words were painstakingly memorized.

"The queen has killed herself. She betrayed you to the Romans, and in her guilt, she took her own life."

Antony stood very still, hearing the words echoing, and then fell to his knees, the room spinning around him. Though they'd talked of suicide, planned for it, he never imagined her dead. His mind filled with an image of her desecrated body, bruised and battered, held in the air as a trophy by Octavian's centurions.

She loved him, or she would not have died for him. If she betrayed him, it no longer mattered. He would not be apart from her for long.

"Eros," he said. His servant ushered the boy out the door, giving him some coins for his toil.

Antony removed his armor, piece by piece, until he stood before his servant in only his tunic. He passed the man his sword.

"Do you remember your promise?" he asked.

"I do," said Eros, but his eyes were uncertain. They'd been together for years, and Mark Antony had been a good master to him. He hesitated.

"Then fulfill it," Antony said, spreading his arms, exposing his chest. "Go to Octavian when this is done. End the war before any other men die. He will reward you, and you may go then and do as you will."

Eros nodded, and drew up the sword over his head, but at the last moment, he turned the blade, and stabbed it into his own body.

"No!" Antony yelled, leaping forward to catch the hilt, a second too late.

Everything was crumbling. All the precision of the Roman army, all the years spent as a general, and it had come to this: chaos, desperation, his city invaded, his beloved dead, and his manservant sprawled on the floor, blood trickling from the corner of his mouth, his eyes glazing over even as Antony knelt beside him. Antony felt his mind twisting, felt the walls tilting around him.

Outside the door of the room, another messenger demanded entrance. Antony tried to plan. He'd be taken prisoner. He'd be transported to Rome, put on trial, buried away from her.

Antony pulled the sword from Eros's body. From the pouch at his waist, he took two coins and placed them over his servant's eyes. He could do that much to help the man to his rightful place in Hades.

"I come from the queen!" The door rattled. "Cleopatra demands that I speak with Mark Antony!"

Antony swayed against the wall, hearing her name. She'd never call for him again, never laugh with him again.

"*I am yours,*" he had told her, wherever she was. "*I am yours.*"

With all his strength, he drove the blade into his stomach. A fiery pain, his body resisting death, just as his mind had. Despite the pain, he felt a sense of deep satisfaction. There would be no more uncertainty. It was done. He closed his eyes and lay slowly back on the floor, thinking of his wife.

The door shook again, someone throwing himself at it.

"The queen requests that Mark Antony join her at their mausoleum! She informs him that all is not lost!" the messenger shouted from outside the room.

"The queen is dead, you fool," his soldier shouted in return. "The queen has killed herself."

"She has not!" said the messenger. "I have just left her company. I was delayed in the city!"

The door burst open, and a horrified soldier stumbled over Eros's body and to Antony's side.

"He's wounded!" the legionary cried to the other guards outside the door, and they crowded into the room.

"No," said Antony, calm now, feeling his life running out. "I am dead."

"But I recognize the man," the soldier said. "He is the queen's secretary, Diomedes, and he says that the queen lives! The first messenger lied. She calls you to come to her."

Antony took a shuddering breath, trying to bring himself back to consciousness. It was too much to make sense of this. A false message? She lived?

"Carry me to Cleopatra," he ordered, and when he noted the hesitation on the men's faces, he used a stronger voice. "You will take me to the queen. This will be your last duty in my service. Perform it well."

They dressed the wound as best they could, covered Antony to protect him from the eyes of enemies, and then lifted the pallet carefully onto their shoulders, and proceeded into the street.

The mattress was a boat, and there was a stormy sea beneath him. Antony laid his hand over his eyes to shield them from the sun. The lighthouse rose into his vision, smooth and white, a perfect thing. He'd lived on Pharos island for a time, in a small house away from the city, at the foot of the great stone tower. It was just after his return from Actium, when his sorrow at his own betrayals was too much to bear in company.

At the top of the tower, so high it could scarcely be seen, a golden statue of Zeus glittered in the sun. Antony smiled, seeing it still shining there even as he passed through the city, a witness to his own funerary procession.

The only sounds he'd heard while he stayed in that house were those of waves crashing up against the shore. There was no Rome, no legions, no love. He'd never felt so peaceful. He might have stayed forever in that little house, like a philosopher in his cave, but he craved company, drink, and jokes, and he dreamed of his wife. He walked back across the causeway and found everything at the palace as though he'd never left. Back into her arms he went then, and back to them he would go now. If he had died for her, let her see it done. Let there be an end.

An Egyptian soldier, drunken and disheveled, bowed his head as Antony was carried past, thinking him dead already.

"Is it the king you carry?" the soldier asked Antony's men.

"It is Mark Antony," they answered.

"You carry the king of Egypt, the honored husband of our queen," the soldier said.

Beneath his covering, Antony's lips curved into a painful smile. He'd never imagined that he would die a king.

5

The boy darted back through Alexandria, singing to himself. He'd delivered his message to Mark Antony and seen the great man in person. He was still heroic to look at, despite the dirt of battle upon him. His dark hair was iced with silver. The boy had seen it in the dim light of the building. But his arms were still ropy with muscle, and his chest was wide and armored.

One day, perhaps, the boy would grow up to be a warrior, and if he did, he hoped he would be tall and strong like Mark Antony. The great soldier looked down upon the boy, and the boy saw that he controlled the sun and the moon. He patted the boy's shoulder. His body still vibrated with the honor.

By the time he reached the boundary of the city, the Gate of the Sun was open, and the boy skittered through it, toward the Roman camp. A tall, broad-chested man emerged from the tent and looked at him carefully, his lips tight.

"Did you see him?" he asked the boy.

"I did," the boy said proudly.

"You're certain?"

"It was Antony," the boy insisted. "He fell to his knees when I told him the queen was dead."

The man shook his head, and the boy wondered if he was angry. He turned and led the boy back to the tent where he'd first received his assignment.

A slight, light-haired man sitting on a three-legged stool waited there. He appraised the boy with pale gray eyes.

"Your messenger has returned," the boy's guide said tersely. "I would not have had it done this way. Antony was outnumbered. It was only a matter of time."

The gray-eyed man lifted his chin and shot a fierce look at his general. "Do you question my honor, Agrippa?"

Agrippa did not answer. He looked steadily at his cohort for a moment and then turned on his heel and left the tent. The boy nervously watched him go.

"I did not ask for your advice," the boy's benefactor called after Agrippa.

His expression changed as he looked at the boy. "You've delivered my message to Antony?"

The boy blushed with pleasure at having completed his mission successfully.

"It is done," he said.

"Good," said the man, and winced slightly. He closed his eyes for a moment. "Good."

➤6➤

There was a sharp clattering from above, rocks being thrown against the window bars. Cleopatra jolted up from where she was kneeling, the knife still clutched in her hand. Who was coming for her? Antony? Or Octavian?

Charmian ran down the stairs, her face pale.

"Your husband is here," she whispered, her voice panicky. "His men have brought him."

Brought him? What sort of phrase was this? He'd lead his men, not be led. And why did he not come through the passage?

"Tell me what the matter is!" Cleopatra snapped, gripping the girl roughly by the shoulders.

"They've carried him here on a stretcher. He's covered."

Cleopatra was already running up the stairs to the window, her heart pounding in terror. This was her fault. She should never have let him go back to battle. She'd known better, after what she'd witnessed at the window the night before. Antony's gods had left the city, declaring the war a loss. There'd been an invisible celebration as Dionysus departed through the center of Alexandria, his procession unseen but raucous with trumpets and harps, the beat of dancing steps, drums, and trills.

In the room behind her, Antony had stretched out his arms to her.

"What are you doing out of bed?" he asked.

"Looking at the moon," she said. "Full and golden. A good omen." She did not say for whom.

"We will win this war," she told him, thinking of Sekhmet, imagining herself more powerful than any omen. "We will win this war."

"Come back to me," her husband replied, getting up from the bed as if to see for himself what drew her attention, but she pushed him back. They made love as though time had stopped, as though they had no battles to prepare for, no danger in the morning, no end to nights like these.

Cleopatra had sent her beloved out into battle unprotected and now she was paying for her arrogance.

She threw open the barred shutter, her body leaning out the window, a target for any archer. Antony's personal guard was below. She knew the men well. And there, on a litter, covered in a cloth—

Cleopatra felt herself swaying. There was a bloodstain on the sheet, the crimson spreading on the ivory ground.

The leader of the guard looked up at the queen. Cleopatra could see the grief on his face.

"There was a false message," he said. "He believed you killed yourself, and he sought to join you."

"Is he dead?" she whispered, scarcely able to make the words leave her lips.

Antony's hand rose to push aside the cloth that covered his face and chest.

"Not yet," Antony said. His face was gray with suffering, his hand bloodied where it pressed the wound.

Cleopatra clenched her teeth to keep from screaming. How could this have happened? Had she followed her original plan, had she not stayed, thinking to tame the gods, she should have been beside him shipboard, the green and silver sea, the coast of India, their children safe in their beds belowdecks.

"I come to die with you," Antony said. "Will you have me?"

Sobbing, she threw down the rope and let his men rig him in it. She and her handmaidens pulled him up to the window, the wound in her hand opening again as she held the fibers. She watched his face as he rose toward her, feeling every pain he did. He would not cry out in front of his men. By the time she had him in the mausoleum, her garments were covered in blood. Her limbs felt dipped in wax, slowed and numb.

"Antony," she murmured, stroking his face, his chest, his arms. She knew every part of him. The old war wounds, white stripes in his sun-dark flesh, and this new wound, still gaping. His eyes focused on her suddenly.

"Why did you betray me?" he whispered. "I would have done anything for you."

"What are you saying?" she cried, but he was not listening.

"Wine," he called.

He was too weak to lift the cup. She held it to his lips, hoping to ease his pain.

"You must not die without me," she told him, but he looked at her, unseeing. Never, in all the years she'd known him, had he looked through her. She was always his focus, and when his gaze landed on her, she felt her skin warm, as though she walked through a ray of light sent from Ra himself.

"I will see you again," Antony said, and smiled.

Then he was still.

Everything was still, the air, the smoke of the incense, Cleopatra's own heartbeat. The maids stood, wide-eyed, watching for a breath, and none came.

A tear fell from Cleopatra's face to Antony's, and she watched as it rolled down his skin. The bloodstain on his tunic spread, larger and larger, and he did not move.

A scream rose up in Cleopatra's throat.

"You will not die without me!" Her throat convulsed with sobs, and she doubled over, holding him tightly, her hands gripping his bloody tunic. Her body shook, every place he had touched her, every place he had kissed her.

This could not be the end of their story.

Running feet and shouting outside the building, swords clashing, Antony's men engaging with Octavian's. They were coming for her.

She staggered up from Antony's side and ran into the sacred circle, her hands dripping with his blood. She'd made the paste of honey and ash, added the lion's fur and cobra's skin. Now the potion awaited the final ingredient.

She knelt, her knees cold against the stone of the floor. She threw back her head and sang the spell, her voice rattling the air itself, calling out to the heavens, her hands steady now as she held the agate goblet filled with her own blood.

Forbidden.

The warning of the Egyptian scholar appeared in her mind, and she shook her head frantically to rid herself of it. Nothing was forbidden. Nothing. This was her love.

Though this goddess was meant for vengeance, today she would be called to raise the dead as well.

Cleopatra drew a shuddering breath and performed the final step of the spell, pouring the blood of kings over the bared teeth of the icon. She watched as the red dripped down into the icon's throat.

There was a rushing sound. Time spun around her like a sirocco, a searing, razing thing. The air charged with sparks, and the edges of the treasure glowed out of the darkness.

In the darkness, there were soft steps on the stone.

Cleopatra turned, and the goddess was upon her, tremendous. She shone in the endless night of the sealed chamber with the fire of the sun, her head that of a lioness crowned with a twisting, living cobra, and her body that of a woman, her arms decked in jewels, her fingers ending in talons. Her gown, tight to her form, was bloodred with rosettas over each breast, and the fur of her throat and face was golden.

She rose to the ceiling, and beside her all the glow of Egypt's treasure was overshadowed. She was the daughter of Ra, Nicolaus had told Cleopatra, created from the sun god's fiery eye. Her heat shimmered in the air.

"Sekhmet," Cleopatra whispered, and the goddess roared, the sound rattling the coins and echoing from the walls of the mausoleum.

Where were Cleopatra's servants? Fallen against the stairs, sleeping as if drugged, guarding the room from intruders. How could they sleep in the presence of this?

Antony slept as well, his skin pale and cold. Dead. A pang of grief stabbed through the queen's chest, a sudden sense of doom. This was the end of everything, and she'd brought it on herself by thinking she could have everything and pay no price.

"Bring him back," she ordered Sekhmet. Her fears did not matter. "Bring him back to me. Help me to avenge this."

Cleopatra lifted her crown from her head. Egypt would belong to the old gods again. Farewell to Isis, farewell to the Greeks and the Romans. She would give the country back to its beginnings, to its lions and crocodiles, to its jackals and falcons and cobras.

The goddess gazed at her, a flicker of amusement in her wide, yellow eyes.

Not enough, she said, or didn't say. It was known. More would be required. The heart's blood of the last queen of Egypt, Cleopatra knew suddenly. That would be the sacrifice required to bring him back from the Duat, Egypt's Underworld.

"Take what you wish," Cleopatra said, throwing her arms out from her sides, offering her throat, her breasts, and her wrists. She'd survived worse than this. She was surviving it now.

The goddess leapt over the treasure, her teeth bared, her talons extended, and her skin began to shine with the pitiless glare of the noontime sun. Her fingers and limbs smoked, blurring with heat, and Cleopatra steeled herself for the agony that was to come. A burning brand, a sizzling impact, she thought. But this was not to be.

Sekhmet transformed. A tremendous serpent coiled before the queen. It looked deep into Cleopatra, assessing her weaknesses.

Cleopatra was grateful. Serpents were the sacred creatures of her line. They were beautiful things, snakes, and this one was no exception. Its scales were gilded emeralds, the eyes cruel rubies.

Cleopatra glimpsed a flash of diamond fangs as the goddess struck her throat. Still no pain. Only a sense of time stopping, a spinning, the sound of air rushing past. Then her neck burned with a pain that was not pain but a brilliant heat. An overpowering sweetness swept over her.

Cleopatra discovered that her feet were no longer touching the floor. Her body—she felt such tenderness for it now, for this fragile, mortal body—hung from the serpent's teeth, and as though from miles away, she watched her own skin pale. Her fingers clenched and then released. Her vision filled with the places beyond the night sky, the blue-white shine of the edge of the moon. She was dying, and yet she cared nothing about it, nothing about anything that had ever happened or that would happen in the future.

Then the goddess pulled away, and agonizing pain tore through Cleopatra. She was a tree, and each leaf was on fire. She was a city, and every building was pillaged. The streets ran with boiling oil, citizens fleeing, their hair clouds of smoke, their clothing gusts of flame, orange and blue. She was a volcano erupting, and her skin was furrowed with the passage of lava, deep tunnels of searing, searching heat. The soles of her feet melted where they touched the floor, and she staggered to keep from collapsing. The goddess was the light of a thousand suns, and Cleopatra felt her skin peeling away, exposing her very bones. She was turning to ash. No human could live in flame. Her eyes dilated, blinded.

You think to summon me to serve you? You, who have forgotten your gods?

The words appeared in Cleopatra's mind, echoing there like the sound of men stomping over decks, readying themselves for war. She could smell her own blood slipping down her throat and over her breasts, and she could smell the scent of rage as well, emanating from Sekhmet to wrap about the queen's arms, binding them to her sides as though she were mummified already.

You are not one of our kind. Do you think I wish for your blood?

"That is all I have," whispered Cleopatra, her voice ravaged by smoke and pain.

Is it? The goddess laughed, a horrible sound. Somewhere in the room, a glass goblet shook, shattered, and turned back into the sand from which it had come. *I think you have something more.*

"Anything," Cleopatra managed, looking at Antony. "Anything I have is yours."

And then Cleopatra felt a change. The pain was blinding but uncertain. Where did it come from? What had been taken? A sudden sense of loss, a hole at the center of her being. Her body convulsed around this absence, and she screamed and could not stop screaming. She was a husk, as thin as eggshell, and inside her was nothingness, black night, rushing chill, the frigid glow of dying stars. She gasped, searching for air, and found nothing. She was drowning, and her heart, her heart—

Her beloved moaned.

She spun toward him and saw his eyelids flutter.

Joy rose up inside her, replacing the emptiness that had been there only moments before. She was whole, with him beside her. She was herself again.

She flew to Antony and knelt at his side, her hands on his chest, feeling it expand as he took his first breath. She ran her fingers over his bare skin and felt it warming under her touch. Her pain, if not gone, no longer mattered.

Antony's dark eyes opened, and she kissed him. She brushed her fingers over his stomach, felt the edge of the wound that had killed him, and sensed it healing. The goddess had done as she'd promised.

"*Te teneo*," she whispered in Latin. "You are mine."

His hands rose to cup her face, stroking her jaw, her lips, her earlobes, her hair.

"You followed me," he said, and smiled. "I did not think you would."

She realized that he thought they were both dead, traveling together to the Duat.

"No. We live," she told him. "I've brought you back."

She laid her face against his chest, listening to his heartbeat. "I am yours," she said. Her eyes brimmed with tears.

Antony moved uncertainly, restless, silent. His hands brought her face up to his, and he looked into her eyes.

"You betrayed me," he said.

"Lady! You are taken alive!" Charmian shrieked from the staircase, and then flew from the stairs to the opposite side of the room, pursued by one of Octavian's legionaries. He'd somehow penetrated the sanctuary, scaled the walls, removed the bars, and fitted himself through the window.

Cleopatra spun, searching for Sekhmet, but the goddess was gone. Gone! How dare this man, this plebeian, break into her sacred place? How dare he force the goddess out?

Cleopatra threw herself in front of her husband, blocking the soldier's access to him.

"You are in the presence of a goddess," she told the invader, and her voice did not shake. She was herself again, the queen of Egypt, fearless. "Leave this place or face the consequences."

She needed only a few minutes more for Antony to recover himself, and then they would go forth, together again. She would show compassion. She would let this man go.

If not—she grasped her ritual knife. It was a once-in-a-lifetime act, the summoning of such a power, and she had lived through it only by luck. She'd given all the blood she could give and still walk the earth. She could not bring her love back a second time.

The legionary rushed toward the queen and her beloved, his sword drawn.

Suddenly, Cleopatra was racked with *knowing*. She could smell the legionary's sweat, the sweat of an endless, unpaid march, of years of battle. And more than that. She could smell his children back in Rome, their hunger and hope. She could smell the sea in his hair. She could smell his longing for a woman, any woman. *The Whore Queen*, that was what he believed her to be. She heard it now, his thought of taking her as a chained captive to present to his master. He thought her weak.

The fool. He was nothing to her.

Her heart swelled with a clean, white fury. Her limbs shuddered in their sockets, her spine became a sword of flame, and her lungs filled with the heat of the desert sand.

She heard herself gasp, felt herself consumed, and then the world went black.

Cleopatra looked down at her hand, feeling something strangely heavy. Her head spun, racked with pain, and she narrowed her eyes, trying to focus on what she held.

What was it? She gazed at it for a moment, uncertain, her fingers pressing into its slippery, scalding edges. The thing ran purple over her fingers, weighty and profane, still trembling with its last life.

His heart.

She'd torn out his heart.

She screamed and flung it away from her, away from Antony. Her servants crept along the wall, their eyes wide with horror.

Against her will, Cleopatra found herself looking down at the legionary's ruined body. She had the taste of metal in her mouth, blood running from her lips to soak her garments.

What had she done?

"Lady," Charmian whispered. "Lady?"

Antony took a rattling breath, a cry of agony. Cleopatra turned and saw the legionary's sword piercing her beloved's body. It had been thrown in the struggle and was pinning him to the floor. The blood. The smell of iron, the taste of honey. She gagged, clutching her mouth in horror, and her hands came away from her lips covered in scarlet.

"Cleopatra," her husband whispered. "Come to me."

She stumbled to Antony's side and touched his skin. Stiffening. Cooling.

"You will not die now," she told him, her voice breaking. "You cannot."

She pressed her mouth to his, breathing her air into his lungs. When she pulled away, the legionary's blood stained Antony's lips.

She'd brought him back from death only to watch him die again. She moaned, listening to the sound that wasn't. No heartbeat. No breath.

The stairs rattled with the steps of legionaries. She turned to see them. Dozens of men, armed, shouting. They were coming to take her to their general. She felt strangely calm. They would not take her alive. Nothing mattered now that he was gone. She'd failed, and this was the end.

The legionaries swarmed around her, their weapons drawn, shouting and shoving, but she was beyond them.

"Surrender by order of the emperor," they yelled, tearing at her hands, throwing her to the ground, but her hand was already on the ritual knife.

She twisted and drove it into her stomach, feeling none of the pain she should have felt.

And when she drew the dagger out of her body, no blood stained the blade.

⟫ 7 ⟪

Three nights later, the conquered queen of Egypt lit the fire that burned her husband. And they reveled in Rome. A prisoner surrounded by enemies, she could hear their trumpets, smell their foul feasting, carried across the water all the way to Alexandria. The world rang with proclamations of the new ruler's name as Cleopatra stood before Antony's pyre stunned, dazed like one in a dream.

"Hail Caesar," they sang as Cleopatra lifted the torch to Antony's shroud. He was as still as a statue, yet he had been warm. She had brought him back and lost him again. He'd spoken to her. He'd thought himself betrayed by she who adored him, she who'd summoned the goddess and given up her—

She did not want to know what she'd given up.

She did not want to know why she remained here, among the living. This was not where she belonged.

The ceremony was held in darkness, to keep the crowds from assembling. Not even the royal children were in attendance. Cleopatra wondered where they were imprisoned. Surely they still lived, or she would have felt it. The funerary group consisted only of Cleopatra and Romans, the general Marcus Agrippa, second to Octavian, and a slew of lesser functionaries. Whether through mercy or insult, Octavian did not appear. It was to be Cleopatra's last act as the queen of her country.

With a burst of brightness, her love went up in flame.

Cleopatra tilted her chin and watched the rising cloud of smoke that had been her king. She wanted only to fall into the flames and join him, but the guards surrounding her kept her from moving.

The smoke obscured the stars, and Cleopatra thought of the gods that had failed her, the goddess that had tricked her. She lived, and he was dead. She lived, and she did not know why.

She stretched her fingers to feel the flames. Someone barked an order, and the Romans pulled her back. They let her—indeed, they *made* her—stay until the pyre went out. When everything was ash, she knelt miserably in the char and gathered what was left of her husband's body. Her tears fell then, for the first time since the horror in the mausoleum.

As she touched the ash, her mind filled with a strange and roaring sequence of images: galleys saluting Rome, herself naked and sleeping in bed, the buckles of Antony's armor as they were fastened, the sword he used to stab himself, the lighthouse shining pale in the sky, her own face, blurry and bloodless, grief-stricken. She heaved with suppressed sobs, but they let her hold him only for a moment.

A stone-faced centurion, a former soldier of Antony's, took the ashes from her and placed them in a silver box, one Cleopatra recognized as having commissioned herself. Isis and Dionysus decorated its sides. She'd had it made as a wedding gift for Antony, and in her foolishness, ordered that the gods depicted on it have human faces. Dionysus had a cleft chin, and Isis a crown of cobras. Their hands were twined together, the marriage of Cleopatra's gods and Antony's.

She was no god. Why had she been so stupid as to declare herself one? All of this, everything, was her fault. She'd started things in motion and now she'd lost control. Her life was a cart careening down a hillside, horses shrieking and stumbling, unable to stop themselves from falling.

The box would be taken back to the mausoleum. The murderers would bury Antony in Egypt. They'd given her that much at least. The proper ceremonies, the rituals. Antony's wishes would be granted. He'd renounced his Roman rites and declared himself a citizen of her country. As long as his ashes remained in Egypt, she hoped his soul would eventually travel to the Duat. Cleopatra would not be there to meet him.

She thought of him wandering alone through the caverns of the dead, making his way toward the Beautiful West without her. They'd planned their lives and deaths so carefully, and now it was all for naught.

She lived.

Still, with these ceremonies, he belonged to this country. Or so Cleopatra hoped. She realized that she knew nothing now, nothing true, nothing solid. Not since the thing that had happened in the mausoleum. Who knew which Underworld would claim him, or what the gods would do with him once they had him? Who knew whom she'd offended?

She watched as they marched away with the box that contained Antony. Too quickly, the legionaries were out of sight, and she was left in the dark with the guards to take her back to the palace.

The Romans kept her caged in her own bedchamber, where she awaited the emperor's summons.

Outside the room, sentries trod the marble, their steps echoing through Cleopatra's mind. Her luxurious bedding had been stripped from the bed for fear she'd use it to strangle herself. All that was left was a bare pallet, but it didn't matter. She'd neither slept nor eaten since Antony's death.

Her mind seeped with an unpredictable darkness. Was it madness? Had she imagined everything that happened in the mausoleum? She saw herself in a horrible flash, a soiled linen shift, muddied feet, tangled hair, wandering the roads, collapsing, her flesh picked over by vultures, yet still living, a shrieking husk. This would be her legacy, not her years of rule, of preserving the city from the Romans, not her pure love of Antony.

The Mad Queen Cleopatra.

She unwrapped her robes and ran her fingers over her skin to confirm what she already knew. Smooth. No evidence of the knife that had penetrated just below the ribs. She was chilled, and she shook as though fevered, but her body, at least, was unwounded. She could not say the same for her soul.

Something, everything, was terribly wrong. She could feel it, but she could not find it.

All night, she lay wide-eyed in her chamber, every sound magnified, the darkness dazzling.

At dawn on the sixth day after Antony's death, she opened the shutters to watch the sunrise, once her particular pleasure. She sought to comfort herself with ritual, standing in the window, watching the indigo sky turn pale gold, but as the sun broke over the edge of the world and touched her face, she felt a searing pain. She gasped and leapt back from the window, her skin burning.

Tentatively, she stretched her fingers back into the light, and they blistered as though doused in boiling oil. She snatched them back, cradling her hand to her breast. Her eyes watered and sparked with the sun. Hissing with pain, she slammed the shutters closed again.

Had she offended Ra as well as his daughter? Might she throw open the shutters and die in the sunlight?

No. As she watched, her hand healed with agonizing speed. Where the flesh had been burned, there was smooth skin again. Soon, it was as though the burning had never happened.

It seemed that even this pain would only cripple her, and that only temporarily. She tried to calm herself by counting her heartbeats, but she could not find them.

She checked again. Nothing. Silence where there had always been motion and song, emptiness where her soul had been.

The goddess had taken her heart, her soul, her *ka*.

Cleopatra curled in the corner of her chamber, shaking, her hands clasped to her breasts, feeling the place where the darkness had touched her. Even if she died, without a heart to be weighed she could never enter Egypt's Underworld. She could not follow Antony. She imagined herself ferried across the water to the Island of Fire, Osiris standing on the shore waiting to judge her. What would she offer him? She had nothing.

She sat in darkness, listening to the sound of nothing, listening to the beat of nothing, feeling the hollow space within her breast.

At last, after days of Cleopatra's solitude, Eiras and Charmian arrived to dress the queen's hair and paint her face for her audience with the emperor. The maids held up a mirror of polished metal so that the queen could catch her reflection. In it, she was beautiful but for the sunken cheeks that no paint could hide, and the mark of Sekhmet's fangs bright against the skin of her throat.

Cleopatra looked into her own eyes for the first time since Antony's death and saw a stranger inhabiting her skin. She drew in her breath sharply.

This stranger hungered to kill everyone in the palace, she realized for the first time. Everyone in the city. Cleopatra's fingers flexed, endowed with strange fire. The thing inside her, the thing she was not ready to accept as her own, hungered to kill everyone in the *world*, and perhaps it was capable of doing so.

Everyone except herself.

She felt a sound rising, humming behind her lips, a roar that might shatter glass, that might avalanche a city, and from deep inside her body, from deep inside her mind, something spoke to her.

You are mine, the voice said, dark and shining as any night.

Cleopatra shuddered, panicked. What thoughts were these? What voice had stolen Antony's words? Flickering images paraded through her mind, lakes of blood, cities destroyed. Things she'd never seen. Things she would never have wished to see.

Charmian took her hand, concerned.

"Are you well, lady?" she asked. Cleopatra straightened her spine, feeling flickers of flame running down it, willing herself to stay seated. Madness. It was clearly madness. She must resist it. She touched her brow, expecting to find it burning, but it was as cold as marble.

Eiras dabbed at her eyelids, painting them the gleaming green of sacred insects, bordering her lashes with warmed kohl.

"Perfect," said the girl, though her brow furrowed as she brushed her mistress's strangely icy lips with carmine.

Together, Eiras and Charmian braided her hair, frowning at the thread of silver that had appeared in it since Antony's death, a glittering ribbon.

She was no longer young, Cleopatra realized suddenly. The sun god had seen her face for thirty-eight years, though he saw it no more. She felt ancient, and yet she was no closer to the grave than these girls were. Death did not want her.

"He is yours, lady," said Charmian, draping the fine linen gown lower on Cleopatra's bosom, arranging the lapis pendants and diadem to better frame her face. "Your Caesar was this man's kin. Surely, they share the same temptations. No man can resist you, if only you smile."

"You'll bewitch this man, as you have every other," Eiras assured her, daubing perfumed oil behind Cleopatra's ears, scattering flecks of gold dust on her naked shoulders. Somehow, the maids had forgotten what they'd seen in the mausoleum, or were too loyal to speak of it.

Charmian twined a jeweled snake about Cleopatra's arm and wrapped a silken veil around her throat to hide the evidence of the goddess. There was that, at least, to prove Cleopatra's memory. Those two fang marks, swollen at the edges, burning with an invisible fire.

She wanted to disappear, to die as she had been meant to die, but instead, the first citizen of Rome desired her to dine with him. He feared that she was planning a death by starvation, a martyrdom that would reflect badly on him.

"Eat something," Eiras begged, offering her a platter of sliced figs, in better days her favorite fruit. The scent, the seeping red centers, revolted her. She would starve to death if she only could. Her stomach twisted with hunger; her mouth was parched with thirst; yet water nauseated her, and wine held no allure. She could not eat.

She'd kill Octavian, she promised herself. He would pay for Antony's murder. It *was* murder. Antony had been alive when the legionary stabbed him. She would make the emperor of Rome pay for her lover's death, no matter what it cost her.

"The emperor approaches," Eiras whispered.

Cleopatra looked up, but it was not Octavian who entered the room. He'd sent her children instead.

The ten-year-old twins, Alexander Helios and Cleopatra Selene, ran toward Cleopatra. The sun and moon, she and Antony had named them, imagining themselves, the royal parents—oh, she regretted it now—to be the sky. The baby, Ptolemy Philadelphus, just four, scampered in behind them, grinning wildly at his mother, his face smeared with sweets.

He had them, Octavian was telling her. They were at his mercy should their mother not provide what he desired.

An icy wave of misery ran through her. She loved her children. She'd often dismissed the governesses and tutors, and spent hours teaching her children to talk and write and read, sharing with them her command of the languages of the world. She'd cooed at them in Arabic, chided them in Greek, praised them in Egyptian, denied them in Macedonian. She'd fed them in Hebrew, and now that they were growing tall, she advised them in Latin.

"Mama," Ptolemy cried, the joy in his voice crumpling what was left of her calm. The cleft in his chin, the tilt of his head—

Her children were the images of Antony. Each face brought his face back to her, the nights spent drinking and dancing, his hands on her waist, his lips on her throat, and the memories grieved her anew. She could see it as if it were happening again, the two of them sharing one cloak, walking the streets of their city, pretending to be common people. They'd thought themselves immortal, but he had been wrong. And she? She had not imagined they would end like this, herself bereft of a husband, her children bereft of their father, and all of them broken.

She could feel the absence blasting through her center even now, the horrible feeling she'd had in the mausoleum, the emptiness, the bleak, black sky, and her heart missing, her skin frozen, her love halting and hopeless.

Ptolemy climbed into her lap, nuzzling into her arms, and though she tried to stay strong, she clutched him. She did not want to show Octavian that she loved them. If he knew this, he'd be more likely to kill them.

"Send them away," she ordered, desperate to keep herself from crying in front of her children. Their father was dead. Did they not know it? Cleopatra had grown up with only a father, her mother having died birthing her. Did her children not feel the strangeness inside her?

"But, Mama," said Ptolemy, tears already streaking his face. He had a toy with him, a small lion carved out of ebony, and he showed it to his mother. His fingers on the toy were chubby, and she knew he would never survive without her. He was a baby still. Tears ran down her cheeks, and she held him tighter for a moment, then let him go.

He stared at her, bewildered. His eyes looked just like Antony's had in those last moments. Antony, who'd been convinced she had betrayed him.

The twins comforted their brother. Cleopatra Selene, the beautiful, black-haired daughter, looked back as she was led toward the doorway. Her eyes smoldered at Cleopatra.

"Who are you?" she asked, her tone sharp. "You are not our mother."

Cleopatra was silent for a moment, though her daughter's words felt as the sun had, searing and blistering. What did her daughter see?

"I am not well," Cleopatra told her finally, her voice shaking. "Your mother is not well."

"They say you betrayed our father," Selene said.

"They lie!" Cleopatra shouted. Her sons cringed away from her, and she pushed herself back into her chair. She should not scream at this child. Her own child. "Who told you that?"

"They say that you killed a man in the mausoleum," the daughter persisted, her eyes wide and scared but her tone harsh.

"Who says that?" Cleopatra asked again. "Tell me who."

"Is it true?"

"You must not speak to your mother that way, Selene," said a voice from the doorway. "It is not respectful. She is your queen."

Cleopatra raised her head slowly.

There the monster stood, a slight blond man with unsettlingly pale gray eyes. He had not bothered to put on formal dress for the meeting.

Ptolemy ran to the conqueror, and Octavian scooped the child up into his arms. Cleopatra stood up, her muscles aching with the effort of remaining on her own side of the room. She must keep them safe. She must pretend she didn't care.

Octavian put Ptolemy down and waved his hand at Cleopatra's twins. They let themselves be led from the chamber, only Selene looking back.

"You betrayed *us*," Selene said. "They say you betrayed our father, but you betrayed us."

Then they were gone.

Octavian sat down disrespectfully in Cleopatra's chair, leaving her standing. He appraised the queen, slowly looking her up and down. Discomfited, she sat on her couch. She would not be forced onto the bed.

"I thought you'd be beautiful," he finally said, "given all the lives you've ruined."

In spite of her pain, Cleopatra nearly laughed. Was this the conversation they'd have, here, now, after all that had come before? Did he think beauty mattered to her? And yet, even as she thought this, she wondered what she looked like. Was she no longer beautiful, even gilded and glittered, wrapped in diaphanous silks like a gift to the conquerors? No. She'd seen herself in the mirror. He was merely trying, in his small way, to wound her.

She was disgusted to realize he'd succeeded.

"Just as I thought you would be a man," hissed Cleopatra. "It seems we are both disappointed."

"You've dallied too long in the company of eunuchs and drunkards," Octavian said. "It is no wonder you do not recognize a man when you see one. Your consort—"

"My *husband*," Cleopatra corrected.

"My sister Octavia's husband, Mark Antony, was a glutton. He never saw wine nor woman he didn't sample. You were an exotic meal, nothing more. He tasted Cleopatra, and then he moved down the table, dipping his spoon in every other dish. You do not imagine your lover was faithful, do you? Not to Fulvia, not to Octavia, and certainly not to you."

Cleopatra was not injured by this liar. Antony had had a queen at his disposal, ready to make love to him and counsel him on battle, all at once. They'd spent countless nights together, their bedchamber filled with soft silks and sea charts, Cleopatra plotting the routes of his ships even as he kissed her thighs. What need could he have had for other women when he was married to an equal? No. It was not true.

"What is it you want from me?" she asked Octavian. "I have nothing for you."

"A friendly meeting," the boy general said, and smiled an unfriendly smile.

In other days, she would have wooed him. Talked sweetly, extended her arms in graceful motions, sung and danced, shown him his importance. She'd done as much in the past and profited by it, with his adoptive father no less, smuggling herself into Julius Caesar's chambers, wrapped in a carpet, then rolling out of it like a spirit and slipping directly into his bed. Time had passed, though, and things had changed. She could not find it in herself to seduce her enemy today. It was as though her past did not belong to her.

And there was something disgusting about Octavian. He smelt of nothing. What was he, this thing adopted into emperor?

"Libations?" she offered.

"I do not drink," he replied.

"I suppose you don't eat, either," she said.

"Not while a queen starves before me," he said, and smiled, revealing small and somewhat crooked teeth. He drew the gilded chair toward her couch.

"Such courtesy is unusual in a barbarian," she commented.

"I am a family man. My daughter Julia is my chief joy. I would not have your children lose a mother," he said. "Bastards though they are."

Her skin prickled with fury. "They are not bastards," she replied. "Their mother is a queen. I doubt the Romans would understand."

Octavian leaned forward, his elbow on his knee.

"Unless you dine with me," he said, his voice and smile unchanged, "I will be forced to slit your bastards' throats."

She inhaled deeply, scenting this nothing man. She would rip out what heart he had, and she would drink his watery blood.

"What would you have me eat?" she asked, her tone savagely polite. "I see no emperor's banquet here. Shall I dine upon *you*?"

She laughed, but something twisted inside her.

It was a joke. Barbed words, that was all. She was not well, she was not well. Her skin chilled. Her robes were drenched. Could he not see it? How could she be expected to sit here and listen while he talked of slitting her babies' throats? The barbarian.

Why hadn't she killed him when she'd first met him? He'd been so weak, that reedy, feverish boy in the bed. So vulnerable.

No, she was not a killer, not in those days; she knew it even as she thought it.

She'd changed.

"I am ill—" she managed, and then gagged, covering her mouth with her veil.

The conqueror waved his hand, signaling his men to bring in trays.

"You are weak with hunger," he said, pressing into her fingers a piece of roasted meat dripping with oils and rubbed with spices.

She felt muscles clenching in her back and arms, clenching against her will. Her thighs tightened. She would spring at him—

She pressed herself back against the hard metal frame of the couch.

No. She'd eat the food he offered. If it bought her children's lives, it was no price. Those dying of hunger, she knew, often hallucinated. Perhaps that was all this was, the voice in her head, the strange desires. She took the meat between her teeth.

Oozing juices. Foul, rotting flesh. Her throat closed against it, and she spat it out.

"You would not allow me to kill myself, yet you try to kill me with poisons? You've already seen me die when my husband was taken from me. You are dining with the dead, even now."

He sliced a piece of meat from the same platter, put it into his mouth, and chewed it.

"It is not poisoned," he said. "And you are a stubborn fool. Is my food not fine enough for you, lady?"

He beckoned to his men, and they approached Cleopatra. One of them came from behind, bringing a chain from beneath his cloak, and before the queen knew what was happening, he'd wrapped it about her wrists.

The metal burned her skin, and she cried out at the unexpected pain.

"Behold, a chain fit for a queen," Octavian said. "Did you not put

Mark Antony on a silver throne while you sat above him, on the gold? And he thought you were naming him king instead of slave, the fool. This chain is forged of that throne."

"He was never my slave," Cleopatra whispered, curling into her couch, willing the pain away. "He is my husband. Summon a physician. I tell you, I am not well."

Octavian gazed at her, impassive.

"Look at the whore's false tears. I know them, lady, just as I know a whore's false cries of pleasure. Force the food down her throat if she will not eat it herself," he said as he left the room. "I will not be seen to starve the queen of Egypt."

⇒ 8 ⇐

In the corridor outside Cleopatra's chamber, Octavian leaned against the wall, panting with the effort of the conversation. He hadn't expected seeing her to be so jarring, unpredictable emotions rising within him and threatening to disable his voice. He thought he'd conducted himself well, despite this, but he was not certain. Perhaps he should not have involved the children. Perhaps he should not have met with her at all.

Octavian groaned quietly, seeing Cleopatra as if she were still before him, the diadem in her hair, the soft gown draped over her breasts. The fullness of her lips. She had not looked well, no, but it had been profoundly shocking to see her so close.

She was his prisoner. He might do as he pleased with her—

No. It was not safe.

Cleopatra was a witch, he knew that much. Antony had clearly been under her spell for years. He'd left Rome for her, left glory, left peace. He'd left everything that made him a man in order to follow her like a slave, kissing her feet and carrying her through crowds on his shoulders. It was shameful.

In spite of himself, Octavian's mind boiled with visions of their love-making. It was only with effort that he put it from his mind. He refused to think of her the way he'd thought of her these past sixteen years. He remembered their single meeting quite clearly, though Cleopatra had clearly forgotten it.

If Octavian closed his eyes, he could still summon every detail of the young queen's weight beside him on his sickbed, of the heavy outline of her milk-swollen breasts, the way they had been revealed when she bent over him, telling him he'd live through the fever that had almost killed him.

It was that sentence that had kept him fighting his way free of the delirium, the hope of seeing her again that had kept him alive.

And now, here he stood in her palace, her conqueror.

When he'd received the news of Antony's suicide, he'd felt a strange uncertainty rising within him. He'd behaved dishonorably in sending that false message, though only Marcus Agrippa knew what he'd done. To his horror, Octavian had begun to weep in front of all his men. He'd found himself pawing through his trunk, unearthing old correspondence and waving it in the air.

"He was my friend!" he'd heard himself shouting. "I warned him! I tried to warn him away from the witch!"

They had never truly been friends, but despite their differences, they had, until this most recent series of battles, fought for fifteen years on the same side. When Antony had disappeared into Cleopatra's arms, Octavian illegally raided the temple of the vestal virgins for his will and discovered proof of betrayal.

Even if he died in his own country, Antony's will demanded that his body be sent to Egypt and Cleopatra. No Roman would ask such a thing. Rome was home and heart. Octavian read the shocking provisions aloud in the Senate, drumming up support for the war. If Antony was so loyal to Egypt that he wanted his soul laid to rest there, what would prevent him from other loyalties? What if Cleopatra desired more from him? What if she wanted Rome for her own plaything?

Octavian had found himself in frantic pursuit, bewilderingly unable to let Antony depart into Cleopatra's bed.

Now, though, Octavian wondered whether his pursuit had been legitimate. Antony had died for Cleopatra. Perhaps he had wedded himself to Egypt for love, and not for ambition at all.

Octavian coughed, inhaling dust from some corner of the palace. He wanted nothing so much as to leave this wretched country. He'd put someone else in charge of Egypt. Some lower general. There was a list in his mind already, of suitable men who were owed reward. Some reward, this mosquito-ridden hell. Octavian felt infuriated that he'd been forced into this war by arrogance, by Antony's disobeying the rules of Rome. The man could have been discreet about his love affair. He should never have divorced Octavia. He'd provoked Octavian, and he deserved what he got.

He stomped down the hallway, relishing the sound of his steps. Let her wail there in her chamber. Let her refuse to eat, even though it was obvious she was hungry. He did not care. She'd destroyed Antony, and now she destroyed herself, and none of it mattered to the soon-to-be emperor of Rome.

None of it mattered in the least.

⇒ 9 ⇐

The soldiers pressed meat into Cleopatra's mouth as though she were a fattening fowl, and then left her, still chained. She vomited again and again, her maid tending her, bathing her face and throat with cool water.

Hours passed, and with each of them, Cleopatra's fury grew stronger. Her wrists burned where the chain rubbed against them, her body revolting against the metal. The voice in her head now sounded like her own. No matter how she struggled with the metal, it did not give, and her skin tore and mended, seared invisibly, scalded and wounded. She howled with exhaustion and rage as dawn came, as the night birds took themselves back to their nests, as the cocks crowed and the city began to speak.

"I will say I have eaten," she growled when the soldiers returned. "I'll swear to it. Release me from these chains. Your master will not know."

One soldier eyed the other and shrugged.

"Some of the food must have gone in," he said. "She swallowed it, at least."

Cleopatra looked into the soldier's eyes. So slender, a boy. A virgin yet.

"Release me," she whispered, and the soldier came toward her. She could smell him now, his sweet flesh, the nick in his skin where the blood had come to the razor's edge. His home, a small structure made of trees his father had felled, high on a hill. The village girl he loved, a cobbler's daughter, and the taste of her lips on his, only once, the day before he left for war. The two of them had lain in a meadow of wildflowers, watching the clouds drift across the sky, just as Cleopatra had once done, long ago, with Antony at her side—

No. She would not think of Antony.

The soldier came closer still, looking at her, his face open as a child's. He reached out a hand.

The other boy swallowed nervously.

"We're not to converse with the prisoner," he reminded his companion. "She's clever, this one. She snared Mark Antony, wrapped her legs around his waist and took him to her bed. You saw what happened at Actium. She deserted him and fled with her own ships, leaving him to die. And what did he do? He left his men and followed her back here. It was no wonder he killed himself."

Cleopatra bit her lip to keep from screaming at him. He was wrong. Everyone was wrong.

"I only want to touch her," stammered the first soldier. "Just to see what a queen feels like."

Cleopatra laughed her most seductive laugh, but from afar, she watched herself, horrified by her own actions. What was she trying to do? Surely not.

"Free my wrists," she cooed. "And see if the stories you've heard are true."

He bent closer, closer still. She felt her lips parting, as she inhaled the smell of his skin.

"She's supposed to be beautiful, but she doesn't look beautiful to me," the other soldier complained.

Her wrists were free. She spread her hands and readied herself. The boy's pale throat was inches from her mouth. His sweet smell was in her nostrils. She pressed her fingers against his chest and leaned toward the glorious, pulsing vein in his neck.

At that moment, the other soldier drew the curtain back, and the newborn sun came in, a blinding rise as it broke over the horizon.

"There," he said. "Now we'll get a look at her."

But the queen was cringing away from the burning light, stunned by what she had almost done. She threw her body into the shadows and turned her face to the wall. Her hands trembled, and with effort, she forced her muscles to be still. She was salivating, and her tongue felt rough, like that of a cat.

"Leave me," she said, and when they hesitated, she screamed the words again. "LEAVE ME!"

They left, disgruntled. Changeable things, women. One moment ready for love, the next for war, and men never knew which was coming. They muttered their way down the corridor, their long bodies banging against the tapestries, the smell of their histories fading.

The queen drew a breath. The danger was over.

In the window, a bird appeared, and before Cleopatra knew what she was doing, her hand had snatched it from the sunrise, its hollow bones shattering in her grasp. The softness of its feathers. The throb of its racing heart. It still lived.

She would not—

She could not—

She sobbed as she drank the swallow's blood.

➤10➤

The tutor stood outside the entrance to the palaces, cursing himself. He could stay in Alexandria no longer. He'd miss the royal
children. The girl was bright, a fiery thing. The boy, her twin, was dull
in comparison, always wanting to play at battle, while his sister read
in seven languages. In the employment of the queen, Nicolaus had set
about training the children into scholars, though only the girl took to
books. Now it was all for nothing. The city was taken, and no matter
what had truly happened, he would be considered an enemy of the state.

Though Cleopatra was imprisoned, he suspected she would not be
for long. Allegiances would shift. He heard she'd met with Octavian,
and perhaps seduced him. The people of the city were convinced that
soon she'd be ruling again, this time with more power than before, new
mistress to the Roman emperor. Their queen was resourceful in such
matters.

There were things about Cleopatra that only Nicolaus knew, however, and they disturbed his sleep.

He'd felt it the moment she summoned Sekhmet. In the air over
Cleopatra and Antony's mausoleum, a flock of birds fell out of the sky.
He knelt in the courtyard of the Museion, and picked up one of them.
Its feathers were mysteriously singed, as though it had flown in the path
of a meteor. Something had gone wrong with the spell.

His spell. Nicolaus took off at a run for the mausoleum and Cleopatra, but he was too late.

When he arrived, it was only to witness the queen of Egypt, her wrists tied behind her, being lowered out of the upstairs window by Octavian's centurions. Her hands, face, and gown were covered in blood, and her eyes were black and bottomless with suffering. Nicolaus quickly turned away so she would not see him.

He'd be blamed, whether the spell had failed or succeeded.

It did not appear that it had succeeded.

Later, though, Nicolaus bribed a physician to view the body of the legionary Cleopatra had killed. In the underground chamber in the Museion, he stood paralyzed with horror, looking down upon the raw wound where the corpse's heart should have been. The queen had been in possession of a weapon of some kind, the doctors concluded. An exceedingly sharp though strangely rough-edged knife.

Nicolaus feared that he knew better.

He'd never understood why he, lowly tutor to the queen's children, had been the one chosen to seek and then to translate the summoning spell, but he'd done it eagerly, nurturing some small thoughts of finding a deeper favor with Cleopatra, even as the city seemed poised to fall.

Before all this had happened, he'd been convinced that she would rise again, regain power over Egypt and perhaps other territories as well, and that when she did, he would rise with her. The queen's historian. The queen's lover, yes, say it, was what he most desired, and the summoning had been too tempting a project to resist. The opportunity to be near her, to meet with her in secret. He'd loved paging through the moth-eaten and worm-bitten records, catching the scents of ancient herbs, running his fingers across the brilliant colors of the hieroglyphs. At last, a crackling scroll of papyrus bound in a red cord. As he spread it out to view, parts of it disintegrated in his hands.

The scroll depicted a summoning, a pharaoh kneeling over an altar, making cuts in his hands. The goddess herself was unmistakable, with her lioness head and the sun disc balanced over it, with her voluptuous female body. Nicolaus made a deep if somewhat rushed study into the elements of the spell, the snake skins and venoms, the honey, the herbs, the pigments and proper designs. The most important thing was, of course, the blood sacrifice. He made some guesses as to what else the spell might contain, some conclusions based on instinct, thinking of it as an academic exercise.

He'd never imagined it could go this far.

Nicolaus was a historian, after all, not a magician. He'd come most recently from Jerusalem, where he was employed as King Herod's personal philosopher, following a dream of greater stature. Cleopatra and Antony seemed like the rulers who would eventually be remembered, while Herod seemed a waning force.

Nicolaus cursed his ambition now. He'd been a fool. His actions had left him one choice: Flee Alexandria or die, and he had no plans to die here, at the beginning of his career.

Nicolaus turned away from the shuttered palace windows and walked into the night, heading for the port. He'd find a ship and leave.

He could never see Cleopatra again, he knew that much. Not if he valued his life.

If she returned to power, he'd be executed. And if the spell *had* worked, as he feared it had, who knew what had been unleashed?

He would not stay in Alexandria to find out.

✦ 11 ✦

The fools thought they had sealed her away from any weapons, but the palace was her home, and she knew every stone. Behind them, beneath them, concealed everywhere were knives and relics. She slashed her palms and watched as the wounds opened and then closed again, bloodless, like gills on a fish. She couldn't summon the goddess back, not the way she'd originally summoned her.

All she could do was listen to the whispers that filled her mind.

You are mine. You belong to me.

"I must speak to Nicolaus," she ordered Charmian. "You must find him and bring him to me."

Drink.

"He's left the city, lady," the girl told her hours later. "No one can tell me where he's gone."

I hunger.

She'd executed the only other scholar who might have helped her, the Egyptian. She saw his face now, his admonitions against the summoning. Forbidden, he'd said. Forbidden.

The bird quenched her thirst for only a few hours. With Charmian, she had to will herself not to act. Her teeth were razors in her mouth. She clasped her arms about her knees and shook, pressing her spine into the corner of her chamber.

She was a murderess, if not yet, then soon.

It was terrifying, this certainty that she teetered on the verge of losing control. Her entire life had been a study in calculated restraint.

Reserve and then seduction. Seduction and then manipulation. The arts of a queen. Only Antony had been exempt. She'd loved him, and that had terrified her, too, at first. Now there was no one to hold her back from doing what the voice wanted her to do. There was no one who loved her enough to save her.

"There's an old temple near Thebes, where the lions come to drink," Nicolaus had told her when they'd practiced the ritual. "The sanctuary of Sekhmet. This spell, the scroll says, comes from there."

The sanctuary was Cleopatra's only hope, but she was here, a prisoner, and if she broke free? She found herself panicked at what would happen if she went among her people. Here, at least she could do no harm to her citizens, but every night, it was worse. Every night, she grew stronger.

Cleopatra had loved her freedom, loved walking among her people, walking with Antony. They'd spent countless evenings that way, strolling the city, watching the swifts at play in the darkening sky, the queen uncrowned, her hair done in the style of a commoner, and Antony without his armor, his face smudged with dirt, an anonymous Roman soldier. Invisible, or so they fancied themselves. They joked and threw dice, sang in the bars, danced amid the people of Alexandria, with no guards, no gold, nothing but the two of them and the breath between them.

Antony stopped in the midst of a dance one night. His face glowed with love for her, and she drew her cloak over their shoulders and led him from the festivities, out into the street and into an alley. They made love in the half dark, her back pressed against the wall, and she cried with sheer pleasure. This man, king of all she held dear.

Nothing could take him from her, she'd thought then, feeling herself ecstatically in charge of her destiny, powerful, certain. So human, and so foolish.

Now the freedom she'd taken for granted was gone. The palace walls contained her, and worse than that, the stranger lived inside her, thirsting, all claws and teeth, all hunger. She knew she'd lost things that could not be regained.

The palace physician brought her prescriptions, ground herbs in his mortar, smeared honey on her skin. She could not tell him what was wrong. She held her breath and clenched her jaw as he came near.

"I cannot eat," she told him.

"Drink, then," he said, offering her pomegranate juice and muttering magic words.

She thrilled momentarily at the color, the deep red, and then laughed bitterly.

"I cannot drink," she said, but she could cry. Tears ran from her eyes as hunger racked her body. The muscles in her back felt like blades. Her ribs grew prominent.

Outside the palace, her conqueror held a special audience, forgiving the citizens of Alexandria for crimes committed against Rome during the war. Debtors were received in grace. He'd win her people while she still lived, convince them that it was better to be ruled by a Roman than by a queen. That was his goal.

They chained her, six guards straining to keep her from breaking free, and Octavian visited her again, demanding an accounting of her treasures.

What treasures had she left?

"My children," she said.

He sighed. "And what would you have me do with your children?" he asked. "Shall they fend for themselves?"

She had not expected him to negotiate. She stumbled, unprepared, then came upon a solution. "Send them to their brother, Caesarion. Only then will I tell you what I possess."

She'd kill him as soon as she knew her children had left the city. He'd come for this final accounting of Alexandria's gold, and she would lean in, close, closer.

He looked at her, his face smooth, his eyes untroubled.

"I am a family man," he said again. "I'll consider it."

Could it be he meant to do as she asked?

"But where would I send them to meet him?"

She hesitated. Could she trust his honor?

"Koptos," she said at last. "We sent Caesarion to Koptos with his tutor, and then overland to the Red Sea, and Myos Hormos. He will not have arrived yet."

Octavian smiled. She could glean nothing of his thoughts. Nothing of his fears. Nothing of his plans. It made her uneasy.

"Son of Caesar," he murmured. "I should like to meet him. Does he take after his father?"

"He does," said Cleopatra. Her bones rattled, hollowed. Her skin burned where the chain wrapped about her wrists. Her mind felt blurred at the edges.

"He is just as Caesar was," she continued, impatient to reach agreement. "Anyone would see it. He is Caesar's only son."

Octavian leaned back, his jaw tight. She saw his eyes darken.

"I think not," he snapped. "*I* am Caesar's only son. Your children are mine. Your gold, your palaces, your books? Mine. You are no longer the ruler here. I heard that Antony gave you the libraries of Pergamon, which were not his to give."

She looked up at him, her eyes blazing.

"Your own dear Caesar burned the library of Alexandria, and I was owed a replacement," she retorted, still bitter, even in this dire state, about the loss of Alexandria's treasure. Tens of thousands of scrolls set afire as Caesar sacked her city. Had the library not been burned, had the summoning scroll not been damaged, perhaps things would be different.

"You're owed nothing," Octavian said quietly, enjoying himself, his calm returned. "You're conquered. Do you not know what it means to surrender? You've surrendered to me, and all the world knows it. *You* are mine, Cleopatra. *You* belong to me."

Antony's words. Antony's rights.

She screamed a wordless sound of rebellion, threw herself forward, straining against her bonds, and spat in Octavian's simpering face. He stepped back in disgust, beckoning a servant to wash his skin.

"I have what I need, in any case," he said. "You're not the only one who knows where your treasures hide."

Cleopatra's secretary was summoned, and he searched through the accounting in front of them both, finding mistakes and crying them out, betraying her who had brought him from the countryside, taught him his trade, kept him from the squalor of the poor.

The guards, the secretary, and Octavian retreated from her chamber, and that, at least, was a blessing. She was no longer cursed with the smell of their flesh. Eiras and Charmian tended her, dressing her hair and washing the wound on her throat, but she heard her maids murmuring outside the chamber door.

"The queen is mad," Eiras whispered to Charmian.

Cleopatra reclined in her chamber, pretending to sleep, but her senses were acute. She could hear every word said in the palaces, from the kitchen depths to the upper towers. She could hear falcons landing on the roof, and men stamping their feet in the courtyard. She could hear rats wending their way through secret passages, and moths chewing at silks. She could hear bats fluttering from the dark, hidden corners, departing for a night of hunting. These women were fools to think she could not hear them talking.

"We must show our allegiance to the emperor if we are to have any hope of outliving her," Eiras continued, her voice a hoarse whisper.

"He plans to kill her?" asked Charmian. There was a note of regret in her voice. Cleopatra had only to listen below the surface of the words, and everything the girl thought was revealed.

The girl had worked her way from village to palace, and now it was all for nothing. She was planning to make off with some of the queen's robes at least, some cloth of gold, and perhaps a piece of jewelry or two, and then offer herself to the emperor's wife as a lady's maid. Cleopatra saw a vision of Rome in the girl's head: glorious spires, handsome men, ripe fruit. She believed she'd no longer be a slave. Cleopatra smiled bitterly at that. The girl was wrong.

Cleopatra herself, a new-crowned queen, had been as good as a slave in Rome in the time she'd spent there as Julius Caesar's mistress. The city assumed her to be whoring herself out to Caesar to buy his sponsorship of her throne. The senators treated her not as a queen but as a simple woman, good only for childbearing. When they met with her, they looked over her shoulder, directing their requests to Caesar.

She'd concocted a fantasy that she controlled them, even with her hair unbound and her baby at her breast, but in Rome, only the vestal virgins had public power separated from the fruit of their wombs. Cleopatra was certainly not one of their kind. This girl would not be, either. A slave she was, and a slave she would remain.

"The humiliation will kill her, if he does not. The men say that he plans to take her to Italy in three days, she and her children. I was told to pack their clothing. As though I were a common maid," Eiras said.

"What will they do in Rome?"

"He'll parade them in chains, and us with them."

"Might he not take her to wife?"

"To wife? To bed, maybe, but never to wife."

The women laughed at this. They did not understand her love for Antony, nor her sorrow, Cleopatra could feel it now. What was love to them?

"She's poxed, likely," said Charmian. "I heard her husband wooed the kitchen slaves."

Cleopatra hissed under her breath. They should fear her, they should tremble, and instead, they chirped outside her door. Hunger gnawed at her stomach.

"I wouldn't mind warming the emperor's bed," said Eiras, preening. "He's a handsome man, even if he is a bit short. He looked at me. Did you notice?"

Somehow the queen could see her, even though a door stood between them. Eiras's hair draped like black silk over her smooth shoulders. In her own village, she'd been known for her beauty. Not so since she'd come to work for the queen. Here, she was forced to unstyle her hair, to simplify her dress so as not to compete. Here, she was no one. Cleopatra could smell her history, even through the stone. The smell was not unpleasant, and beneath it, there was heat, the girl's life thrumming under her skin, like the juicy meat of a grape contained by only the thinnest of coverings.

Cleopatra felt dizzy with starvation and strange knowledge. She could feel every corner of Alexandria, like a creature seeing through the dark to find its prey. She could see things, even as she sat caged in the palace.

Evening fell, shadows dancing over the stones, and the streets of Alexandria lit up with the wildly spent gold of the Romans. Every brothel in the city was busy, and every doctor, too, quelling the poxes that were spreading from whores to soldiers and from soldiers to whores. Goats were being slaughtered for feasting, and bulls were bleeding into basins. A troupe of young men walked below the palace window, drunk and disarrayed, laughing raucously. The smell of blood and lust and anticipation rose through the open windows and filled the room.

Cleopatra could wait no longer. She was caged, yes, but not chained, and suddenly, she felt she could break free. Octavian pretended for the sake of her people's trust that she was in the palace as his guest, willingly surrendering her throne to him, and now she would take advantage of his error. There were few guards. She would be out.

"Charmian," she called, making her voice as sweet as mead. "Eiras. Tend your queen."

They'd fit her out for the night, she told herself, and she'd slip out and leave them. Her cloak dark and rough. Her hair braided as a commoner's. She'd walk the streets, unseen. Inhale the evening air. That would be enough. Surely that would be enough.

The girls entered the room. They were such pretty things, their throats long above their gowns, their cheeks ablaze, nervous that she'd heard them gossiping. She smiled, pretending she had not.

"What will you have us do?" asked Eiras.

The queen rose from her couch, her body suddenly vibrating.

The girl came closer, a questioning look on her face.

Her expression changed as she saw the queen's eyes. They were wide and golden, dilated. They were not human.

Cleopatra felt the maid's shock and saw herself through the girl's sight. She was a monster. An animal.

She inhaled the girl's fear as though it were her own. Her body filled with desire, a searing heat, a slashing hunger.

She sprang.

⇒12⇐

leopatra's teeth were on the girl's throat just as the scream rose from it. The beautiful, unheard sound of Eiras's voice rippled through the queen, absorbed into her body like music.

Her blood was salty and bright, and the queen's fingers spread on her servant's skin, holding her smooth, bronze face. Seventeen, was she? A child. Eiras struggled in her grip, making muted, desperate sounds. Her life was strong. With each movement, Cleopatra drank the girl's youth, her strength, her ambition. She drank her history, her dreams, her hopes, her jealousies and sorrows.

"Help me," the girl whispered, and Cleopatra felt the plea traveling from Eiras's heart and all the way through her lips, the words like teetering boats on a swift-flowing river, before they coursed out of the girl's body and into Cleopatra herself.

Her skin warmed as the blood flowed into her lips, hot and pure, perfect. She heard herself moaning with pleasure, her body trembling as it fed, her very skin tightening, her hips shuddering. This was what she had needed. This was right.

She drank Eiras's desire for the strong soldiers marching into Alexandria, her blushing heat as she stood in the shadows, waiting for the one who would be her lover. She drank the girl's simple hopes of babies, of a home, of a tree and a garden, of food to eat and pretty clothes to wear. She lapped at her throat, at the sweet liquid, the wine of the gods.

Eiras's body began to seize. Her hands grappled hopelessly, but

Cleopatra scarcely noticed her. She was prey, an insect or bird, and Cleopatra was a cat, playing with her as she ate.

The voice inside her sang for pleasure. *Drink*, it sang. *Drink!*

She was the queen, and before that, a king's daughter. Slaves had brought her trays of food, poured her wine, and formed her honeyed cakes.

Slaves had always fed her.

The spark of life began to leave the girl. Her flesh was still pliant, but she breathed no longer. Cleopatra, her hand on the slave's breast, felt the girl's heart stop beating and, her mouth on the slave's throat, felt the blood slow, the pulsing end. She pulled her lips away and laid Eiras down. She gazed upon her for a moment.

Her body hummed with it, a ferocious, glorious sound, a song, a call to reenter the world. A call to feed. Cleopatra looked down at the girl's body and felt as though an army had revealed itself. She was not what she had been, a woman, a mortal. No.

She was more.

The dark voice inside her cried out in triumph.

Her eyes turned to the corner, easily picking the other slave out of the shadows, where she hid, hands over her face, crying.

"Please," Charmian whispered. "Please don't. I won't tell anyone. I should never have said those things. Mark Antony was a good king. You are my queen."

Cleopatra heard her, but these things were unimportant. There was nothing but her body, still quivering with hunger, nothing but the blood that even now filled her, fed her. Her eyes swam with red. She could smell the girl's terror radiating from her skin like perfume.

Her thirst was boundless, deeper than the sea that surrounded her city, and she felt she could drink until the world was empty.

She shook her head, trying to rid it of the image of blood-filled oceans, of corpses. Suddenly, her eyes opened wider. What was she doing?

Why should you be denied? the voice inside her purred. *Why should we hunger?*

"Don't be afraid," Cleopatra heard herself say, her voice soft, the blood soothing her throat. "I will not hurt you. I need you to do some-thing for me."

"What would you have me do?" the girl asked, still crying, trying to regain her composure. She would run, she was thinking, as soon as Cleopatra turned her back. She'd go to the country and never leave it again. She thought of her mother and her younger sister. She thought of the riverbank and the old temples, suddenly dear to her.

Cleopatra heard it all, and yet she could not find herself any longer. The voice inside her was too loud. It felt like her own heart speaking.

"Dress me," said Cleopatra. She'd go into the world as she had planned. The beautiful, throbbing world, the dark, the songs and dances and brothels. She would not go out a peasant, though.

She would go out a queen, dressed in her finest gown, radiant, jew-eled. She had not been a goddess in her previous life. She'd been a woman pretending to be divine, pretending to be immortal. She was a goddess now, and nothing could stop her. She felt the girl's blood filling her, rushing through her, and the feeling was of pure, clean power.

"Dress me in my wedding robes," she said. "And bring me my crown."

When Charmian had tied every ribbon and fastened every clasp, washed her feet and fitted them into her sandals, and veiled her hair with cloth of gold, Cleopatra bent her head as though in modesty.

"How do I look?" she asked.

"Beautiful, my queen," the girl said, a thrum of delicious hope mov-ing through her now. She was to live. She would be free.

"I would pay you for your service," said Cleopatra.

The girl was not accustomed to being paid. She stood on her toes, startled. Then she thought she would take what was offered. Gold, per-haps. Enough to keep her quiet, and certainly enough to make a life elsewhere.

"Thank you," she whispered. "Thank you for the honor."

She held out her hands.

More, said Sekhmet's voice, rising up from inside Cleopatra. *More*.

Deep inside the queen, a tiny human voice cried out in opposition, demanding to know what she was doing, ordering her to stop. She

71

banished it. She was no one's slave. She would not take orders, least of all from something so weak, so powerless.

"I pay you the greatest honor of all," Cleopatra said to her slave. "You feed your queen."

When she finished, she lay back upon her gilded couch, dizzy with pleasure. Her body was sated, and her eyelids felt heavy for the first time in days.

While drinking from the girl's throat, something wonderful had occurred. A reward, perhaps, from the one she fed. Her heart, quiet all these days, began to beat. Slowly at first, and then more quickly.

She had not lost it after all, and with a heart, she could still enter heaven. If her heart was in her breast, it could be weighed in the Underworld. It could tell Osiris of her deeds on earth and bear witness for her in the court of the dead. She would be allowed into the Duat.

With Antony.

It was his death that had given her this power. It would not be in vain. The heartbeat hadn't lasted long, just a few minutes, but it had been enough to reassure her that she still lived, that she was still Cleopatra.

She would avenge his murder. She would fling these villains from her palace. She'd seize her children from their clutches. She would find Caesarion in Myos Hormos and bring him home. She needed no army this time. She had the strength of a thousand, here, in her fingertips.

She would kill everyone who opposed her.

For the first time since all this had begun, sleep swept over Cleopatra like a veil.

She would dream, for just a little while, and then she would go forth into the world.

⇒·13·⇐

At last, the queen of Egypt was dead. Octavian had been uncertain how much longer he'd be able to bear occupying the palace with her.

His official resistance to her suicide had been a mere formality, a necessary evil meant to win her subjects to his side. He'd imagined she would be more resourceful. Every time he met with her, he'd half hoped to find her strangled or stabbed, and instead, she looked at him through sunken eyes, starving herself for all to see.

At last, gritting his teeth, certain that Cleopatra would be forced to kill herself to avoid being taken as a trophy to Rome, he leaked the rumor himself and caused the guards about her chamber to be reduced. Then he waited, tapping his foot, agonizing with both guilt and rapture.

Five hours later, it was done. The spy sent to peer in at the peephole confirmed as much, and now it was time for the official discovery of the body.

He could barely contain the sound that threatened to erupt from his mouth, a sort of gasping sob. He clenched his teeth. It would not do. Marcus Agrippa was looking at him, and as a concession to his general's paranoia of lurking assassins, the new ruler of Egypt sent Agrippa before him to knock down the door of the queen's bedchamber, while he tried to master his emotions. It was triumph, that was all. Triumph long desired, long deserved.

Cleopatra had sent incoherent messages to Octavian in the last few days, demands that she be placed beside her husband in the mausoleum, whether she be dead or alive, begging pleas about the fate of her children, but he would not honor them. They were the requests of a whore. He was an emperor. What use did he have for her last wishes? He had what he needed from her. The locations of Alexandria's treasures, including Caesarion, the heir to Egypt's throne.

Only Marcus Agrippa disapproved of Octavian's methods. He was more tight-lipped than usual, more terse, but the man was a traditionalist. Octavian was the new world. Agrippa would come around. He always did.

Octavian stepped into the room, behind Agrippa. It was aggravatingly dark in here, but a couple of lamps burned low.

He started at an unexpected movement in the shadows, near where he assumed the body of Cleopatra would be lying. His men raised their swords, only to see that the queen's pretty little serving slave was still in the room, on her knees beside the queen's body, adjusting the diadem.

Octavian looked at the girl's trembling hands. No doubt, they'd surprised her as she was in the act of thieving.

She was strange-looking, this servant. Her skin seemed bruised, and her eyes rolled in her head. Her lips were blue.

"What is wrong, Charmian?" one of Octavian's soldiers asked, moving toward her.

She turned toward the men and gave them a look of betrayal.

"The queen is dead," she said. "And I am dead, too. I do my last duty that I may go to heaven."

She slipped to the floor, and Octavian's man ran to her side. He looked up, grim. At his feet, the body of the other handmaiden lay contorted.

Octavian rejoiced internally. All were dead, and at the queen's hand. That made things easier. He'd make a show of sorrow and convince the citizens that none of it was his doing. Tears sprang to his eyes in advance of the performance. He'd trained himself well. Some of the tears, it occurred unpleasantly to him, were real, but he would not think on that now.

He'd bring her corpse to Rome with him. Those mummies of the ancient days were impressive things, in their gilded wooden cases.

Octavian's hero, Alexander the Great, had been treated so, and his grave, near Cleopatra's palaces, contained his body, glittering in a sarcophagus. That was an old tradition, though. Not Roman, not Greek. And he wouldn't do Cleopatra such honors. To be worshipped long after her death.

Octavian would have her corpse draped with plain linen, and he'd place her atop a rolling cart surrounded with flowers, a parade spectacle with her children in chains behind her. They'd all know it to be her that way. There would be no rumors of an empty coffin.

When that was finished, he'd scatter Cleopatra's ashes in Italy, do it himself, make a public ceremony of it. She, who had stolen Mark Antony from Rome, would feed the soil of his country with her dust.

Tensing his jaw, Octavian stepped closer to the queen's corpse, dodging around Agrippa, who stood, ridiculously, with his sword still drawn.

There she was, wrapped in a cloth of sheer, spun gold with a royal purple border. She reclined on a gilded dais, her body as supple and curving as it had been in life, and—

He would not look at her body.

"You will have a long life," she'd said sixteen years before, and now she was dead, and he stood over her corpse.

She was still wearing the same perfume.

Disgusted with himself, Octavian shook the past from his mind.

He would melt this entire palace into money and thank the gods for it. Rome would be rich again, as it was meant to be. He'd pay his soldiers. It had been a near thing, bringing them here unpaid, with all her treasure hidden in that mausoleum, and her threatening to set the place on fire, but Egypt was conquered at last.

Cleopatra's breasts were clearly visible through the cloth, he noticed, one completely bare, the nipple erect, as though recently touched. Or kissed. Her arm was thrown back, the better to display the indecency.

Octavian—no, *Augustus;* that was the name he'd chosen and by which he would soon be known—snorted in revulsion. Whatever poison the queen had consumed, it had treated her as a lover. She was a changed woman from their last meeting a few days earlier, when she'd inexplicably revealed the location of Caesarion. He could only assume she'd been delirious with grief. Why else would she have been so foolish? Gray and gaunt, her eyes blackened, she'd certainly looked ill. Nothing about her had attracted him then. It had been a relief.

In death, however, Cleopatra nearly glowed, and a sheen of perspiration covered her skin. Her position was appalling, one knee bent, the other leg dangling off the edge of the couch. Her back had arched, seizing in her last moments, no doubt.

It was too quiet in this room, far from the noise of the city.

He'd won. His enemies were dead. It puzzled Octavian that he did not feel peaceful.

He moved toward Cleopatra to adjust her draperies, he told himself, to protect her from prying eyes, but in fact, he wanted to run his fingers over her skin, press his lips to her throat. He wanted to—

"Summon doctors," he said, jolting away from her. "Let them determine how she fell."

Agrippa bent over the queen, pulling aside the scarf twined about her neck.

"There's no need," he said. "It was an asp. Here's the mark of its bite."

Octavian leapt back.

"Kill it," he ordered, suppressing the tremor in his voice.

"It has gone already," Agrippa replied. Octavian glanced suspiciously about the throne room. It could be hiding anywhere: in the queen's garments or those of her maids. Beneath the furnishings. How had it gotten into the room in the first place? Smuggled in, no doubt. The queen was sly. He approached her again, willing himself to breathe normally.

"Show us the marks," he ordered. "And summon the Psylli. We will do everything that can be done. Perhaps she is not dead yet."

The marks of the fangs were strangely large, and bright against the pallor of her skin. Octavian looked at them for a moment, disturbed, and then turned away. Whatever had bitten her, it had not been a typical asp but something much larger. It was a painful and strange way to die. Why did she look so calm?

The troupe of snakebite magicians came and knelt to the queen's throat to suck forth the venom, but she did not revive.

"She is dead," the leader of the Psylli said, his dark face grave. "But her soul is not far gone. Something is strange with her. She is not as she seems."

Octavian shrugged at the man's phrasing. What did Rome care for her soul?

He dismissed the Psylli, paying them in gold. Word of the queen's suicide and of the emperor's attempts to save her would be all over the city by nightfall.

Agrippa hesitated at the doorway.

"Go," Octavian said. "I'm nearly done here."

When Agrippa had gone, Octavian bent over Cleopatra one last time, to remove her crown. He let his hand rest on her breast, still amazingly soft. One would think her heart still beat.

He bent closer, inhaling her perfume, telling himself that he was simply taking the measure of his enemy. One last conversation with his foe, before she was gone forever.

"Caesar taught me that true leaders fight with words instead of swords," he told her. "An army hears an order they think is from their queen, and they turn on their commander. A man hears a message that his queen has killed herself, and he acts to save his own honor. Have I done as you would have done, had you come to my country with your army? Now you will travel to Rome with your emperor. You, who said you belonged to no one, belong to me."

He leaned closer yet. He pressed his mouth against her parted lips, and then—

The queen's eyes opened.

⇒ 14 ⇐

For the rest of his life, the emperor would remember what he saw that day, looking into the eyes of a dead queen. Visions, he thought at first. Prophecy, he realized as they went on. He was seeing what would come.

He saw the future laid out before him like polished gems on a black cloth, each moment distinct, each moment vibrating with its own horror.

Black clouds filled with slashing lights. Crippled bodies, skeletons. Ships beached on dying shores. Rats swarming bodies, covering them so completely that no skin was left visible. These were the trappings of war, Octavian tried to tell himself. Though he was a young man, he'd commanded armies. He had seen civilization.

This, this blazing place, this horror, was nothing like it.

Here, soldiers herded women and children into machines, tore away their rags, their shoes, their belongings, held metal sticks at eye level as their victims stood against fences, hands behind their heads, waiting for death to take them. Here, child warriors slew other child warriors, brandishing cleavers and metal rods, throwing something that blasted hearts away, carousing in an ecstasy of violence, singing and whooping as they smashed the skulls of less lucky children. Here, the naked and the dying ran through the roads of some dark city, their skin melting away, their mouths gaping with horror.

Wolves prowled cobbled streets, stalking lanes that still held homes. A baby cried out, only to be snatched up by an animal. He saw a flame-haired, white-faced woman crowned with gold, her mouth stretching in a cry of agony, a bearded man throwing his hands into the air, summoning some vast, horned creature. He saw an island of fire, a river of lava, creatures flying through the sky.

A human heart on a scale, a weighing.

A tremendous serpent thrashed and coiled, its fangs shining in the moonlight, high above an arena strangely familiar to Octavian. Metal monsters flew through the air and ignited, screaming people leaping from inside them, and below it all, the blood ran, scarlet rivers of it surging into the oceans and coloring the waters. The great beasts of the sea rose up, fins and teeth, battling over bloated corpses.

The sky rained fire.

Octavian saw himself suddenly as though in a nightmare, a slight, young man walking down a deserted road, and behind him, a lioness padding softly, her maw dripping with gore.

He shouted from afar, trying to send a warning, and the lion—no longer on the road but, impossibly, with him in the palace—turned to look at him, her body shifting, growing larger.

She was a woman now, with a lion's head, and she gazed upon him, seeing him utterly. He felt his organs dissolving and a red miasma floating over his eyes. The creature's mouth curved into a smile, and Octavian was transported again to a place that seemed, for a moment, peaceful.

A green orchard, a star-spattered sky, and himself, walking the paths between the trees. He was old now, older than his true father had been when he'd died, older than Caesar, too. His skin was as dry as papyrus and his hands, opening before him, were spotted with age. His spine was hunched, and one leg was short, hobbled. He chewed his meal with rotting teeth, and swallowed painfully.

He looked nervously into the darkness, feeling himself watched by a predator. He tried to cry out, but his throat seized, and something burned its way through his center.

Then he saw *her*, Cleopatra, unchanged, standing in the shadows. She stepped toward him, her hands outstretched, her fingers tipped with talons. He saw her pointed teeth bared. He felt her breath on his face.

Above him, the trees spread their darkness against the sky, blotting out the stars, and he was falling backward, convulsing, vomiting fire.

"Guards!" he screamed, and Marcus Agrippa charged into the throne room, leading his men.

Octavian was drenched in sweat, and he found that he was down before Cleopatra. Kneeling to her. He couldn't stand. The men, swords drawn, ran from end to end of the room, searching for the enemy that had upset their leader. Agrippa knelt beside Octavian.

"Are you ill? Do you need a physician?" asked Agrippa, and he couldn't answer.

Her eyes were shut now, as though they had never opened, as though he'd never seen into the depths of—what? What had he seen? He knew one thing, and that was that he never wanted to see such visions—such omens—again.

"What happened here?" Agrippa demanded. "Is there an enemy?"

"She was—" Octavian stopped. Agrippa would not believe him. How could he tell him that a dead woman was not dead? That he'd seen a vision of the end of days in her eyes? Agrippa would think he was mad.

"I thought I saw the asp, but I was mistaken." Struggling to his feet, Octavian commanded, "Bury her." He wanted nothing to do with his previous plan to take her corpse with him to Rome and parade it through the streets as proof of his victory. "Bury her with Antony, if that is what she wants so much. Wall up the tomb with two layers of mortared stone. Make sure there are no entrances or exits. We do not want anything getting out. Set guards around the perimeter. Give them the best weapons."

Agrippa looked at him, bewildered.

"Getting *out*?" he asked.

"Do you question me?" Octavian asked, regaining his authority at last. Finally, he could draw a breath. His damp garments chilled against his skin, even in the heat of the room. He would not look at the queen. He would not.

Her eyes had been bottomless. He had seen in them the very sphere of the sky, the edges of the horizon, and the green, living world, just before it all went dark.

He would burn her body, if he only knew what would result. It might spur the visions to take place, like a spark to kindling, and he'd be the man who begat the end of the world.

No, he thought, his breath coming too quickly, his head spinning, the safest course would be to wall her up with the man she'd wanted so badly. The proper rituals, a funeral fit for a queen, for a wife. That would placate her. That was what she had wanted, after all, this soulless creature, this thing. Love.

"Don't touch her!" he shouted as one of the men laid a hand on the queen's arm. What if she woke? The men, accustomed to carrying out peculiar orders, lifted the couch with Cleopatra upon it and carried her over their heads, making a funerary procession. But Agrippa remained, eyeing Octavian worriedly.

"What happened?" Agrippa asked quietly, and Octavian shook his head. He could not answer.

Cleopatra had stayed motionless as they lifted her, a smile on her lips, as though taken with a pleasant dream.

The monster slept, Octavian knew. She slept. But for how long?

"And chain her," he ordered.

⇒ 15 ⇐

She awoke in darkness. The sound of marching steps encircled the building she found herself inside. High above her, the pale heat of moonlight transferred through the stone. Here, the smell of new mortar and dust. Her mouth was dry. She shook at the cloth that covered her and stretched her fingers. They curled at the touch of teak.

She was naked, she realized now. Naked but for her crown, and a silver chain that wrapped about her body, binding her to the wooden slab.

The pain of the silver had woken her.

The queen knew the place now. This was her own mausoleum, but the room was changed, all its treasure stolen, even the pearls pried off the walls. How had she come to sleep here? How had she come to be bound? Where was her gown? She'd been dressed in her finest garments, she remembered, glorious in her silken wedding clothes, decked in jewels.

The chain scored her flesh, wrapped about her body like a strangling serpent, pressing in upon her tender skin, biting at her. It crossed her at the shoulders and bound her arms to her sides before wrapping again across her breasts and, again, over her stomach. Her legs were chained together, and her entire body was secured to the wooden pyre she lay upon.

Dread filled her. Was she to have her liver plucked out by birds, as in the Greek story? Was she to be immobilized as she was tortured, crying out to the gods, unanswered?

The smell of burning flesh lingered still. Antony's ashes. The silver box sat on the pyre beside her, open to the air. She could taste his bones each time she inhaled, and worse than that, she could taste his sorrow, his great losses, his fears. Until the end, he'd believed that she had traded him for Egypt, given him up to Rome, conspired secretly with his enemy. Her eyes welled, but there was nothing she could do to change it now. Her beloved had died mistrusting her.

There was a movement of some kind, just outside the walls. Leathery wings. Bats returning home after their hunting, hiding themselves in cracks in the stones. It must be near dawn. How many days had passed? How long had she slept? Why had she slept here at all?

She recalled only snatches of what had passed in the hours before she'd arrived here. A hunger. A feeding. The feeling of her body swelling with pleasure, warming. What had she eaten?

She remembered the touch of the emperor's lips on hers. She'd felt the pressure of him against her thigh, his hand on her breast, yet she'd been unable to move. He'd spoken to her. She struggled to remember what he said.

A confession. He had told her how he had sinned against her, but she could remember only the taste of his words, not the sound of them.

Something had terrified him. He'd lost his pride and confidence and turned back into a boy scared of the dark. He knew she lived, and he had buried her because of it.

She quivered and then cried out as her skin shifted against the chain. Each link burned and cut her flesh. She tried to still herself, hoping that her body would cease screaming if she were immobile.

It was airless, or nearly so, in this crypt. They'd bricked up most of the air holes near the roof. The window upstairs was gone, too, she could sense that much, and when she stilled herself and stretched her senses— what strangeness, to be able to feel the edges of things far beyond her sight—she knew more. They'd placed a layer of stone outside the mausoleum's walls and then a layer of alabaster, sparing no expense, finishing the structure as she herself had meant to do. She could feel the chisels, the inscriptions carved into its surface. She could feel the march of the guards, several of them, encircling the building, armored as if for battle.

Why would they have done such a thing, after they'd placed her here, still living? Tricking her people, she guessed.

Octavian Caesar had stood on the steps of the mausoleum, looking over the crowd. Cleopatra could smell his fear still lingering there.

The queen is dead, Octavian told her people. *She killed herself in grief for Mark Antony. It was an honorable death, though it went against the wishes of Rome.*

Her people would have suspected her murdered but not dared challenge him. Cities that resisted the Romans ended in ashes. The people of Alexandria would have mourned instead, torn out their hair and knelt, processed about the mausoleum, singing and drinking. She could still hear the echoes of it.

The queen is dead. Long live the emperor. Hail Caesar!

This was a Roman city now.

She heard a man breaking into drunken song out on the street, the guards hushing him. She was suddenly filled with wrath. Would she be doomed to listen to the world forever, trapped away from it?

She screamed in fury, there in the dark, but all she heard was the echo of her voice, bouncing from the high ceiling, rattling against the walls.

Antony's ashes shifted with her scream. She breathed him in, another gasp of betrayal and sorrow, of his blood on her hands. She'd be here forever, beside the ruined body of her beloved, unless she did something to escape.

"FREE ME!" she screamed, every muscle straining and crying out against the chains as she pushed herself up from the slab. She was not strong enough to break them. Her skin was seared, and she felt the metal slipping beneath it, slicing into flesh. Rage boiled inside her and she howled her order out to the ceiling. The guards would hear her. Someone would hear her. "Release me! Your queen lives, and you serve a monster!"

She heard a high call, a keening song. A pulse of sound from outside the building, and another sound, of something creeping, fluttering through a small space. A rustling.

Something was coming.

⇒16⇐

Octavian visited Alexander the Great's grave, crippled with unease. He'd long looked forward to paying his respects at his hero's burial place, nearby as it was to Alexandria. It was the heroic thing to do, after all, a scene that might be written about by the poets of Rome, the young emperor standing beside the tomb of his predecessor, inheriting his power. *Augustus the Great*, he'd thought secretly, tasting the name on his tongue.

The simpleton slaves and keepers of the necropolis insisted that he see the endless Ptolemaic tombs as well, and he was forced to descend an unpleasant stone staircase into a black pit, but he immediately turned and ran back up into the light, fearful of more creatures like Cleopatra, dead and yet not dead.

"I came to see a king," he snapped, "not a pile of dead bodies."

This was to have been a reward for Cleopatra's death after all, a final triumphant act in her city before departing for other places, other kingdoms, but what he'd seen in Cleopatra's chamber had drastically changed the tone of the visit.

All he could think of now was her glowing eyes, her smiling lips. She lived, she lived, and he'd buried her that way. Too late, he realized that she would not stay buried. She would come for him. He must flee the country.

Before he could, though, he must do this or regret it forever.

"Open the sarcophagus," he ordered. "I wish to see him."

He sent the slaves away the moment the case was open, and then forced himself to look into the coffin. Alexander's features, which Octavian had long venerated, dreamt of, were nothing but fragile leather. Nearly three hundred years had passed since Alexander's death by poison at Nebuchadnezzar's palace. His corpse had originally been transported from Babylon in a vat of honey, as though he were a queen bee. The sweetish smell still lingered, along with that of the cinnamon used in his embalming. The odor confused Octavian's mind, twisting his memories. In Egypt, the precious inner bark of the cinnamon tree was used on the dead, but in Rome it was used on the living, as an ingredient in love potions. Octavian himself had wandered the darkest alleys of his own city, sniffing out magic in the corridors, witches brewing potions for hire.

A flash of fury blasted through Octavian's center. His problems here in Egypt were certainly the result of a witch. Were it not for her, he would not be looking at a corpse and wondering if it lived.

"Great Alexander," he shouted, the walls echoing around him. "I pay you tribute."

He'd brought with him a golden diadem, discovered in the queen's treasure, and flowers to fill the sarcophagus, but first, he must make certain that Alexander was truly dead. Octavian put out a tentative finger, breathing unhappily through his mouth, icy sweat breaking out over his body. The hand shook so gravely that it knocked against the corpse's face, and with a faint, dusty sound, the flesh gave way.

Octavian jumped away, horrified. The nose hung crookedly now. He squeezed his eyes shut, waiting for the awful sound that would herald the rising of a wounded god, but no sound came.

The eyes of the corpse were closed. No black depths, no shining end of the world there. No life inside the body of his hero. Thank the gods.

Octavian permitted himself a small sigh of relief. He would not have wished to contend with both Alexander and Cleopatra. She was more than enough.

"What should I do?" he whispered to his hero, praying for a revelation, though now he knew there would be no answer. "What should I do with her?"

Alexander the Great would never have trembled in the face of magic.

He would have attacked Cleopatra, living corpse or no, monster or no, ferocious with his sword. He would have summoned sorcerers to plot against her, researched potions and poisons. He would have done whatever was necessary to conquer her.

Octavian ran his fingers over the great man's burial garments. He tore off a small section of fabric and hid it on his person, hoping to absorb some of Alexander's godlike courage.

Octavian was himself the son of a god, or so his mother, Atia, had always claimed, swearing Apollo had come down from Olympus in the form of a snake and impregnated her. According to legend, Alexander the Great had also been fathered by a god in snake form, the Egyptian king and magician Nectanebo, and so Octavian had never seen reason to dispute Atia's politically useful story. It made Alexander and Octavian the same sort of hero, the same sort of man.

Octavian did not feel heroic at present. He felt queasy, thinking of Cleopatra's chamber and the missing asp. Might the snake have been a god? What else could explain the queen living and dead at once?

No.

Surely the opening of her eyes had been an aftereffect of the snake's—the *mortal* snake's—poison. Did not dead men's members stand erect on the gallows? Did not the beheaded stare in wonder? Surely, were he to look into Cleopatra's mausoleum now, he'd find her decaying, just as Alexander was.

And if not—

He'd do as his hero would have done. Alexander had won the world through bravery and perseverance, through resourceful actions, and Octavian would follow his lead. He would not flee.

He was the man who controlled Rome, and Rome controlled the world. His enemies were dead, all but her. He had the power in his hands. He would run her through with his sword. Either that, or he'd burn her, a thought that seemed more and more attractive. He'd been childish, imagining that she would set the world aflame. It was his own fears controlling him. What witch could survive a burning? He'd turn her to ash, and let her try to rise from that.

Octavian stood up from Alexander's tomb and looked down one last time at the shriveled figure lying within. Alexander had been killed at twenty-nine, long before he'd reached his full potential. Octavian was thirty-three. He did not plan to die this day.

"There is more world out there than you knew," he told Alexander, testing a certainty he did not wholly feel. "More things than you ever dreamt of. I've seen the world, and it belongs to me. All of it is mine."

He turned to march up the stairs. The room echoed with his last exhalation, the dust of empires rising and falling behind him.

"Mine."

⇢·17·⇠

They filled the room, arriving from beneath the floor, slipping through impossibly small cracks and portals. They came from above, nearly deafening Cleopatra with their shrill song.

She cringed, her rage gone as quickly as it had arrived. Now she was terrified of the pain that would surely come. They'd tear her skin, and she'd live. They would wound her flesh, and she would remain awake, feeling each ripping movement. Feeling each creature—and she knew them now, not birds but bats—diving toward her heart. Their tiny fangs, their scrabbling claws. Her body, though it was changed, was still hers. It was her only possession, and these were thieves coming to break it apart.

They would find her empty.

Something else was coming, though. She could smell a musky, dry odor. Snakes slithering across the stone, their sleek bodies blending into a rippling surface, roiling as a storming sea. And rats, their skeletons bending against the narrow passages, their fur glittering black, their eyes glowing.

Her subjects.

She laughed, the sound mixing with a sob. Queen of Egypt, in her lost, gilded robes. Naked before her true citizens, she must offer them her last words. Oh, the proclamations she might make, here in the dark.

"Save me," she whispered. "Your queen commands you."

She laughed again, feeling hysteria rising. Nothing to calm her here, no wines or potions, no Antony to press his fingertips against her lips.

She felt the rasp of snakeskin on her ankle. The brush of leather wings on her face. The lash of a rat's tail, whipping through her fingers.

This is how it would end, then. This is how it would be, from here until the end of time. The queen and her creatures. Eaten, but not consumed.

A snake pressed its skull beneath her breast, fitting its triangular head under the chain and then flowing over her skin. It slipped up her throat, and appeared before her, its eyes glittering in the dark, gazing at her with what seemed to be intention.

She was mad to think the snake might understand her. More were coming. She felt them writhing across her limbs like a living mantle.

The snake stared into her eyes, waiting for something. She tried to move but could not.

"Free me!" she shouted, giving in to the madness. "I am your queen! The queen of Egypt calls upon you!"

The snake slithered away, and Cleopatra laughed and cried at once. She was insane, and worse, she knew it. Her predictions had come true. She, who was the daughter of generations of kings, now thought that she could talk to animals.

The rats began to gnaw at something. Let it not be her bones. She couldn't feel anything anymore, couldn't tell where the animals were.

The chain shifted around her, burning, burning, but she didn't care. Let it burn. Anything was better than this, these beasts of the night pressing against her body, the sounds of hissing and hungering. Another serpent slithered across her abdomen, pressing into the curve of her waist, where once a jeweled belt had hung, tempting kings, tempting warriors.

The chain shifted again.

She could hear the rats gnawing at the wood beneath her, furrowing its surface. She'd commissioned the pyre, just as she'd commissioned the box that held Antony's ashes. Now the rats were turning it to dust. Everything would go to dust, everything but Cleopatra.

The chain loosened. She stretched her arm and touched a serpent. She moved her leg and felt another. The room was dark, but all around her was the sound of movement.

Bats rose through the dark, singing. A moth glowed in a sudden spark of light and was taken, struggling against claws.

The chain lifted from her skin and hung in the air above her.

She lay there for a moment, amazed, and then she felt the creatures waiting, all around her.

"Thank you," she whispered.

The only reply she heard was the soft swishing of serpents making their way back to where they'd come from, bats singing their way back out into the sky, and rats channeling their bodies into the cracks in the walls. Like ghosts, they returned invisibly to the waking world, populating the hidden spaces, filling the shadows. She realized that she was as good as a ghost herself, and as she listened to the departure of her saviors, she learned from their quiet. There were secret places in her city, places the Romans would not think to look for her.

She eased herself up from the slab, naked and exultant. Whatever it meant, whatever it would mean, she was free.

It was a simple matter to leave the mausoleum, pressing the stone with her fingers and waiting for the hidden tunnel to the palace to open. How had they imagined she'd gotten into the place to begin with? All the tombs were connected to the palaces, and had been for centuries.

She slipped back in through the slave's quarters, taking only the silver box that contained Antony's ashes, wrapped in a cloth to protect her fingers from the strange, scalding pain the metal caused her skin. She hid in a cellar. It was daylight, and she could not go out into the sun, particularly not as she was. She would need dark clothing, and something to swath her face.

She found herself confused, uncertain where to go next, and so she stayed hidden. Her city was a great unknown, though it had always cradled her in the past. She had no servants, no trusted friends, no messengers. She had no dresser, no woman to paint her skin and braid her hair.

She was dead to all of them.

She thought of this with a kind of wonder as she crouched, naked and filthy, against the cool stone wall of the cellar. She was no longer a queen. She could do exactly as she pleased now. No more politics, no more advisors, no more declarations of war.

What was it she wanted? What would she do now that she was dead? She *was* dead, that much was certain. Dead to her country, in any case.

The things she loved had been taken from her, but some of them still lived. Her children. She would find them. Her enemies still lived as well. A whisper of memory came back to her as she thought of Octavian. She saw him as he knelt over her in her bedchamber, thinking her dead, speaking to her as though she could forgive him. He'd confessed his sins to her. He was the one who'd told Antony she was dead. He was the one who had told her armies to desert her husband.

All of this had been set in motion by Octavian's lies.

When she found him, she would hurt him as he had hurt her.

The palace seethed with activity when first she entered, servants running from room to room, the foul scent of roasting meat, excited gossip, but as the day passed, the place quieted. Octavian had left the palaces just before she'd arrived, or so she gleaned from listening to the chatter. He'd taken a mass of his soldiers, bodyguards, and armor, kindling, and firepots, and gone out into the tombs. Starting a tiny war somewhere in her city, she imagined.

When at last she emerged from the cellar, creeping along a kitchen wall, the place was nearly empty. The creature she finally spoke with was ancient, a blind crone hovering over a basin, scrubbing away at some vile root.

"Where are the other servants?" Cleopatra asked her.

"Are you not one of us?" the crone asked.

"I've been away," Cleopatra said, trying to repress her regal tone. This was not the sort of conversation she would normally have with a slave.

"They've gone to the execution," the servant said.

This was a stroke of luck, though who might Octavian be killing now? His own soldiers? She would not be surprised by such an act. He *would* kill his trusted allies. Antony had been his friend, his teacher, and look at what he'd done to him.

There was no one left to war against. The city had surrendered. Mark Antony was dead, and so was she, for all Octavian knew. She looked forward to seeing his face when she proved that assumption wrong. Her mouth filled with saliva. Hunger. She still could not remember the last time she'd eaten. Something about the shock of her false burial, she concluded. There were gaps in her memory. It was a blur of light, a glimpse of red that failed to resolve into anything clear.

Cleopatra found a kitchen knife. In the dark, she held out a lock of her hair and sawed it off, shuddering as it drifted to the floor, braided strands and loose ones. A single shining twist of silver. Her hair had been beautiful, and the coif she'd been buried with, dressed by Charmian, was complex, each knot signifying something specific. Those things were gone. She grieved them as much as she gloried in her new state. *Free*, she reminded herself. *Free*.

Soon, it was all sheared, cut into a rough tumble, and her head bound up in a swath of dirty cloth. She washed the paints from her face with cold, greasy water. She looked like a slave. None of the assembled would know her for their queen. Still, she would cover herself fully, for though the day was waning, the sun shone low in the sky, and she did not imagine she would be immune to its rays. She wrapped the box containing Antony's ashes in a piece of cloth and slung it over her shoulder before dressing herself in a robe, a pair of leather sandals, and a rough traveling cloak stolen from one of the cook's chambers.

At last, she veiled her head and made her way into the city, following the sounds of reveling.

Her enemy would be at the execution. She looked forward to seeing his face when she appeared before him.

⇢18⇠

Octavian strode onto the platform where the accused awaited him. Cleopatra was the reason for this. The only reason. She'd forced Octavian's hand, and he resented it, but he had to find her.

It had taken only a moment to determine that the queen was gone from her mausoleum. The chain that had bound her draped the pyre like a glittering veil, and the fastenings that had bound the chain itself to the teak were destroyed.

Something, or someone, had clawed the wood away.

As for how she'd escaped the building, he could not tell. Octavian himself, claiming that he sought some forgotten treasure inside the mausoleum, had required stonemasons to break into the covered window at the top of the building, and there was no other way in or out, not that he could see. The witch had spirited herself away.

Well, he would spirit her back.

Somewhere out there, she was watching him. He seethed, despite his dread. He was surrounded by guards, and it would not be he who died today. Marcus Agrippa stood beside him, and though he remained bewildered by the episode in the mausoleum, the general was the most reliable defender a man could ask for.

Octavian caught a glimpse of the criminal's liquid golden eyes, those long limbs beneath the Roman toga, and he feared that he was not making the right decision.

The boy gave him a pleading stare. Octavian turned away and cleared his throat.

"Citizens of Alexandria," he said, looking down into the wild-eyed crowd. She was not visible, if she was here. "Your emperor addresses you."

The crowd cheered for him, and though he knew it to be false—they were Egyptians, after all, cheering for a conqueror—it pleased him.

"This man stands accused of treason," he continued. Treason? He made up the accusation as he said it. "He is Caesarion, son of Cleopatra, who herself conspired against the Roman Empire and against her own people."

Octavian had sent riders to Koptos and Myos Hormos as soon as Cleopatra revealed where the boy had gone. His messengers caught up with the boy's trusted tutor, Rhodon, at a roadside inn, and as the boy slept, innocent of betrayal, the price for a peaceful delivery had been negotiated. Five days before, even as Cleopatra was being buried in her mausoleum, Caesarion had been delivered back to Alexandria by Rhodon, who was paid a bounty in Egyptian gold for the task.

Octavian had been undecided about what to do with Egypt's heir. He could see his own adoptive father in the shape of the sixteen-year-old's jaw, and it unsettled him.

"How did my mother die?" the boy asked Octavian during dinner the night he arrived, a strong set to his mouth, sitting straight and true in his chair.

"Suicide," Octavian replied, and the boy nodded bravely, asking no further questions. Octavian straightaway took him out for weapons training, and the boy excelled, his smooth, copper skin shining in the sun, his form perfect. This boy, this Caesarion, was so obviously Julius Caesar's son, Octavian could hardly bear to kill him.

Octavian had slept restlessly, dreaming of taking Caesarion back to Rome and installing him in his own house. His wife, Livia, would protest, of course, but what place did Livia have to protest anything? She'd married him while pregnant with another husband's child, and who would blame him for adopting a male heir when Livia had not provided one for him? *This* boy was Caesar's own blood! Far better than Octavian's stepson, Tiberius, who carried no heroic line in his ancestry. Just as Octavian had been adopted by Julius Caesar, Octavian would adopt Caesarion. It was fitting.

The symmetry had pleased the emperor, and he'd been on the point of announcing his decision when the absence of Cleopatra's body from her mausoleum changed things.

Octavian needed a lure for the queen, and the son must serve. He announced that he'd changed his mind, that Caesarion could not be trusted.

A bewildered Agrippa resisted this sudden shift in Octavian's plans, insisting that if Caesarion had to be executed, it should be done in private. He feared a riot, angry Alexandrians resisting the death of their prince.

Octavian could not bring himself to explain that the execution was a trap for a dead woman.

Where was she? He scanned the crowd again.

Perhaps she'd appear in the final moment. He signaled to his forces to remain on guard. The sun was setting, and he must kill the boy or lose the light. The crowd, whatever their loyalties, desired a death. All this was Cleopatra's fault, and Octavian resented her for it.

He took a deep breath and nodded to his centurion. He would not do this dirty thing himself. The crowd screamed with bloodlust, recognizing the gesture.

"Traitor!" they cried, and pushed closer, some of them attacking each other in their excitement.

His men raised their shields in a ceremonial gesture, and he searched the crowd one last time. No one. Only an old woman wrapped from head to toe in rough veils struck his eye, and she was at the farthest edge of the throng, pushing her way forward. Not the queen.

Octavian glanced toward the boy, questioning his haste in condemning him. Scarcely Cleopatra's son at all. Far more the son of Caesar. He looked toward his advisors, wondering what excuse he could use to render this afternoon forgotten, wondering how he would calm the crowd should he not give them what they expected.

Just then, the boy's eyes blazed open, and he lurched in the grip of the centurion, flinging his arms upward and his body back. He kicked and connected with the older man's leg, and the centurion lost his hold. Caesarion began to run, launching himself off the platform like a gazelle, and even in such dire circumstances, Octavion could only look upon him in wonder.

Here was a warrior. Everyone had seen his bravery. The boy was a credit to his father's country. Octavian moved his hand to call the execution off.

"Pardon him!" he managed, but the noise of the crowd was too loud.

They surged forward, fists in the air, throwing punches and bellowing, surrounding the boy.

"Kill him!" they shouted, and Octavian's centurion, now recovered, leapt off the platform with a roar of fury.

⇒19⇐

People kicked about Cleopatra, pulling and tugging at her robes. The scent of flesh seared her nostrils. She inhaled deeply, feeling the press of limbs against hers, the weight of bodies. Her fingers curled, hidden beneath her robe. Cleopatra could almost see the emperor, almost see his intended victim, whoever it was. She pushed her way forward, craning her neck for a view.

She hungered, troubled by the gaps in her memory. Surely, she had last eaten weeks ago, before Antony's death. She'd dined with her love, that was it. The night before he died.

But somehow, she was not certain of that. There were flashes in her mind that felt like memory, pale skin, blood trickling.

The last light of the sun shone directly on the shields ahead, reflecting into her eyes. Her wrappings were not enough to keep it from burning. She felt weak, with both hunger and heat, her skin sparking beneath its coverings, her eyes filling. She needed to get out of the light, but there was nowhere to go. She pushed herself deeper into the crowd toward Octavian.

Odd. She caught a glimpse of someone she knew, close to the platform. It couldn't be he, though. Rhodon the tutor was long gone, to Myos Hormos with her son Caesarion. She was mistaken.

Drink, her body called, urging her onward.

Octavian was somewhere up there, and even if she could not see him, she could smell his strange absence of odor. The smooth grayness of him, like a gap in all the other scents and thoughts. Ahead.

She pressed forward, her mouth filling with saliva.

Feed.

A shaven-headed centurion appeared on the platform, his short toga newly white. Bleached in urine, and then rinsed in water until it passed for clean. Cleopatra wrinkled her nose, sniffing the foul Roman odor from where she stood, even if no one else in the crowd could smell it. The centurion leapt off the platform in pursuit of the victim, and then, suddenly, through a gap in the crowd, Cleopatra caught a glimpse of her son.

Caesarion.

His panicked face, his slender brown limbs scrabbling as he ran from his executioner. Cleopatra staggered with shock even as she shoved herself deeper into the crowd, toward him, toward him. It could not be.

Why had he returned to Alexandria? He'd been safe, taken from the city by Rhodon. How had they found Caesarion? Who had betrayed him? It came to her, in a devastating realization.

She had.

"*I am a family man,*" Octavian had sworn, and she'd trusted him, thinking to save her other children, thinking to bargain with a fiend.

She'd led the Romans to her son.

"KILL HIM!" the crowd screamed, pummeling one another in their desire to snatch at Caesarion's garments. Cleopatra saw knives flashing out of concealment and smelled blood being shed all around her.

With the bloodshed, everything came rushing back to her, all that she had done, her maid arching backward, struggling to free herself from Cleopatra's clutches. The other girl, paling quietly, as her body dropped like a shed garment to the floor of the queen's chamber. Cleopatra gasped, convulsing with the memories, but she could not afford to let them stop her.

She threw herself forward, clawing her way closer to her child, her voice drowned by the rioting around her.

"CAESARION!" she screamed, fighting the crowd. The last rays of sun shot through a gap in the buildings, and light flared off the raised shields of the legionaries, momentarily blinding Cleopatra and amplifying the heat. She lost her balance and stumbled to the ground, stunned and weakened, her clothing in disarray, her veil sliding off to bare her face to the glare, blistering her skin instantly.

Fingers tore at her clothes, and sandaled feet kicked her trapped body. Her bones shifted in her skin, crushed and then repaired. Her cheekbone shattered under a heel. She felt her arms break and then knit themselves back together.

She knew the mind of the crowd then, with that horrible *knowing*. They hated her, hated the royal family for their neglect, for their distance, for their scandal, for their Greek ancestry. They hated her for losing their city to Rome. It was her fault that they were inflamed now against her child. They demanded a sacrifice.

She screamed wordlessly from the ground, pushing herself up, rising, rising.

Her son threw his hands into the air and shouted a desperate proclamation.

"Hear me!" he cried, his voice cracking, speaking in Greek. "Hear me! I am your king! I am son of the Ptolemies! I will rule over you! I will keep you safe from the Romans! They will enslave Egypt! I will keep you free!"

He repeated his declaration in Latin and then in Egyptian, to prove that he was a man of the people, but his voice was drowned by the sounds of rioting. His words were exactly the wrong ones.

"I AM YOUR KING!" the boy shouted again, and Cleopatra struggled to her knees, the sun still searing her flesh, her eyelids blistering, glimpsing her son mere lengths from her now, almost within reach.

Just as her fingers touched him, a centurion appeared behind her child, raised his hands to Caesarion's throat, and placed them on his perfect skin.

"Kill him!" the crowd screamed, and she tore at the centurion's tunic, desperate to get to her son before he did. This could not happen. Not this. Not while she watched.

Someone kicked her in the face, throwing her back to the ground, and her eldest child disappeared, dragged into a sea of hungering, murderous bodies as she was dragged in the opposite direction.

She could not reach him.

She saw, fleetingly, pale gray eyes, light hair, a laurel crown, as the emperor fled the platform. He would not even watch what he had set in motion.

She heard the sound of bones giving way as the centurion wrapped his fingers around Caesarion's throat. She heard her son's last breath as the Roman broke his neck.

Her howl of agony shook the buildings of the agora, calling the crows in chaos down from the sky, but it did not stop what was happening. It did not stop anything.

⇒ 20 ⇐

The boy died quietly, gracefully, in the manner of a king. Octavian was able to watch only a moment of it before he was forced to turn away. It had taken twenty-three thrusts of his betrayers' daggers to bring Caesarion's father down, and Caesarion was more a man than Octavian himself, who vomited from the platform as he heard the bones in the boy's neck shatter.

Then, there was that sound, that unearthly, animal howl, which came from no discernible place, from no discernible person. The crowd boiled before him, and crows filled the sky, circling and shrieking.

Octavian was suddenly aware of how exposed he was.

The crowd erupted before Octavian, rushing toward the body of the boy, and the centurions pulled their leader away, pressed him into a litter, drew the curtains. There was blood on Octavian's white toga; he could see it, scarlet droplets standing out from the ivory linen.

The queen had not appeared. Where could she be? What army might she be raising against him? Octavian secured an extra slave to taste his food, in case she thought to poison him. It was a faint protection. She could be anywhere. She could be part of his own army, hidden in the guise of a man. He called his troops to order and had them inspected. Agrippa, his only trusted general, tore their tunics from their bodies, revealing all their scars and puckered battle wounds.

She was not among them, though part of the emperor now desired to execute everyone who had accompanied him to Alexandria. Any of them could be guilty of hiding her. Any of them could have been seduced by her magic. They could be plotting against him even now. He well remembered her beauty, echoed in that of her son. Now the son was dead and the mother was not, and Octavian could neither sleep nor eat. Dread overcame him in his bedchamber, and when he sat at his table, his fear of poisoning was too great to allow him to partake of anything more than a dry crust of bread.

He remembered a hideous story involving the queen of Parthia, who had dined in peacetime with an enemy. The enemy, watching the queen's robust consumption of her meal, had believed he was safe.

He was wrong.

The queen had coated one side of the serving knife with a lethal dose of poison and left the other side clean. When she sliced the meat, the poisoned side calculatedly went to her foe, while she innocently served herself the other half of the dish.

This queen, Octavian's enemy, was easily as intelligent and crafty. He trusted nothing, not until he was safely ensconced in Rome, though he knew that there was no way to be entirely protected, not even in his own city. How could he have let her escape him? She'd been his, conquered and killed. And yet she lived.

He had *let* her live, and every moment she lived ensured his death.

He sent patrols in search of her, turning up every paving stone, investigating every secret passage. Agrippa's men searched the kitchens, the far warrens of the palace rooms, the Soma itself, and there was no trace of Cleopatra.

"*Who* is it we seek?" Agrippa asked him, for the hundredth time.

"The body of the queen," he said. That it was a living body, he did not add.

The emperor instituted blockades on the roads and river, announcing that the body might have been transported by a solitary woman, smuggled out of Alexandria, but he knew that she would evade any such measures. What need had such a creature to travel by land and water? She could as well be traveling in the sky, taking flight like a sacred falcon or, more appropriately, like a vulture.

"Bring the children," he ordered. He had them under guard, deep in the palace, and now he thought they might know something he did not.

He pressed his back against Cleopatra's golden throne, cursing the discomfort of his position. The twins, when they came, unnerved him.

The boy looked down, as was proper, but the girl tilted her head to look at him. She was the image of her mother, black hair rippling down her back, though her lips held none of Cleopatra's sensuality. The girl's mouth reminded him of Antony's, drawn tight in a moment of petulance, and below her lips was Antony's own cleft chin. Cleopatra Selene's eyes were large, black pools, also inherited from her father, who'd used his limpid gaze to seduce half the wives in Rome.

"Where is your mother?" he asked her, abandoning the canny line of questioning he'd prepared. Her glare discomfited him.

The girl spoke in an unknown language, a torrent of bewildering, crackling sounds. She then looked at him as though he ought to understand everything she said.

"Interpreter," he called. It was ridiculous. Surely, someone had been aware of this problem before now and failed to alert him of it. Perhaps the girl was simple.

She took a step closer toward him, and involuntarily he drew back. She seemed to be taking his measure.

"There is no need for a translator. Our mother is dead," Cleopatra Selene announced in Latin, her voice unexpectedly deep and rasping. "I am surprised you do not know where she is, as we were informed that you'd buried her."

What fool had told them the details of their mother's death? He'd ordered them sequestered. It would not do to have them grieving their parents and blaming him for their deaths.

"Where is my brother?" the boy asked, speaking unexpectedly. The girl put out her hand to silence him.

"Ptolemy is sleeping in our bedchamber," she reminded him, and then turned back to the emperor. "Do you not speak Egyptian?"

"Of course not," he said. "I am Roman."

"As is our father, but he can speak the tongue of our people. How is it that you do not?"

"I'd like to visit Rome," Alexander Helios interrupted, his eyes bright. "I'd like to train in the army."

"I will take you to Rome," Octavian told him. "In exchange for information."

"We do not wish to go to Rome," Cleopatra Selene interrupted. "We will await our father here at the palace. He is traveling, and we would not like to leave without his knowledge. He will grieve over our mother's death, and we will comfort him."

A stroke of luck. She did not know everything.

"If you tell me where your mother is," he tried, "I'll let your father live."

The girl smiled a nasty, vindicated smile.

"So you are a liar as well," she said, this time in Greek.

Octavian straightened his spine and put on his most regal air.

"Do not question me," he said.

The girl laughed, a short, harsh bark, and continued in Greek.

"My brother doesn't study when the tutor comes and so he cannot speak any language but Latin. He does not know that our father is dead. I heard the slaves talking, while everyone else slept. I do not wish to stay in Egypt. The people will kill us."

Octavian was taken aback. The girl no longer looked like a ten-year-old, but like a full-grown woman, and it appeared that she was attempting to negotiate with him.

"Ask him where Caesarion is," the boy whimpered, and his sister pinched him.

"He is dead," Octavian said, resigned. "He was a traitor to Rome."

The boy looked shocked. The girl did not, though Octavian caught her face wavering for a moment.

"A traitor? He isn't a traitor. He's the son of Julius Caesar! Our mother says he is as good a man as his father," cried Alexander.

"He wasn't a man," Octavian said. "He was a boy."

"Then why did you kill him?" Alexander asked. His eyes were wide and disbelieving.

"*I* did not kill him. He was killed in battle. No more of that. This is war." The boy's eyes were leaking tears, and Octavian felt disgusted.

"We will not need to be killed *in battle*," Cleopatra Selene informed him. "I will go with you to Rome. I will walk in your procession, behind her body. Is that not what you are planning? My mother's body displayed with the asps that killed her? I will salute you as my emperor. My parents loved each other more than they loved anyone else. My mother planned to live forever with my father, but she did not plan anything for my brothers and me. They forgot about us."

The girl's lip wobbled slightly, the first real indication of weakness Octavian had seen. She was nearly the same age as his own daughter, Julia. A child.

"What do you know about living forever? Did she consult with a magician? A witch?" Octavian asked. He could not help himself.

"I know nothing of my mother's whereabouts, but perhaps I know other things," she said, giving him a steady look. "My mother did nothing to keep us safe. She left it to me. I will give you my allegiance, and I will tell you what I know, if you will protect us."

A small movement caught Octavian's eye, a flutter in the tapestry. His heart rattled against his ribs. He leapt from the throne and dashed across the room, sword pointed into the fabric, at the spot where he knew she would be. He stabbed through it and blunted his blade against a stone wall, seeing only a rat disappearing into a crack therein.

Octavian could barely keep from screaming. Egypt was that wall, full of cracks, and Cleopatra could be in any one of them. The queen could be on her way to Rome. He might arrive home in triumph, crowned with laurel, and find her awaiting him in his own bed, his wife and daughter murdered and their blood staining her hands.

"I will protect you," Octavian managed, even as he wondered why he felt compelled to make promises to a child. And what did he propose to protect her from? What foes did she have? It was he who was in danger.

"Then I will kiss your hand," she said, and a moment later, he felt her lips brush his fingertips. "It is settled. We will be Romans. You will want to find our tutor, Nicolaus the Damascene. He knows what she summoned."

Octavian felt his heart shudder. *Summoned.* He'd suspected it was something like this.

"You asked if she consulted with sorcerers," the girl said. "I do not know the answer to that. I do know she consulted with scholars, and she practiced a spell to summon a goddess to our city. It was meant to be a secret, but our tutor helped her. If you can find him, you may find her."

"She is not missing," Octavian said. "She is dead and buried."

The little girl looked at him.

"Then why are you so afraid?" she asked.

⇒21⇐

Cleopatra pulsed with fury and grief, with guilt and despair, and most of all, with rage. Her empty heart was a hornet's nest.

The Romans had taken both of her loves. She remembered the songs she'd sung to Caesarion in the womb. She remembered the feel of him suckling at her breast. Cleopatra twisted, her body pounding with visions of destruction. Of revenge.

You are mine, said the voice in her head, a whisper now, a voice that sounded like her own.

"I am yours," Cleopatra said aloud.

She would tear Rome to the ground. She'd make the streets run with blood, pile bodies wherever Octavian walked, in the Forum, in the Circus Maximus. His wife, his generals, his sister, his friends. Would the citizens scream in the streets, saluting their brave emperor, killer of children? She'd fill the temple of the vestal virgins with blood. All the gods of Rome would bow to her. All the leaders of Rome would beg her mercy, and she would not grant it. Antony and Caesarion would be avenged. They would be avenged.

All around her, during the execution, she'd sensed the goddess, felt her bloody smile, heard her rumbling breath, but she couldn't see her anywhere. As she fell to the ground, as her child was murdered, she'd realized that the goddess was not in the crowd but inside her own body.

Cleopatra could feel her, furious, blinding in her desire. She could not tell what part of these feelings were her own and what part belonged to Sekhmet.

She hungered now, so desperately that had there been blood pooled on the stones, she would have lapped it up. As the stars appeared and she healed from the damage done by the sun, her strength increased. A tongue of fire made its way up her spine, licking at her like a lioness, rasping away any resistance she had left.

Feed, her body commanded, and she would not deny it. There would be no more forgetting what she had done. Her eyes were open now.

There were people sleeping behind easily entered windows, her body told her. There were people drunk in the streets, easily harvested. She stopped herself, with effort.

She did not know enough about what she had become. The sun had thrown her to the earth, weakening her, breaking her power. It was only luck that the Romans hadn't found her there, lying in the dirt, and brought her back to their prisons.

She must learn what she was. She must understand how to control it. She could not afford to surrender completely, to lose herself in hunger and fury.

It seemed a thousand years ago, those metal bowls, the lighting of incense, the scrolls. Sekhmet's order, Nicolaus had said. In Thebes, there was a temple to the goddess. Priestesses to the old gods. A place where she might find knowledge.

Cleopatra did not plan to leave her enemies for long. Just long enough to put them at ease, to make them think themselves safe.

She'd once felt safe.

A soft sound made her spin, searching the darkness for soldiers, but all she saw was a dog wandering the open area, its ribs visible, its nose pressed to the ground. It raised its head and looked toward her with a dry whine. She would not kill an animal, not now.

No. This was a city full of Romans, and she could smell them, feel them, and hear them everywhere.

This was a city of betrayers, too. Her son had been under the protection of one of them. At least she might avenge herself on *him*.

She picked her way over the cobblestones, watching bats flying about the sky, listening to birds shrieking their hunting calls. Eventually, she stood at the Museion's gates. With one leap, she was over them and inside the courtyard.

Another few steps and she stood outside an open window, inhaling the history of Rhodon, Caesarion's tutor. The scent of libraries, of languages learned and forgotten. The scent of gold, of promises, of ambition.

A lantern flickered in his window, and the man packed his bag, preparing to leave for Rome. Cleopatra stood in the dark, watching him for a moment. Rhodon's robes were finer than they had hitherto been. She saw a gleam of gold beneath his linen and the ruddy flush of good health on his face. Her son's sacrifice had made him rich.

When he stepped out into the courtyard, his step jaunty, his jingling bag slung over his shoulder, she was waiting for him.

An hour later, east of Alexandria, she slipped into a seaside bar, listening to the jokes and shouts of drinking men.

"A felucca?" she called, showing only her arm from out of her cloak, having veiled the rest. In her hand, she held a piece of gold, stolen from her victim. Cleopatra's own face was printed on one side with her name. The reverse was Antony. They'd laughed when they saw them for the first time. She'd thought him far more handsome than the coin would suggest, and he'd felt the same about her image, though her profile had conveyed power.

She held the coin tightly in her hand, letting the image of Antony's face press into her flesh. In better days, she'd traveled to her beloved in her own golden barge, a purple silk sail stretched above the ship, and the sides fitted with silver oars. Now, she was reduced to hiring a rickety felucca with a drunken captain.

A man approached her, his eyes gleaming for gold, and she withdrew it into her cloak.

"You will take me to Thebes," she told him. "Immediately. There will be more when we arrive."

She saw him smirk at his fellows, telling them wordlessly that he'd love to take a woman aboard his vessel. To Thebes? Hardly. Thebes was days away. They'd have to proceed east along the Mediterranean, to the Canopic branch of the Nile. He'd take her a few miles down the river and see how long it took her to spread her legs.

Every man in the bar had similar ideas; she could hear them echoing.

She strode across the dock and leapt into the small, wooden vessel, accompanied by the captain and his single crewman.

The moonlight soothed her injured skin, healing the remainder of the wounds of the earlier sun. She put her face up toward the stars and felt their cool radiance as the ship set off. A cat wound itself around the rigging and stalked toward her, purring as it approached. She stroked its golden head and looked into its clear, yellow eyes. It gave a small cry and leapt into her arms.

Within moments, she'd settled herself into the vessel, though she could not afford to sleep as deeply as she had before her burial. With the dawn, she would conceal herself belowdecks, wrapped in her cloak. The vessel was sun-tight enough to suit her, and she would know if the men sought to harm her there. The motion of the water rocked her to sleep, and she dropped into blackness, losing track of time and place, dreaming of the Underworld, of Antony taking the form of a falcon and soaring up into the light, of the Beautiful West stretching before her.

A ll ships searched by order of the Emperor!"

The shouts woke Cleopatra from dreams of heaven, tears running down her cheeks, and she nearly cried out. She pressed her back against the ship's side, panicked. They were looking for her. They'd stretched a chain across the Nile to block the passage of any vessel.

There were several dozen soldiers on the shore, all armed. Battle-hardened, for the most part, but young and excitable. Romans. She kept herself still.

"Are there passengers aboard this vessel?"

The captain of her ship answered in the affirmative. "A woman, traveling alone."

"Have her show herself," one of the legionaries commanded.

The other soldiers laughed raucously.

"Have her show everything!" one yelled. "By order of himself, the Emperor of the World!"

"Lady?" the crewman asked, pulling aside the curtain Cleopatra had drawn to protect herself from prying eyes.

There was no one there.

The legionaries searched the ship but found only a tangle of linen, a rough cloak, and a small silver box of what seemed to be dust.

Beneath the water, the queen of Egypt waited for them to depart.

Her hair streamed in the current as she laid the flat of her hand against the hull of the ship, feeling the smooth grain of the wood. Soon enough, she told herself, she would be back on board with Antony's ashes. She did not like leaving them, but she had no other option. She'd slipped into the river as the soldiers came toward her hiding place.

All around her, fish coursed through the water, their mouths gaping as they consumed tiny living things. She could feel each of their bodies, their scales shifting as they moved, their gills opening and closing silently. She could feel the crocodiles as well, slithering from the banks and melting themselves deep into the teeming waters. A yellow eye opened beside her, and she felt the corrosive friction of the beast's skin against her thigh.

She'd slipped into the dirty water only out of desperation, used to the pure, rain-filled cisterns beneath the city of Alexandria, but now she stretched in pleasure. She had not recognized the life that filled the Nile, the tiny creatures and the large, the plants and sands and scents of faraway places. She began to silently raise her head above the level of the water to take a breath, but the boat rocked with legionaries boarding it, and the wooden hull struck her skull. She was driven downward, inhaling burning fluid, her lungs protesting, gagging, but as she sank, something began to change in her body.

Her eyes widened under the water, and she felt her nostrils close. She felt her spine thrash and elongate, her throat stretch endlessly. Within moments, her shape was that of the river itself, long and narrow, limbless and yet pliant. Her bones fit together like a perfect necklace, an articulated chain, and each motion heralded the next.

She slithered past the legs of a legionary who'd entered the water to hold the rope detaining the felucca.

She let her midsection appear above the surface, lashed her tail for a moment, and felt them nervously wielding their swords, trying to predict her next position.

"Serpent!" they shouted. "Serpent! Onto the bank!"

⇒ 22 ⇐

Two hours later, the felucca's captain and his crewman hunched over a table in the captain's quarters, counting the coins they'd gained from their missing passenger. She must have leapt from the ship and been eaten by a crocodile, stupid thing. She'd have been better off staying aboard. The Romans had been too fearful of the water to reboard the vessel after seeing the serpent, and so they'd waved it on. Now the felucca was on its way past Damanhur. No matter what the captain had planned to do with the woman, it would have been better than jumping into the Nile. Who knew what she'd been running from? The legionaries weren't seeking her, surely. They were looking for a dead body, and there were certainly no corpses aboard the felucca.

"That, or any oddity," the leader of the legionaries had muttered. "Any feminine oddity." They did not seem to have any more specific description than that.

The felucca drifted lazily in the current. The captain had decided to press on to Naukratis and visit the whorehouses there, spend some of their Cleopatra-marked currency on women before the new emperor declared it worthless and demanded that it be reminted into coins in his own image. A warm breeze propelled the ship down the river at a reasonable speed, and the moon rose high in the sky.

"I hear the redheaded whore came back," the captain said.

"I don't know about her," his crewman replied warily. "The last time I saw that woman, I had to visit a physician and drink something made of moths and frankincense. Cost me half my wages."

The captain laughed.

"There's always another whore. Five more, each one better than the last."

The seaman nodded in agreement and then looked up, the expression on his face changing. The captain glanced at him, curious. The pox must have been a terrible one to warrant such horror.

"Look," the crewman whispered, pointing over the captain's shoulder.

The captain spun lazily in his seat and then leapt to his feet.

There she was, shining in the moonlight, their passenger, naked to the waist.

"Lady," the captain began. Where had she come from? She balanced her arms on the rail, her body still partially in the water. Was she injured? "We did not mean to leave you behind."

Something in her eyes transfixed him. They glowed, that was it. Even her short black hair seemed to shine. Her breasts hung heavy over the rail, the smooth skin glittering with droplets of water. She smiled.

The captain smiled back, nervous. She was angry, he could feel it. It would be better to throw her off the vessel now, put her back into the waters and leave her to die. There was no explanation for her appearance here, two hours after she had fallen overboard. Surely, she could not swim as quickly as the felucca could sail.

She shifted on the rail, pushing herself up higher, the better to climb aboard. The captain admired the rosettes of the woman's nipples, the precise curve of her waist, her navel. It was most unusual to see a naked woman outside of a whorehouse. His gaze roved downward and then stopped, unbelieving.

His passenger undulated her hips to push herself over the rail, and the captain jumped backward, feeling his gorge rising. He opened his mouth to scream, but the sound died. Impossible.

The woman was half snake.

"I hired you," she said, too calmly, "and you left me."

The crewman, with startling presence of mind, laid hands on an axe normally used for rope cutting. He heaved it high in the air and swung it with all his strength toward her throat.

Her tail whipped up out of the water and lashed around him, crushing him in its coils just as the blade touched her skin. The creature arced gracefully onto the deck, her body slithering from the depths, an endless serpentine length.

The terrified captain pushed the pile of coins across the table, but she paid them no attention. He fell to his knees to beg for mercy. Surely, this was a deity he'd failed to ferry, and now he would die for his offense. She was a monster with the face of a goddess, scales catching the darkness and turning it to light.

She rose up on her coils, high above him, and looked down upon him without benevolence. Her body writhed, nearly covering the entire deck. He felt her tail twist around his ankles, an icy strength.

Would no one save him? There were no villages nearby. Out there in the dark, all that would hear him would be crocodiles and lions, bats and snakes.

She wrapped about him, and his last thought was that she felt like a woman still, a strong and lovely woman, clutching his entire body as a woman would clutch him between her thighs. Her beautiful face was inches from his. He could almost forget what she was.

"But you shouldn't forget what I am," she whispered, her voice bitterly sweet, her hair soft as silk as it wrapped about his fist. He tried to pull himself free, but he was already too weak.

She looked into his eyes just before her fangs sank into his throat.

→ 23 ←

Cleopatra emerged from the river near Thebes and lay on the bank of the Nile, her naked skin basking in the darkness. She'd left the vessel behind hours before, still shocked by the glory of her transformation. Traveling underwater, her body skimming the silted floor, absorbing stories from every creature she touched, from every droplet of water that had come to the river from elsewhere in the world, she'd felt the histories of the raindrops that had fallen from the sky to become the Nile, and of the grains of sand that had once been the shells of animals. She'd felt the stories of the crocodiles and the fish, the water snakes and the creatures that drank from the river.

She thought of the destruction she could wreak on the Romans in this new form. She could slip through underground passages, through places her human form could not travel. She could speak to animals, feel their needs and hungers. She could rise from beneath the Tiber, and the Romans would never know she was coming.

She thought of the power she now possessed.

Her mind had shifted while she was in the form of the serpent. The things that mattered to her human form suddenly meant little to her. It wasn't until she surfaced at Thebes and her body became human again that she realized she'd left more than just her clothing and coins behind. She'd left Antony's ashes as well.

She should have left him in the mausoleum, safely buried; she knew it now, but it was too late. She moaned, imagining him without her. He was dead, she knew, but holding him had comforted her. His body was still in Egypt, she realized at last, and thus his soul remained here. The silver box that contained him would surely sink to the bottom of the river and never be found. His soul would be safe. She tried to calm her unease.

She stood and walked toward the temple, a ghostly white skeleton perched on the horizon. As she walked closer, she could see that brush had grown up around it, and parts of the walls had crumbled. The temples to the old Egyptian gods were now largely abandoned, and Cleopatra knew that she herself was to blame. For twenty years, she'd largely ignored the native religions in favor of the Greek and Roman gods.

A sleek, black granite statue of the ibis-headed god, Thoth, still stood sentry. She looked at the statue for a moment. This was the Egyptian god of knowledge and resurrection, the god who'd given Isis the magic words to bring her husband, Osiris, back to life, uniting the pieces of his body that had been scattered from end to end of the world. Why had Cleopatra not summoned *him*?

She'd acted with only the spells she had, she reminded herself, trapped in the mausoleum as she had been. Osiris had not survived, in any case. Isis had lost him again, just as Cleopatra had lost Antony to a second death. Osiris had become the Lord of the Dead, and Isis had been left to grieve him.

The New Isis. Cleopatra moved slowly toward the temple, all the rapture of her transformation forgotten.

She entered one of the seven doorways, once resplendent with cedar and copper trims, but now empty of wood. The world and all its creatures might come in and out as they wished here. She made her way through the temple rooms, hearing nothing. The wise woman—the *rekhet* of this temple, the reason Cleopatra had come—was gone, or hidden.

At last, she entered the sanctuary of Sekhmet and stopped, her breath coming quickly. She could feel the power here, different from that contained in the other rooms. There'd been recent sacrifices. Her nostrils flared. She could smell the blood. Nothing large. A hare. A bird.

Against the back wall of the sanctuary was a tremendous statue of the goddess, smooth black stone carved into the shape of the familiar lioness with the body of a woman. A sun disc with a uraeus balanced atop the statue's head, and over this, a portal in the stone admitted moonlight to illuminate her figure.

Cleopatra stood in front of the statue, uncertain. The light glinted off the goddess's pitiless features, and though Cleopatra knew that the statue was not the actuality, she still found herself trembling. The statue reminded her too clearly of the summoning, and the things she'd done in the mausoleum. The man's heart in her hands. The brilliant absence of her own heart. She heard her voice giving Sekhmet *anything*. *Anything I have is yours.*

It had been the right thing, surely. She had power now, beyond anything she'd dreamed. Enough to avenge Antony and Caesarion, enough to destroy her enemies.

Why, then, was she afraid? What was there for her to fear?

It was horribly quiet. There were not even any birds. She looked into the flat eyes of the icon, remembering the shining light within the living version, the sharp white teeth, the talons.

Was this what she wanted to be?

Did it matter? This was what she had become. She could feel it.

Suddenly, the hair rose all over her body.

"There is no need to fear me," said a voice from the room behind her. "I am the last priestess of this temple."

Cleopatra spun, placing her back against the statue, feeling its stone claws digging into her shoulders. "I do not fear you," she said, her voice clear and queenly. But somehow, she did.

A white-haired woman stood before Cleopatra, gazing at her with thin-lipped reserve. She walked forward and draped Cleopatra's naked body with a pale, red-bordered robe.

"This is your home, and you are welcome here," the priestess said quietly, but there was a note in her voice of something other than welcome. Cleopatra looked at her, but the woman's eyes revealed nothing, and her thoughts were veiled. "Come with me."

The priestess led her from the sanctuary and into an open area. In any other temple, there would have been soft carpets, goblets of wine. Here, there was only the darkness and the chill of the marble floor. A tiny animal, some rodent or lizard, skittered across the stones and was gone. Cleopatra felt her head snapping to the side, following its progress into the night. Her tongue rasped against her teeth.

"I have been waiting for you," said the priestess. "I felt it when you joined her. The earth shook, the animals fled, and I knew one would come. What is it you seek?"

"Knowledge," Cleopatra managed through the hunger that had over-taken her.

"What knowledge? Two have become one," said the priestess. "You share your soul with the goddess I serve. Though I am certain you know that already."

"I do not know enough. You will tell me what you know of her," Cleopatra said. "Where she came from. What she desires. I came only as a courtesy."

"You came to learn how best to kill those who have offended you. You know already what kind of deity the Scarlet Lady is, or I mistake you," the rekhet said.

"Tell me," Cleopatra insisted, and the priestess relented, speaking slowly and deliberately, as though she'd long ago memorized the narrative.

"Sekhmet was born out of Ra's divine eye, a messenger sent to light up the waters of chaos and to find lost things. Her first task was to locate Ra's two disloyal children, Tefnut and Shu, who'd abandoned their father. The tears Ra cried upon being reunited with them created humanity, but Ra cried no tears of gratitude to Sekhmet. Instead, he created a new eye to replace her, and placed her in his crown as a cobra spitting fire. The humans created of Ra's tears prospered, filling the earth with their lovemaking and children, with their eating and singing. The gods prospered, filling the firmament with *their* lovemaking and children, with their sacrifices and their magic, with their rituals and with the singing of their acolytes. Sekhmet was left spitting fire from Ra's crown, the only one defending her father from his enemies, the only loyal child.

When Ra was old and weak, and humans began to rise up against him, he sent Sekhmet to the desert as a lioness to slaughter the traitors.

That day, she created pain and death, which had not existed in the world before. She killed everything she saw, drinking the blood of the world indiscriminately. Ra changed his mind in the middle of her massacre, taking pity on his dying human children. He tricked Sekhmet by mixing the Nile with drugged pomegranate juice. She saw its color and thought it was blood. When she staggered and fell to her knees, when she slid beneath the Nile's waters, crying as she fell, Ra threw her back into the heavens, and there she stayed. Until you brought her to earth again.

"I am the last of my line," the rekhet continued, looking out into the darkness beyond the temple. "Here, we have honored Ra and pacified the Lady of Slaughter with sacrifices. We've worked for centuries to keep humankind safe from her fury. The believers have become few, and the land changes around us. The Roman gods have come to our land. You know this much. Were you not once a queen?"

The rekhet took her hand and touched her palm. Cleopatra flinched at her expression.

"You were," she said, her fingers traveling over the skin, her tone increasingly hostile. "Though you are not now. Did you not invite the invaders into your bed? Did you not call to the Romans, worship their gods, sacrifice to their altars? All that has happened was your doing. Did you not proclaim yourself a goddess? Now you are dead, or so they say."

The priestess dropped Cleopatra's hand, poured something from a tiny, elegant bottle into an alabaster goblet, and sipped from it.

"Are you dead?" she asked.

"I am not!" Cleopatra cried, fighting the urge to strike this crone, this woman who knew nothing about what she was saying.

"Are you certain?" the priestess asked.

Cleopatra's mind spun. Dead? She was not dead. And a betrayer of Egypt?

What did this woman know about power? What did she know about the demands put on the powerful? She was a priestess of a forgotten religion. The rekhet should be thanking her queen, not judging her.

"What does Sekhmet desire?" the priestess continued, as though Cleopatra had not spoken. "She desires the end of everything. Can you not feel it? There is no place for her in Ra's boat, no home for her in the Duat. She was banished by her family, and she lives in endless hunger, searching for prey. You brought her sacrifice. You gave her enough to revive her, enough to bring her from the heavens. She desires an ocean of blood in payment for the wrongs that were done her. She will use you to get it. There is no peaceful end for you. You will wander with Sekhmet."

Cleopatra felt an echoing loneliness rising inside her.

"This is a passing form. Until I have my vengeance on Rome," she said.

"And then?" the priestess asked.

"Then I will die," said Cleopatra. "I will join my husband in the Duat."

The rekhet laughed, a laugh as old and sad as the temple itself. "You will not," she said. "You are her slave now, and she does not die."

"Surely, there is a ritual, a spell of separation," Cleopatra said.

The rekhet shook her head.

"You cannot reclaim your *ka* from her," she said. "You gave your soul willingly. She grows stronger each day with your sacrifices. You are a rare prize for one such as she. A queen of Egypt. She'll fulfill her nature with you. Together, you will make war. Together, you will kill. The rivers will run red, and you will drink the blood in them. You are an immortal now, and you will serve her."

"I will not," said Cleopatra, surprising herself, her voice shaking. "I will not be a slave."

"Yet you will hunger. Will you stop yourself? Can you?" The rekhet looked deep into Cleopatra's eyes, judging her. "You've shed blood. You've started wars. It was your nature long before she found you. She chose wisely. Together, you will return the world to chaos. This is your destiny."

"Is there not a poison?" said Cleopatra, desperate. There must be something that would separate her. Something that would kill her. Her revenge must be done, but she could not live this way forever, hungering. Murdering.

Alone and enslaved.

"You are past poisons," said the priestess, and her face shifted into what might have been a smile. "I am not."

The rekhet indicated her goblet, drained of the liquid it had contained, and then closed her eyes and leaned back against the pillar. She was ancient, Cleopatra saw now. The power that had filled her had made her look younger, but now her skin was wizened.

"I, and my sisters, have sacrificed at this temple for thousands of years, to keep the goddess at peace, to keep her at rest," the rekhet whispered, her voice ragged, as the poison began to take effect. "You have undone our work. She is released to do her will, and you with her, hand in hand, heart in heart, soul in soul. You belong to her."

Cleopatra leaned forward to hear her final, rasping words.

"I will not stay to see the world you make."

⇒ 24 ⇐

The ghost ship drifted near Damanhur for two days before Octavian's men brought it to his attention. The villagers refused to approach it. There'd been sounds on the night the ship appeared, screams and struggling. One of the children of the village had seen something tremendous and dark lashing in the water.

"No doubt the captain fell overboard and was eaten by crocodiles," Octavian said, disgusted anew at the notion of governing this superstitious, illogical country, even from afar, but his messenger, having visited the villagers, disagreed.

"They say it was something else," he insisted. "Something they've never seen before."

One of Octavian's legions encountered something in the area as well, some sort of serpent. He felt mildly curious upon hearing the report, though the incident clearly had nothing to do with the missing Cleopatra. A snake, not a woman.

As the hours and days wore on, however, with no sign of either the queen or Nicolaus the Damascene anywhere in Alexandria, he began to feel a disquieting sense of something familiar about descriptions of that snake.

When he looked into Cleopatra's eyes, had he not seen some sort of serpent thrashing? In memory, it appeared to him again, its mouth stretched wide and filled with sharpened teeth. Venom dripped from them. The beast in the vision had risen up from an arena, which now he realized he knew all too well.

The Circus Maximus. He'd seen Rome.

Octavian cursed. He would go himself. His men could clearly not be trusted to find her. They did not know what they were looking for. He ordered his barge prepared and filled with armed soldiers. At least shipboard he'd be safe from her. There was no way to sneak onto a ship unnoticed, not unless one could walk on water. And this barge, repossessed from the queen's personal fleet, was a glorious thing, shining in the sun as if it were made of pure gold, silver oars flashing, a royal purple canopy awaiting the emperor as though it had been made for him.

The odor overwhelmed him as he stepped aboard the felucca at Damanhur, covering his nose and mouth with a cloth. The sickly sweet smell of rot was everywhere. The sun blazed down upon the emperor's head, but even the bright daylight did not improve his nerves.

A hot breeze stirred the air, shifting the deck and causing Octavian to temporarily lose his footing. He leaned against a table to recover and planted his weight on something that gave beneath his hand. It hissed, and there was a high-pitched howl of fury.

The emperor flung himself to the opposite rail, willing himself not to vomit. It was a cat, that was all.

A cat that had been making a meal of a corpse.

"The crew did not abandon ship," he announced to Agrippa, carefully averting his eyes from the body. He would not look at the mess the cat had made of the man's face. "Determine what killed them."

The cat looked up from the body with shining yellow eyes and licked its lips. The emperor had always hated cats, but he dared not injure this one. In Egypt, the vile carrion eaters were worshipped as gods.

He was being ridiculous. It was a ship's cat. Every vessel had one. He swatted at it, he hoped surreptitiously. Still, he was the ruler of this place now, he reminded himself. If he banished cats, it was his business.

The cat skittered up into the rigging, where it looked down upon the emperor as though it knew his deepest secrets. It opened its eyes wide, flattened its ears, and then, very deliberately, showing all of its needle-sharp fangs, it hissed.

Octavian's face had broken out in a cold sweat, and he mopped his brow with one of the purple-embroidered handkerchiefs from his barge.

The other body lay pale and strangely withered on the deck, just behind the first. The cat had not seen fit to eat from this one, so it was possible to view him. Octavian knelt, breathing through his mouth. He and Agrippa would be an example to his troops, all of whom were showing signs of superstition and fear.

He put out a hand—now gloved—to prod the flesh and found it as stiff and unyielding as he'd expected. The man's head was turned to the side, and the cause of his death was clearly visible, though the withered flesh was peculiar.

"Snakebite," Octavian announced.

"This one was crushed," Agrippa commented. Agrippa pushed at the corpse and all assembled watched in disgust as it shifted. It was as though the body were a cloth sack filled with small stones. Every bone seemed to have been broken.

A large—a *very* large—snake had slithered aboard the vessel, bitten one man and smashed the other in its coils. Octavian swallowed hard. It was too much coincidence.

He noticed something on the snakebitten man's arm. There was another mark, this one clearly that of the cat, but there was something odd about it.

"Open the corpse," he said, and Agrippa pulled out a small blade and slit the corpse's belly.

Octavian was horribly reminded of a sacrifice. Everything inside the body cavity was pale. The emperor had seen enough battles, attended enough deathbed rites, to know that this was not a side effect of death. This was something else.

The man had been drained of his blood.

"Gods," murmured Agrippa.

The day after Caesarion's execution, the body of the boy's tutor, Rhodon, had been discovered in the Museion. It had surely been the action of thieves, nothing unusual in a port city, but the man who reported the death had been terrified. He claimed the body was strange. Shriveled.

Octavian shuddered as he remembered. He had not connected it with the queen, not then.

One of Agrippa's men shouted, beckoning them to view a heap of women's clothing he'd found on the deck. A rough cape and a linen gown. The emperor caught a whiff of a familiar scent, perfume emanating from the fabric.

He suddenly realized that he was trapped. He looked frantically around. Would she come from the river or the sky?

Another legionary directed Octavian to the small pile of gold coins on the table. They were marked with Cleopatra's face. Octavian felt his pulse racing. His eye fell on something else.

A silver box engraved with images of Isis and Dionysus.

He'd last seen this box in Cleopatra's mausoleum. It was a companion to the pyre he'd had her chained to, and inside it was all that was left of her husband.

Octavian stifled a moan. She'd been here. Now she was gone, and he had no way of knowing where she would appear, or who would die next.

He lifted the box of Antony's ashes. She would not have carried it so far only to leave it behind on purpose. It had to have been an accident. Sooner or later, she would realize that she'd lost it, and then—

He wrapped it carefully in his cloak. It was more precious than gold to him now, more useful than his weapons or any hostage. According to Selene, she did not care about her children but only about her husband.

The box might be the one thing Octavian had that Cleopatra wanted.

That and his own life, he knew that well enough. The only reason he was still alive was that he'd been exceedingly lucky. He could stay no longer in this country. He'd depart for home, where he might have enough time to assemble his own forces and the forces of others against her.

His stomach lurched in a most undignified fashion.

"We return to Alexandria," he announced. "And then to Rome, as quickly as can be arranged. We do not go toward peace. Marcus Agrippa. You and your men will go in search of something special."

Agrippa looked at Octavian, his eyes unreadable.

"What is that?"

"Sorcery," the emperor whispered, thinking of Alexander, thinking of what his hero would have done if faced with such things as these. "Magic to defend Rome. We cannot fight without help. You will find the most powerful sorcerers the world can give you."

"And how will I know them?" Agrippa asked, clearly hoping that this was a whim of Octavian's and not a true order.

"You will find those who are most feared in their villages," Octavian told him. "The ones whose fires light the woods, who dance with demons, who summon shades."

He thought of the stories, of Circe and Calypso, of Medea. Powerful things. There were witches in Rome, yes, but they worked only simple magic.

He dreamed of something larger, something stronger. Surely the world was wide enough that it might be found. The future of his country depended on it.

The visions he'd seen in Cleopatra's eyes would come true unless he fought them back into the darkness.

"To your knees," he said. "All of you. We pray for strength. We pray for Rome."

≫ 25 ≪

Cleopatra bent to touch the rekhet's shoulder. Dead, like everything died, the birds and insects, the animals, the fish, the plants. Cleopatra was the only thing in the world that would not go to dust.

She was chained to Sekhmet.

If she ever wished to join Antony in the Duat, if she ever wished to die, she'd have to kill her. There was too much Cleopatra did not understand still, too much that was strange. Even as she thought it, she felt the hunger surging through her. Flashes of red. Her blood boiled with fury and resentment. She would find the emperor, if she had to follow him around the world.

If she'd sold her soul, the soul of the last queen of Egypt, if Antony and Caesarion had died, it could not be for nothing.

The Romans would call to the Scarlet Lady, they with their leavings of metal and blood. Cleopatra could smell them now, though she was far away. The followers of this emperor who'd killed so many. This emperor who had murdered her son, whose men had murdered her husband. It would not be possible for Octavian to hide her remaining children from her. She was their mother. When she found them, she would destroy their captors.

She would eat the heart of the man who had forced her to sell her own heart.

She turned quickly from the temple and looked out into the empty desert. Dawn was hours off still. The moon was high and white. *Selene*, Cleopatra thought. Her daughter's name and that of the moon as well. *Alexander Helios. Ptolemy Philadelphus.* Her children were still so small.

The silence had ended with the death of the priestess. Night birds cried, and a wind whipped over the sand.

Outside the temple, a lioness lowered her head to drink from the river. Cleopatra could see the blood on the animal's mouth from here. She'd been hunting. A gazelle, perhaps. The lioness raised her head and looked toward the temple, yellow eyes ablaze.

So she had no will of her own? The priestess was wrong about that. Cleopatra was a queen of kings. She was stronger than any the goddess had taken in the past.

Caesarion, she thought. *Antony*.

Once she avenged herself upon the Romans, once she reclaimed her children and made certain that they were safe, she would find a way to separate from the goddess. She was going to Rome, and in Rome she would be born again. She could feel the human wonder that had been her own heart, filled now with teeth and claws.

She would use them.

She shrugged the red-bordered garment from her shoulders and stood for a moment naked beneath the million shining stars of her country. The woman she had been was gone, and in her place was something more.

Cleopatra dropped to her knees and placed her hands in the dirt, stretching her fingers, feeling the glory of her coming form, the grace, the power. Her back arched and her legs gathered beneath her. The tawny fur on her spine rose into a coarse ridge.

Her tail whipped back and forth, and she bounded into the night, across the desert and toward the sea.

BOOK OF DIVINATIONS

Alas, alas for thee, ill-wedded bride,
Thy royal power unto the Roman king shalt thou give,
And thou shalt repay all things which thou aforetime didst with
  masculine hands;
Thou shalt give thy whole land by way of dower,
As far as Libya and the dark-skinned men, to the resistless man.
And thou shalt be no more a widow,
But thou shalt cohabit with a man-eating lion, terrible, a furious
  warrior.
And then shalt thou be unhappy, and among all men unknown;
For thou shalt leave possessed of shameless soul;
And thee, the stately, shall the encircling tomb
Receive . . . is gone . . . living within.

—The Sibylline Oracles, circa 30 B.C.E.

Translated from the Greek

Milton S. Terry, 1899

Translator's note regarding the last line: "The text is so mutilated at this point as to leave the exact sentiment of the writer quite unintelligible."

In a tiny cave high on the rocky coast of Thessaly, a priestess of Hecate raised her gaze from the water she'd been using as a scry.

Ships were coming north from Africa. The scry showed blood, oceans of it, cities falling and corpses heaped in the streets. Ghosts and their grievances. Beasts and their hungers. The scry showed something tremendously powerful, risen.

Chrysate smiled. Her dilated eyes were as black as the sea below her cave, and her hair hung in a tangled nest of knotted plaits. Her mistress, Hecate, was a patroness to witches and drew her sacrifices from their activities, but they had reduced in number as Rome's influence shifted the ways of the world. High on this cliffside in Greece, Chrysate was one of the few priestesses left, and her mistress had fallen from favor with the gods and with mortals alike. Hecate was an old god, a Titan who'd once held vast power over earth and sea. In protesting the abduction of Persephone, however, she'd gained an enemy in Persephone's husband, Hades.

What was abduction became marriage, and now the Lord of the Dead kept Hecate chained near the entrance to the Underworld, presiding over hounds.

Chrysate had waited for this day.

The scry showed that the horizon was scarlet. Soldiers marched overland, searching not for battles but for those like Chrysate, who trafficked in dark magic. Rome sought allies, but the Romans had no notion of what Fates they tempted. No notion of what ancient things they drew.

In chaos, there was opportunity for change, opportunity for reversals of power. Hecate, who had been trapped for centuries, her influence limited, might be released. She'd lived far longer than the gods who now presided over Hades, and her powers were as simple and deep as those of the Earth herself, the scalding of lava, the ice of winter storms. Hecate's heart was made of lust and hunger, of murder and rapture. The powers Chrysate saw in the scry were similarly ancient. If Chrysate could find a way to channel such power, Hecate might rise up, and her priestess with her.

Chrysate worked her opal ring, engraved with the face of the goddess she served, over her twisted knuckle and dropped it into the basin, breaking the scry. She'd seen enough.

She glanced quickly about her cave, her gaze flicking over the heap of bones in the corner. She took only a few things in tiny leather pouches, balms made of rare ingredients, some beeswax, a knife so ancient and well used that its blade was a mere whisper of metal.

Murmuring to herself in Greek, she walked barefoot down the rocky trail and toward the soldiers.

As she made her way into their path, the knots in her hair untangled themselves. Her slender body became curvaceous, her crumpled skin silken, and her eyes greener and more glimmering.

By the time she reached the legionaries sent by Marcus Agrippa, she looked almost human.

⇒ 2 ⇐

The ship tossed in the storm, the wood singing and creaking, salt water seeping through the cracks. This was a transport bringing goods and slaves from Africa to Italy, and beneath the deck, wild animals destined for combat at the Circus Maximus could be heard howling and shifting. Once they were delivered to Rome, they'd be housed in tunnels beneath the city, and the sounds of beasts would be heard, faintly, by pedestrians walking above them, as though Africa had become Rome's Underworld.

The sailors trod the deck, uneasy, trimming the sailcloth and swarming the ropes, peering out into the night, suspicious of omens. Swallows had nested in the rigging, and a monster had been sighted off the stern. Its dark shadow and sharp fin trailed the vessel, not deep enough in the water to be harmless. The sailors had felt unsafe since they'd left port, what with their shrieking, roaring cargo. And those whose duty it was to feed and tend the animals felt more nervous still.

Something was not right in the darkness there, and lanterns were not enough to illuminate the corners.

A goat skittered across the deck, its white fur standing out in wet tufts.

A swallow wheeled and twisted in the air.

The smell of heated fur and trampled grain, the smell of hungering.

Something was not right.

A lion roared. A rattling, rippling sound, and then a tiger answered. Plaintive bleating of captive goats. The sound of large wings, rising, catching the still air, and then collapsing. Hooves clipping across wood, the jangle of chains. Six lions. Six tigers. Gazelles. Zebras. Crocodiles. Ostriches. A rhinoceros and a hippopotamus, the last captured with extreme difficulty. The Egyptians both revered and dreaded the animals as earthly embodiments of the evil god Seth, and even caged, the hippopotamus was dangerous to everything that came near it.

Elsewhere in the hold, slaves claimed in battle were being transported, the men into the fighting trade, the women into laundries and brothels and kitchens. All of the passengers traveled as one flesh, humans beside beasts, beasts beside humans. Soon, their blood would entertain Rome, red ink pouring out and writing a tale in the dust.

A forlorn strand of song spiraled up from the slave quarters below, and the ship's boy shinnied farther up the mast.

In his miserable cabin, Nicolaus the Damascene sat huddled, moaning with seasickness.

He'd been delayed getting out of Egypt. Three months had passed since the night he'd stood outside the palaces ready to flee.

"The queen is dead," criers had suddenly called in the streets, and Nicolaus was flooded with guilty relief. She'd killed herself. His problems were solved. Eventually, he'd ended up in a brothel, grieving and celebrating at once. The woman he bought was neither young nor lovely, but she was glorious flesh and bone, nothing of the spirit world about her. Wide hips and round breasts, perfumed and veiled in cheap fabric. He pressed his face into her hair, inhaling her smell, reveling in the life before him.

He had dallied in the city, wondering if indeed it was necessary to leave, until he heard nervous whispers in the streets that Octavian had searched the queen's mausoleum for her body, and that she'd disappeared without a trace. Quickly thereafter, he heard that the Romans were looking for a scholar, one Nicolaus of Damascus, tutor to the royal children.

The walls outside the Museion were papered with his name and a reward, and he knew the other scholars would as easily turn him in as hide him. Everyone's purse was empty now that Alexandria was occupied. He had to leave Egypt, and leave it now.

The port was closed and under guard. Nicolaus smuggled himself out of town in the company of a bribed musician, hidden inside a drum. When he finally got free of the city walls, it took him more than two months of dangerous travel to make his way to an open port. He back-tracked through villages, fearful he was being watched. Roman patrols were everywhere, and Marcus Agrippa's men were particularly tena-cious. He heard about the missing Damascene scholar in every village he passed through. It was good fortune that his pursuits had taught him languages far beyond his own. Nicolaus very quickly learned to say that he'd never been to Damascus. No. And scholarship? He was apprenticed to a baker.

In his unhappy journey, he was witness to thousands of statues and engravings of Cleopatra being smashed and then covered over with stone. They were all being destroyed, all but the few the emperor had sanctioned.

The workers who were laboring over those images reported strange requests from the conquerors. The emperor had ordered completion on a temple the queen had begun, the outside of which was decorated with a depiction of Cleopatra and her son Caesarion making an offering to Isis.

The temple and its decoration were traditional, the boy depicted with a miniaturized version of himself traveling behind him. The souls of royalty were always portrayed this way.

The depiction of Caesarion was traditional, but that of the queen was not.

At the temple of Dendera, Octavian had ordered that the queen be depicted unaccompanied by her *ka*, her soul.

Most imagined it to be an act of libel, a mockery of the woman Rome had conquered. Cleopatra, robbed symbolically of her soul, no longer royal. It was an elegant metaphoric insult.

Nicolaus the Damascene suspected otherwise.

What did Octavian know?

When, at long last, he arrived at an open port, he was so desperate to get out of Egypt that he leapt aboard the first vessel he saw, *Persephone*, a Greek transport full of slaves and animals, destined, he assumed, for

Athens. He bought his passage with coins marked in the queen's image, paying more than he'd expected.

"Those are being melted down now," the captain told him. It had been nearly two months since the queen's death. The coins were the easiest portraits to obliterate, stirred into a slurry of metal and then recast. The new ones had Octavian and his general, Marcus Agrippa, on the front. The reverse was marked with a chained crocodile.

"Then have them all," the scholar said. "They are of no use to me."

They'd been at sea for a week before it occurred to Nicolaus to ask what exactly their destination was.

"We travel to Rome. The animals are to celebrate the emperor's triumph over Egypt."

Nicolaus would have laughed had it not been so idiotic. Of course. He'd placed himself aboard a ship sailing into the arms of those who hunted him.

Now he stood aboard this ship of animals, watching the vessel breach the waves and wondering if, despite all his fleeing, despite all his planning, his end was coming. He'd seen things as the ship tilted, visions in the green depths, and none of them were bright. Sharks, with their dull, gray eyes, and more. Tentacled things, nothing beautiful. None of the sirens of the great epics. He thought for a moment of his idol, Homer, who had simply lived a poet and died a poet. He had not been a fool, as Nicolaus had. He hadn't trafficked in magic he didn't understand.

Nicolaus sighed and rubbed at his eyes. He could have disappeared into the desert or returned to the court of King Herod, from whence he'd come.

Instead—

The Fates had arranged things differently. He was following her to Italy, however against his will. She'd pursue her enemy and her remaining children. He had no doubt that if she lived, that was where she was headed.

Nicolaus ran his fingers through his long hair, tugging at it in an attempt to galvanize his mind and keep himself awake. Here he sat, on a rocking ship, on a tossing sea, helpless to stop the thing he'd unleashed.

Somewhere in the depths of his knowledge, surely there was a solution. Somewhere, there was the right story, a story of triumph, of mortals conquering the gods. Years of reading, years of learning, and yet he couldn't think of what he should have done.

Suddenly, he sat up straight, listening.

From somewhere below, he heard it again. A wailing cry. A moan. A scream.

Somewhere, deep below him, someone was dying.

→ 3 ←

The chieftain of the Psylli tribe watched the sand rising on the horizon as he milked the last droplets of venom from his viper's fangs. He coiled his serpents into their traveling basket.

"Hush," he told them, looking into their bright, arrowhead faces. "Sleep, sweet ones."

Usem was already painted for his employment, his ebony skin smeared with reddish pigments and precious violet inks. His ceremonial headdress was in place, and his coral ornaments. There was no point in trying to avoid the Romans. The nomadic tribe was regularly employed by them, for matters relating both to poisoning enemies and to healing those who had been poisoned. Usem himself had been drawn into Roman service only three months before, brought to Alexandria to attend the dead queen Cleopatra. Though Usem tried, his fingers on her heart, his lips on her wound, he was not able to resurrect her.

It was not snake venom that had killed her, he knew that even then, though he could not determine why she lay so still, a shining thing in her shining room. She didn't seem entirely dead, or if she was, it was a kind of dead he'd never encountered before.

Something was terribly wrong. Usem had tried to tell the man who was now their emperor, but the Romans had ignored him, and eventually, he'd given in, taken their payment and departed.

Upon his return from Alexandria, Usem had consulted the wind, who went everywhere and saw everything. Now he understood. A dark goddess had risen, one of the Old Ones, and Cleopatra was her earthly vessel.

The forces of chaos were stirring.

All across Africa, serpents seethed from their nests, and lions padded through villages. Elephants stampeded. One of Usem's own tribesmen had seen the queen walking down a dusty road in the South. The man reported that the very air shook with her power. She killed several villagers before moving on, and nomads picked up the bodies on the roadside, shriveled and pale, bloodless.

The signs had ceased a few days before, but Usem was not foolish enough to imagine that this meant peace. The queen might have left Africa, but it did not matter. Where she went, the world shifted, and what she did was enough to disrupt the balance. The rising of such a force was to no one's benefit.

The seas tossed, higher and higher. Angry waves crashed upon the walls of Alexandria, and strange beasts were washed up from the depths.

Though it was the Romans who enraged her, the violence of such a creature would not be confined to her enemies. Still, Usem was not afraid. His people were warriors by nature. And there were things to be gained in this fight. More than gold, though this was the usual form of payment for a Psylli's services. No. This fight was a matter of life and death, and Usem sought to use this to his advantage. The Romans were desperate. He would drive a harder bargain. If they wished to employ a Psylli to battle with an immortal, it would cost them more than they were accustomed to paying.

Usem, as it happened, had a price in mind.

He looked about him, at the smooth desert, at his camels, at his home. His children, three daughters and three sons, huddled in the tent, and their grandmother stretched her arms to encompass them.

Usem threw the leopard skin over his shoulder as the soldiers rode up to his camp. It represented the starry night sky, and his possession of such a thing would show his power to those who sought to use it.

"I will ride with you against your enemy," he told their leader, his words precise.

"You have no choice," said the centurion, looming over him. The fact that the legionaries were mounted meant that speed was required.

Otherwise, it would have been a march. "It is the will of the emperor that you come."

The Psylli laughed, a dry rattle of mirth that shook his ornaments and caused the sand around him to rise into a small tornado. The winds were his dear ones, and he called them to stand with him.

Out along the horizon, the sky grew black and whirling, the shapes of great and horned beasts forming in the dust. Their eyes flashed heat lightning as they began to move toward the interlopers.

The soldiers drew back from this spectacle, quaking and disbelieving, just as Usem intended them to be.

"There is always a choice," said the Psylli, as he leapt atop the horse, kicking his bare heels into its sides. "I have made mine. We ride to war."

≫ 4 ≪

The scream was repeated, high, desperate, desolate, and then there was a deep, rattling roar. Nicolaus ran onto the deck, where the sailors were surging about in panic, swearing.

"If the lions are loose," one said, "I'm going up the mast."

"They can climb," said another. "Didn't you see them draped over the trees? We'd be better off jumping into the water."

They looked over the rail at the dark, finned shape still accompanying them. More had joined the first, and now the vessel was trailed by a shifting underwater cloud of predators. The captain, a stout, weather-worn man with a lifetime's worth of steel-gray tattoos on his shoulders, looked down at the sharks, spat, drew his sword, and attempted to instill order.

"If the lions are loose," he said, "we'll kill them or we'll cage them back up. Nothing to be afraid of, boys."

Another roar, followed by screaming.

Screaming.

Screaming.

And silence. Which lasted much too long.

The swallows launched themselves off the rigging. The moon slid across the sky, and the sun crept about under the horizon, its bright fingers grasping at the edge of the sea. Still, the crew stayed on deck.

No one wanted to be the first to investigate what had transpired below.

"The lions sleep," said the captain, though he was not entirely convinced of this. There had been something about that roar that had stayed in the pit of his stomach. "The lions have eaten, and now they sleep."

No one moved. The gladiatorial slaves were an expensive cargo, if nothing else. No one wanted to go below and discover carnage. Least of all, if the creatures that had created it were still hiding there, hungering.

"I'll go," said the lone passenger just as dawn broke.

The sailors looked at him.

He was mad, clearly. The passenger talked in his sleep, swinging fretfully in his hammock, and he spoke in languages the sailors had never heard before.

Still, he was not one of them, and so they were willing to let him go to his death.

"How many lions are below?" Nicolaus asked, standing over the locked hatch that led to the animal's hold.

"Six," said the captain.

"If one is loose, then they all are?"

"Exactly."

The captain had armed himself with aconite-smeared arrows. He passed Nicolaus a sword and shield, and then the sailors stood in formations, waiting for the lions to be chased up onto the deck.

Nicolaus eased himself down the ladder, at each rung expecting hot breath on his back. His lantern was not bright enough to illuminate the darkness to his satisfaction. He might only travel in a small circle of light, and beyond the edge of it was something horrible.

What was he doing, climbing down a ladder into a dark and haunted hold?

He was as good as dead anyway, a wanted man traveling to Rome.

He could hear breathing, there, in the far darkness. He held the lantern out in front of him, the sword in his other hand overmatched by trembling.

A lion, tawny, amber-eyed, enormous, stretched on the floor, his mane streaked in gore. The beast regarded Nicolaus calmly for a moment, and then, just as casually, lifted his lip and bared his long teeth. The historian felt his bowels liquefy. There were bars between them, though. This lion had not escaped.

There was a sound behind him. The sound of air displaced in a silent leap.

Nicolaus whirled, the lantern swinging, catching a glimpse of golden fur before it disappeared into the shadows. He smelled the silk of the creature, the sleek fur, the musk.

He turned his head slowly, counting them. There were six lions in the cage.

But there had been seven lions in the room.

He suddenly heard the muffled sobbing of a woman. Nicolaus walked cautiously toward the door that led to the slave quarters. His lantern went out as he entered the room, and then he could see nothing at all. His other senses compensated, attempting to draw understanding from invisibility.

The pungent, smothering smell of bodies kept too close, sweat and salt, feces and blood.

The dripping heat, radiating from the walls and floor.

The sound of sobbing. Only one voice. A female voice.

He could see light coming in from somewhere, a fissure in the side of the ship. He walked toward it, stepping carefully, his feet slipping on something he chose not to think about.

He could not find her at first. The ground was covered in straw and—

His feet nudged against solid objects, strangely frail. His eyes began to adjust, and he recoiled.

Bodies.

The sobbing continued, softer now.

Nicolaus pressed his hand over his mouth, swallowing bile. The lion had killed all the slaves. All but one, and here she was, crying in the darkness. Every nerve in the historian screamed for his departure, demanding that he bolt up the ladder and into the light.

But where was the beast?

Something moved quickly in front of him in the dim light, a form barely visible and impossible to define. He pressed his sword out before him, slicing the air. Nothing there.

"You will not be able to kill me that way," someone whispered from close behind him. He felt breath on his ear.

He whirled, the blade cutting through the place the sound had come from. His shoulders clenched. His heart pounded, and he suddenly realized that—

He knew the voice.

It was ravaged, changed from the silvery thing it had been, but he knew it. He'd listened to her tell tales, listened to her sing, listened to her call to her children. He'd listened to her spell chanting, teaching her the pronunciation of the words.

"Shall I kill you, too?" the voice asked him, and then there was another choked sound of pure misery. "I cannot stop myself. Leave me if you want to live."

He moved toward her. There she was, curled in a coil of rope.

"How can you be here?" he managed to ask. An inadequate question.

She looked up at him, and he saw, in the dim light, her eyes glittering, her expression weary. Her face was streaked with misery, her mouth with blood.

"You do not know me," she said. "I am nothing that lives in light."

What had his life become? Here he was, on a slave ship in the middle of the sea, with the creature who had been the queen of Egypt.

"Queen Cleopatra, I am Nicolaus of Damascus. I was tutor to your children," Nicolaus said. He could not lift his voice above a whisper. "I know you."

She made a sound that was a cross between laughter and sobbing.

"Knew," she replied. "You knew me. You know me no longer."

She lifted her hand toward him. Her long limbs, her delicate fingers, all of it smeared with red. She cradled something covered in cloth.

"What have you done?" he asked, his voice strangely high and sharp. He was near to swooning, and yet anger tripped up from within him, triumphing over fear. "There were a hundred slaves aboard this ship."

"Did you think they were people?" she asked. She raised her chin, and there was a trace of the old pride. "They were not treated as people. They were animals on this vessel. The Romans feed them the same food they feed the lions. Less food. I was a queen, and now I am a lion. I was a lion and now I am a slave. I was a slave, and now I am a beast. As a beast, I hunger. Should I not be fed?"

"Where are the rest?" Nicolaus asked.

Cleopatra moved her hand to indicate the hole in the ship's side. There was, Nicolaus noticed now, a shred of fabric clinging to the splintered wood.

The sharks. Nicolaus understood it suddenly, the mass of silver flesh tracing the route of the vessel.

"If you knew me once, then help me now," she said.

Nicolaus stepped back. He did not want what she had to give him.

Cleopatra pulled the cloth in her arms aside and revealed the face of a small boy, perhaps four years old. Ashen cheeks, dark, knotted hair.

The child's eyes opened and he looked at Nicolaus, terrified. The historian snatched him from Cleopatra. The boy was unwounded.

"This was his mother." She touched a corpse with her fingertips. "My hands were on him, when I realized."

She opened her fists and revealed long scores in the flesh.

The grief on the monster's face crippled Nicolaus with guilt. She was not wholly a monster. He could see the Cleopatra he had known, still inside.

"I would not kill a child. You must believe me. *She* takes my body, and she hungers. I thought I was strong enough to resist her."

The historian wrestled with his soul. He'd helped to do this. She was here because of him.

Sekhmet cared nothing for gold, nothing for gems. All she desired was blood. Once she began to kill, she could not stop. That was her nature. Cleopatra had killed not of her own volition but because he'd translated that spell, translated it badly, and summoned the goddess with no protections for the summoner.

Had he not, the queen would have been dead and buried these months. Had he not, Nicolaus would never have found himself aboard this vessel, hunted by Romans, a criminal.

"What do you want from me?" he asked.

"My children are in Rome with the emperor. Help me find them. He killed my husband. He killed my son. He killed *me*."

"And yet you live."

"Then you do not know what the living are."

She grabbed Nicolaus's hand and placed it on her breast. He tried to pull away from her, but she held him there until he felt the absence of her heartbeat.

"I will help you," he managed.

→ 5 ←

Auðr was kneeling beside a bed deep in the northern forest, when she heard the legionaries approaching. The girl she was tending gasped, her swollen belly bluish and rigid, the pallet beneath her soaked with blood, and Auðr hissed in frustration. The horses outside were distracting, and she needed all her powers for this. Her arms trembled with tension. Too much time had passed.

Outside the doorway, snow drifted over the pines. In her own land, the gods came in the northern lights, glancing their fires across the skies, spinning clouds from their looms, singing with the thunder. Here, they did not even know that her homeland existed. *Oceanus*, they called it, as though it were not a true place, as though the water stretched to cover the world apart from them. Still, she had been here for years, had come across the ocean to this forest. Her part in the pattern had dictated that she place herself here. The sound of hooves on the frozen land was distinct, and Auðr cursed quietly. She had not expected the Romans so soon.

Auðr was a fate spinner, a *seiðkona*, but for the first time in her life, she was unable to see the entirety of the future. Something grave had changed in the world, and for months she'd tried in vain to understand what it was. She knew only that there were torn threads in the pattern, a dark disturbance in the tapestry of time.

Destruction and bloodshed, old gods rising.

Death.

If all humanity was fated to die or to descend into pain and chaos, it was not the place of a seiðkona to try to change it, Auðr knew; she was not supposed to interfere in the fate of the world, but she could not stop herself. Though she was not as strong as she had been in her youth, Auðr had spent her life keeping chaos from finding purchase in an orderly universe. She did not fear death, but she feared that it would take her before she finished her work.

She was far from her home, far from her people, and she had broken the rules.

Two days before, she'd irrevocably transgressed by braiding the threads of her own fate to the ones that began the tangle.

Before her, the girl's head lolled back, her eyes rolling like those of a terrified animal. The seiðkona curled her aching fingers about her distaff, her *seiðstafr*, twisting and arranging the threads of destiny about the girl and her child as quickly as she could. The girl screamed, and then writhed, arching up from the bed, her body controlled by Auðr's power.

The fate spinner caught the baby between her hands. A girl child. Still. Pale as a fish. Lips and eyelids deep blue. No spark of life there, no heartbeat.

She'd been dead three hours, perhaps longer.

Pounding on the door, shouting, horses. The seiðkona clenched her hand around the distaff. Her fingers worked, reweaving the child's threads into a new pattern. Everyone had a place in the tapestry, and this soul would have one. She would have a life filled with ordinary miracles. The seiðkona would give it to her. It would be the last thing she did in these woods.

Auðr pressed the baby's lips to her lips and said one word, breathing it into the infant's mouth, just as the door of the hut burst open, and the soldiers swarmed in, shouting. The new mother screamed, and the seiðkona looked up, seeing only the silhouettes of the men against the door frame.

A pair of hands dragged Auðr from the hut. Someone threw her onto the horse's back, ripping her leather cloak and tearing her hood from her white braids.

From inside the hut, the baby's wail rose up, frail at first and then stronger. Hearing it, the seiðkona smiled, but a sharp object hit her hard in the skull, and that was all she knew.

Hours later, light slashed into her eyes, and she found herself sitting bound in the saddle—the smell of leather, the salted scent of horseflesh—an armored man behind her.

The soldiers came at her own request, though they did not know it. Auðr's manipulation of the fates had ensured that she'd soon be in the center of the darkness, a part of whatever would happen there. She would die there, she knew. There was no other choice.

Blood trickled from the wound on her forehead, dropping onto the pale skin of her thigh. The man's hand moved on her waist, and she bared her teeth to growl.

"She wakes," he said, his command of the forest language rudimentary at best. "I am Marcus Agrippa, and you are summoned to Rome."

➤ 6 ⬅

The sun blazed down upon the emperor's head, burning his scalp. His chariot was pulled by four white horses, and the laurel wreath was on his head, his gold-embroidered toga perfectly arranged over his tunic. He looked evenly, confidently over the Roman crowd, as though he did not imagine an enemy in their midst, as though he did not expect the world to shake and the city around him to crumble. If a horrible, unnatural war were coming, Octavian needed his allies to believe that his power had been granted by the gods.

Where was Marcus Agrippa? He and the legionaries had gone across the world in all directions to find the assistance Octavian needed, but months had passed and there'd been no word from any of them. What if Agrippa had encountered *her*? It was Octavian's fault. He'd been too cowardly to tell his general of Cleopatra's resurrection.

Octavian smiled tightly and processed forward into Rome, behind the conquered corpse of Egypt's queen. A sculptor had rendered the image of the dead Cleopatra, incredibly lifelike, an asp clasped to her breast. She was carried on a flowery pyre, and her twins walked on either side of it, holding heavy chains, the younger son at the front. Selene moved regally, her hair loose and straight down her back. There was no grief on that face. It might as well have been carved of the same marble her mother's was.

It was a cruel irony. Mark Antony, who had no need for heirs, had fathered at least four sons and several daughters, but the gods had given Octavian only one child, and that a girl, incapable of succeeding him.

His eleven-year-old daughter, Julia, sat in the chariot beside him, but she would not inherit. There could be no female rulers in Rome, no queens.

Octavian thought for an unpleasant moment about queens. He'd been awake every night since Alexandria, pacing his rooms, troubled by the visions he saw in Cleopatra's eyes. Flying creatures and lightning sticks, heaps of bodies shoveled into ditches, children fighting, women fighting, men fighting. He might doze for an hour, but then he'd jolt out of bed, screaming himself awake. He employed storytellers and musicians to sit beside his bed and sing, to spin tales of heroes and victories, anything to keep him from falling fully into sleep. Even in daylight, carried in his litter, he feared the nightmares that might overtake him if he leaned too heavily against the cushions and napped.

He wondered now if he'd been mad to send his chief defender seeking something that might not even exist. Witches. Sorcerers. Saviors.

He tried to calm himself. Agrippa and his men would find what Octavian needed. Marcus Agrippa had neither approved of Octavian's instructions nor understood them, but Agrippa was not in charge. If this was to be war, Octavian must be prepared, just as Alexander the Great would have been. And if his methods were unusual? There could be no shame in fighting an unnatural creature that way. Rome had legions, yes, a hundred and fifty thousand men at the ready, and over three hundred fifty thousand if he added the soldiers stationed in his client states, but what good would legions be against her? He needed something more. He himself had banned witchcraft in Rome, but this was a special situation.

At the conclusion of the procession, Octavian stood before his people to be given his new name. It was the moment he'd imagined for years, and yet he took no pleasure in it. He'd chosen the name Augustus for augury, suggesting that augurs had seen his reign in the signs, and today he renamed Sextilis, the month in which he'd conquered Egypt, after himself. August, he thought, would yearly remind the people of Egypt's submission to him.

Now he regretted everything about this. Egypt had not submitted.

Instead, Egypt was on the move.

The throngs before him cheered, waving banners and scarves, throwing flowers, singing his new name in the sunlit streets of Rome. The last time he'd been so exposed before so many people had been at Caesarion's execution. Today, he took the name of Caesarion's father for his own.

Gaius Julius Caesar Augustus.

His skin prickled and his stomach shifted uneasily. On the voyage out of Egypt, he'd felt his hair turning gray, strand by strand, and during dinner on the seventh night at sea, he'd experienced a disastrous sensation, lifted his hand to his mouth, and pulled out an entire tooth.

A horrifically bad omen. He shook himself. He did not believe in omens.

He rushed back to the Palatine when the ceremonies were finished, sprinting up the marble steps and into his study, waving off advisors and pouring himself a cup of unwatered wine, pausing to remove the top of a small vial of something his physicians assured him was an antidote to every sort of potential poison. It was theriac, made from Julius Caesar's own recipe, which had protected Octavian's benefactor from everything but the treachery of his friends. The potion contained, among other rare and distasteful substances, cinnamon, frankincense, scarab beetle dung, acacia and rhododendron, aconite and iris, anise and turpentine, pulverized bones of kings, viper venom, and, most important, tears from the poppies that bloomed on the great glacial fields of Italy. As a final addition, the emperor had provided his physicians with the powdery piece of cloth stolen from the mummy of Alexander.

The resultant potion smelled like a battlefield after three days' decay, but Augustus eased a few drops of it down anyway, drained his cup and poured another.

One could never be too careful.

Augustus gazed out his window, his pale eyes squinting in the light. All the emperor could think of was darkness. It would come, no matter what he did to resist it.

He hoped Rome would be ready.

⇒ 7 ⇐

The port of Ostia teemed with activity, legions of soldiers arriving and reporting to the emperor's forces, shipments of grain, cloth, and slaves, and groupings of sailors, soldiers, and whores conducting business.

A transport ship with a cargo of long-awaited animals, imported to celebrate the return of Rome's first citizen, was being unloaded in the midst of this, the creatures harnessed, muzzled, and then prodded into the crowd.

The zebras descended the planks first, their hooves stamping so hard after long captivity that the wood splintered beneath them. The gazelles followed, their eyes rolling up to show white. Even in the chaos of the shipyard, the ostriches drew attention, with their high-stepping, with their long, wavering necks. Crocodiles, low and dry and scraping, heaved themselves slowly onto the stones, their tails lashing as they went, several sailors clinging to the ropes that bound each one. A set of jaws snapped and a feathered thing was gone.

The most dangerous creatures were the last off the vessel. First, the rhinoceros, its horn tipped with cork in a hopeful attempt to blunt it, and then the hippopotamus, which opened its jaws and bellowed, to the entertainment and awe of the crowd. There'd never been a hippopotamus in Rome before. Then, the tigers, each as long as two men, with their glossy, variegated pelts and flashing, dismissive eyes. Finally, the lions appeared on deck, sailors wrangling them into submission.

"One of the lions went wild and ate up all the slaves that ship was carrying," a young sailor bragged to his whore. "I got it from the ship's boy."

"Which lion?" she asked.

"That one." He pointed at the largest of the lions, a male with a twisted mane and rheumy eyes.

"That one looks old," she replied.

The lion chose that moment to roar, revealing a gummy, toothless mouth. The whore looked at the sailor and smirked.

A slender woman wrapped entirely in a dark, hooded cloak and veil too heavy for the weather made her way down the *Persephone*'s plank. Her gloved hand was roped to that of a young and handsome man, who was draped in scholarly robes. His chin jutting, his other arm supporting a small child, the scholar pushed his way through the crowd.

As the trio of passengers moved alongside them, the lions and tigers began to roar, rearing up onto their haunches and struggling with their captors. It seemed that they were trying to follow her, though surely this was an illusion. The animals that had already been unloaded began to cry out as well, the ostriches looking about in alarm and flapping their useless wings, the gazelles and zebras bolting in terror to the ends of their ropes and then snapping backward. A crocodile broke his bonds and barreled forward, his teeth snapping, as sailors danced about him, trying to wrestle him back into servitude.

The woman in black looked over her shoulder as the scholar led her, and the whore caught a glimpse of her face. A dark-smeared eye, a flash of brightness. Something strange there. And beautiful, too. The whore was intrigued.

She tugged at the sailor's arm and pointed in the woman's direction. "Who's she? And the boy?"

"The only slaves the lion didn't kill. The scholar bought them for a couple of coins. She's bad luck. The captain wanted to be rid of her, and I don't blame him."

The whore craned her neck after the woman. What sort of thing might she be, that a slave-selling captain would throw away his prospect of profit? She took a half step in their direction, but the sailor who'd purchased her for the hour pulled her the opposite way, his hands already burrowing into the folds of her gown.

Marcus Agrippa and a small group of his soldiers, ragged after months of travel, marched past a moment later, agitated by the delay the animals had caused their vessel. They bore with them the seiðkona, her long white hair tangled and her eyes as silver as polished metal. She looked about the port, her expression chilling to any who inadvertently met her gaze.

Auðr's head suddenly whipped to face the woman in black. The old woman hissed in surprise.

"What is it?" Agrippa asked the fate spinner, stumbling over her guttural language.

The seiðkona shook her head, her fingers twitching. Agrippa followed her stare, his face scanning the crowd until it landed on two travelers. Something about the man was familiar, and the woman, too. The way her arm moved, the way her feet seemed scarcely to touch the earth, caught his attention. There was a strange grace about her.

Agrippa's eyes narrowed and he took a step in their direction, but as he did, the man took the woman roughly in his arms and kissed her.

Agrippa's attention faded. She was nothing, a whore or a slave, and no business of Marcus Agrippa's. He was overdue in Rome. Besides, the woman she reminded him of was long dead. Agrippa laughed at himself. The way his heart raced, you would think he'd seen a ghost.

Agrippa's company marched on, only Auðr looking back. She'd seen something in that woman's eyes. Something old and dark and familiar.

The seiðkona had seen its like only once before, when she was a girl of thirteen, sold as an unwilling talisman to an exploring ship, but she had never forgotten it. Her ship had capsized in a storm, leaving none but Auðr alive, clinging to a piece of wreckage in the middle of an icy ocean. At last, certain she was dying, she saw something in the waters: a great eye, a long and whirling tail, a creature like the dragon her ship had been carved in imitation of.

The monster hung there in the blue depths, and she looked into the eye for what seemed like thousands of years, seeing its history, a world of water, a melting sea. Worshipped by sailors and by kings, and then forgotten.

She had seen a god living deep beneath the world. An Old One, something from before the beginning. She felt herself falling into darkness and gave herself over, but the god sent her back.

She had stumbled onto the foreign shore, clutching only her seiðstafr, which she'd tied tightly into the cords of her dress as the ship had gone down. Alive. She had not known why, not then, but she knew there was a reason.

The universe worked according to its own laws. She was meant for something, some great task.

This task. She wished it had come sooner, when she was stronger, but the Fates had their own timing.

Auðr whispered to herself, twisting the threads of fate between her fingers as she was pulled through the marketplace and toward the emperor.

A moment later, the scholar and the queen parted from their embrace, and within a few steps, they and the child disappeared completely into the crowds and chaos of Rome.

8

Cleopatra caught her breath, trying to control herself as Nicolaus turned away. The scholar's kiss had awoken her hunger, and now she wanted only to be away from him before she did something she would regret.

He wanted to be away from her as well; she could feel it. He wanted to run, but he had promised he would help her. His brave words were false. Nicolaus trembled before her, and yet he managed to turn his back on her, pushing through the throngs, wending their way through the slender, dusty streets of Rome, the child sleeping in his arms.

She had no pity for him. He was the one who'd insisted they depart the ship at dusk and walk into a sea of people, the sights and sounds of Rome, the animals flanking them, the whores and sailors. She could see only the back of his neck as he led her through the crowd, the slender vertebrae above the scholar's cloak. It would be easy. The rope between them was pulled taut. He was already tied to her, though to observers, it would look as if she was tied to *him*, his property, his slave.

It would seem to the crowd that he was a trainer and she was his beast, a lion barely tamed by a leash, she thought, bristling, and then remembered that she was not a lioness but a woman.

"Never do that again," she managed to say. "Never touch me again. I would have had him."

"It was quick thinking on my part. Agrippa's men would have captured us. I saved you."

She was not something to be saved, the voice of Sekhmet whispered. She was something to be worshipped.

Did she need him, truly?

Yes, Cleopatra reminded herself. He could go out in the day when she could not. He could seek her children where she could not. Her face was too easily recognized in this ugly city.

"I *wanted* him to see me," she said, rebelling against her own thoughts. "I would confront him. Agrippa was the leader of the army in Alexandria. It is because of him that Antony is dead. And he was there when they killed my son, standing beside Octavian. He gave the order."

"Confront? You do not mean confront. You mean kill. You would have fought him there, in the port? There were citizens everywhere."

"*Roman* citizens," Cleopatra said. What if a Roman was hurt? Did it matter so much?

"And your own people, perhaps," Nicolaus reminded her. "There was another boatload of slaves coming in, and who knows where they were seized? The emperor's men have been all over Africa."

The scholar touched her hand, and she pulled away from him, barely suppressing a hiss. Was this what it would be from now on? No one to touch her? No one to love her?

It did not matter. Antony was dead.

She should be entering the city with her ancestral crown atop her head, and instead she'd climbed up from the slave quarters and into the dirt. Rome was a colorless city, somber in comparison with Alexandria's brilliance. At home, everything was draped in silks, every surface ornamented. Here, decoration was seen as weakness. The last time she'd walked off a ship and into this country, she'd had Caesarion in her arms, newborn and perfect, and Julius Caesar beside her. Caesar, at least, had respected Cleopatra. He believed that women were as capable as men, and when, in the course of his long career, his foes had mocked him as being "womanlike," he'd retorted that the Amazons had once ruled over Asia, and Semiramis had reigned supreme and ferocious over Babylon for a hundred years. If this was womanlike, let him be a woman. Caring nothing for gossips, disregarding his betrayed wife, and scoffing at the way the senators talked, he'd installed his mistress in his own garden house on the Tiber, and there she'd walked, surrounded by roses that reminded her of home.

They passed those same gardens now, given to the people at Caesar's death.

"I am a queen," she told Nicolaus finally. "You are a servant. You will not touch me."

"Keep quiet. We do not need to be captured just as we arrive," said Nicolaus without looking at her. He pulled her into a doorway as a patrol of legionaries marched past.

In the shadows, Cleopatra shifted her veil. Her eyes were dilated, she knew. Beneath the veil, she examined her fingers. The nails were long and curving, the claws of a lion. As she watched, they receded.

Antony, she thought. *What have I become?*

Talking to him was the only thing that kept her human. She thought of their marriage ceremony, their hands entwined, all the lamps lit, peacocks parading, their children seated around them, his shaggy mane of hair, the feeling of his muscles beneath his skin as she held his arm. Cleopatra was not gone when she thought of her husband. She had not lost herself entirely, she kept trying to remind herself. Part of her was still human.

But she feared this was untrue.

Amongst the cats, she'd stayed quiet enough, forgetting her history, forgetting everything. Vengeance and Rome had seemed far away. She slept curled around the lions and tigers, soothed by the sound of their purring. In the cat's body, she scarcely noticed what she was doing, and the slaves seemed to expect what was coming for them. They hardly resisted.

Only slaves, Cleopatra thought, still troubled by what had happened aboard the ship, but it was no comfort. She hadn't known about the child as she took the mother, as she took the father, as she took everyone, frenzied, glorying in hunger and satisfaction. She'd nearly killed the child, too. Her mouth was on his throat when she realized what she was doing and forced herself backward, screaming into the darkness for discovery. She'd thought herself in control of her hunger by the time she boarded the ship, but she was wrong.

You will be her slave.

Half through the voyage, she'd found herself crouched with the cats in the hold, running her fingers over a tiger's coat, certain she could read the markings on it. *The future*, she'd thought, believing, if only for a few hours, that her own acts were written here, her own hopes, her own solutions. The tiger's stripes were hieroglyphs, she'd thought, as she'd sat in the dark, reading in the language of the gods. It was only now, walking through the streets of Rome, that she saw the madness in this.

Her future, whatever it was, was written nowhere but in her own body, and the writing was unclear. All she knew was that she had arrived in the city of her enemies, and that they were all around her.

Nicolaus placed the ship's child in apprenticeship to a scribe he had known in Damascus, and at last, they arrived at their destination.

"No one will look for us here," he said as he pried the lock from the door. He hid her in a library, the home of a poet, Virgil, a great favorite of the emperor. Nicolaus had encountered him in Alexandria months before and learned that he planned to be in Campania for some time.

She tried to study Virgil's library instead of dreaming of fire and bloodshed. The scholar brought incense to the room, and she burned the resin, but it gave her none of the pleasure it once had. It reminded her of Alexandria, the smell of the cedar planks imported from Cyprus. Those same dockyard planks had caught fire and ignited the library filled with the knowledge of every traveler, every scholar, medicines and magic, maps and death songs, in all the languages of man. Now all that true understanding was lost, dispersed as ashes into the air of Egypt and settled into the sand. Cleopatra had inhaled the ashes herself—she remembered walking the city as it burned, the smoke low and black—and they had not taught her anything.

Nicolaus went out into the city to glean the location of her children. This was what a queen should do, she knew. Wait for her servants to get her the information she could not herself obtain. She knew that Rome was traitorous, that assassins could appear out of nowhere. She knew she should be reasonable. She would resist Sekhmet's voice. She could not take revenge until she knew where her children were. She would not run the risk of hurting them more than she already had.

Cleopatra opened the scrolls, spreading them on the marble floor before her. Studying them as once she had studied her language lessons. Poems and histories, books of myth, romance, and medicines. Words were the things that had made her a true queen of Egypt. They were her power. No longer. The vellum of certain, more precious texts radiated nothing but the lives of dead things. She could scarcely pay attention long enough to absorb the stories in the scrolls.

Even in this windowless room, Cleopatra could feel the moon crossing the sky. She thought of Ra, an ancient with bones of silver, flesh of gold, and hair the pure blue of lapis, traveling the waters of the sky in his day boat, creating the stars and constellations so that when night came, and he traveled into the Underworld, his path would be lit.

Now endless night was what she desired. Night was best for murder, and her enemy, like all men, surely slept when the sun was gone. She could feel Sekhmet surging through the world, fueled by Cleopatra's rampage aboard the ship.

She bent again over the book before her, searching for distraction.

She happened instead upon an unpublished poem about her own marriage. Virgil had obscured it somewhat, and grafted a new and terrible ending onto the story. She was gossip now.

Virgil had disguised Cleopatra as Dido, the foreign queen of Carthage, in love with Aeneas, who left her behind to return to his own people. In this poem, the queen's suicide was successful. Aeneas watched the smoke of her pyre from the deck of his homebound ship.

It was as though Antony had fled her at Actium and gone back to Rome, leaving her to burn.

Cleopatra threw the pages to the ground, furious. She would not wait here, in this library, in this poet's house, no matter what Nicolaus said.

An old city filled with temples. A city filled with people. Her children and her enemy awaited.

⇒ 9 ⇐

Augustus spilled his drink, startled by the sound of someone in the hallway. He'd raised his glass as a weapon, thinking to smash it in the face of the intruder, when Marcus Agrippa's face, grim as ever, appeared in the doorway. Augustus leapt to his feet and embraced the man.

"It's been six months since Thebes," he said, nearly overcome with relief. "I thought you were dead, or worse."

"What would be worse than death?" Agrippa looked at him irritably. "My men have been from end to end of the world on your orders, and I still do not know why. I have three magicians for you. I might have recruited three legions of warriors in the same amount of time."

"Magicians?" Augustus grimaced. "I can find magicians in Rome."

"Witches," Agrippa amended. "Sorcerers. Whatever you call them, they are all the same kind of creature, and nothing I trust."

"I wish you'd brought them more quickly," Augustus said.

Agrippa sat down opposite him and leaned over the table.

"Just as *I* wish you'd tell me what you plan to war against with *witches*. This is not the Roman way. Are we threatened by Parthia? Scythia? You need not fear them. We have legions, ready to serve, here in Rome and more abroad."

"It is not Parthia," Augustus said.

Agrippa was somewhat relieved. Campaigns in Parthia—notorious for its archers and lack of ready forage—had taken many lives.

"Scythia, then?"

"Neither is it Scythia."

"What is it that threatens us? Long-haired Gaul? Britannia? Is it something sprung of Oceanus, something we've never seen before? We can fight anything, be it monster or man. We are Romans!" Agrippa wiped the sweat from his forehead and poured himself a drink.

"Yes," said Augustus wearily. "It is something we've never seen before."

Agrippa drained his first cup of wine, recoiling at the aftertaste.

"I assume you know your wine is foul," he said, and served himself another cup, taking only one sip before he grimaced and poured it out, shaking his head. "Is it peace that frightens you, then? I grant you, it's unusual, but Egypt is conquered, and Rome is fortified against any enemy."

Augustus looked at him with a pained expression on his face. He shook his head.

"You know me, Octavian," Agrippa said, his voice softening. "You've known me since we were boys. Do you not trust me enough to tell me what is wrong? You've not been right since we took Alexandria, since the business with Antony. I have forgiven that. It was wrong, but it is long since finished."

There was a moment in which Augustus thought he might tell his friend everything, but it quickly passed. He was the emperor now. There was no one he could truly trust, not even his closest associates. He'd learned that much from Caesar.

"My name is Augustus, not Octavian. I am no longer the boy you knew. See that you remember that," Augustus said coolly. "Bring me the witches."

Agrippa looked at him for a bewildered moment, and then left the room, shaking his head. Augustus poured himself another cup of wine, and with it, theriac. He felt the ingredients edge into the back of his mind. His fingertips tingled.

The first witch presented to him was a tall, slender, white-haired woman with silvery, slanting, wide-set eyes, her fingers gnarled at the knuckles, her lips pale and thin, like those of a fish. Augustus could not tell her age. She might be seventy or a hundred. She was clearly agitated, and in chains.

"Her name is Auðr, and I found her myself in Germany," Agrippa said. "The villagers there relied on her to bring babies, but she came to them over the water, from the frozen lands where nothing lives, and they swore she had other talents."

"A midwife?" Augustus barked, disgusted. A midwife was not what he had asked for.

"That is not all she is," Agrippa insisted, motioning to a soldier, who handed him a long package wrapped in a cloak. "She involves herself with the Fates. She's chained for a reason."

The woman's eyes opened wider, a sudden strange light in them, and she made a purring sound of anticipation. With covered hands, Agrippa unwrapped the item, a slender wooden staff with a narrow, rounded top. The creature's eyes began to shine in earnest. An unpleasant glow, to Augustus's mind, like those of an animal sighted in the dark. Augustus pulled on his gloves, and his general passed the distaff to him. He could see nothing thrilling in its composition.

Agrippa brought forth a legionary who'd been standing at the back of the room.

"What is your name?" he asked the boy.

The legionary's face crumpled in consternation. He thought for a moment, his fingers grasping and then releasing some invisible object.

Agrippa looked pained.

"She tapped the boy's forehead with this distaff, and since then, he knows nothing of his own history, and little of anything else. He's been riding since before he could walk, and yet we've had to tie him to his horse all the way here. I would have her pay for this."

The old woman looked at the boy and said a few rough words in an unknown tongue.

The legionary spoke, blank-faced.

"She says that my fate was dark. She has changed it. Now I do not remember the man I was, and my path has shifted to one of less trouble."

"He did not speak her language before she touched him," Agrippa informed Augustus. "Now he functions as her translator."

The woman spoke again.

"She says she is a seiðkona, a fate spinner," the boy said. "She does not serve Rome but the Fates. There is trouble here and she seeks to understand it."

Augustus was distracted. Her skills had sparked his hopes.

His *own* fate was dark, he knew. When he shut his eyes, the visions were there again, red waves rising over red waves, the roaring and tearing of beasts, serpents, that river of blood. His death at Cleopatra's hands.

This woman, this seiðkona, might change his destiny.

"Rome welcomes you to her defense," he said. "Take her to her bed-chamber down the corridor, and bring me the rest."

"You would have creatures such as these staying in your house?" Agrippa asked, his brow furrowing. "They would be better kept under guard in my quarters."

"I need access to them at all hours. And I need their protection."

"I ask you again, from what?"

Augustus had no answer. He tried to ignore Agrippa's expression. His friend's temper had always been slow to ignite but long to burn, and Augustus was slightly surprised to find it directed at him. He drank deeply until Agrippa returned with the second witch.

"The chieftain of the Psylli, Usem," Agrippa said. "My men brought him from Libya."

Augustus recognized the very man who'd incorrectly declared Cleopatra dead. He'd answer for that, in any case. Black as a burnt field, black as a crow's plumage, his skin glinting with that same dark, bluish iridescence. His chest was decked in strands of stones the color of fresh blood, and over his shoulders, the spotted skin of a leopard was draped, fixed with golden clasps.

He placed a woven basket on the floor of the chamber, and Augustus instinctively raised his feet from off the stones.

"I bring my serpents to battle," Usem said, removing the cover from the basket. Several snakes slithered from the basket as the Psylli moved his arm into the air. The snakes arced their bodies in mimicry of it, coiling themselves into a rippling design.

"These are my warriors," the Psylli informed Augustus. "They can travel anywhere you desire. They can seek out the traitors who hide your enemy from you. They can find those who serve your enemy."

Augustus let himself relax, slightly. "And what else do you have for me?"

"Is this not enough for you, emperor of Rome? I see you are an intelligent man. My tribe controls the Western Wind."

"Like a slave? Does it always obey you, then?" Augustus asked.

"Just as we obey Rome," Usem said, and smiled. "When Rome fattens our purses. Still, it pleases the wind to serve our friends and plague our enemies."

"And which are we to you?" Augustus asked him.

A sudden breeze appeared in the room, guttering the candles. In the flickering light, Augustus saw Agrippa's hand tighten on his sword. The shuttered window flew open, rattling in a quick and drenching storm.

"We are friends," said the Psylli. "Or have I misunderstood?"

"Certainly," replied Augustus, shaken. "We are friends."

"There is a price for my service," Usem continued.

Of course. The emperor had been prepared for exactly this eventuality. He signaled to a slave, who wheeled in a barrow of treasure taken from Alexandria, but the Psylli laughed.

"I do not desire gold," Usem said.

"Your people have always taken our gold."

"Not for this task. It is too large," the Psylli said. "If I deliver what you ask for, you will close the Gates of Janus. My people will no longer cower in their tents when they hear hoofbeats. We will no longer travel our desert fearing war, fearing poisoned waters, fearing kidnapping and slavery. My people do not fear the wind, and we should not fear Rome."

Augustus was shocked. He looked at Marcus Agrippa. What had the man been thinking? This should have been negotiated and refused already. Since the founding of Rome, the nation had always been at war, fighting off invaders, yes, but also invading and gaining territories through bloodshed. The closing of the Gates of Janus by the emperor of Rome would announce that the empire was at war no longer. The Psylli demanded peace from end to end of the Roman world.

Agrippa shrugged.

"It was not for me to refuse. You requested sorcerers, and you knew that it would not be inexpensive."

The emperor could not imagine it. The gates had been open his entire life. It was a ridiculous request.

"You require my assistance," the Psylli said, standing before Augustus, his jaw tight. The wind whipped about Augustus, shifting his garments. "The wind has told me of your trouble with the queen Cleopatra."

Augustus jolted. How did the man know?

Agrippa stared at Augustus for a moment and then collapsed back into the chair, where he rubbed his temples.

"I might have guessed this wasn't finished," Agrippa muttered. He raised his head to look at Augustus. "Her people may wish her alive, but we all saw her dead and buried. Her body did not walk from that mausoleum. Her people took her corpse, and I am sure it was for some rite common to Egypt. The dead are enemy to no one."

Augustus ignored him.

"She walks," Usem continued, and smiled, showing his keen, pointed white teeth. "And she is more than she was. You will not conquer her with soldiers."

Augustus wavered for a moment, and then hurriedly thrust out his hand to the Psylli.

"Yes," he said. "I swear it. I will close the Gates of Janus, if you deliver me the queen."

Usem took Augustus's hand.

"It will be done. Now I require accommodations and a meal. My snakes hunger, and so do I."

"Take him to his room," Augustus ordered. "And let him give his directions to the kitchen on the way." A legionary led the Psylli from the chamber. Out of the corner of his eye, Augustus could see Agrippa seething.

"You make promises to such a man?" Agrippa asked when he was gone. "You swear to give him something you will not deliver? You ask him to hunt something that does not exist? Cleopatra is dead. What has gotten into your mind? This man will pretend he has conjured and beaten her, and then he will demand that you keep your promise. It is all a sham."

"Are you a fool? I have no intention of closing the gates," Augustus snapped.

Agrippa looked at him, his gaze steely. "We do not want the Psylli as enemies," he warned. "They have warred against the strong many times before, and won."

"They will not win against Rome. I have not yet met the last of our warriors," said Augustus.

"This discussion is not finished," Agrippa warned.

"Nicolaus the Damascene, then," Augustus said. "What of him? Where is he? You say I have no enemies, but you have not brought me the man I asked for."

"He is nowhere to be found. My men have sorted through every grain of sand in Egypt. He's likely cowering in a cave somewhere. The man you seek is a tutor, Octav—Augustus. He is no assassin."

"The night is filled with enemies. You know that as well as I," Augustus said. "Where is the last witch?"

Agrippa surrendered for the moment.

"You will not enjoy her company," he said. "She offered herself into our service. This one comes from Thessaly, and my men say that the village near where they found her was filled with tales of her deeds. The men thought she was a whore, but she is not. She is certainly not. I met her tonight, and I do not think Rome should trust her." The general's face rippled with distaste.

"Who are you to say whom I should and should not employ?" Augustus asked.

The third of Rome's defenders was led into the room. There was a moment of silence before Augustus could find his voice.

"Your emperor welcomes you to Rome," he stammered at last.

The third witch was an Aphrodite, her body curving and generous, her limbs perfectly formed and draped in indigo-embroidered linen. Her hair fell to her knees, braided in thousands of complicated plaits, each knotted with beads and shells. Her eyes were wide and emerald green, and her lips, unpainted, were the color of the roses in Caesar's gardens.

The girl—for she could not be older than seventeen—had the grace of a dancer. She stretched her arms over her head and yawned, catlike.

"It has been a long journey," she replied in Greek. Her voice was deep and rough-edged for such a fragile creature.

"What is your name?" Augustus asked.

"What is yours?" she replied.

The emperor leaned forward. "Do you not know?"

"Rome is nothing to me," the girl said. "I live by my own laws."

"You may call me Octavian," said Augustus, though he did not know why. It was no longer his name. He felt Agrippa staring at him.

"You may call me Chrysate," said the girl.

"She is a priestess of Hecate," Agrippa interjected. "And a *psuchagogoi*. You should not get too near her."

A summoner of souls. Augustus did not believe in such things.

"I will not harm you," the girl said, and Augustus believed her. Such beauty could only hold goodness.

"Leave us," Augustus said, and when Agrippa did not immediately move away, he repeated the order in a voice that left no possibility of resistance. "*You will leave us, Agrippa.*"

Marcus Agrippa looked defiant, but he sheathed his weapon, nodded his head in a somewhat brusque display of surrender, turned on his heel, and left the room. He slammed the door behind him.

"Have her if you will," Augustus heard his old friend call, his angry voice fading as he marched down the corridor. "She is nothing good."

Chrysate came closer. Augustus could see a ring on her finger, a huge, shining opal flashing shades of rose and blue, green and purple. It was carved with an intaglio of some kind, an image of a woman's face, perhaps.

Augustus reached out and laced his hands around the girl's tiny waist.

He could smell her scent: salt, wood smoke, rosemary, and sex. He put out his tongue to taste her skin.

She threw back her head and laughed, reaching over him to lay her hands on an object on his shelf.

"Is that all you think I am?" Chrysate asked. "A woman?"

"I know you are more or you would not be here," Augustus replied, though in truth, he did not think she was much more. He smiled into the girl's throat, and then took her breast in his teeth. This was exactly what was needed to make him forget about the misery to come. What was war without a woman? He pulled the girl onto his lap.

She leaned back, away from him. He noticed that her eyes were greener than they'd been a moment before, her cheeks brighter.

"What is this?" she asked, showing him the object she'd taken from his shelf. "It's a pretty thing. I might use it for my jewelry."

It was the engraved silver box containing Antony's ashes.

"Not that one," Augustus said. "Let me give you something better. Something made of ivory and rubies, to suit your complexion."

She smiled. Augustus noted a fleck of gold in one of her eyes. Her skin was the color of milk. Her lips were like warmed wine now.

"What shall I do with this, then?" she asked.

"You'll put it back where you found it," he said, smiling.

She was a tease, this girl. Augustus thought about the things he would do to her. He had some ropes here, and a whip braided of soft leather, which would leave lovely marks on that pale flesh. His body hummed pleasantly.

"I think I will not," Chrysate said.

Something changed in her. Her thighs clasped his, and Augustus felt, all at once, as though she were made of iron. The softness of her waist became something live and brutal beneath his palm. Augustus caught a glimpse of her face as she arched her spine, her throat toward the ceiling.

The green of her eyes had been eclipsed by black.

Augustus gasped beneath her, pain coursing through him. His hands scrabbled at her skin.

She opened the box, curled backward and drew her fingernails, almost lazily, along the stone of the floor. With a wrenching sound, a fissure appeared, a trench in the very earth. The priestess poured a measure of ash into the soil.

Augustus watched, horrified and paralyzed.

Chrysate pulled a pin from her braids and stabbed it into her fingertip. She held the finger above the ash for a century-long moment, before a glob of blood formed and fell into the trench.

With her terrifying, dilated pupils, she looked into Augustus's eyes.

"Watch," she ordered. "Listen."

A wailing moan came from deep beneath the house. The floor tilted. The books spilled from the shelves, and Augustus himself fell to the floor, his face inches from the trench. He could not see to the bottom of it.

There were more sounds, shrieks and wails, indistinct calls in unknown languages, sounds of hunger and lust, sounds of despair.

A chill filled the room, and something began to move in the frozen dark down there. A dusky thing, twisting and rising like vapor over a river, a scrap of mist.

"Come," the witch said to the mist. "Come to me."

The thing rose, a creature taken from some deep ocean, and reeled into the air.

And then, before them, in Augustus's chamber, was a man, transparent, strange, his eyes wide and black and terrified. A wound in his stomach, the blood itself transparent.

Augustus could see through his chest and into his motionless heart.

"Tell us your name," Chrysate said. "Tell us who you are."

There was a long pause. The man raised his hand slowly to his mouth and removed a metal coin from his tongue. He looked at it for a moment, and then clenched his fist, holding it tightly in his palm.

"I was," the man said at last. "I was Mark Antony."

"And so you are again," the priestess said. "I have opened the gates of Hades for your shade to pass through."

➤10⬅

The shade wavered, the light of the candles pouring through the place where his wound had been. He held his hand to the spot, pressing his fingers against his lost flesh. He moved his hand from the wound and held it up, gazing at it. There was blood on the fingers, but it was immaterial, like a faint residue of ink washed over with water.

He was a flickering presence in the now frigid room. Augustus had to narrow his eyes to distinguish the man, and even then, he moved in and out of clarity, as though he were a sunken ship glimpsed deep beneath rippling waters.

In spite of his state, he was certainly Mark Antony. There was no doubt. The unruly hair and trimmed beard, the cleft chin, the wide chest, the handsome, weathered face. Augustus recognized the ragged, coiled scars, evidence of battles they'd fought together.

His enemy was more man than he, even as a ghost. Augustus picked up his goblet in trembling fingers and refilled it with wine, taking care not to meet Antony's eyes.

"Is this safe?" Augustus asked Chrysate, taking care that his voice did not wobble. "You've brought my enemy into my house. I trust you know how to control him."

"He is a shade," Chrysate answered, smiling. "Not the man you knew. They are the perfect servants. Their will begins to slip away from them the moment they enter Hades. The river of forgetfulness beckons them, and they always surrender. Look at him. He is nothing of what he was. He cannot take up arms against you. But he may be useful."

174

"What have you done?" Antony asked, the full darkness of his gaze upon the emperor. "Where is my wife?"

His voice seemed to come from far away, an aching echo propelled from the depths of the earth and into the room.

In spite of the witch's assurances, the emperor clung to his chair, his entire body desirous of flight. He wanted the sun to rise, and it did not. The only glow came from the stars outside the window, and that light was cold. The soul-drawing witch—the *psuchagogoi*—stood beside him, her fingers resting lightly on his shoulder. Augustus did not like the way they felt.

"Where is she?" Antony demanded. "Where is Cleopatra?"

Augustus glanced nervously at the witch, at her gleaming, bone-white skin, her phosphorescent eyes and bloodred lips and the tongue that ran hungrily over them. He mastered his voice with another deep draught of wine and theriac.

"First, you must tell us where you have been," he informed the shadow before him. "Tell us of your time in Hades."

The ghost stood straighter, clearly angered. He shook his shoulders, and ripples of gray light came off him.

"Is this why you have summoned me?" Antony asked. "To tell you of the Underworld? You will go there yourself one day, and knowing will not ease your mind."

"Tell us," Augustus insisted.

Antony laughed, a short exclamation of disgust. "Do you think you will find yourself in Elysium, soothed by the light of Elysium's stars, basking in the glow of Elysium's own lovely sun? No. You will not go to Elysium, Octavian, though you call yourself a god on earth. Only heroes go to Elysium."

"Your emperor orders you to tell what you know," Augustus said, his voice cracking and betraying him.

Antony smiled, only his lips moving. His eyes remained bleak.

"My emperor? You are not my emperor. I live in the land of the dead now. I'll tell you something, though, if you insist. In Hades, you starve. You perish, and you perish forever, without cease, without respite, without home. I am of Egypt. My love is of Egypt. I should not be in Hades."

"And you are not," Augustus retorted. "You are in Rome."

"I should be in the Duat," Antony said. "My body should be in Egypt, and it is not. Where is my wife? What have you done with her?"

Augustus started to speak, but the witch interrupted him.

"Your wife is why we have called you here," she said. "She lives."

Antony's eyes narrowed.

"If she lived, I would have felt her tears filling the river Acheron," he said. "Cleopatra would have sacrificed on my behalf. Her sacrifices would have fed me. She is certainly dead. What have you done to her?"

"She does not live," the witch corrected. "And she does not die. She is here."

"Cleopatra is in Rome?" Antony asked, looking up with focused eyes for the first time.

"In Rome," Chrysate confirmed. She glanced at Augustus and tossed her hair back. "What is wrong, Emperor of the World? Are you afraid? Protected as you are by women, snake charmers, and shades? Do you fear for your life?"

"No," said Augustus, lying. "I fear nothing. Rome is well fortified."

So she was here. He had felt as much.

"She is in Rome," Antony murmured to himself. "And yet she betrayed me in Egypt. Is she here? With you?"

Augustus glanced at him impatiently. The emperor's hands were now quite numb, and his lips felt frozen.

"You will guard my home," Augustus instructed the witch.

"I will find her," Antony murmured. "If Cleopatra is here, I will find her." He moved toward the window.

"You are my creature," Chrysate told him sharply. "You'll abide with me."

The witch opened her hand to reveal a carved stone. A *synochitis* meant to hold shades in the upper world once they had been summoned. "You are held here," she continued, moving her hand in the air. The stone disappeared from view.

Antony looked at her for a long moment. Augustus felt nervous, seeing the look on his face. He had known Antony, known him well, and he knew him to be no one's creature.

At last, the shade bowed his head in assent.

"I am yours, then," he said. "My lady."

Chrysate smiled, fingering the carved box of ashes she held against her breasts.

"You are mine," she repeated, and there was something rapturous in her tone. Something triumphant. "We are done with you, emperor of Rome. Octavian, is that your name? You may go to your bed."

She gazed at Augustus steadily, until he was forced to look away.

The emperor left the room, swaying with unaccustomed wine and theriac. He could not say why he allowed himself to be dismissed from his own rooms by a witch. Perhaps Agrippa was right. There should be more soldiers, more Romans, not these unnatural things. Everything about this made him uneasy.

He made his way to his daughter's bedchamber and stood in the doorway for a moment, his eyes filling with strange tears. He would protect Julia from all of this, these creatures in his house, this monster in his city. She moved in her sleep, pressing her rosy cheek to her pillow. What did Julia know of the powers of an emperor? What did she know of trouble?

Augustus envied her, blearily, for a moment.

He gently closed the door and walked to the next bedchamber, that of Cleopatra's daughter, Selene. She'd been of service to him, and she might be of more. Selene was superior to his own daughter. Smarter. Perhaps Julia might learn virtue from his enemy's child.

Augustus wavered in the corridor, uncertain, intoxicated. He was tired. So tired.

He made his way to his own bedchamber and lay upon his bed without even undressing. He shut his eyes and slept. In his dreams he walked through a fig orchard, ancient and miserable, knowing that his life had come to nothing.

In his dreams, Cleopatra came for him, as she did every night. He saw her teeth and claws.

➤ 11 ⬅

The Psylli crept from the Palatine and wound his way through the wealthy alleyways of Rome, considering his position. Certainly, this came at the proper time. The Psylli tribe had fought against enslavement for centuries, and they'd won, but the Roman Empire's power was on the rise.

If Usem served Rome and won against Rome's enemy, he would guarantee his tribe's independence. Still, the Psylli felt uneasy. He did not trust Augustus. The man had agreed too easily to the bargain.

What if Augustus did *not* want to destroy Cleopatra? What if he wanted to harness her power instead? Currently, the Psylli might work for whomever they chose, but if the Romans added Cleopatra's strength to their arsenal, Usem suspected that the emperor would claim the Psylli tribe as his personal poison ministers.

As Usem walked, his dagger in hand, he plotted his course. The best thing would be to find the queen before they did, and take her unaware. When she was dead, he would bring them her body and claim his reward. It did not occur to him to be afraid. The wind traveled with him, kicking up straw and clay dust, dancing into windows and out again, seeking the house that was sheltering her, and the wind was an immortal defender.

The wind whispered into his ear, telling him of the things it saw in Rome, the secrets kept behind grates and up chimneys. One house had a murdered corpse beneath the floorboards. Another had a fortune stuffed into a straw pallet.

The wind entered, finally, at a narrow window and fluttered through the rooms behind the bars. It emerged, and told Usem what it had found therein. A library, filled with all the poems of Rome and Greece. The wind had browsed the pages, flicking through the vellum and papyrus, turning inks to powder and stories to dust.

A woman, said the wind. *Perhaps the woman you seek. She is dead.*

"Does she move?" Usem asked.

She does.

Usem's snakes emerged to twine around his neck. The serpents looked impassively at the building, and then slithered back into the folds of his garments. The wind began to blow in earnest, swinging the laundry hanging on the lines, spinning the weather vanes on the rooftops, and sending the chickens balancing on the fences up into the air. Usem placed his hand on the door handle, and felt the wind pushing him away from it.

I am not strong enough to protect you, the wind whispered.

Usem hesitated. The wind had never said such a thing before, and he took it seriously. A failed attempt would mean disaster. He would wait until he had more power at his disposal, then, even if it meant trusting in Rome a little longer. He need not fight her alone. There would be legions of soldiers, and the two other sorcerers as well, though Usem was not convinced of their intentions.

He wavered at the doorway, considering again. His dagger had slain many foes in the past. He had done the impossible and survived it, over and over again, though he wished he had his own men behind him, following his commands.

You will not kill her, the wind insisted. *You can only die.*

A thought occurred to him.

"Where are her children?" he asked the wind.

With the emperor, she answered.

"And her husband?"

The emperor has him, too. The scorn in the wind's voice manifested as small whirlwinds. Ghosts were creatures of breath and spirit, like the wind itself. Usem could tell that the wind wished to set the shade free.

"That is not our place," Usem told the wind.

He thought of the legions of soldiers who marched on behalf of the emperor. If he failed here, if he *died* here, it would be all too easy for them to march upon his people.

For a moment, he wondered if it would be better to let Cleopatra destroy the Romans. With the threat of Rome removed, the world would function as it once had.

Still, the queen had been a conqueror herself. His people had lived beside hers, but Egypt had not always been an easy neighbor. Once she had Rome, she would want more of the world. Once she had *that*, she would want everything.

At least the emperor was mortal, and he had sworn to the bargain. It was a once-in-a-lifetime opportunity to barter for independence. Usem could not let it go. He turned back to the Palatine, his cloak whipped about by the wind.

You must not trust him, the wind insisted. *He lies.*

"Then I will lie, too," he finally said as he entered the house and made his way down the corridor to his room.

The wind left him then and made its way through the residence, slipping beneath doors and through windows, listening to conversations, exploring hearts.

Selene tiptoed into the hallway, her eyes alert, her nightdress barely rumpled. She'd been awake for some time, plagued by bad dreams. Her parents had appeared to her in a nightmare and then abandoned her to a mob of Alexandrians, all of them waiting to tear her apart.

She heard noise from down the hall, and paused. She was surely not supposed to be roaming the emperor's house. In Alexandria, a nursemaid would have followed her. In Julia's room, there were two women stationed to tend to the girl's every need. Here, no longer the daughter of a queen, Selene had strange freedom. She pressed her back against the wall, breathing shallowly, but it was too late.

At the end of the passage, a door opened, and a beautiful woman stepped out, smiling.

"I thought everyone was sleeping," she said. "Everyone but you and I, it seems."

The girl hesitated, on the verge of running back to her bedchamber.

"There is nothing to fear. I am a guest here, too. You are daughter to Cleopatra, named after her, are you not?" the woman asked.

"No. My name is Selene, and I am a Roman now," Selene said, stumbling slightly over the words. "My parents are dead. I am no longer anyone's daughter."

"You cannot change your parentage so easily," the woman said, smiling. "Your blood is royal. There is no need to apologize for that. It is a precious thing, not a shameful one. *You* are a precious thing, though they may treat you like a prisoner."

"They don't treat me like a prisoner," the girl protested. "No one watches me at all. I can do as I please here."

Chrysate stepped into the hallway. It would not do to let the girl see the shade of her father, his angry spirit kept in her rooms.

A bouquet of wildflowers appeared in the priestess's hand, and Selene gasped in delight.

The flowers transformed before her eyes into a bouquet of songbirds, their feathers jeweled in every color of the sunrise, every color of the ocean, every color of the deepening end of the rainbow. In spite of her uncertainty, Selene was flooded with desire. The colors in them reminded her of home.

Chrysate smiled hungrily at the girl. Nothing in the scry had indicated that she might find a child of royal blood in Rome, orphaned. The child was everything Chrysate had been once, long ago. She was everything Chrysate would be again. Selene would be the missing piece of Hecate's summoning.

It had taken most of Chrysate's remaining power to bring Mark Antony from the Underworld, and she was significantly diminished. The gods of the dead did not approve of such transactions, and shades tended to descend back to Hades the moment their summoner released hold.

Once, she would have sacrificed an entire animal as part of her spell, a black-fleeced ram. Now, with her patroness Hecate so weakened, a drop of her own blood was all she could spare to bind Antony to her, and she was not sure that it would be enough. The holding stone was a precautionary measure until she regained her strength.

Chrysate was limited by her depletion, and so this final spell, bringing the birds out of nothingness, conjuring them out of feathers and words to woo the girl, was a slow-acting dream, a soothing song, the most rudimentary of love spells.

It would do what was needed, however, even if it took more time than Chrysate desired. The body the priestess occupied had been used for much too long, but gifts such as these had to be willing or the spells would fail.

"Selene," she purred. "These birds came all the way from Greece to sing to you. Would you deny them?"

The birds opened their golden throats and sang.

The wind flickered down the hall, listening as the songbirds sang to Selene of poisons drenched in honey, of corpses dancing beneath starry lights, of bears raising themselves up onto their haunches to orate, and of the moon, dipping itself into blood and drowning there.

All these words were sweetly sung, but the wind heard the darkness in them and watched as Selene walked toward Chrysate, entranced, her hands outstretched for the bouquet.

The seiðkona, locked in her chamber, was suddenly alert. Currents of power whipped about the building, slithering down hallways, simmering over hearths, broiling beneath flesh, scalding to the bone. The magic of night and of day. She could feel both sorts. Someone in the house was casting a love spell. The wind was wandering the hallways, and below the ground, the currents of cold fire and death were massing.

Auðr's head spun to the window, but she could see nothing.

Without her distaff, she had not been able to accurately divine the other witch's roles in the events to come. The man was here for the money, she assumed. Rome was rich in Egypt's gold, and the Psylli would be paid his weight in it if his services proved useful. The woman was here for other reasons. The threads of her fate, the ones the seiðkona could see, were barbed and bloodied. Chrysate served an old god. It was she who had summoned the dead and set them to intervene in the affairs of the living.

The seiðkona smiled. This was not a bad thing. A soul whose thread had been cut was now restored to the tapestry, and its presence changed the pattern. It might be useful.

Auðr stretched her arms out in front of her body, gazing on the knots that bound her wrists. Panting with exertion, she watched as the ropes gracefully unlooped themselves and fell to the floor. Her captors had not understood her nature. She was a spinner of fates, and the strings of destiny obeyed her. The ropes they'd bound her with were just another form of thread, just another sort of spinning. Her fingers stretched like the legs of a spider, kept too long twisted about a web.

Her distaff was under guard, somewhere nearby. She could feel it, if she could not see it.

Now that she had seen Cleopatra, she knew that she would need it. If there was any hope at all, it rested in Auðr.

She was seized with a spasm of coughing, raw and painful, and when it finally ended, her hands were spattered with blood. She felt about on the tapestry, testing the strength of her own thread. Cleopatra was coming, no matter the seiðkona's health. Without the distaff, Auðr could be of little use.

She opened the door into the corridor and made her way through the marble complex. As she walked, she brushed aside the threads belonging to all those who lived in Rome. Her own thread was knotted with these destinies, its golden span tangled and braided in ways she had not imagined it could be. She might ensure the fall or the rise of Rome with her actions here. She might break bloodlines, or make them. Most of all, she might find the source of the chaos, the thing that was twisting the pattern, the reason she'd come.

The queen, and whatever it was that twined with her.

Cleopatra's fate rippled, a strong strand, weaving itself against the souls of those in this house. She was coming, then. She had decided to act.

The seiðkona found a barely bearded youth standing uneasily against a wall. Her distaff was inside the room he guarded. She bent her back, a crippled old woman in need of an arm to hold. As the youth approached her, she worked a small magic.

The boy smiled upon her and opened the door.

⇒·12·⇐

Cleopatra crept out of Virgil's doorway and into the city. She moved quickly over the stones, wending through alleys as though she carried the map of Rome in her bones. She did not know this sector, but she could smell the Theater of Pompey, and she went toward it. Julius Caesar's heart's blood, shed there so many years ago, gave off a metallic, vinegary tang that was instantly recognizable.

She heard the sounds of the inhabitants of Rome, even though she did not see most of them. The splashing of chamber pots emptied over balconies, the terrified cries of those in the grip of nightmares, the coos of Parthian courtesans to their clients, the stretching joints of acrobats preparing for the next day's employment.

She trotted past Caesar's rose gardens and across the wooden bridge over the Tiber, her body regaining memory with each step. Before her was the enormity of the Circus Maximus, the chariot racing and gladiatorial arena, with its high wooden walls and oblong shape.

There, on the other side of the arena, was the Palatine Hill, crowned so thickly with white marble structures that it looked like a snow-capped mountain. Atop it, gilded, and shining even in the darkness, was the Temple of Apollo, newly built since her last visit. There were more new buildings, too, chief among them a complex that she knew housed Octavian. *Augustus*, Nicolaus had told her, but she did not care that her enemy had changed his name.

Cleopatra began to make her way stealthily around the boundary of the circus, planning to slip up the side of the Palatine unseen, but she paused, startled. The sounds of workmen sweating and heaving were nearly deafening after the silence of the night.

Up above the fence line, they were levering an object with a slender red granite surface and clean lines. A sacred Egyptian obelisk, looted from Heliopolis? She could see the inscriptions from here, praising Ra and wishing him safe passage through the Duat.

They had stolen it from Egypt, stolen it from under her nose.

Her mouth opened in a hiss of fury. They would not destroy her country. They would not take its ancient objects and use them for decorations. Her mind filled with Sekhmet's voice. *Ra's tributes, stolen.*

She was over the lower fence, her teeth exposed, her body ready, before she knew what she was doing, and then it was too late.

These were not workmen but legionaries, and she had flung herself into their midst.

How many were there? Twenty at least, surrounding her, and for a moment she was afraid, but then she laughed. She could see them looking at her, bewildered that a woman could have done such a thing. One of them took a tentative step toward her.

"My lady," he said. "These grounds are off limits."

They were no match for her. This city was no match for her. She had been kept too long belowdecks, and now she wanted to run. She took a step toward the soldier, smiling at him, and then, with a soft leap, she was before him.

The men shouted in surprise as her claws tore into their fellow's shoulder. She threw him to the ground easily, using none of her true strength.

"They are not off limits to me," she said, and then she leapt to the top of the high fence, daring them to follow.

After her!" shouted the centurion who'd been supervising the installation of the obelisk. His men, still reeling, charged though the gate, their swords drawn.

The creature had leapt from the fence top and down to the street without any warning. She would be gone if they did not get to her quickly.

There she was, atop a building. He could see talons from here, long and silver in the lamplight, attached to her slender human fingers. Her face was shadowed, but he had seen her fangs, her shorn black hair. He could not tell what manner of thing she was.

She laughed again, a terrible sound, and then she was gone into the shadows. The centurion cursed the darkness, signaling to his men to spread down the street.

Cleopatra waited above them, looking down at their bodies creeping through the alleyways. She could see their every move, but they could not see her unless she wanted them to. She was seized by the glory of her form once again. All the sorrow of the ship seemed far away, as she leapt from rooftop to rooftop, taunting her pursuers.

They could not catch her. They could not hurt her. This was her city now and she was a god in it. She was faster than any soldier, stronger than any Roman, and she would find their emperor and kill him. They could do nothing to stop her, with their shouting and swords. Night was her power. She would kill Augustus in front of them and show them how weak they were.

She sprang from building to building, her steps rattling the rooftops, and the soldiers struggled below her, smashing doors and sprinting up stairways moments too late.

"There!" shouted a legionary, charging at the figure before him, a slender, barefoot woman. For an instant, the soldiers saw a lioness and then she whirled and was gone again, running ever faster, closer and closer to the emperor's dwelling.

There were guards there, but not enough. The legionaries did not understand what it was they were chasing, and they did not want to. They had never seen anything like it.

His heart pounding, sweating with panic, a centurion crept out of a doorway, leading his men, just in time to see the woman's garments flutter around a corner.

"Get her!" he shouted, and his men raised their swords and shields and ran for the end of the alley, but when they turned the corner, all that awaited them was another group of wild-eyed legionaries, looking up into the sky in disbelief.

"Where is she?" the centurion demanded.

"Gone," his counterpart replied.

"We must report this to Marcus Agrippa," the centurion grunted.

"Report what? That we lost something in the dark? That we can't say whether it was an animal or a woman?"

Cleopatra watched their argument from her perch at the top of the Temple of Vesta. There were too many lives in Rome, and she felt them all. She wearied of the chase.

She slipped off the roof and back into the streets, cutting through the Forum. There was nothing to see there, not at night, but it comforted her. She'd strolled there many years before with Julius Caesar, holding Caesarion in her arms. She walked aimlessly through the square, listening to the night birds and the sounds of legionaries running through the city, seeking her. Her mind was so occupied with the past that when she stumbled, she did not at first understand what was before her.

Her own face, ghostly pale, frozen in the darkness.

Cleopatra almost screamed, thinking she encountered some new horror, but her fingertips touched marble. A statue perfectly made in her image. She saw herself dead and broken, close to naked, an asp slithering over her breast, her head thrown back, eyes shut as though in ecstasy instead of death.

Thus is Egypt Conquered, said the inscription. The statue was decked with laurel garlands and, below that, covered in graffiti. It stood in a pile of refuse.

Her entire body recoiled, her throat convulsing. This was their triumph, this frozen thing. They had carried her through the streets and shown her nakedness to everyone.

She rocked the statue on its base and pushed it until it fell to the earth, unbroken. Only the serpent's tail was cracked. The rest remained. Her voice betrayed her, and a wail became a roar.

It took only moments to ascend the Palatine and arrive, panting, outside the emperor's residence, her skin icy, her rage cloaked in darkness. She pressed her hands to the stone of the outer wall, feeling the fractures within it. It was vulnerable.

She might slip in, take the form of the snake, and pass through the hall, silent as death, sleekly moving over the paving stones. To Octavian's bedchamber. To Octavian's bed. She would strangle him there.

Feed, Sekhmet whispered. Cleopatra jolted.

Her children were inside the house as well. She could feel them dreaming. Alexander Helios playing at weapons in his sleep. Ptolemy, little Ptolemy, dreaming about her. She saw her own face in his mind, her own arms holding him. He dreamt of his mother, but not as she was now. The mother he remembered was dead.

Where was Selene? Cleopatra could not hear her dreams, and after a moment, she realized that it was because the girl was awake, somewhere in the house. Awake, or not quite. She seemed to be in a waking dream, her thoughts drifting out of the residence as birds and flowers, and the face of a woman Cleopatra did not recognize, a green-eyed girl with braids to her knees.

Cleopatra realized with a start that Selene was dreaming of a new mother.

She slipped around the outer wall, searching for Selene's room. She could not face her sons, but the thought of her daughter had sustained her aboard the ship. She was so like Cleopatra, and the rejections she'd shouted in Alexandria were exactly what Cleopatra herself would have said had their places been switched. Selene was ambitious, truly royal. She might understand why her mother had done as she had, even if her brothers could not. Cleopatra suddenly wanted desperately to explain, to woo her child back to her side. Her daughter was near. She moved silently along the building, ever closer.

She imagined herself as she was, bounding into Selene's room. The girl would rise from bed, and run to the windows, and—

She halted in confusion, scenting something she recognized. A musky smell, mint and night, wine and sweat, blood and metal. She turned slowly, looking into the dark.

"Antony?" she whispered, her body straining for a reply. But there was nothing. After a moment, she realized she was a fool. With her heightened senses, she must have caught an echo of long ago. This was Antony's city, after all.

Whose bedchamber was it coming from? She looked up to the second floor of the residence.

The shutters stood open, and from them she could hear the emperor's nightmares. He dreamt of Cleopatra. She saw her own face in his sleeping thoughts. Her *dead* face, like the statue he'd had made in her image. All thoughts of her children forgotten, Cleopatra fit her fingertips into a crack in the stones, and began to climb, her claws scraping against the rock. It took only a few moments before she was in the window itself, and there he was. Her enemy in his bed, his pale hair lit with moonlight, the lines in his face deep and contorted. Tears ran down his face. He cried in his sleep.

She thought of the taste of tears.

She stepped over the sill, her feet silent. She dropped to the floor, her body shifting as she moved toward Augustus.

She could hear the legionaries coming up the hillside, resolved to tell Marcus Agrippa what they had seen. She could hear them pounding on his door. They had no idea where she was.

She undulated across the silken carpet, the sound of her passage a mere whisper. She fit her pointed jaw beneath the counterpane and slithered, cool and slender, into the emperor's bed. He stirred, murmuring as her body slipped over his ankle, over his wrist, over his chest.

She swayed above his face, looking at him through a serpent's gaze, her spine arching as she drew back to strike. His eyelids fluttered. Yes. She wanted him awake.

Feed.

A sound from the hallway startled her, and she turned to see her daughter in the open doorway, her steps as slow and light as a sleepwalker's, her hands filled with a bouquet of what first seemed to be flowers and then seemed to be birds. A strange fragrance followed the girl, something dark and ashen.

Selene turned to look into the room, her eyes dazed, and Cleopatra felt herself falter.

Her daughter took a step forward, blinking into the shadows at the serpent that coiled atop the emperor's chest.

Selene's eyes widened. She dropped the bouquet, and the songbirds scattered to the ceiling.

The girl screamed, her piercing voice tearing through the Palatine.

Cleopatra tore herself from the emperor's bed, disobeying Sekhmet's hunger.

She was gone before Augustus's eyes were fully open.

☞13☜

Agrippa spun and raced from his quarters at the sound of the screams, certain that it must be the Greek witch in Augustus's room. He knew he should not have left him alone with her the night before. The emperor was a fool when it came to women. But why was she screaming?

The general sprinted down the hallway and into the room, his sword drawn, only to stumble over Selene crumpled on the floor. Augustus was still in bed, staring out the unshuttered window, tightly wrapped in his coverlet and shivering. He remained there even as Agrippa shouted his name. No one else was visible.

The Psylli was close on Agrippa's heels, and when he saw that there was no enemy in the room, he fell to his knees beside the girl, checking her heartbeat.

"What is it?" Agrippa shouted, spinning in search of the villain. Selene took a gasping breath. The emperor said nothing, and Agrippa turned his attention to her. "What did you see?"

The little girl shook her head weakly. Her skin was too pale, and her eyes were oddly dilated.

"A snake," Selene said, her voice quivering.

"A snake," Augustus whispered, and Agrippa tore the coverlet from his bed. There was nothing there.

Agrippa took a threatening step toward the Psylli.

"Have you let a serpent loose in the emperor's house?"

"Not one of mine," Usem said. "They are all accounted for, safe in my chamber. I told you. You do not know what it is you fight."

"It went out the window," Augustus managed, pointing his finger. Agrippa crossed the room at top speed, placing himself beside the window frame. He angled his eyes cautiously downward, scanning for threats.

All he saw was the clay-daubed hut of Romulus, founder of Rome. The emperor had built his house in order to be near the landmark. The hut was his special prize.

"Is someone concealed there? Tell me where he is," Agrippa whispered.

Augustus did not answer for a moment, and Agrippa shifted, grasping his sword more tightly and raising his shield to barricade the window.

"*She*," said Selene. "It wasn't a man."

"No," Augustus interrupted. "It was nothing. Take the child away. I did not sleep well, and I scared her. I thought I felt a serpent in my bed. I thought I saw someone climbing out my window."

"I saw it, too," Selene protested.

"Take her to her chamber," Augustus insisted. "She does not belong here. This is a conversation for men, not children. This is a discussion of war."

The Psylli took the child from the room, looking over his shoulder at Agrippa and Augustus. A breeze stirred the girl's hair, and in the emperor's room, the curtains blew suddenly out from the window.

In the hallway outside the chamber, Auðr stood against the wall, trembling. She had felt the line of Cleopatra's fate slithering into the residence, and shifted the emperor's fate just in time, pulling Selene's thread to bring her past the bedroom door. Now she would pay the price of working such magic without preparation. She felt as though she were drowning. The Psylli gave her a sharp glance as he passed, noting the distaff in her hand. He nodded tightly at her.

"There is no enemy out there. There is only Rome," Agrippa said, his voice terse. He'd spent an infuriating night, first walking the corridors and then consulting with a group of legionaries who reported a strange intruder in the Circus Maximus. The men were at a loss to describe what the intruder had done, insisting she had been able to run more quickly than they, that she'd leapt from street to rooftop with ease, that she'd seemed one moment an animal and the next a woman.

Agrippa accused the men of drunkenness, not unusual after a return from a long sea voyage, and sent them back to their quarters. But only moments after their departure, the screaming had started.

Augustus looked up, startled, as his general slammed the chamber door and threw his weapons down upon the stones.

"What exactly is it we seek to war against?" Agrippa roared. "Why do you have me dealing with the blackest creatures in the world? Why do you insist that such things stay in *your own house*? You will tell me what all this means or I will be gone from you."

His friend looked up at him, and sighed. Agrippa noticed that Augustus's face had developed new lines. His eyes were grimmer than Agrippa had ever seen them, the whites streaked with red. Though it was early morning, there was wine on Augustus's breath. Wine and something else, something herbal and caustic. He'd lost weight in the past months, and his hair had the ragged look of a badly shorn sheep. In Alexandria, he had sent false messages. Now he called for witches. Perhaps the guilt over the sabotage of Mark Antony had made him ill.

"Cleopatra lives," Augustus said. "I swear it. I should have told you long ago. What the Psylli said was true. She is not dead, Agrippa. She was here last night."

Agrippa leaned closer to his friend. He would summon a physician discreetly, and immediately upon leaving this conference.

"She is certainly dead," Agrippa said, attempting to soothe Augustus. "Look out that window, not at Romulus's hut but at the Circus Maximus. Have you not noticed what is being erected there by your own army? An obelisk, taken from Alexandria. See the point, rising over the fence? Would we have such a thing had we not won the war?"

"She lives, and she is in Rome. I swear it. You think I'm mad," Augustus said, his mouth twisting into a wry smile. "I am not. I saw her, just now. Selene saved me by screaming."

"Such visions come of fever." Agrippa brushed the emperor's icy forehead with his hand, worried enough to defy all protocol. The room was strangely cold suddenly, though it had been warm enough when he entered. He would order a fire lit.

"I am as well as any man could be, knowing that his enemy stalked him, knowing that his enemy resisted death. There would be no witches in Rome if I were not desperate. She lives, and she is not human."

The emperor brought forth a mound of rough fabric. A linen tunic. A cloak such as a peasant might wear. An agate goblet.

Agrippa looked at the objects, bewildered. He could see no meaning in them.

"I took this from the queen's mausoleum in Alexandria," Augustus said, picking up the goblet and holding it to the light. The sun glowed through it.

The residue of something dark lay in its well.

"Once, there was a queen of Egypt," he began. "A queen who became through magic something else."

When Augustus was done speaking, Agrippa pushed himself back from the table, furious.

"I passed her yesterday at the port," he said, his voice hoarse with frustration. "She was just arriving in the city, and had you seen fit to inform me of all this earlier, I would have had her, and her scholar, too. A patrol of my men saw her an hour ago and gave chase, but they did not capture her, because you had not told me what we were looking for. Now she's hidden under our noses. I thought I imagined things. A dead woman walking through Rome."

"A dead woman walking through Rome," Augustus echoed.

"You misunderstand me," Agrippa said. "Cleopatra never died. The snake venom counterfeited death. We should have burned her body. I believe you when you say that she was aboard that boat in Egypt, but I do not believe she worked alone there to kill the crew. She had an accomplice, the scholar perhaps, or a hired warrior. Perhaps a magician to manufacture the illusions my men described. Alexandria is full of magicians, all of them dealing in fragrant smoke and mirrors. It would not take much. You've let superstition take hold of you, and everyone else in this city has done the same."

"I told you! I saw visions in her eyes, Agrippa, visions of dark things!

She's a serpent! A lioness! Her daughter swears she and the tutor summoned something in Alexandria, something powerful, and I saw blood—"

"Now that I know what I am to fight, we will defeat her," Agrippa interrupted. "She is only a woman. A single enemy who has lost everything she once had. She has no army, no weapons, no friends beyond the tutor. We'll hold a *venatio* tomorrow night and trap her in the Circus Maximus. What could be better than an arena, enclosed, with a moat about its edge and lined with my soldiers? We'll capture her easily, and this time we will kill her."

"And how will we attract her there?"

"Her children," said Agrippa.

"She did not oppose us when we executed Caesarion. If we use only the children, we will fail."

"She is their mother," Agrippa insisted. "Think of our beginnings, when everyone in Rome thought we would fail in attacking Caesar's assassins. We did not fail. Look around you."

Augustus looked around the room, at the trappings of an emperor. It all looked fragile. He thought of his great-uncle, stabbed twenty-three times at the height of his power, by men he called friends. Augustus felt dizzy.

"We won those battles when we were boys," he said. "And now we have much more to lose."

"Not today," Agrippa said. "We fight a woman and a scholar."

"We'll have the witches," Augustus said, remembering, with relief, his defenders.

"I do not recommend that," Agrippa said. "We will bring what Cleopatra loves, and bait the trap with it. My soldiers are well trained."

"Her husband," Augustus said, his voice suddenly taking on a liveliness it had not previously possessed. "Antony is what she desires."

Agrippa was certain that the vision Augustus swore the Greek witch had produced was merely a trick, a creature made of smoke. Nevertheless, such a skill might prove useful.

"Yes," he agreed, a concession. "We will offer Cleopatra her husband."

⟫·14·⟪

The shadow detached itself from the stones and moved invisibly along the wall, slipping out beneath the door of the emperor's bedchamber.

They all thought he was a hopeless wisp of soul, locked in the Greek priestess's rooms, but they were wrong.

As Chrysate slept, exhausted by the spells she'd cast, a wind had gusted suddenly into the room, whipping at the witch's coverlet. The holding stone fell loose in her hand, and Antony was free, at least until she woke. It was well that Chrysate's chambers were far from the emperor's. She had not wakened when Selene screamed.

The witch did not know as much as she thought she did about shades. Antony was no one's servant. She'd told them he could be deployed at Rome's whim, his price a droplet of blood, his memory emptied of all his old grievances, but Antony had not forgotten who he was. Though he'd spent months in the Underworld, he'd repeated Cleopatra's name over and over, willing himself to remember even as he watched spirits fumbling toward the rivers, seeking to forget the ones they'd loved, the lives they'd lost.

His heart filled with fury as he thought of the things he'd overheard. The false messenger sent by Augustus to swear that Cleopatra was dead. The bribes paid by Augustus to sway the Egyptian army and tear them from Antony's service. The fact that Augustus had knowingly buried Cleopatra alive.

The fact that she *still* lived. Antony paid no attention to the other things Augustus swore, the visions he said he'd seen in Cleopatra's eyes. They were the visions of a coward. If he had been as drunk in Alexandria as it seemed he was now, it was no wonder he'd hallucinated Cleopatra into a monster.

Where was Cleopatra? It had been Antony's only question in Hades, and it was his only question here. Augustus swore she was in Rome, swore she'd just left his rooms, and as Antony stood against the wall, shaking with wrath, the emperor and Agrippa had discussed their plans to trap and kill her in the Circus Maximus.

What could he do to save her? He was nothing, an echo of his former self. He had no body, no hands to pick up a sword.

Antony thought about his wife's extraordinary resourcefulness. Long ago, in a betting game, she'd informed him that she could serve him a meal worth ten million sesterces, more expensive than any banquet that had ever graced *his* table.

He took the bet, scoffing, and she promptly called for a cup of *vinum acer*, removed one of her tremendous sea pearl earrings, and dropped it into the goblet. It dissolved, rendering the vinegar free of acid. They drank that wine together, and he laughed, awestruck at her invention.

"A glass of wine with you," she told him, "is more valuable than anything else I possess."

She had transformed vinegar to wine for him, no matter the price, and he would do the same for her.

It meant nothing that Antony's hands could not hold a sword. He could still declare war against her enemies. There were many ears in Rome, and not all of them were devoted to the Boy Emperor.

Augustus thought that Antony was only a ghost, and no longer a warrior.

It was not the first time an enemy had fatally underestimated Mark Antony.

He smiled as he emerged from the Palatine and made his way down the hillside, his body nearly transparent in the afternoon sunlight.

It was not hard to find the men who had once been his soldiers. With Rome at peace, they congregated in bars and brothels, and the city was filled with them, in various phases of inebriation. Egyptian gold filled their pockets.

What would be difficult was finding men who would be loyal to him again. Most of the men Antony saw had shifted to the side of Octavian after Actium. He did not need disloyal soldiers. Antony had hoped to locate Canidius and the rest of his senior officers, the best-trained men in the army, but his lieutenant had been executed in Alexandria. Antony listened to the men sing bar songs of the bravery of Canidius Crassus. Of course his officers were dead.

He stood in the dusty street, cursing himself. He had no idea when Chrysate would wake, and when she did, his time for searching would be done.

At last he found a few men, strong and scarred, napping in the back-room of a bar. He shouted, and the men's heads lurched up from their table. It was not the entrance he would have chosen.

"Attention!"

They blinked in the dusty air. Drunkards. Antony had been a drunk-ard himself on occasion. He knew how they felt, and so he made his voice all the louder.

"Defenders of Alexandria!"

The men squinted.

In a flash, Antony appeared before them, and they gasped, pushing themselves back, stumbling over chairs in their haste to escape him. He looked suspiciously at the state of their muscles. The year since Alexandria had made them fat, but this was the best he could do on short notice. If he'd had time, he might have searched throughout the world, located his true friends, found the strongest men, but he had only until tomorrow evening to save Cleopatra.

"Your commander calls on you," he said. "Your commander charges you with action."

"How do we know who you are?" asked one of the soldiers, his cup spilled before him.

"Do you doubt me? I am Mark Antony," Antony said.

One of the legionaries grinned.

"You look like him, I won't deny that," he said. "And you sound like him. Who's playing us for fools? Show yourself!"

Antony grimaced. Soldiers were not easy to force into sobriety, nor were they impressed by the impossible.

They would be easier to bribe than command, in this condition.

"I want to hire you," he said. "Tomorrow night, at the Circus Maximus. You will appear there, armed, and await my signal. There is a woman—" He hesitated and decided not to name Cleopatra. "Who must be protected from other soldiers. You will keep her safe."

"How much?"

"Enough to keep you in whores until you die," Antony said.

"And drink?"

"Who do you take me for? It will keep you in drink as well," Antony said.

"Then I'm your man," said the legionary, "whoever you are." The others nodded, and Antony explained what he needed from them. At last, when he had made himself clear, sworn them to sobriety, and promised gold to them, he made his way from the bar and out into the street. He had more to accomplish, and this time he would improve on his performance.

In the private, tiled room where the senators sat, taking their afternoon steam bath, the walls were warm and slippery with oil. The vapor surrounding the men hung as thick as fog, and their voices echoed, disembodied, from out of the clouds. The senators had installed themselves far from the ears of the emperor and his dearest general.

"He claims to be descended from Apollo, though we all knew his mother, Atia, and she was nothing a god would touch, even accidentally in the dark while fumbling around on the temple floor, looking for something better," muttered one of the senators.

Another senator splashed his hands in the water to make his point.

"Caesar Augustus is only a lowly great-nephew, and yet he dares to call himself Caesar, as though that drop of Julian blood were enough to counterbalance his moneylending grandfather!"

"And the slave!" cried another. "I have it on good authority that his great-grandfather was a freed slave who spent his life twisting rope in the South."

The senators were appalled.

They shifted themselves on the mosaic-tiled benches, dangling their large, complaining feet into the scalding water below. They mopped sweat from off their shaven heads and muttered further.

"Augustus—"

"Call him Octavian!" shrilled one of the eldest. "He is a tiny child, scarcely sprouted from out of the earth! He is a spring asparagus!"

The other senators looked indulgently upon their elder and continued their lament.

"Augustus will destroy the system of logical discourse. He will shrink Rome until it is under the control of one mind, one voice, and one emperor."

Emperor.

The thought made their testicles shrivel, and yet there was nothing to be done about it. They missed the old days of the republic, when they'd run things. When they'd run everything. The glorious days of speeches and arguments, scrolls and debates. The days when the Senate needed to be persuaded, for days on end, before coming to any decision. And perhaps bribed as well.

"Senators!" boomed a voice. "Senators of Rome!"

The men stopped what they were doing and peered into the steam, confused.

It was certainly some trickery, some pageant created to frighten old men. Something done with a trumpet or an actor, falsifying the tones that each of them knew very well.

And yet.

They'd heard him orate. They had heard him address the crowd, offering Caesar's funerary speech. They had heard him cry battle. The voice was an impossible voice.

The man they knew was dead.

The temperature of the room began to drop as a figure emerged from the steam, dusky and faint, as shifting as any vapor. His chin was cleft, and his hair fell in dark, silvering curls over his forehead. His gilded armor was strapped upon him, and there was a wound in his abdomen. A bloody, mortal wound.

The senators murmured in terror. Mark Antony was dead in Egypt, dead nearly a year, and yet here he stood. His sandals did not touch the ground.

Three senators surged in the direction of escape, but cold clouds of fog blossomed over the doorway, and they could not find their way out. A skim of ice had formed over the tiles, and one senator slipped on it.

Another three pressed themselves against the walls of the bath-house, hiding in the steam and praying to the gods that the spirit had not noticed them.

"I come to you from Hades, with tidings of dark deeds kept from you by the one you call Caesar," the ghost said, his lip twisting up in a smile of satisfaction. "Will you hear me, who was once a man like yourselves? I come to you with news of your emperor."

"Augustus?"

"The same."

That was enough to change their minds about fleeing. Dispensing with the minor matter that their messenger was from the Underworld, the senators leaned hungrily forward on their benches to listen.

"Speak," they urged. "Tell us everything."

"There is a price. A small matter. Nothing that such powerful men would find difficult. There is an object I require. A piece of green glass, a *synochitus*, must be stolen from a woman tomorrow night at the Circus Maximus and destroyed. You will send a man to do it."

"Yes, yes, that's easy enough. Get on with it," said a senator, and Antony nodded.

"There will be games held tomorrow night, and at the games the emperor's betrayals will be revealed to you. He has bound himself to witches, against the ways of Rome. His defeat of Egypt was false. Cleopatra is not dead. Would you have me speak further?"

The senators leaned forward, shivering in the newly frigid room.

One of the pools was entirely ice now, and a thin rime of frost covered the men's pates. Still, they were eager for more information. Rome was powered by such things, and always had been. A rumor of an emperor's betrayal was worth as much as this and more.

"Continue," said a senator, and the rest nodded.

"You must each give me a drop of your blood, so that I may speak fully," the shade told them, and the senators held out their hands, willing.

Blood was a small price when one was offered information about the powers that ran Rome.

Blood was nothing.

Antony smiled. All the memory of Rome was contained within these men, and he took it, seven drops of blood, as snowflakes drifted gently from the ceiling of the room.

He told them all he knew, and then, together, they made a plan.

⇒15⇐

Cleopatra was maddened by her failure. What had stopped her? Fear? Her daughter's face?

She thought at first to return to Virgil's house, but then the thought of Nicolaus kept her out in the city. She hungered too much to trust herself to return to him. With daylight, she'd hidden in a root cellar, but the sounds of Rome plagued her nonetheless.

As soon as the sun dropped, she was out again, scarcely managing to pass the doorways, the stones, the temples that Antony had once visited, without stopping to look for him. She could almost feel him, but she knew he was dead. She'd burned his body.

Nothing was ever entirely gone; she knew it now.

A cryer sprinted past her, shouting his announcement.

"PRIVATE VENATIO, an hour past sunset, tomorrow evening! To be attended by Caesar Augustus, celebrating the arrival of the children of conquered Egypt and offering a special curiosity: a vision of Mark Antony, brought from beneath the earth to bow to Rome."

She hissed, hearing it, but thought she imagined things. Her hunger was great now, and she could scarcely contain it. A group of legionaries stumbled from a bar and past her, and she thought she heard them say Antony's name. She shook her head to clear it.

In an alley near a bathhouse, she caught the scent of Antony, stronger this time. Her eyes filled with tears as she inhaled. It was as though he were beside her. If only that were true.

A legionary passed her, pasting notices of the venatio onto a fence. She paused to look at them. A drawing of a man, his body familiar,

broad-chested and tall. She looked more closely. The man in the drawing had a cleft chin. He bowed before a drawing of Rome's emperor.

Cleopatra tore the notice from the wall and then followed behind
the man who was posting them. How dare they mock Antony this way?
It would be an actor, painted and costumed, a theatrical show exploiting
the memory of her husband.

Still.

She would not stop this time. It had been a mistake. She'd had the
emperor, and she could have killed him. This would all be done.

Now it would be in public. That might be better. There would be
so many people there that her children would not be in any danger. No
frenzy could take her and injure them, not with so many Romans present. Sekhmet craved the blood of enemies, Cleopatra convinced herself,
not the blood of loved ones.

The animals Cleopatra had traveled with would fight here, to celebrate
Conquered Egypt. She could feel them beneath her, in the cages that had been
installed in the catacombs beneath Rome. They'd be prodded up into the
light and given shouts and applause when they surfaced in the arena to
meet their fighting partners, the *bestiarii*, gladiators doomed to fight the
doomed. Lions, tigers, and crocodiles pitted against men.

She would attend.

The poster hanger paused, looking behind him nervously.

She leapt at him, her talons slashing, her teeth in his throat before he
had time to make the slightest sound. If he broadcast the emperor's filthy
lies about Antony, then he deserved to die.

From the shadows, Antony watched his wife tear savagely into the man's
throat. He'd searched every corner of the city for Cleopatra, and now
he had found her. In shock, he watched her drink the workman's blood.

What the emperor said was true. Was she under a spell or sickened
with some sort of poison? He did not know what she had become, but he
was horrified. He turned and disappeared into the shadows of the falling
sun. He could not talk to her. Not now.

➤16➤

Chrysate woke suddenly and looked quickly about the room. It was empty but for the shade of Antony, who sat beside her, quiet and still. She had slept most of the day, and she still felt weak from the spells she'd cast the night before.

She felt magic around her, and not her own. The house was filled with it. She had not seen the other witches in the scry, and the old woman in particular made her uneasy. Chrysate had slept like one drugged, dreaming of threads, of being entangled in a sticky web spun by a tremendous spider. She stretched, reassuring herself that nothing had changed in the room, and then turned to look at her captive.

Antony stared beyond the ceiling, his eyes dark.

Had she not known better, she would have thought he grieved over something. This was impossible, though. No shade Chrysate had ever seen was strong enough to resist the forgetfulness of Hades for long, even if the shade was that of a previously formidable man.

"You may eat," she instructed Antony, though he looked strangely substantial.

He passed to the table, dipping his fingers into the honey and milk all shades craved. Was her memory flawed? His skin had been ashen, and now it seemed less so. His arms had been nearly transparent, and now she could swear there was blood moving through the faded veins.

Had he left the room while she slept?

"What has changed?" she asked him.

"Nothing, my lady," he answered.

She shook her head. The holding stone was tight in her hand, but something was not right, and her powers were not strong enough to understand what it might be. She wished the girl was ready, but that spell was not complete yet. There was no time to do what she planned for Selene, not before the venatio. Chrysate would have to suffer through the night in this condition and perhaps longer. It would not do to be interrupted.

There was enough power contained within Cleopatra to remove Hecate from her lowly position and bring her to rule over Persephone herself. There was enough power there to do anything Chrysate desired. She had only to capture her, and the change foreseen in the scry would be set in motion.

Chrysate smiled.

Sekhmet must have been foolish or desperate, to tie herself to a human, like a hawk to a chain. If the human was captured, the chain might be reeled in and the hawk seized, or so Chrysate hoped.

She did not expect it to be easy. She'd have to sacrifice more blood to keep Antony in her power. She needed him to lure his wife.

Wincing, she took a long, keenly pointed ritual knife from her garments and ran it across her wrist. Even after all these years, even across the white line of scar first put there when she was a girl, on a body long since abandoned, the necessary sacrifices remained unpleasant. Her skin felt frail and furrowed under the tip of the knife, though it appeared as smooth as silk.

She held her wrist to Antony's lips.

Antony pressed his mouth to the cut, licking the blood from it. His color improved as he drank, her blood running through him.

Oh, he was hers. There was no doubt about it.

Why, then, did she still feel that something was wrong?

⇸17⇷

The night before the venatio, the emperor was too frightened to sleep. The thought of Cleopatra in his city caused his heart to race. He kept seeing her outside his window, outside his door, in his bed, her scaled skin slipping across his naked chest.

He tossed for hours, his eyes clenched shut, the pillow lumpy beneath his head, his cot as tight and hard as a stone-covered hillside. At last he rose. It had been months since he'd slept through the night, since his ship waited outside the Alexandrian harbor. He cursed Cleopatra and Antony. They had stolen his sleep, and now he walked, half waking, half delirious, through the halls.

Usem, patrolling outside the emperor's chambers, heard bare feet shuffling across the stones toward him.

He turned and found the emperor behind him, dressed in only a thin tunic, his eyes wild, his skin clammy.

Augustus blinked, as though looking at a bright light.

"You will live a long life, she told me," he whispered. "Now she means to take it. She smells of lemons and fire. Her perfume is the same as it ever was, and I smell it in Rome."

"She is not in the house," Usem said, taking pity on the man, but the emperor shook his head frantically, as though trying to rid himself of an insect.

"Tell me a story," he asked the Psylli. "Tell me something to make the night come."

Usem laughed, a dry sound of curious pleasure, something that calmed the emperor vaguely. If the man still laughed, all could not be lost.

"It is night already," the Psylli told him. "It is hours until dawn."

"It is not night in my mind," the emperor replied.

"I will tell you a story," Usem said. "But there is a price."

"There is always a price," the emperor said wearily. "I will pay it."

Augustus was now convinced that any fee owed to the Psylli and his tribe would never need to be paid, at least not by him. His death would no doubt occur long before he paid his debts, and Usem wanted peace. Who could promise such a thing in a world where creatures like Cleopatra existed?

The two walked back to the emperor's room, where Augustus lay down again and Usem settled into a crouch beside his cot. The Psylli began to speak, his voice low and even.

"A young man was in the desert one day, walking over the sand and dreaming of his future. He had reached the age of marriage, but the neighboring tribes would not surrender their daughters. They were afraid of his people, who consorted with poisonous serpents. When other tribes saw the Psylli coming near, they fled, leaving even their camels behind. The Psylli grew rich on abandoned possessions, but their own tribe became smaller and smaller. This boy longed for a bride, but he did not wish to take a woman against her will. He knew that he would have to walk for days to find a tribe who knew nothing of his people, but he swore to himself that he would not return to the snake people until he had found his wife.

"He walked for seven days and six nights, sleeping in caves dug amongst the serpents. On the seventh night, as dawn neared, the boy saw something spinning on the horizon, dancing and throwing light across the darkness. The boy walked closer, wondering."

The emperor turned his head toward the Psylli and saw the man's eyes glitter.

"As the young man neared the tornado, he could see a graceful hand twisting in and out of the sand, its long fingers bedecked with sparkling rings, the source of the light he had seen.

"As he got closer still, shielding his eyes to protect them, he saw a slender form in the center of the sandstorm, her long hair twirling and whipping through the air to cover her naked body. The young man cried out in wonder, and a rapturous, startled face turned toward him for only a moment. Then she was gone, across the desert, away from him.

"The boy had caught a glimpse of the youngest daughter of the Western Wind," the Psylli said. "She was the most beautiful woman on earth, and he was instantly determined that he would take her for his bride."

Augustus shifted in his coverlets. The moon outside, though it was but a crescent, crept through his window, leaving a slice of brightness on the Psylli's face. He could see only the man's eyes, which were so black he could not discern their expression. The Psylli continued.

"The young man chased after the wind, but she disappeared from his view, whipping the sand into new dunes to block his passage as she fled. The sun laughed from above as the young man walked the day long, sizzling in the still air, searching for his love. At last he saw her far across the sand, but she blew away as soon as he was close enough to ask her name. This time, however, she smiled at him before she was gone, and he heard her laughter echoing over the desert. The young man kept following, sometimes seeing flowering branches from far-off places left in the sand, and sometimes watching exotic birds ride on the wind's back, high over his head. Once, she left him an empty ship dropped gently from above, with its sails billowing, but she would not speak to him, nor would she come near enough that he might touch her hand.

"At last, after twelve days and nights without sleep, without water, with nothing but his hopeless love to sustain him, the young man collapsed on the sand, exhausted, his skin parched and his tongue swollen. He closed his eyes."

Augustus's eyes closed as well, though only for a moment. He lay back against his pillow, cursing silently, his very soul twisting inside him. Love stories. What did he care about love?

"When the young man woke, he found himself in the center of a tornado. All around him was the daughter of the Western Wind, and she lifted him into her arms and held him to her lips. She kissed him, and her kisses filled his lungs with air. She brought him to an oasis and poured water into his mouth. She wrapped herself around him and took him high into the sky.

"With her, the young man traveled from end to end of the world. He listened to her whispers and howls, her screams and laughter, and he fell more and more deeply in love with her.

"In the North, she blew up a blizzard, sending white drifts across ice floes, whistling a trilling song as she sent enormous blue ice mountains crashing across the sea. He watched a pale bear and her cubs swimming across the freezing water and then capering in the snow. The daughter of the Western Wind played with them, flinging herself in and out of the water, making waves that splashed over the ice, bringing fish to their shore, until the young man, unused to the cold, was nearly frozen to death.

"She picked him up and carried him South, to an island where the trees bent to make a leafy bower for their wedding bed. There, the daughter of the Western Wind and the son of the Psylli made love, and the young man gloried in her, watching her inhale and exhale gently, her skin smooth and warm, her long hair wrapping around him. The young man asked his bride about her family, and she told him that she did not wish to share him. It was her nature to travel over sea and land, and she could not be still for long. If she stayed in his arms, the oceans would go still, and the bees would cease drinking from the flowers. If she stayed in his arms, the storms would stop filling the rivers, and the snow would stay in the sky. She told him that she would have to leave him soon, or risk the wrath of her father."

Augustus had fallen into sleep at last, his dreams dark and twisting, as ever they were, his hands clenching invisible weapons and his mouth forming inaudible words. Around him, the world exploded and showered down upon itself, shining and searing. Inside him, the world ended, again and again.

"The young man did not wish to let his wife leave his side. He tied himself to her body as she slept, and he was thus entwined with her when her father appeared, a roaring rush of fury, tearing the palm trees from the sand, and sending tremendous waves crashing over the shore. Those who lived on the island ran out from their homes and over the beach, but the Western Wind was merciless. He lifted his daughter up from where she lay sleeping and soared into the sky with her. As he flew, waves shook themselves up from the oceans and broke over the land, destroying everything in their paths. Entire forests were uprooted and flew into the clouds, landing in the heavens, where eventually they settled and became shelter for the stars. The young man clung to his bride as she warred against her father, screaming at him and beating him with her fists. Three mountain ranges turned to plains. Seven rivers turned to rain. A shooting star found itself blown off course and into the fingers of a child, where it became a shining plaything.

"At last, the father landed on the sands of Libya, where the young man's tribe was camped. He swept their camels into the air, and threw their tents from end to end of the desert. He strew their possessions across the mountains and tossed their serpents into the sky. Later, they would rain down, poisonous, mysterious, and full of rage, onto the heads of a neighboring tribe.

"The Western Wind turned his wrath onto the wells of the Psylli, and directed his hot breath into them until they were dry. The young man's tribe was left without water, and they spoke angrily to their wayward son. He knew he'd hurt his people by falling in love with the Western Wind's daughter, but this did not stop him from loving her."

A soft breeze began to blow into the emperor's windows, rattling the shutters and easing them open.

"The young man refused to give up his bride. Her father snatched her from his arms and took her back to his home at the edge of the world. The young man spoke with his tribe and convinced them to go to war. Though they were angry with him for inciting the rage of the Western Wind, they were angrier still at the wind, for drying their wells and for stealing a rightful bride from one of their own."

Augustus thrashed in his sleep as the breeze passed over his bed, tearing his coverlet from his body and chilling him to the bones. Usem looked up and smiled as the breeze passed over his face.

"The Western Wind had stolen not only a bride but a baby, for the daughter of the Western Wind was with child. The tribe of the snake people armed themselves and rode out across the desert, with their serpents beside them. They rode day and night and never saw the Western Wind's daughter. The Western Wind himself tormented them with sandstorms, pushing waves of dust up over the desert so that they engulfed the warring tribe, their mounts, and their serpents. Convinced that he had buried them so deeply they would never recover, the Western Wind went off to his other business at the far side of the world. The warriors and their serpents dug themselves up out of the sand and rode on until they reached the world's edge."

The window was opened entirely to the elements now, and the wind blew in, tossing the curtains, ruffling the scrolls. It blew into the emperor's mouth, and out again. It perched on the Psylli's shoulder.

"They stood looking out across the nothing that awaited them there, and far in the distance, balancing on a platform of the thinnest air, they could see the lighted castle of the Western Wind. In the doorway of the castle, the young man could just see his bride, her hair twirling around her, her eyes flashing lightning. She was tied to the castle wall. The young man despaired of reaching her. He did not know how to walk on air, and the distance was too far for him to leap. His bride's voice, however, was light enough to travel across the distance between them, and she whispered into his ear that she loved him.

"The young man thought hard for a moment, and then he called to his serpents. They twined themselves together, tail to throat and throat to tail. Soon, the young man and his tribe had a coiled rope of snakes as long as the distance from the edge of the world to the castle of the Western Wind. The young man threw the rope across the divide, and his bride pursed her lips and gave the rope a breeze to carry it the last few lengths across the gap and to the castle doorway. The young man did not hesitate. He stepped instantly onto the serpent's backs, and ran across the tightrope to his beloved.

"Thus it was that the tribe of the Psylli traveled across thinnest air and arrived at the castle of the Western Wind. Thus it was that the tribe of the Psylli waited for the Western Wind and captured him with their ropes and their magic, slicing at him with their swords until the wind surrendered and gave over his daughter."

The Psylli stood, his body shining dark and lean in the moonlight. He looked down at the emperor's form. The man's eyelids fluttered, and Usem knew he was only pretending to sleep. The Psylli placed his hand on Augustus's chest.

"Thus it was, by going to war against the Western Wind, that I won my wife. We became parents and I came here, to Rome, to protect my family from war and trouble, from pain and sorrow, as any father should protect his children."

The Psylli looked at the emperor, and his jaw clenched slightly.

"Any father," he repeated. "Any ruler of any tribe, any ruler of any country. That is the responsibility of a leader. But a leader should understand that the loss of love can be more dangerous than the loss of a kingdom. He should understand that he risks himself when he tangles his city in such a thing. A broken heart can destroy as surely as a knife, and there are broken hearts in Rome. There are stolen lives in Rome. It would be no shame to give her children back to her. My wife believes that it would calm Cleopatra, and a calm enemy is easier to best. It would be no shame to relinquish the ghost you hold captive. She wants peace for him and for herself. She wants it more than vengeance, at least for the moment."

The emperor stopped breathing for a moment, feeling the Psylli's gaze upon him. He said nothing. Then the man removed his hand from the emperor's chest and turned away.

The breeze became a woman, her hair twirling, her hands outstretched to touch the snake charmer's. Together, the wind and the Psylli left the room.

In the dark, Augustus's eyes opened. His heart felt broken and furious at once. Love. Who was this man to talk to him about love? Who was this man to say Augustus did not understand it?

Cleopatra had not been broken by love. She had been broken by her hunger for power, and by her desire to be the queen of more than her own country. Augustus knew it, just as he knew that he himself had the same hunger. He ruled, just as she had. He'd climbed up over obstacles of kin, of friends and warriors, just as she had, and now, here in the Palatine, he stood at the top of the world. She was far below him. He had only to kill her now.

The emperor stepped out of bed, weary to his bones.

He had never loved anyone but Rome, and Rome needed him.

⇒18⇐

The witches met in the corridor outside the emperor's chambers, Auðr's silver eyes glittering dangerously at Chrysate, who feigned disinterest. Usem, Chrysate noticed, was armed. His dagger had recently been sharpened, and it was a strange metal, something she had not seen before. She smiled at him. He was a man. Her spells would surely work on him. Never mind the Northerner.

Usem glanced at Auðr. Since he'd seen her in the hallway outside the emperor's bedchamber, he'd wondered what her goals were. She did not look well, but something about her radiated force.

We will capture her, she said, looking at Usem, and he heard her voice in his own language. *Do not let the other know. We are strong enough to do it together. She must be destroyed. We are here for the same reasons.*

Usem looked away. What sort of thing was this voice in his head? He did not care for it. Magic and mind control. He wanted to get to the Circus Maximus with his dagger. The emperor refused to surrender the children, and the longer they waited, the angrier Cleopatra would be.

Usem was the first through the door when it opened.

Augustus awaited them, already dressed in ceremonial garb, his gilded laurel crown gleaming on his head. Agrippa stood beside him, rigid with discomfort.

"You will be positioned around the emperor," Agrippa said. "Each of you will defend him from his enemy."

"From Cleopatra," said Augustus.

"From Cleopatra. My men will be positioned all around you. The circus will be filled with them. There will be no danger. She is one woman."

Agrippa turned his gaze to Chrysate.

"You will bring the illusion," he said.

"He is no illusion," Chrysate replied. "He is the queen's husband."

"You will use Antony to attract Cleopatra to us," said Augustus, and smiled, though his lips wobbled. He did not wish to let them see his nervousness. It would be done soon.

"And how do you propose to destroy her once she is captured?" Usem asked.

"That is not for you to know," Agrippa said, and Augustus shook his head.

"No," he said. "Some things are better kept secret."

⇻·19·⇺

Above the arena a pale moth fluttered, tempted by the torchlight. The moth twisted, stretching its antennae, batting itself about on currents of wind, floating suspended and desiring over the chaos of the crowd.

Hundreds of thousands of people were gathered there, chanting and shouting, and the heat of their bodies called up to the insect. Outside the walls of the arena, more people pummeled each other, pushing themselves up onto the hills in order to look down into the circus and see the animals and fighters.

Below the moth, each torch looked like a glorious lake of fire.

It swept itself closer, hovering over the starry earth.

The passages below the city were dark, despite the torchlight. Holding her breath to avoid inhaling the too tempting smell of blood, Cleopatra pressed herself against the clammy wall of a slender passage. She could feel every stone through the thin tunic she'd worn, imagining herself more easily concealed if she appeared to be one of the animal tenders.

Still, she received some suspicious looks. There were few women below the ground, and the queen had an unearthly glow about her skin.

"What *are* you, lady?" a manure sweep stammered, and fell to his knees in worship as she passed him.

She broke his neck for the question and threw his body into a bundle of straw. She could not afford screams.

The bestiarii occupied special quarters, and the queen smiled as she passed them. The gladiators caged there were chained until needed. Some of them would be permitted to kill the beasts they fought, provided with weapons or with hobbled opponents, and others would be sent naked before Rome to be executed by beasts. Something in their looming mortality pleased the dark parts of her heart. The parts that were not her own.

She heard the bears, smelled their ripe odor. The crocodiles were familiar, caged in a muddy pool to keep them wet. The quarters for the wild cats smelled of goat meat.

In Egypt, to kill a lion or a cat of any kind without the proper ceremonies would be death to the murderer. Here, things were done differently. In Rome, the animals were not gods.

Or maybe it was simply that the Romans did not know that they were.

In the air before the queen, a pale feather floated downward, caught in an unknown current.

The feather of Maat, she thought convulsively, though the better part of her mind knew that it was nothing more divine than a goose feather. Cleopatra could hardly ask for assistance from Maat. The Goddess of the Weighing of the Heart, of Truth, and of Justice kept chaos—*isfet*— from reigning. If the heart that had once belonged to Cleopatra were weighed now, she knew it would fail the test. Sekhmet was Maat's opposite, desiring a world of blood and violence. The scales would drop, and her heart, leaden, would be given to the Eater of Souls, who crouched beneath the scales, lion-haunched, crocodile-jawed, fangs shining. Still, Cleopatra whispered a word of blessing to Maat, for whatever little good it might do her.

There was too much death in her memory. Caesarion, leaping from the platform, his neck breaking in the hand of the emperor's man. She remembered each moment of her son's murder, just as she remembered Antony's death.

She hungered for the heart of the emperor of Rome. She imagined him pleading for his life. She would not grant him, nor any of the others who had fought with him in Alexandria, mercy. They would each be consumed. She was the Eater of Souls here, she realized.

She was the decider of fates.

Cleopatra hurried into the area of the lions, sighting familiar cats from the voyage. She leaned against the lion's cage for a moment, enjoying the darkness and the sounds of eating and grooming. Her presence calmed the cats. Aboard the ship, she'd slept as an animal beside them, feeling part of a family as she never had in her childhood. She'd never been able to reach out her fingers in her sleep and touch another person, not until Antony and her children.

Cleopatra stayed a moment, thinking about her lost life, and then shook the sad thoughts away. She slipped through the bars.

➤ 20 ⤐

Outside the arena, Nicolaus sprinted through the arcade, his robe catching on the splintery stalls as the vendors packed up their items and began to depart. Somehow, he'd found himself opening the door of Virgil's house and running through the streets, thinking, perhaps delusionally, that he would convince Cleopatra not to do what she planned.

He knew better than to trust her. He'd searched the city for her to no avail the moment he realized she was gone, and when he saw the posters announcing the venatio, he knew where he would find her.

Help me, she'd said, and he'd felt so guilty there in the hold of the ship, his hand on her empty heart, that he had helped her into Rome, telling himself that if he found her children, she would be satisfied. Telling himself that she was only a woman, a mother, that she could be talked out of vengeance.

He was a fool. Sekhmet controlled her.

His quest through Virgil's library had unearthed little of use, though he'd read for hours about immortal battles, about immortal monsters. Eternal life might sometimes be relinquished, but this was a dispensation given only by the gods. There were no stories of mortals working such spells. Immortals might kill other immortals in certain circumstances, but that was not helpful either.

Nicolaus was helpless, and he knew the queen suspected as much. He'd thought, in the ship, that she desired separation from the goddess, but now he wondered if she had simply used him to smuggle herself easily into Rome.

The entire city was in or outside the Circus Maximus. It was a trap, he knew. There was no other explanation for the nighttime *venatio*, the display of the emperor and of Cleopatra's children, the mention of Antony. They knew she was in Rome and meant to draw her out.

Nicolaus wavered, nauseated. Had he any sense at all, he'd flee this city.

He knew that she would not stop before she killed Augustus, and to kill the emperor, she would have to go through hundreds of people. If this was a planned event, a trap for the queen, Augustus would be guarded by the entire arena.

He saw the imperial procession, litters being carried down the Palatine on their way to the circus, directly in his path. The procession was surrounded by guards, and he shifted his course away from it, dashing in the opposite direction. Agrippa's men were everywhere, some of them in civilian attire. He could tell the soldiers by their posture. All of them were on alert.

He slipped into the arena with a group of senators, their robes crisp and their bald heads shining. Once he was inside, he spun, searching the crowd. Thousands upon thousands of people were already in the stands, shouting and craning their necks, hoping for a glimpse of the animals. The arena floor was empty as the emperor entered high in the stands, being led to his private box. No sign of Cleopatra in the area surrounding Augustus, but her children were there, positioned around the emperor. Alexander sat on the emperor's left, and Ptolemy in his lap. They were decked in golden headdresses, their faces painted as young kings of Egypt.

Selene sat in front of Augustus, her eyes lined with kohl, but a tiara of gilded laurel on her head, the better to emphasize her allegiance to Rome. Nicolaus shook his head miserably. Their costumes would only incite Cleopatra more.

Where could she be?

He heard muffled roars from beneath the ground, the tunnels under the circus.

With a sinking heart, he realized. He would never get to her in time.

Chains rattled against the stone ramp as the cats ascended it, and Cleopatra felt her ears flatten. The fur on her spine stood up in a ridge. There was danger here.

She was chained, her leg secured to another lion with iron. This was how the bestiarii were given a chance to win over the animals. Otherwise, the games would have been over too quickly, the human combatants left ruined on the circus floor, and the animals rampaging in bewilderment and terror. She could smell the fear of the bestiarii, and taste their histories.

They were convicts, but many of them were not criminals. They had just happened upon legionaries at the wrong moments and been accused of crimes they had not committed. One of the newly crowned bestiarii was the father of a beautiful daughter, who was a virgin no longer. Now the father was guilty of assault, having tried to beat back the Roman who'd sought her favors. Another of the bestiarii had owned a gilded shield that had been desired by a centurion. Now the man was a convicted thief.

These were not fighters by trade. They had once been Egyptians, and Cleopatra had once been their queen. She tried not to think about them, their souls, their pains. They did not matter. They could not. She was here for a reason, and in order to get close to the emperor, she must kill them in battle.

She would do so if it meant she could get close to the emperor. She could smell his absence, the gray nothing of his soul, high up in the stands. She thought of his throat, the pale skin, the veins pulsing beneath it. She thought of his head crowned with laurels. She would tear into him. She would uncrown him. She thought of his heart, or what passed for a heart. What would it taste like? Dust. Stones.

Her teeth grew sharper in her mouth, and her breath quickened. She looked up into the torchlight and saw thousands of faces glowing with anticipation.

Waiting for her.

⇒ 21 ⇐

Augustus sat in the covered confines of the imperial box, looking down over the circus and attempting to keep himself still. All the power of Rome and beyond awaited Cleopatra.

Where would she come from? Where was she now?

Auðr sat behind the emperor, watching his thread spin out around him. The seiðkona drew a deep breath, willing herself not to choke on it. She needed all her strength. The battle was near. She moved her fingers, spanning a fine length of Augustus's fate. She twisted it gently, snaring it in her sharp fingernails. All around her, fates spun out, and she could touch each one. It was as though the entire arena was covered in a web of drifting threads, snarling and tangling, floating and braiding. And here was the queen's thread, twisted together with Sekhmet's, stronger than all the other fates combined, and endless. How many threads had Auðr cut over the years? How many lives had she ended to keep the pattern from disorder? How many fates had she changed?

She tried once more, her fingers twisting, but she could not shift Cleopatra. She could not unknot her from the goddess, and neither thread would be cut. All Auðr could do was manipulate the fates surrounding the two immortal strands, and hope that this shifting would draw the queen into her hands.

It was too much, she thought, afraid for the first time in years.

Augustus leaned forward, scanning the faces of the crowd. None of the witches seemed to have sensed Cleopatra, but that did not mean she was not near. She'd never escape. Everything and everyone was in place.

He was still nervous.

Was there enough space between the arena floor and the imperial box? Years before, twenty elephants imported by Pompeius had charged the stands here, breaking down the iron railing that had protected the crowd. Julius Caesar had dug a moat as deep as a bull elephant around the edge of the circus to keep such a thing from happening again.

The moat was too wide for anything to leap across, and the newly constructed imperial box—the *pulvinar*—was situated high up on the Palatine Hill, to offer the optimal views of the chariot races, venatio, and gladiatorial games, which had been held here since the founding of Rome. The rape of the Sabine women had been held here, too, according to legend, though this was an event to which no tickets had been sold. The ground had a bloody history, but Augustus and Agrippa had taken precautions to ensure the emperor's safety. All around the imperial box were seated Agrippa's soldiers garbed as common men. Thousands of them had been called to order here tonight, and all of them had the same orders. *Protect the emperor.*

The emperor glanced back at Chrysate. She was too striking to display publicly without proclamations that she was the emperor's new mistress. He had her face covered in a sheer black veil, but he could see her eyes through it even now. Green as the sea but lit from below with something yellow. He congratulated himself on her presence. The shade would bait the trap, along with the children. He gave Selene a pat on the shoulder, feeling slightly guilty for bringing her here. She was a girl and should not see such things, particularly after the scare she'd had with the serpent, but she was necessary.

Under Augustus's hand, Selene leaned forward in her seat, trying to contain her emotions. What had she seen in the emperor's rooms? The vision blurred in her memory. A serpent with her mother's face. The physician had come and dosed her with something that slowed her mind.

When she woke, the bouquet of flowers Chrysate had given her was there waiting, though she knew she'd dropped it in the emperor's bedchamber. Now Chrysate sat beside her, her only friend. Augustus had denied Selene, sworn that she had not seen the thing she knew she had.

Only Chrysate believed her. She felt a sob rising in her throat as she looked down at the arena floor. The thought of animals reminded her of home, that was all. She did not miss her family. How could she? They had abandoned her to this. Beside her, Chrysate smiled and took Selene's fingers in hers.

"There is nothing to fear," she told the girl. "I will protect you."

Something inside Selene told her to trust the woman.

Chrysate glanced at the emperor and smiled at him. A calculated smile. She watched as he smiled nervously back at her, his crooked teeth showing.

She considered the other witches. The Northerner sat beside her, clearly ill. Chrysate had heard her coughing all the way down the corridor of the Palatine, and the old woman's skin was sallow and feverish. Nevertheless, she sat with her spine straight, her strange silver eyes watchful. She should not be hard to kill, should she become a nuisance tonight. Chrysate was prepared. The snake charmer, on the other hand, was a stronger foe. Perhaps he was on her side, however. Or could be bought. His tribe was known to practice sorcery for hire. She leaned toward the man.

"I may need you," she said.

"As I may need you," he replied, his jaw tight. "She will not be taken easily."

The wind informed Usem that the queen had arrived, and though he could not see her yet, he knew that he soon would. He regretted this already. A sleek, copper-patterned viper slithered itself about the Psylli's two arms, its body thick as a limb. He glanced over at the Northern witch. The Romans had taken her distaff from her, but he could see it now, well concealed against her side, hidden in the folds of her garments. He suspected that he was the only one who knew it was there and that he was also the only one who knew that her wrists were not actually bound. The wind had whispered all these things into his ear. He was not sorry that the seiðkona had her weapon, however. They would need whatever they had. He planned to kill Cleopatra himself. He did not trust anyone else to do it.

He touched his dagger, testing the blade with his fingertips. It was sharp enough to slice through thinnest air, he knew, having used it for that purpose once before. He'd treated it with the venom he himself was immune to. It would be sharp enough to slice through either of the witches' flesh if necessary and kill them quickly. He was not so certain that it would kill Cleopatra. The wind wrapped around the Psylli's shoulders like a cloak, watching and waiting.

An ostrich paraded below, its beak thrust high and prideful into the air. The Romans scarcely took notice. They'd seen ostriches before.

Augustus's gaze fell on a large grouping of senators, their bald pates shining in the torchlight. They were accompanied by scribes. He nudged Agrippa.

"Why are they here?"

"I don't know," Agrippa answered.

"They're old men," said Augustus.

"And not armed," said Agrippa.

Augustus looked at them again, wondering what their purpose was. Senators did not typically attend such events. They ought to be sleeping, but they were rigid with excitement. One of them glanced over as the emperor looked away.

The senator's gaze made contact with the eyes of a slender man in the guise of a servant, who'd fallen into position just behind the imperial box, unnoticed by anyone in it. The man slipped sideways until he stood directly behind Chrysate, and the senator, almost imperceptibly, nodded to him.

The sun was setting, and the torches were lit. It was about to begin.

Augustus filled a goblet of wine, took the vial of theriac from his tunic, and poured some into his cup. A rough hand took the wine from him. Augustus turned to the intruder, infuriated.

"You must remain clear for this," Agrippa told him.

"I will do as I wish," Augustus replied, annoyed. The theriac hardly tasted bitter to him now. It was nearly sweet.

Music played from beneath the bleachers, and the gladiators began to proceed up from below, for their presentation to the emperor. Augustus looked down at them, displeased. They were a wan and ill-looking group. Beaten. The bestiarii bowed their heads before him, prodded by their handler.

Had it always been this way? In his boyhood, Augustus had gloried in the strength of the gladiators, the polished muscles, the shining— though brutish—armor and weapons. These men looked feeble. They were criminals, of course, condemned to serve out their sentences in the ring, but this was no excuse for their ashen faces, their skeletal limbs.

Augustus removed Ptolemy from his lap and stood, and the crowd, seeing him, quieted.

"Citizens of Rome!" he shouted. "I, for one, would like to meet the wondrous rhinoceros and the great hippopotamus rather than these! These slaves are only animals, when we have been promised wonders!"

The crowd roared with approval.

Augustus's mood improved. He gave a flourish of his toga, a gesture of presentation. Now he would bait the trap. Now he would entice his prey. He put his hands on the children's shoulders, beckoning them from their seats.

"As I welcome the animals of Africa," Augustus shouted, "I welcome three children into Rome. These were not children of Rome before today. They were children of Egypt!"

The crowd booed and hissed. Agrippa shifted beside Augustus, his hand on his sword.

Under Augustus's hands, the boys shifted as well, uncomfortable with the attention suddenly directed upon them. Selene looked straight ahead. Regal. Octavian approved. Would that she were his own daughter.

"They were children of that country's queen. You may remember her name. *Cleopatra*. Perhaps you saw her in my procession?"

The audience laughed and jeered at the name of their defeated foe.

"She is dead, and her children came willingly to this country."

The booing became louder. The emperor let it build to a crest of wrath and disdain before continuing.

"They are no longer the children of Egypt, however," Augustus said. "For *Egypt* is now the child of Rome."

Applause and laughter at the emperor's wit. Augustus stood straighter, delighting in this moment. He loved his citizens. They were beings of intelligence. They obeyed the rules of discourse. They stood and shouted their support.

The senators, he noticed, were quiet in their seats, watchful. What did they await?

"I present to you Cleopatra Selene, Alexander Helios, and Ptolemy Philadelphus, children of Rome and special favorites of your first citizen. I've forgiven them their parentage, and so shall you.

"And now . . . a unique entertainment, never before seen in Rome."

The emperor smiled in satisfaction. This would draw her if nothing else would.

"You may remember a betrayer of Rome," Augustus said. "A man who left his country behind in order to woo a foreign queen. A man who abandoned his soldiers, abandoned his wife and family, for that same queen."

The crowd booed on cue.

"The gods blessed Rome and struck our foe down. Tonight, our former enemy visits this arena from the Underworld."

There was a hush of expectation, a nervous giggle, quickly quieted.

Augustus inadvertently caught Selene's gaze. She was staring at him, bewildered, her eyes wide. It occurred to him that perhaps this had not been a perfect plan. Children were unreliable. But there was no turning back now.

"I give to you Mark Antony!" Augustus shouted.

Chrysate opened the silver box she held in her lap, and the ghost of Antony unfolded from it, fully armored, his eyes dark and unwilling, his wound visible even from the floor of the arena.

There was a moment of total silence and then the audience erupted in applause at the wondrous illusion.

"Father!" Selene screamed a bloodcurdling scream, high and terrified. Ptolemy joined her. Alexander reeled, staring at his father, disbelieving.

Antony, his body controlled by Chrysate, bent at the waist to bow to Caesar, and with that gesture, the lions were released.

➤ 22 ⬅

Cleopatra opened her throat and roared into the brightness, her body vibrating with the sound. She was still in the tunnel's mouth, and could not see what was happening in the arena. She could hear only the emperor's voice claiming her children, mocking her husband. The other lions surged forward with her, the dust flying behind her paws as she charged into the Circus Maximus.

The bestiarii awaited her, each with his sword and trembling knees. Some were brave, standing firm in the face of the wall of charging wild cats. Others tried to flee, though there was nowhere to go. A trench surrounded the fighting floor. Cleopatra judged it, assessing the leap.

There.

High in the stands, his toga shining, the evildoer. And beside him, on either side—

Her children.

Selene in the center, her hands grabbing the boys, the little one wide-eyed, and the elder, looking equally startled. Selene grappled with them, tugging their hands.

The emperor, between them, looked straight at the fighting, his gray eyes glinting and lustful. Beside him, a dark-skinned man stood, his dagger drawn, his face watchful, a serpent twining about his arms.

What was standing on his other side? A very young woman, glowing with some strange inner light, had her hand on the shoulder of a man. Cleopatra could not quite see him. He flickered, transparent. An actor, painted to look like Antony. It must be.

Cleopatra lashed forward with a paw, clawing the arm of the

230

bestiarii before her. She did not desire to kill him, and so she dodged his sword. He did not wield it well, in any case. Some of the fighters were screaming and slashing with their eyes closed. Dust flew up and obscured the bleeding lion beside her. The rhinoceros heaved his way up from below the stadium, its great ivory horn as sharp as a dagger, and its eyes flashing black and beady as it began to run, thundering across the circus.

Cleopatra caught sight of a sword, slicing directly at her head, and leapt forward to tear the fighter's throat, savoring, even if only for a moment, the heat of his blood.

She gathered her haunches and lunged at the stands, feeling the dead weight of a lioness beside her, anchoring her to the ground.

She gloried in her invisibility, straining at the chain that bound her and feeling the links stretch, the metal protesting. They did not know her. They had no idea she was coming. At last, she felt the chain break, whipping out from her throat and lashing across the ground. Red splattered her eyes and the moans of the dying rose around her.

Her muscles tensed for the leap over the trench, and for a graceful moment, she was in the air, high above the crowd, higher than any true lion could leap.

Augustus's face was shocked and upturned. She could see his heart beating through his throat. Terrified of her at last. He had underestimated Cleopatra.

The force of her landing threw the emperor to the ground, and he cowered on his back before her.

"You took my family!" she screamed, her voice still that of a lioness. She dug her claws into his shoulders, relishing his terror. "You took my country!"

"Get it off me!" the emperor shrieked. His eyes were wide, and reflecting in them, Cleopatra could see two female figures. First an old woman, and then a young. The elder had a distaff in her hands, and she raised it in the air, spinning it so swiftly, Cleopatra could scarcely see it move. The old woman looked into the queen's lioness body and *saw* her. Her eyes flashed silver-white, and Cleopatra felt her body begin to weaken as though she was suddenly bound with ropes, caught in a web.

The young girl rose up from her seat, smiled and lifted her hands, throwing some glittering substance into the air.

It showered over Cleopatra, and for a moment, Cleopatra was no longer a lion. She felt herself melt back into her human form, crouched atop Augustus in his laurel crown, her fingers bloodied.

She did not care.

Everything ceased to matter as she finally saw the face of the man who stood beside the witches, the man she'd thought an impersonation of her husband.

"Antony!" she screamed.

The knowledge ripped through her. It could be nothing but dreaming—but she reached out her hands to touch him. Did she imagine it? Did he cringe back from her?

She did touch him, an almost him, a faint him, with her fingertips, just as someone leapt upon her and tore her from her husband again.

➤ 23 ⬅

Agrippa and Usem both threw their bodies between that of the emperor and the monster. Agrippa locked his hands about Cleopatra's throat, feeling the woman's flesh in his fingers, even as the lioness growled before him. Her fangs grazed his shoulders.

He clung to her, screaming wordless obscenities against a world wherein something that should not exist, that *could* not exist, could suddenly be before him, attacking his emperor. He howled invective against magic and its unpredictability, the witches surrounding the emperor even now, and yet here he was, fighting the monster, and he was not a witch at all, but a soldier. Agrippa did not believe in magic. He did not believe in witches.

He did not believe in the thing he was doing.

Usem attacked the lioness from behind, his arms locked about her shoulders, his dagger seeking purchase. Would its poison kill her? He had no way of knowing. The Psylli clung to her back, feeling her toss him from side to side, feeling her sandpaper fur and, at the same time, her silken skin.

She was one moment a lioness and the next a woman, and Agrippa held her ferociously, pressing his thumbs into her jugular vein. Even a monster could be killed. Monsters died in the stories, their heads chopped off and buried, turned to stone by the sight of their own hideous aspects, poisoned by their own venoms.

He would kill this queen, this beast, this fury.

Her lips were pink, and then black and feline. Her eyes were golden and slitted, and then dark and long-lashed. Her fingers were dainty and pale, and then curved and taloned. Her waist was tiny and her hips were round, and her thigh came up beside his and wrapped around his back. He gasped, feeling suddenly deranged, and losing his grip on her throat.

Was he killing a woman, a defenseless—

No. He was killing a monster. He saw her jaws opening for him.

Out of the corner of his eye, Agrippa saw the man who was and was not Antony lift his hand in a gesture of command.

"Now!" Antony yelled, and suddenly there were men running toward them. Soldiers. Agrippa could see the flash of their swords.

He felt the Psylli pressing the hilt of a weapon into his fumbling hand. Agrippa looked up and saw Usem yank Cleopatra's head back. Agrippa thrust the serpent-poisoned dagger deep and hard into the monster's breast, feeling nothing but her demonic body engaged with his, hearing nothing but her shrieking roars. Her breast. At once creamy and bare and tawny-furred, both lioness and queen, and the blade had struck true, he knew.

He felt the dagger penetrate deep into her chest, and he twisted it, grunting with the effort. Surely, she would die. Surely.

He could hear swords clashing, men surrounding them, his own men, he thought, but he was not sure. Someone tried to wrest Cleopatra from his arms.

Chrysate muttered under her breath, whispering darkness, trying to bind the queen. She was strong enough to weaken her but not to break her. She called to Hecate, but Hecate was bound herself. The priestess clutched her holding stone. The shade was resisting her, too, and beside her, Cleopatra's daughter trembled in terror, barely contained. She turned her head to look for Auðr and saw the Northerner, her hands high in the air, moving rapidly, spinning, the distaff nearly invisible between them.

Agrippa's men were fighting Roman soldiers who had come from nowhere, and who seemed to be trying to defend Cleopatra. The shade of Antony shouted encouragement at them.

Cleopatra's face was pinned upward, the general clenched about her throat like a chain, muscles heaving and sweating, blowing like a bull. She hissed, air slipping from her lips.

Something was weakening her. Cleopatra shuddered, feeling a chill rising inside her, dragging her back into her human body.

Her husband, a false vision. An illusion. It could not be Antony.

She tried to convince herself, to banish it. They were tricking her. She'd seen something that could not be true. The man she had seen could not be Antony, but with every part of herself she knew it was. The smell of mint and wine. His smell.

She could feel the magic coming from the old woman, with the strange motions of her distaff, and the other, the one whose hands rested on Antony's shoulders, chanted words in a language even Cleopatra did not know. Any sorceress who had sway over the dead had sway over Cleopatra. She was not alive enough to resist it.

She struggled against Agrippa's hands and against the other man clinging to her shoulders. How could a mortal man hold her so tightly? Usem's dagger lay in her breast like a hornet's sting, maddening. She wailed, not for pain but for Antony. She had touched him, and now he was gone. She had touched him, and yet he was dead. He had cringed away from her. His face had shown her things she never wanted to see.

She terrified him, and with good reason. She terrified herself.

She let her body go limp, and Agrippa released his grip on her throat slightly, thinking her dying. She felt herself gripped by several other men, the soldiers who had appeared fighting Agrippa's men. She shook them off.

"NO!" Usem shouted, but Agrippa had no time to move before her tail whipped up and wrapped around his torso, flinging him deep into the stands, and Usem down through the crowd. Agrippa landed on his back, feeling ribs crack, an arm splinter. He gasped, unable to breathe, and then, choking with horror, he watched as the snake's tail lashed around the paralyzed Augustus and lifted him from where he stood.

She twisted the emperor's body before hers, bringing his struggling form to a level with her eyes.

Augustus looked into them, strangely calm. It was happening at last.

He should have died in Alexandria. Human. Snake. Lioness. None of these things, and all of them. He had not been mad, nor had he been preparing all these months for no reason.

As the pressure of her coils grew greater around him, he felt his heart trying to leap out of his throat. He gagged on bile. This would be the end of Augustus. He knew it with every bit of his soul. All these years of surviving intrigue, surviving Rome, for nothing. For this.

Her mouth opened wide in a hiss. Her cobra's hood spread wide, the torchlight shining through it, and where were his defenders? The circus was half empty now, he could see from his vantage point, and the people who had not been quick enough to flee the stadium were trampled and dead in the stands. His soldiers were engaged in battle with the wild animals, whose assigned human combatants had fled the circus for the streets. Agrippa lay across a row of seats, possibly dead himself. Usem crawled up the aisle.

Augustus's eyes began to close, the world dimming before him. The snake surrounded him, pressing in on his bones and blood, chilling his heart. He'd been a fool to think Agrippa would kill her with a dagger or with any of the other weapons they'd assembled. She was not of this earth.

He felt his body giving over to her.

"No," he whispered. Cleopatra looked into his eyes, caring nothing for his life.

"*You killed my husband,*" she hissed. "*You killed my son. You took my home.*"

Augustus felt his bones beginning to crack, his ribs splintering inside his chest. The serpent coiled tighter about him.

Then he saw the Psylli stand, his eyes dark and wrathful. A whirlwind hung beside him and then dispersed, whipping through the air of the circus. The warrior shook his head furiously, and a sound suddenly began to echo, swooping and whirling from end to end of the stadium.

Cleopatra, in the throes of her triumph, felt herself falter, her body transfixed. She began to lose her grasp on her prey.

Amplified by the wind, Usem stood in the stands, singing the song he'd learned as a child in the desert to make snakes forgive the sins of humans. He sang, his throat open to the sky, his hands thrown out into the air, his feet stamping in the dance of the Psylli.

The serpents of Rome heard him.

All over the city, people leapt from their doorsteps in horror, watching serpents surge from tunnels and secret holes, watching the streets of Rome fill with a slithering, tangling mass, all the snakes proceeding to the circus. They continued to come until they ran like water down the Appian Way, stacked ten deep in every slender alley. They swam the river, their heads bobbing over the surface of the water like eels. They poured through marble hallways and over the tombs in the graveyards. They slipped through secret doorways, coursing over the unsuspecting bodies of illicit lovers and spilling across their beds and out of their windows.

There were more serpents in Rome than there were human souls.

The snakes danced for Usem the Psylli, and in the Circus Maximus, the great serpent that was the queen rose up as well, her green scales shimmering. Augustus fell from her grasp, tumbling end over end to the ground beside Agrippa, who lay transfixed, looking up at the serpent that had almost killed him.

Cleopatra's tremendous form undulated helplessly, senselessly, as though the Nile had been made flesh and now stood on end before the emperor of Rome, enslaved to his will.

Usem sang the final notes of his song, and the serpent ceased weaving. She stood frozen before him, before the wounded emperor, before her stunned children, and then, with a motion like the shrugging off of a veil, her head fell back, and she collapsed onto the floor of the circus, her body naked and human once more.

She was beaten.

Usem hesitated for a moment. Around him, the wind surged insistent, whipping his garments, informing him that he must capture and kill Cleopatra now, or risk further damage. He could not leave it for Rome to do, but Usem found himself uncertain of anything. He had spent too much time looking into the queen's eyes, had seen her there, lost and alone. He was not sure who his song had worked on, the serpent or himself. And his dagger. The poison on it had not even wounded her. What could he do?

Chrysate stepped behind Usem, remaining hidden. There was an opportunity to take what she wanted, weak as she was. Even the small spells had nearly broken her.

Auðr stayed at attention, her fingers moving in the air, spinning the greatest thread, that of the queen herself, now fallen in the dust. She'd tried again to cut it, but she could not. It was still too strong, too twined with the goddess's. The seiðkona pulled at other tense threads, tightening them into a web. The Psylli and the Greek priestess. The shade of Antony. Panting with exertion, her chest rattling, she twisted them together with the fate of the queen. And with her own fate. Always her own fate.

Antony cursed, his legionaries beaten. Half of them were dead, and the rest had been captured by Agrippa's men. What had he been thinking? His plan had been terribly flawed. He had failed Cleopatra, hired drunken soldiers, and not enough of them. They were scattered now, holding their heads, raving. The men had not been prepared to do what they should have done, taken Cleopatra from the circus as quickly as possible. He could not blame them. When he'd hired them, he hadn't known she was what she was. They'd had no warning.

Augustus's private guard surrounded Cleopatra, their spears and swords poised to attack her should she move again. Marcus Agrippa struggled to his feet, gasping for breath, lifting the emperor from the ground, wincing at the pain in his fractured arm.

The Egyptian boys ran from the stands to Cleopatra, crying out her name. Selene stayed where she was, looking down upon her mother as if frozen. Her mouth hung open, and her eyes were wet. Antony took a step toward his daughter, and then, seeing the horror on her face, he shifted and took another step down the stairs and toward his wife.

Chrysate exulted, pulling him back, her fingers laced around her holding stone. Behind her, the man in the employ of the senators stood, waiting, biding his time, even in the midst of chaos. She did not notice him.

"You are dead," Chrysate told Antony. "You have nothing more to do here."

"My wife is here," Antony said, his voice low and dangerous. "And I will go to her."

He tore himself from Chrysate's side, his face twisting with the pain of resisting the holding stone. Moving without touching the ground, he was nearly at Cleopatra's side within seconds. A shred of his soul remained in Chrysate's fingers. She clung to it fiercely, and Antony screamed with rage.

"I am no slave! You will release me!"

On the floor of the arena, Cleopatra trembled, her body still ruled by the snake song, though she'd shed the snake's form. She looked up, her face unbelieving.

"Antony," she whispered. "I thought you were dead."

"He is," Chrysate said, and swiftly twisted the edge of Antony's soul in her fingernails, crushing him back into the wisp he had been when he first rose from Hades. She smashed him back inside the silver box, and then she moved toward Cleopatra, swift and graceful as a wolf assessing wounded prey.

The legionaries moved closer to the stricken queen, prodding her with their spears. Her two sons huddled beside her. Antony was gone. Surely, she'd hallucinated him. She stretched her arms to touch them, but the elder cringed, fearful of her hands. Ptolemy crawled into her arms, crying, and she held him tightly against her. She would not have long with him. She kissed his face, and whispered into his ear.

"You are the king of Egypt now. You and your brother. You must behave like kings."

"There is no Egypt," her elder son said. "Egypt is dead." But he came to her anyway, and burrowed into her arms. Cleopatra held her children with all her strength and looked back up into the stands. Selene was still seated above her, looking horrified.

"I came for you," Cleopatra said. "You are why I am here."

Selene shook her head. Cleopatra looked into her daughter's eyes, at her small copper face. It had been over a year since she had seen her in the light, and the girl had changed.

"You are not my mother," Selene said, and Cleopatra felt the words stinging her skin, breaking her memories of joy.

Her face a mask of confusion, Selene reached out to the witch who stood beside her, the witch who had captured her father. She took Chrysate's hand, and the priestess laughed. Strength flowed into her from the girl, even now.

The emperor hobbled down the stairs and appeared at Cleopatra's side, his eyes lit with triumph, despite his pain. In his hand, a silver net glittered.

Augustus threw the net over her, and she gasped at its scalding touch. The pain shone through the center of her bones, nearly intolerable. Her children were pulled from her arms, and she was left alone, tangled in silver.

"Did you think you could win over Rome? We will burn you this time," he sputtered, rage and pain choking his voice. "Make no mistake, we will burn you."

"You cannot burn me," Cleopatra told him. "I will not burn."

Augustus signaled to a grouping of soldiers, who stepped forward, their arms filled with clay vessels. They poured the contents over Cleopatra's body.

A sleek liquid that shone in darkness.

"You will burn this time," Augustus said.

The queen writhed, tormented by the silver, and by the liquid drenching her hair, her hands, her fingers. The legionaries piled wood about her, a circle of kindling, and those assembled stepped back.

The emperor took the final vessel. He tilted it over Cleopatra's head, and a single spark leapt from it and into her hair.

There was a rushing sound, and Cleopatra was aflame.

Her children screamed in horror, Ptolemy's face hidden in Alexander's shoulder, Selene unable to keep from looking. From the corner of her eye, though, Cleopatra's daughter saw something on Chrysate's face. The witch glorying in the flame. As the light reflected off Chrysate's skin, Selene saw into her for a moment. Something ancient clothed in a beautiful body. Something was not as it seemed. Selene gasped, and dropped Chrysate's hand, trembling, but the witch did not notice. The power of the fire was too compelling. She let the heat warm her face.

High in the stands, Nicolaus watched, his face wet with tears. They were making a grievous mistake, and he was powerless to stop them.

Augustus shouted with triumph as the inferno grew hotter and hotter still, white and blue, and at its center his enemy twisting, her body lit from within, incandescent with heat. This was the end, and he had won. This was the end, and he was watching her die.

Cleopatra struggled against the net, her body heated past pain, the silver melting into her skin, and yet she was not consumed.

She screamed in agony and felt the earth shake as her bones glowed, and her voice filled with thunder. Something was changing. The flames were not burning her but feeding her.

The sky tore open with lightning, and from it came the roar of a goddess. The legionaries looked up, terrified at the sound of the storm's voice, and in the sky they saw a tremendous fireball crossing the heavens. Another roar, this one of resurrection. Romans fell to their knees, praying to their own gods, but it did no good. Sekhmet slashed the sky above them.

Augustus himself stared at the comet. An omen. But of what? He did not know.

Cleopatra burned brighter and brighter until through the flames, she saw a single living creature, a moth with a red coral body and enormous pearly wings spotted in black flecks, like hieroglyphs.

The moth was drawn toward the inferno, its flesh singing in anticipation, its wings spreading, its destiny certain.

At last, it was there, its delicate membranes heating, its creamy wings catching fire. She could see it, illuminated in the last moment of its life.

As it died, Cleopatra was carried through the net and high into the air on a sudden current.

A metamorphosis. She spread her wings and flew, aiming herself at the comet.

High in the stadium, the Psylli shouted a few furious words to the wind and signaled to the priestess. The wind changed direction, and

Chrysate leaned forward as though this had been her plan all along. She held out her silver box. She had seen this moment in the scry months ago, though she had not known how it would come. She had waited for it. Auðr leaned forward as well, her eyes flashing. She would have only one chance. In her hands, she held the fates, trying to keep them controlled.

"*Bring her to me*," she told the Psylli, but the man ignored her.

Behind Chrysate, the man sent by the senators moved for an instant, his hand outstretched to snatch the holding stone from Chrysate's seat. In its place, he left a piece of green glass. He slipped back into the darkness, gone before the priestess saw him.

The newborn moth fluttered, caught in a current, helpless, rising, rising, and the wind, angrily following the orders of Usem, carried her into the priestess's clutches instead of the seiðkona's.

Chrysate's face contorted as she fought against the power the fire had lit in the queen, using all her strength to close the silver box around the moth.

Everyone in the arena watched light wings disappear into the dark, and Chrysate cried out with triumph.

Beside the priestess, a small girl with long black hair cried out as well, a broken, despairing cry, and then, disregarding the emperor, disregarding the witch, disregarding the soldiers who tried to stop her, she ran out of the arena.

She did not look back.

➤ 24 ⬅

Nicolaus rose from his crouch high in the stands and looked down into the dust where the bloodstains were still bright and the bodies of bestiarii and animals lay. There was a tremendous blackened circle in the sand at the center of the arena, and the smell of fire still lingered in the air.

How could he have been so foolish?

On the ship, he had seen what she had done, but he had not seen her *do* it. He had not imagined what she was capable of, not truly. A lioness, he knew, but tonight, with every flicker of torchlight, she became a new thing, and all of them equally savage. With every move, she lacerated skin and wounded innocent victims, without conscience, without care. Nowhere in the stories, nowhere in the histories, was there anything comparable. And the sky. He knew that the Romans had called the goddess back to earth with those flames, as surely as he knew anything. Fire was Sekhmet's family. She was a daughter of Ra.

Now a lowly witch held her in a box.

Did they not understand that a witch could not cage a goddess? Cleopatra would escape, and when she did, she would tear the world apart.

Nicolaus knew that he should take to the sea and disappear beyond the horizon. He was a scholar and a fool, and she was a monster.

Instead, he ran down the stairs, trying to force himself to do what needed to be done before he had time to regret it. He sprinted through the Circus Maximus and out the gates, saying a silent good-bye to any life he'd had as a historian. His fate had changed, and he must follow it.

He climbed the Palatine Hill. He would go to the emperor.

He'd lost hope of separating Cleopatra from Sekhmet. The queen he'd known was gone.

Now, in spite of his conscience, in spite of his guilt, in spite of his fear, Nicolaus sought a weapon that would kill her.

The senators convened in a secret chamber, quickly accessed from the Circus Maximus, all of them nearly frantic with excitement and shock.

"There is opportunity in this!" cried the first senator. "Augustus employs powers far beyond his control. The emperor will say the fire in the sky was an omen for his success, but Cleopatra lives, and our emperor marched through Rome declaring her dead. He is a liar and a betrayer of the republic. He deals in the very things he decries."

"More than that. He battles against something Rome has never seen before. What is she?"

"Nothing Rome should provoke."

"We have all seen her captured."

"Who can know what we saw? We saw the witch take her. We did not see her destroyed. Who knows who the witch truly serves? Perhaps the emperor seeks to turn Cleopatra to his purposes. To kill his enemies."

"We are the Senate," scoffed one. "He would never dare."

"Do you feel so safe?" asked another.

"The emperor is not as protected as he once was. It was only sorcery that saved him," said another, still trembling from the proximity of the serpent, from the searing heat of the unnatural fire.

"What emperor of Rome encircles himself with witches?" howled the eldest.

"Even his uncle would never have dared traffic publicly in magic," said the first, and the group nodded, certain of that. Even aside from all else they had seen that night, it was indisputable that Augustus had gone beyond his predecessors, beyond any code of Rome. Now it was a matter of using the emperor's error to the advantage of the republic.

"A rebellion."

"We are too old to rise up," said the eldest, but even he, with his papery skin and quavering head, felt his hands drawing into fists and his young man's ambition rising within him.

"We will not be alone in this," said the final senator, and the rest nodded. "Augustus is not a general. He does not command the military cleanly. They were Antony's men once, and they may be ours now."

"And the common people?"

Surely, the events of the night were a sign of disaster for Rome. Surely, they were omens that might be found in the Sibylline prophecies or if they could not, they might be written there, given the proper connections.

The senators possessed such connections.

Once a story was told, it would catch the ears of the people. *This* was a story that might change the course of Rome.

The senators nodded at one another and walked off into the city, each in his own direction, each with his own instructions, each with his own set of weapons.

These men fought not with swords but with sharpened tongues.

They would wound Augustus with words, and then, when he was suitably damaged, they would kill him by more conventional means, just as his uncle had been killed.

Outside the arena, the Psylli stood at the center of a whirlwind, arguing with his wife. Against her will, she had helped him force Cleopatra into Chrysate's prison, and now the whirlwind filled with hailstones and rain.

"The queen is captured," Usem protested. "What they do with her is none of my concern. We were brought here to help them trap her, no other reason."

The wind twisted around him, and he suddenly felt his wrists bound by hurricane. Hailstones pelted his face. He shut his eyes, frustrated. The voice of the West Wind's daughter whirled through the buildings and pressed into his ears.

"I did *not* enslave her," Usem said, his voice taut with fury. "Rome will be at peace through my efforts, and my tribe will be safe. Our *children* will be safe. They will never be at the mercy of Rome."

The wind tossed dust in the street.

"She was already entwined with the Old One. If anyone has enslaved her, it is the goddess, and now they are both captives."

The wind whipped Usem into the air, lifting him until he could not breathe. On the horizon the fireball crouched, shining bright against the edge of the world.

Usem stared at it, miserable. His wife was right. The queen might be captured, but Sekhmet lived. He was not finished. There were things he did not know, and he had not been paying enough attention.

The wind about him faded, dropping him slowly to the earth. The air was still and heavy. The summer night settled around him, hot and thick, and above him, the stars gazed down, careless.

Usem looked up, wishing to apologize, but his wife had gone.

Gasping with exertion, Auðr made her way from the arena, surrounded by Agrippa's men. As she went, she laid her distaff against the brow of each legionary, and they forgot what they had just seen. Knowledge increased chaos.

Things had gone horribly wrong. Auðr had not been strong enough to keep the snake sorcerer from acting outside the fate she'd woven for him. He had been meant to deliver the queen to the seiðkona, and instead, Cleopatra had ended up in the hands of Chrysate.

She'd lost control of several strands, and the chaos still showed, dark and twisting, larger than it had been. Nothing the seiðkona did seemed to change it.

Auðr knew only that her own fate was tied to that of the queen. It all fit together in the tapestry, each thread twisting with others, each warp to each weft, and the knots and spaces were part of the whole.

The queen still lived, Auðr knew, and the goddess was stronger than she had been. As the flames rose around Cleopatra, Auðr had felt the Old One feeding on the heat, on the violence.

She was here now.

Auðr touched the night air, sensing gleaming strands of fate strengthened by the bloodshed. Darkness was rising in Rome. Violence and destruction. Other old gods stirred, strengthened by this one.

She could feel it happening, and she could not keep them down. She coughed, bent over, her lungs racked by exhaustion and powerlessness. Why did she still live if she had failed? Her eyes hazed over with smoke, and she choked, dropping to her knees and trying to draw a breath.

The legionaries, stumbling over her, picked up her limp body and carried her up the hill and back to the Palatine, her distaff, even in her unconsciousness, clenched tightly to her chest.

⇒·25·⇐

Augustus sprinted up the hill, wincing at his bruised ribs and denying the men who were supposed to carry him. He reached his study, slammed the door behind him, and vomited out the window. What had happened? He had only a few minutes before Chrysate and Marcus Agrippa would arrive, bringing with them the box that contained Cleopatra.

In those moments, he tried not to see what he had seen, the lioness springing at him, her talons stretching for his throat. The serpent, whose eyes had reflected his own small and fearful face. The queen, her naked form quivering in the dirt, looking up at him with grief and hatred in her stare. Her children torn from her embrace. And the way she had wailed Antony's name.

The fire had not killed her. He saw her body again in his mind's eye, turning white hot in the net, surrounded by flame. She'd looked into his eyes just before she flew.

He tried to convince himself that this ordeal was finished, but he did not believe it. The things that had happened tonight were only the beginning of the visions he'd seen in Alexandria.

He drank the last of his vial of theriac, swallowing convulsively.

He thought of Agrippa, flung by the snake, a weak man, a flawed defender of Rome. The terror Augustus had banished began to return as fury. Was he not the emperor? He'd nearly been killed, and everyone around him had watched it happen. He saw the box closing around Cleopatra, his witches succeeding where his warriors had failed.

By the time Agrippa opened the door to the emperor's study, favoring his fractured arm and grimacing with untreated pain, Augustus was in a righteous rage. Chrysate followed the general into the room. Her wrists were bound, though she still clutched the silver box.

"Why is my defender being treated like a prisoner?" Augustus asked, his tone frigid.

"She cannot be trusted," Agrippa said. "She refuses to surrender Cleopatra, if Cleopatra is even inside that box."

"You saw her trapped in it," Augustus seethed. "We all saw it. She is captured."

"Witches traffic in illusion," said Agrippa, looking bitterly at the fiend as she curled herself into a chair, her bare legs delicate, her lips roses, her eyes an innocent, luminous green.

"I am no witch," Chrysate said. "I am a priestess. The thing from the North is a witch. She tried to take the queen from me. I suggest you watch yourself around her. She is a dark creature, and I serve the light."

"Hecate is not a goddess of light," Agrippa muttered. His ribs ached, and the pain in his arm was severe. It would have to be splinted. "She stands at the gates of Hades."

"You know nothing about her," Chrysate said serenely. "Nor about what she will be."

Agrippa reached out his good hand for the box and tried to wrest it from her grasp, but her fingers were like iron. His hand slipped from the box, and he caught hold of Chrysate's arm. He recoiled, stunned by what he felt. Her skin was withered, though it looked smooth.

He glanced quickly up at her face, seeing, if only for a moment, a crone, her teeth long and pointed, a single eye bulging from her face, staring at him.

Then she was a beauty again, virginal and dewy-skinned, transformed back into the girl she had seemed a moment before.

She smiled at him.

"Who are you to say the Underworld may not become this one? Who are you to say the dead may not one day walk in the sun, and the living in darkness? Who are you to say that *you* will not, Marcus Agrippa?"

The words, though spoken quietly, were a curse. Agrippa's center twisted. He felt like screaming.

"Do you fear the dark, Marcus Agrippa?" the girl asked. "Do you fear my mistress? Do you fear Cleopatra? Then you should leave us. I, and my kind, kept the emperor of Rome safe tonight. You and all your men failed."

Agrippa felt himself sagging, her words piercing him. She was not wrong.

"What is the matter with you?" Augustus asked, looking sharply at him.

Agrippa would not fail again. He must protect his emperor, even if it meant protecting him from things Augustus himself had invited in.

He knew this witch before him would not go easily back to her cave in Thessaly now that she'd tasted power. And the queen of Egypt would certainly not stay imprisoned in that box, not if she could survive fire, not if she could transform at will. If the priestess found a way to control her, Agrippa did not want to imagine what would happen. Together, Cleopatra and Chrysate would be even more formidable than each was alone.

"Do not trust her," he managed, and then he saluted Augustus, mastered his fears for his friend, and left the room.

His task was set. He must find a new weapon, one that could destroy the indestructible. And he must act outside his orders. Agrippa had always believed in his friend, had served at his side for most of his life, but now, Augustus was wrong. The consequences of his error would be severe. If Augustus trusted Chrysate, what else would he trust? What other foolish decisions might he make?

The emperor watched his general depart, feeling the panic rising up again. He certainly could not leave his savior bound. He walked across the room, knelt before Chrysate, and untied her wrists.

The girl was motionless, her skin glowing from within, her eyes greener than ever. Despite his vow to the contrary, Augustus felt himself desiring her again. She was ruthless. To keep her in his employ would bring him power. What might she do in a city built over the bones of so many dead? There were heroes buried in Rome, warriors of legend-ary prowess. And why stop with Rome? He might take Chrysate to the battlefields of Troy. He imagined it for a moment, himself commanding an army of the glorious dead. What need would he have for Marcus Agrippa, when he had Achilles?

"What have you done with Antony?" he asked.

"He sleeps inside this box," she said. "And his wife sleeps beside him as long as I hold the stone that keeps him from descending to Hades. They are mine."

Chrysate could see by the way the emperor's pulse throbbed against the thin skin of his temple that he was thrilled by her as much as he feared her.

She held in her hands the box that contained the end of the world. The monster within would be like a drop of aconite in a cistern, spread-ing through a city's water and killing all who drank. Chrysate could feel Hecate's strength growing. She'd be satisfied with this, and the goddess long ago sent to the Underworld would rise, feeding off Cleopatra and Sekhmet.

Hecate would rise.

For that, though, for the summoning spell, Chrysate needed Selene. Chrysate's powers were dwindling even as she sat here in the emperor's rooms. Despite the love spell she'd worked, the spell that should have made the girl her slave, Selene had run from her in the Circus Maximus, terrified, and who knew where she was now?

Chrysate smiled. At least Selene was not a stupid child. This was good. Intelligent children were more valuable.

She ran her fingers over Augustus's cheek. He startled at her touch, but she saw his color change, his eyes dilate.

"I saved you," she told him. "Without me, your enemy would have escaped. Without me, you would be dead. I want the Egyptian girl. Cleopatra's daughter."

She licked her lips, moistening them.

Augustus looked at her, bleary, his brow furrowing.

"Selene?" he asked.

Chrysate placed the sealed silver box carefully on the table and untied the sash of her robe. She heard the sharp intake of Augustus's breath. She wore nothing beneath, and the spell she'd worked had made her body into one that could easily make a thousand ships refuse to leave port. She was well aware of the emperor's weaknesses.

"Give her to me," Chrysate whispered, leaning over Augustus, pressing him back onto the floor, letting him feel her softness, letting his hands linger on her skin. "Give her to me, and you will have everything you could desire."

The emperor's hands came to life, grasping her thighs. She'd never met a man who could not be manipulated with the simplest tools. They were all the same. She prayed her illusion would hold long enough to accomplish what was necessary. The body beneath the spell was nothing the emperor would want to touch.

"I want only one thing," Augustus said, resisting her hands. "Cleopatra must be destroyed, by order of Rome."

She'd thought him more easily controlled than this.

"I cannot destroy such a thing," she informed him, kissing him hard enough to bruise. "And I do not choose to."

Augustus sat up suddenly, his hands grappling with her wrists, knocking her off balance. Chrysate was startled to find herself swiftly immobilized beneath him, her wrists held behind her, her cheek against the stone floor. He was stronger than she'd imagined. His injuries should have weakened him sufficiently, but the magic she'd used tonight had weakened her. It had been a hundred years since she'd felt anything like this.

"Do you serve me, Chrysate?" he asked, his mouth next to her ear, the rasp of his beard against her face. "Or do you serve another?"

"I serve you," she said, and then stretched beneath him, emphasizing the point. She had not lost him yet. "You and I are not so different. We both want more than we've been given. Do I misunderstand you, emperor of Rome?"

"You do not," he said. She could feel him hard against her. One of his hands stroked her throat, pressing roughly. She wondered if he would try to strangle her. There was a thrum of thwarted violence in him, a weak boy made into the ruler of the world, and all she needed to do to rule *him* was to make him think he'd won.

"Everything in Rome is yours to command," she said. "And the world is Rome. *I* am yours to command. Will you give me what I want?"

She slowly lifted her hips off the ground until he was nearly inside her. She felt his pulse quicken.

"Selene," she said.

"Yes," Augustus said, and laughed softly. "You could ask for gold, and instead, you ask for a girl. You can have Cleopatra's daughter if you want her so desperately. She'll make a good apprentice."

Chrysate arched her back, and he groaned, pulling her closer.

He thought that he controlled *her.* Chrysate nearly laughed, but then she found herself moaning. She had not expected to enjoy this. Perhaps she had not been lying when she'd told him they were two of a kind.

"The box that cages Cleopatra must be locked away," he said. "There is a room lined with silver, here in my house. I had it made for her. You will place the box there, and it will be guarded."

"I agree. She is precious. She should be guarded," Chrysate said, smiling. Locks and silver would not bar her from the queen, not if she wanted to reach her.

"Do you not fear her?" he managed.

"I do not," she said. "She cannot touch me. You can."

They were finished talking.

⇒ 26 ⇐

Elsewhere in Rome, the senator's man stood looking at the piece of green stone he held in his hand. It was such a small thing, to have had so many people going to such trouble over it. Nothing precious at all. It looked like old glass.

Still, he had his instructions. He placed the holding stone on the ground, taking little notice of the way it glimmered and shone in the dark. He was paid well for this task.

The senator's man picked up the hammer he'd brought, and with a single blow, he smashed the witch's stone. Shards of it flew everywhere, but it was broken irrevocably.

With his heel, he ground the remaining bits of magic into the dirt of Rome, and then, with a grunt of satisfaction, he walked on.

Suddenly, she was falling, pulled deep into the darkness, deep into the cold. The burning of the silver net where it had melted into her skin disappeared. The walls of the silver box itself disappeared, and the bed of ash beneath her body was gone as well.

She was adrift in the night sky, or falling through the earth, but she was not alone. Someone held her hand in his, and as they fell, she felt his grasp tighten. Every part of her demanded that she turn back, told her that she did not belong where she was going, but he pulled her deeper, deeper, until she lost herself in his determination. Her body resisted, but there was nothing to be done. Around the hole where her heart had been she felt ice crystals forming.

She gasped, and then darkness took her.

She awoke to cold fingers on her flesh. She was being carried, her body held in rigid arms, her legs dangling. Cleopatra's head lay against a shoulder she would have known anywhere. She tried to sit up.

"Stay still," a voice—*his voice*—whispered. "Don't open your eyes. Trust me. I am yours. You are mine."

"In life," Cleopatra whispered.

"And thereafter," her husband answered.

Together, they walked downward in darkness.

BOOK OF LIGHTNING

And thereupon shall the whole world be governed by the hands
Of a woman, and obedient everywhere.
Then when a widow shall o'er all the world gain the rule,
And cast in the mighty sea both gold and silver, also brass and iron,
Of short-lived men, into the deep shall cast,
Then all the elements shall be bereft of order.
When the God who dwells on high shall roll the heaven, even as a
*   scroll is rolled,*
And to the mighty earth and sea shall fall the entire multiform sky,
*   and There shall flow a tireless cataract of raging fire,*
And it shall burn the land and burn the sea, and heavenly sky and
*   night and day*
And melt creation itself together,
And pick out what is pure.
No more laughing spheres of light,
Nor night, nor dawn, nor many days of care,
Nor spring, nor winter, nor the summer-time, nor Autumn,
And then of the mighty God, the judgment midway in a mighty age
Shall come, when all these things shall come to pass.

—The Sibylline Oracles, circa 30 B.C.E.
Translated from the Greek
Milton S. Terry, 1899

⇒ 1 ⇐

Sekhmet, daughter of the sun, Lady of Slaughter, crouched high above Rome, looking out at her new terrain. Her body quivered with anticipation. It had been so long since she'd had a true form, so long since her strength had been more than a shadow.

She remembered the day the Nile had turned crimson, when human blood had first filled her hands, her mouth. She remembered the beauty of her task. *Kill the betrayers*, her father had told her, and she had done his bidding, until Ra forgave them and betrayed his daughter.

He flung Sekhmet into nothingness, gathered his human children into his arms, and soothed their fear, kissing them and singing to them, while his daughter suffered.

The goddess had barely survived, fading with the passage of time, the sacrifices made by her few remaining priestesses growing smaller and smaller until she was fortunate if a rabbit was killed in her name. Ra forgot her, grew ancient and frail, and fled the bloody, joyful, rageful earth for the sky.

Egypt forgot her.

Everyone forgot her, except Cleopatra.

It had been three thousand years, more, since Sekhmet had felt so strong. A queen as her worshipper. A queen laying waste to the world on her behalf. A queen set on fire. The heat of the flame had brought Sekhmet back entirely. It was as though she dwelt in Ra's eye again.

But Cleopatra was invisible to her now, gone somehow beneath the earth to Hades, the dwelling place of the Roman dead. Sekhmet was banned from the Underworld, and in any case, there was no blood there.

The goddess could wait for her servant to emerge, but still, she needed sacrifices.

Her father had promised her things, but he had never given them to her. Now Sekhmet had only the tears she'd shed after her father's abandonment. Those tears had created seven companions for her loneliness. Seven shining children.

She'd given them names, one by one as they were created, each stronger and more beautiful than the next. Plague and Famine, Earthquake and Flood, Drought, Madness, and Violence.

The goddess looked down over Rome. There were so many bodies there, and all of them would be her prey. She'd destroy their temples, destroy the places their gods received sacrifices, and take their worship from them, whether they believed in her or not. They would ask her forgiveness, but she had no forgiveness for humans.

Gods were meant to destroy.

Sekhmet stretched her arms and pulled the quiver from her back, glorying in her newfound strength. It had been thousands of years since she'd seen her children. They'd weakened along with her, but now, fed by Cleopatra's sacrifices, fed by the fire in the arena, they strained for release. She could feel them humming. She had strength enough only for one thus far, but there would be time. She would see the others again.

She removed the first of her Seven Arrows, feeling it shudder in her hands as it woke. It opened its glittering eyes, and the goddess looked into them, welcoming it back from its sleep.

She kissed the Slaughterer's sharp face, feeling its many rows of needle-sharp teeth, feeling its hunger, feeling its ferocious claws stretching for prey.

She fit it into her bow, pulled taut the golden string, and loosed Plague into the world.

The thing was beautiful, a glowing streak, a glinting, flashing, fiery star making its way across the heavens. A young woman pointed up into the clouds, and she and her mother watched it come. There was no tremor with its fall. It disappeared, and the village did not connect it with the illness that came upon them.

First, an elder of the village fell sick, spiking a high fever that left him trembling in his bed. The old man's skin blistered, as though he'd been exposed to a blazing desert sun, and then it turned black, charred as if over a cook fire. The old man looked out from his body with bright, horrified eyes, screaming in agony as his wife tried to soothe him. The room filled with smoke and smelled of burning, and at last, the old man was dead.

He would be the first but not the last. Within a few hours, the town, from the tiniest children to the elders, had been taken ill, and within a few days, they were gone.

The neighboring villages packed their belongings and headed into the hills, where it was cooler, but Plague traveled with them, killing rapturously, killing indiscriminately, killing hungrily, and those who were well shut their doors to the sick, and those who were sick ran through the streets in search of comfort, throwing themselves into wells and springs, spreading their disease.

Townspeople became terrified of one another, fighting their neighbors for food and space, fighting their friends, fighting their families, and dying all the while.

The Slaughterer's mouth stretched into a tight, fanged smile. It fed its mistress, and this was a new and vulnerable country, with no understanding of the goddess and her ways.

There had once been protective spells, but the world knew nothing of such things now.

The Slaughterer traveled, streaking through the blue and shimmering sky, lighting the countryside afire in places both known and unknown.

It visited India and Gaul, Parthia and the iced-over countries of Oceanus. It fell upon an island, where it was worshipped. It was a god for a time, and then it did as gods do and killed every inhabitant. It swept the dead out to sea, where their bodies would tangle in nets and bring disease to fishermen.

Heat smothered the spheres. Lightning crackled in the heavens. A soft cloud of black smoke filled the clouds as the Slaughterer flew, and it inhaled the smoke, expanding the razor-sharp feathers its body was fletched with and spreading them in the air. It did not need the wind. It did not need anything but Sekhmet.

The Slaughterer made its way over the earth, feeding here and there, leaving only Rome, the center of the world, untouched for its mother's pleasure.

Overhead, the Sun Boat shone brilliantly down on the world, but Ra saw nothing. He was old, and he crossed the sky with his eyes shut, prostrate on his cushions, flying blind.

It was a beautiful day.

⇒ 2 ⇐

In her bed in the imperial residence, Auðr sat up with a choking gasp, her heart racing. The fates were suddenly shifting more quickly than she could spin them. She felt the Old One's thread divide, and another strand arc away from it. Where that strand went, lives ended.

The tear in the tapestry of the fates, once centered in Rome, had begun to spread throughout the world.

Frantic, Auðr focused herself to search for Cleopatra's fate in the tangle. The queen had been tied to Sekhmet. Had she escaped from the box she was caged in? Was this how the goddess drew new strength? The seiðkona's fingers twisted in the air, plucking at strands, but she could find nothing. Where Cleopatra's fate had been, an endless thread too strong to cut, too entwined with the fates of the world to remove, there was now an absence.

The queen was gone.

Auðr felt Cleopatra's thread descend into the world of the dead, and disappear there.

For the first time, she wondered if Sekhmet and the queen could truly still be their own beings. Though Auðr had not been able to separate their fates, for the moment Cleopatra was free. What she did now might shift her destiny.

The future was open, and Auðr watched, her eyes wide in the darkness, as the Slaughterer flew through the world, destroying everything in its path. She watched as Sekhmet's fate grew stronger.

After a moment, she focused herself on what she should have been thinking of from the beginning. A weapon to destroy an immortal. She did not possess such a thing. Even at the height of her strength, Sekhmet would have been beyond her, and she knew it now.

Others were working on the same thing, she realized. She felt in the dark for their fates and found them, one strong and warlike, the general Marcus Agrippa, and the other a historian, fearful and confused. She began to twine them together, quietly, slowly.

Cleopatra was free of Sekhmet for now, and that meant that the goddess had a weakness. Auðr sought to find it.

The Psylli sat on the roof of the imperial residence, looking up at the sky and listening to the wind. Her predictions had come true, and now she returned, furious, to tell him of the plague that Sekhmet had brought to the land. She blew across the world, and in some places, she swept through empty villages, over forgotten thresholds, through broken windows. She whipped across deserts and over seas and found that the plague had touched everywhere. She flew beside the Slaughterer and watched its rampage, helpless to do anything. Sekhmet's arrow rode on the wind's unwilling back, shrilling with pleasure, flinging itself through the clouds and into the world.

"What would you have me do?" Usem asked.

The only way to hurt the Old One is through the queen.

"And how might I wound the queen?"

The wind did not have an answer. The silver box that was Cleopatra's jail waited inside the residence, but Usem's dagger and poison had only pained her, not wounded her. He did not know what to do. He sat, sharpening his dagger, his snakes coiling about him.

⇒ 3 ⇐

They crossed Acheron in Charon's ferry, Antony telling the reluctant boatman that the spirit he carried was a gift for Persephone and that her passage was paid. Cleopatra lay silently as wizened fingers passed over her, determining, after some examination, that she was lifeless. Her skin was cold enough to pass for that of a corpse and scarred with silver veins. The boatman threw a ragged blanket over her body.

Antony kept his hands on her, and where he touched her, she lived. She knew she'd left her body behind somehow, trapped in the witch's hands. She knew that she was traveling in the land of ghosts, an Underworld not her own. Still, she was content.

She was with her love again, and nothing else mattered.

The boat rocked beneath her. A drop of river water splashed onto her wounded skin, and she felt the tears of tens of thousands of mourners sobbing over graves, strewing flowers and libations into the soil. There were no tears for Cleopatra in this river. The tears of Egypt flowed through the caverns of the Duat.

Eventually, after what seemed hundreds of years of travel, the boat scraped rock, and Antony carried her onto a bank dotted not with colored wildflowers but with poisonous plants, dark and ashen. The dead approached, slavering at the sight of one from the world of the living, but then backed away, bewildered by her bloodlessness.

"How did you get us away from the witch?" she asked, hearing the vessel recede back into the river.

Her beloved grinned, a strange, sweet expression here in Hades.

"She may be able to draw a soul up from Hades, but she does not understand Rome," Antony said. "Everyone is willing to bargain if you have something worth bargaining for. I told the Senate about the emperor and his hiring of witches, and in return, they gave me their blood and stole the stone the witch was using to keep me tied to her in the upper world."

"What do you mean when you say they gave you their blood?" Cleopatra asked sharply.

"A drop of blood reminds us of what we were and makes us feel human, at least for a time. Now I've tasted the blood of seven senators, and my bond to the witch is lessened."

Cleopatra thought for a moment. Perhaps he would not mind what she had become.

A ghost approached them, its eyes wide and blank. It offered them a sprig of asphodel.

Antony pushed it away, and it spun on its heels, bowing back into the grasses, plucking flowers and pressing them into its mouth. The spirit moaned with hunger.

"He was a philosopher," Antony said. "Now he is nothing. The longer a soul stays in Hades, the more longing it feels for its past. Most of them wade into the waters of Lethe and drink until they've forgotten the human lives they left behind."

Cleopatra shuddered. She was not human. She knew it, and so did Antony. He had seen her a snake, a lioness.

"Am I dead?" she asked, looking at the painful streaks of silver on her skin, a netting melted into her flesh. "Am I a shade? Is that how I come to be here?"

"You are not alive, and you are not dead, either," Antony answered, his face unreadable. "Your body is above us, trapped in Chrysate's hands, and your soul—"

"I sold my *ka*," Cleopatra whispered. "I sold it to Sekhmet to bring you back."

Antony looked at her, his eyes filled with sorrow.

"When I first came to Hades, I could still taste the wine you gave me in our mausoleum. *Who are you?* the dead asked me. 'Mark Antony,' I answered. *No longer. You are no one here*, they said. 'Where is my wife?' I asked. *She belongs to another*, they answered."

"They lied to you!" Cleopatra shouted, infuriated. "I am yours," she said more quietly. "I swear it. Octavian sent a false messenger to you and bribed my army."

"They were not wrong," Antony said quietly. "I saw you in Rome."

Cleopatra felt as though part of her mind had been left behind with her body. Of course he'd seen her, in the arena.

"I saw you kill a servant in the street. I saw you drink from him until he was dead."

Cleopatra had a fleeting thought of throwing herself into the river. She started to stand, but he took her hand and held it tightly in his.

"Then why did you bring me with you?" Cleopatra managed. If he did not want her, she should be in that silver box. She should be in Rome, a captive.

Antony touched her chest, the place where her heart had been.

"*Te teneo*," Antony said simply. "No matter what you are, no matter what has happened to you. I love you. That was my pledge. I tried to keep you safe in the living world, but I did not understand what you were. I was a fool. I thought soldiers could protect you. We go to Hades and Persephone, the lord and lady of this realm. They will know how to help you."

Cleopatra looked quickly at him.

"You risk yourself," she said.

She knew enough about his Underworld to know that the throne room of its gods was not a place for lowly spirits to visit. There was no petitioning in Hades. The gods were not sympathetic.

"Then I risk myself," Antony told her. "I am not afraid."

She could see thousands of other spirits now, in the gray light, making their way about the terrain, dark and dusty, hungry, bewildered. She couldn't hear their thoughts, if they had thoughts at all, and this was a blessing. They smelled of nothing, and their histories were unknowns. There was no blood here, and it was endlessly dusk.

She thought of her own Underworld, and the sun that shone there for one glorious hour each night, waking the dead from sleep. From the Duat, the blessed dead could go forth amongst the living during the day. The dead flew through the clouds as hawks and basked in the sun as cats. The dead swooped as owls and trotted across the sand as dogs and jackals. At night, they went back to the realm of Osiris, fulfilled. Had she and Antony both died, they would have been together in the Duat, and perhaps, had their souls been judged happily, in the Beautiful West.

Home.

Now her only home was Antony.

Her husband laced his cold fingers together with hers and drew her to her feet. They walked on, into the mists of Hades.

⟫ 4 ⟪

The walls of the prison oozed filthy water, and there was no food but thin, weevil-ridden mash. Nicolaus comforted himself. At least he still lived. It was a miracle he had not been crucified.

A group of legionaries had caught him breaking into the emperor's chambers at the Palatine, and he had been arrested immediately. He demanded to see the emperor or Marcus Agrippa, but the legionaries took him to the prison without hearing anything he had to say.

He'd languished here for days, surrounded by madmen.

The prisoners, mainly soldiers who had collapsed or betrayed Rome by serving Antony in the battle at the Circus Maximus, compared visions of the queen's transformation, gibbering and wailing from their cells. They told one another tales of Mark Antony, once their fellow, walking as a shade and hiring them to defend his queen, and of wild animals slavering. They spoke of serpents that swarmed through the streets of Rome.

They spoke of the queen dancing in the center of an endless fire, undamaged.

He had to get to the emperor. His life was already ruined, and if he did not wish to spend the rest of it rotting belowground, he must tell his story to the Romans. He must get access to other materials, other libraries. Something to find a way to defeat Sekhmet. It must exist. They did not understand that though they had Cleopatra, they did not contain her. Sekhmet still walked, and she was the daughter of the sun. It was very likely that the burning had made her stronger.

He was tormented by a scrap of memory, something he'd read in the

Museion about Sekhmet's Slaughterers, seven ferocious children in the form of monstrous arrows, who served as bringers of chaos, plague, and destruction. They had been punished along with Sekhmet, and if she was free, they were, too.

In desperation, he begged a guard for writing materials, hoping to craft a letter to the emperor, and when they scoffed at him, he mentioned Virgil's name.

Days later, a visitor arrived. He was a head taller than any of the guards, draped in a dark, hooded cloak. Nicolaus watched hopelessly as the man passed coins to the guard. He expected this was some assassin buying his way into the cell, but when the man took off his hood, Nicolaus recognized the poet's face, long and grim.

"You should not have used my name," Virgil said. "Augustus does not know I am in Rome. Someone else summoned me here, but the emperor wrote me in Campania, begging me to come to his bedside as a storyteller. He is having difficulty sleeping."

"As well he should," said Nicolaus. "A monster sleeps in his house."

"I heard that," said Virgil. "The emperor's servants leak secrets. A miracle, is it not? They captured a shape-shifting creature. A wonder."

"It is not a wonder," Nicolaus said. "It is horrifying. You are fortunate that you have not seen what I have seen. You must get me out of this prison. I have to speak to Augustus."

Virgil looked at Nicolaus for a moment, measuring him. "I've brought you writing materials, at considerable risk to myself."

Nicolaus reached out to grasp the scroll, but Virgil held it back.

"I have a price."

"I have no money," Nicolaus said, frustrated. "Perhaps you misunderstand my position here."

"There is a request for a forgery, from high up in Rome, and if I value my life, I cannot do it."

"Why should I be capable of something you are not?"

"You are dead already," Virgil said simply.

The Sibylline Books, Virgil explained, were a complicated fiction: The original texts, purchased by Tarquinius from the Cumaean Sibyl, had been destroyed in a fire at the Temple of Jupiter fifty years before, and since then, Rome had searched the world to replace them with copies. Naturally, it had quickly become clear that the copies might be edited to reflect favorable omens for Rome. The Sibylline prophecies were now largely, albeit secretly, the work of hired scholars pretending to be long-dead prophetic priestesses. They were consulted whenever Rome's rulers wished to justify something with an ancient prophecy. This forgery, however, was a delicate assignment.

"A group of senators desire a doomsday prophecy relating to the rise of Cleopatra and the fall of Augustus's Rome. They wish to sway the public's opinion of Augustus. It seems that the facts support them," said Virgil.

"To what end?"

"The story you will write might aid them in restoring the republic. It might create a revolution against Augustus. It might merely make for entertaining reading. I cannot tell the future, Nicolaus, but a story like this is difficult to resist, even for a man like me. Sometimes, I miss the days when I wrote what I pleased."

"You do not miss those days much," Nicolaus said, snorting. It felt as though they were scholars debating in a courtyard, and for a moment, Nicolaus forgot that he was behind bars in a dungeon and that Virgil stood at liberty, the richest poet in Rome.

"True," said Virgil, and smiled. "I will visit Augustus when I am finished here. I have become the emperor's lullaby singer, but he pays me in Egyptian gold."

"What am I to write?" Nicolaus asked.

"And you were once such a promising scholar," Virgil said. "Can you not guess? The texts are kept under key in the Temple of Apollo, and everyone claims they're incorrupt, but every leader has commissioned his own version of the prophecies, dependent on what he needed the world to believe. The Sibylline prophecies are a creation of convenience and full of lies. *You*, on the other hand, will write the truth. The emperor has employed some sort of witch to steal the memories of those who witnessed the chaos in the Circus Maximus, and the senators fear that the stories will not travel as easily as they need them to."

"I want to write to Augustus," Nicolaus insisted.

"He reads the prophecies," Virgil said.

"Augustus has put Rome in danger. He has put the world at risk by capturing her."

"Then write that," Virgil said. "Terrify him. Terrify Rome. Make them think their doomsday is coming, and all because of what Augustus has done. Is that not what you believe? This is an opportunity. Didn't you dream of becoming a historian? This is a history, though it claims to be prophecy. Tell them what they have done, and if it serves the senators, it serves you, too."

Thus it was that Nicolaus the Damascene began to write prophecy, passing each page to a bribed guard as he finished it. His mind was vague and scattered, but writing kept him from falling over the edge of sanity. He wrote the truth, or at least as much of it as he could, in the guise of a sibyl, thinking back on the various books he'd scanned in Virgil's library and the tone of the prophets' voices.

"Then shall all declare that I am a true prophetess, oracle-singing, and yet a messenger with maddened soul. And when thou shalt come forward to the Books, thou shalt not tremble, and all things to come and things that were, ye shall know from our words," he wrote, pretending that these same words had been written centuries before.

The prophecies would be published as newly discovered, unearthed from an ancient ruin, scrolls found rolled into an amphora or entombed with some hero. They would be read aloud in the Forum and all across the country, drawing support away from Augustus and toward his foes. If the emperor would not deal rationally with Cleopatra, if he would not understand that he caged an immortal, then perhaps someone else would. She must be destroyed, and though Nicolaus did not know how to destroy her, he hoped that someone who read his words might. As for Sekhmet, Nicolaus could only hope that if Cleopatra were killed, the goddess would go back into oblivion, back to where she had been before they summoned her.

Nicolaus was not permitted to use Cleopatra's name—even oracles could not know everything—and so he named her "the widow."

He was not permitted to speak directly of Augustus, so he referred to him obliquely. *"And then shall come inexorable wrath upon Latin men. Three shall, by piteous fate, endamage Rome. And perish shall all men with their own houses, when from heaven shall flow a fiery cataract."*

Three men and the eye of Ra. Augustus, Antony, and Agrippa, he meant, though he might as well add himself amongst that group. Sekhmet, a flaming vengeance making her way across the heavens. They all would perish, and it was all of their fault. Antony for inciting Cleopatra into trading herself for his life, Augustus for warring against her in the first place, and Agrippa for serving as his general.

As he wrote, his mind chewed over the possibilities. Somewhere in his reading, somewhere in his books, there was an answer.

Immortals had been killed before, he knew it, though their deaths were portrayed only in myth. Hercules had used his sword to chop off forty-nine of the heads of his enemy, the Hydra, and then cauterized the wounds with fire to keep them from renewing. He'd buried the furiously immortal head deep below the ground on the road to Lerna, and placed a boulder over the spot. Poison seeped from it and into the darkness, but the Hydra lived now only in Hades. It had not come back to the surface. Thus far.

The thought of the Hydra spurred some memory deep within the historian's mind. He pressed his hands to his temples, searching for the connection. Some fragment read in Virgil's library, something in the tasks of Hercules. Deaths of immortals. The Hydra's venom.

Nicolaus looked down at his task and discovered that he had heedlessly signed the prophecy he'd been writing with his own name. He swore, dropping it on the floor. He would have to begin again.

He paused, still thinking, and at last, the idea he'd been searching for came swimming into the light of his consciousness.

He knew how to defeat the queen. Immortal to immortal. Chaos to chaos. There was a way.

≫ 5 ≪

The queen lives" went the refrain whispered in the streets of Rome. "Cleopatra has returned from the dead to kill the emperor."

The scrolls said as much. A newly published set of oracular texts informed the public that the fall of Rome was imminent, that *Despoina* had risen from her imprisonment, and that her anger at Augustus would destroy everything in the world.

A centurion read from the text, sitting beside a campfire on the shores of the Black Sea. *"And thou shalt be no more a widow,"* he said, and one of his young legionaries laughed.

"They only mean Cleopatra was a whore who went to our leader's bed after her husband killed himself," he said. "Trying to buy freedom for Egypt. Augustus likes a conquered woman, too, just like Caesar did before him. I was in Alexandria. I guarded the queen in her private chambers."

"How did you guard her?" another legionary snorted. "From your knees?"

"She was the one kneeling," the first legionary boasted.

The centurion looked sharply at them.

"These are ancient prophecies, god-given. Have some respect. Listen. *'But thy soul shalt cohabit with a man-eating lion, terrible, a furious warrior. And then shalt thou be happy, and among all men known; for thou shalt leave possessed of shameless soul.'"*

"What do you make of that?" another legionary asked, a feeling of unease creeping through his belly.

"Cleopatra is not a mortal woman, if she ever was. Some say she was a witch and that was how she got Mark Antony to do her bidding."

274

The company made a sign against witchcraft. Antony had been their idol, and then he had betrayed them. It would be a comfort if that had not been his fault. It would be a comfort if, in fact, Augustus, who was known to be no warrior, who had fled several battlefields, turned out to be a liar. Stranger things had happened in the history of Rome.

The commander read the rest of the prophecy.

"And thee, the stately, shall the encircling tomb receive, for he, the Roman king, shall place thee there, though thee be still amongst the living. Though thy life is gone, there will be something immortal living within thee. Though thy soul is gone, thy anger will remain, and thy vengeance will rise and destroy the cities of the Roman king."

He put the scroll down, his face grim.

"In Alexandria, I was with the emperor when we went into the mausoleum. The queen's body was not there, though we had carried it to the pyre and chained it in place three days earlier. We thought it had been stolen, but the emperor went pale. This prophecy says she lives, and I believe it. The prophecy says that Augustus has inflamed her wrath—"

"It doesn't say Augustus," one of the men interrupted.

"Destroy the cities of the *Roman king*," the commander said. "There is a plague, or haven't you heard? Everywhere but Rome. She is saving Rome for last."

The men stared into their campfire, sobered.

"Perhaps she saves Rome for something worse than plague," said the young legionary who had guarded Cleopatra.

Elsewhere in the new texts, the oracles implied that a return to the republic would save Rome. Messages began to be exchanged, from end to end of the country, from legion to legion, from commander to commander. Soon, the senators and their emissaries traveled to these distant legions, soliciting their support, working their way through country villages and ports, where the rumor of the emperor's misdeeds had already spread.

The new Sibylline prophecies did as the senators hoped they would.

An army constructed of legions that had once been loyal to Antony, and of legions that were commanded by allies of the seceding senators, began to rise.

⇒ 6 ⇐

Augustus sat in his chamber, staring out the window at the strange glow that remained on the horizon even in the dark. The night was live with shooting stars, and watching them cross the sky, and cross again, Augustus felt an irrational terror. He had been awake too long, sitting at the window too long. Marcus Agrippa had stayed away from his chambers since the battle at the Circus Maximus, and lately, his only company had been the priestess.

Chrysate practiced spells of binding, spells which, she told him, would serve to keep the queen under her power, but for now, it was best to keep the box under Roman guard, in the silver-lined room.

Augustus trusted Chrysate. Though perhaps not entirely. Strangely scented smoke trailed down the hallway, and when Chrysate kissed him, her hair smelled of burning balsam and damp sand, of honey and cinnamon. The smell reminded him of Egypt's tombs.

They had won, he told himself, but Augustus still could not sleep. He thought of Cleopatra slithering inside the silver box, twisting and looping around herself, and Antony, his eyes burning embers. Every night, he stared at the paintings on his ceiling, fearful of things he could not name. The fireball he'd seen streaking across the heavens, perhaps. The roars that still shook Rome. His servants called them thunder, but he knew better.

There were petitioners and senators, armies and advisors, and all of them demanded his attention. On the table beside him was a tall stack of oracular prophecies, discovered in a cave and newly unrolled from amphorae, along with a message from Agrippa stating that they must be read.

Augustus did not feel like reading.

Augustus had even summoned his favorite poet Virgil from Campania, but the man failed to bring him rest. Nothing Virgil said, no matter the beauty of the words, could keep Augustus from thinking about Cleopatra. The poet seemed to have a special liking for poems about Hades these days, and the verses only made Augustus think of Antony. At last, the emperor had dismissed his poet.

He poured theriac into his cup and drank. His original dosage of two drops had begun to seem ineffective, and now he poured it in equal proportion to his wine. He'd lost his appetite for food other than this. With each sip, he felt his twisting mind smoothed and relaxed.

In her chambers, Chrysate lit the fire. With the queen captured, with Selene in her possession, Chrysate should have been at her most powerful. Augustus had given the girl to Chrysate three days after the battle at the Circus Maximus, transferring her sleeping chamber to the one beside the priestess and telling Selene that she was to be an apprentice. But the girl was resistant to her spells. After her flight from the Circus Maximus, Selene had spent two days hidden somewhere in Rome, finally sighted by a centurion and brought back to the emperor's house. It should have been easy to woo her, but Selene looked at Chrysate with dark, suspicious eyes, and the priestess found herself scarcely able to accomplish the simplest things. She'd spent the past nights trying to communicate with Hecate, to no avail. Her goddess was still bound in the Underworld, and nothing Chrysate did brought clarity. The scry was blurry, everything bloody, but the future was invisible. Now that she had Cleopatra, she did not know what to do with her. There was no clear way to bind her, and the power contained within Cleopatra was inaccessible.

Had she captured the queen for nothing? Was she no longer linked with the goddess? Was there anything inside the silver box at all, or had it all been an illusion? Had the Northern witch tricked her? Did *she* have Cleopatra? Or did the Psylli? The box rested in its silver room, and Chrysate left it there. At least if something went wrong, Cleopatra would be trapped in the second prison.

Chrysate opened her hand and looked at the green holding stone. She shut her eyes, clenching her fist, and said the name of the man who was tied to the *synochitus*. She might send a message to Hecate through him. He could pass through Hades and find the goddess.

Her call should have brought him, but it did not. Her powers had ebbed too far, she assumed. She could not find Antony, and she could not understand what had happened.

She did not dare go to the silver room and open the box to find out. She needed Hecate if she was to use that power, and to summon Hecate, she needed royal blood.

She needed Selene to submit. Every day, Chrysate grew weaker. The effort of keeping herself disguised was wearing on her. Finally, the deteriorating condition of her body had become too obvious. The spell she was about to perform was necessary. If she appeared as she truly was, Selene would never give herself over willingly, and that would invalidate all of Chrysate's efforts.

Beauty was a tremendous part of her currency, both with Augustus and with Selene. Who would trust her as she truly was?

She scarcely trusted herself.

Groaning with effort, she opened a small leather pouch and pulled from it a bronze cauldron large enough to hold a boar. She settled the cauldron atop the flame, and tugged open the pouches that held the supplies she'd brought from her cave. Crystalline sand from the beach at the end of the world, and a pinch of frost gathered from beneath the shine of a thousand-night moon. The feathered wings of a screech owl, struggling against her hands and threatening to fly from her even as she crushed them into the cauldron. Nectar from a star torn from the sky one night long ago, when Chrysate was only a girl. The powdered liver of a stag that had once been a prince. The entrails of a man who had once been a wolf. The eyeless head of a crow, which opened its dry black beak and spoke to her as she brought it from the bag.

"Murderer," it said.

She no longer listened to it. She brought out a dry olive branch and stirred the mixture, letting it come to a boil over the fire, and as she stirred, the branch grew glossy green leaves. Chrysate let a bit of the contents of the cauldron boil over, and where they landed, the stone floor became grass, and flowers began to bloom.

It was ready.

She removed her gown, shuddering at the condition of her flesh. She was withered. She'd let it go much too long, trying to conserve her power, trying to contact Hecate, and it was a miracle Augustus had not noticed. Of course, his theriac had something to do with that. She had introduced a few ingredients to it. Nothing that would disable the man permanently. She did not seek to topple Rome. She sought to use Rome's power, and for that, Rome needed to be stable. Selene, on the other hand, seemed to notice everything. Chrysate reassured herself. After this spell, Selene would not see through her. Things would be easier.

She lifted her knife and, wincing, pressed the point into her flesh just below one ear. She drew it beneath her chin, and a long wound appeared across her throat. Blood ran in torrents from it, thick scarlet down the pale skin. The witch's eyes rolled back, and she swayed before the cauldron, blood pooling at her feet.

She wavered, and at last, she slumped forward, her body slipping over the lip of the cauldron as she fell.

The boiling potion closed over her head.

The surface of the cauldron bubbled for a time, dark and tarry, and beneath the liquid, nothing moved.

⇒ 7 ⇐

Cleopatra and Antony walked hand in hand toward the entrance to the city of the dead. Birch trees quavered around them, pale things veined with black, like the ivory bones of giants. They were followed by thousands of shades, all of them murmuring quietly, all of them hungering.

Cleopatra shuddered as they drew closer to the doorway, possessed by a fear she had not imagined herself capable of feeling. She heard something, a faint echo of Sekhmet's roar, calling her back from the Underworld. A glimmer of wrath and hunger, a god's voice calling down to a place that did not worship her. She thought of her children left behind in the world above, and then, in spite of herself, she thought of Sekhmet, alone and starving.

Cleopatra looked at Antony and found herself unable to speak. Every part of her insisted that, without her soul, she did not belong in any Underworld. She could scarcely keep from turning and running to the river, so great was the certainty that she should go back.

At the same time, she knew that her own world did not want her. In that world, she was trapped in a silver box, and all around her, suddenly, she could feel its walls.

"I shouldn't be here," she said. She could not say that she yearned for the thing she hated. She could not say that half her heart was Sekhmet's, that she craved the darkness and fury she'd left on Earth. The vengeance and bloodshed, the destruction. How could she desire those things over this? Hades was still and cold, but she was free. How could she long for her enemies?

"We are here together," Antony said, holding her shoulders. "You are safe with me."

He was the only person who had ever seen her heart. Perhaps he was the only person she had ever trusted.

Her husband pulled her into his arms, his hands touching her beneath the ragged covering. She stretched her fingers tentatively to run them over his chest. His wound was still there, and she could see it, though she could not feel it when she touched him. He lifted her off the ground to kiss her. She caught herself thinking that nothing had changed, that none of this had ever happened but had been merely a terrible dream.

His lips were cold, but they were his, and she lost herself, forgetting everything, her body against his, her hands in his hair, the curls twisting in her fingers, the coarse silvering strands.

"It is not over," Antony told her, kissing her eyelids, and she had a flash of memory, back to Alexandria. She had said the same words to him. It felt like centuries ago. "We are not finished."

"You will go to the end with me?" she asked. "Whatever it is? Whatever we must do?"

"I will not leave you," he whispered. "I never have. How could I?"

She kissed him, feeling his hands caressing her, feeling his arms supporting her. She could forget the echoing sounds she heard, calling her back to Rome. She could forget the pain and hunger for now.

Antony was hers again, and as she lay back on the frozen grass, his lips on her throat, she knew that she would do anything to keep him safe. Snow fell above them, stars of ice disappearing as they touched the ground. The tree branches were heavy with frost, and her husband held her tightly as they made love, no space between them.

He knew what she was, and he had chosen her.

She felt the trees leaning in to cover them, and the grasses bending to offer them comfort.

The wandering spirits of Hades drifted closer, drawn by the sudden warmth, a fire lit in the midst of a wintry world. Soon, Cleopatra and Antony were surrounded by hundreds of pale shades, their eyes large and wondering, stunned that there could be love in the midst of darkness, that there could be lovers entwined so, here in the heart of the land of the dead.

At last, her sight dissolved into a thousand stars, her head falling back into the snow, her body liquid around him, and he moaned, moving faster now.

"I love you," he said, holding her face in his hands so that he could see her eyes.

Neither of them were whole, Cleopatra knew, but they were together, and together they would petition the lord and lady of Hades.

They would try to reclaim her soul.

☞ 8 ☜

A grippa marched down the corridor to the Northern witch's chamber, the scrap of treasonous prophecy clutched in his hand.

Nicolaus, it was signed. Agrippa had his spies, in the prisons and in the merchant houses, in the legions and even in the brothels; never mind that he himself never entered the places. One of Agrippa's men had delivered him this shred of papyrus, claiming that the prisoner had been writing piles of the stuff.

The Damascene had finally surfaced.

He'd been arrested by Agrippa's own men, the general discovered, on the night of the venatio, but in the chaos, no one had said anything about it.

Agrippa had searched Rome for days, seeking something stronger to fight with, forging new swords and testing new poisons, and all the while, the man who had given Cleopatra her power waited in Rome's own dungeon.

Now Agrippa needed the assistance of the seiðkona. Auðr might not be a Roman, but she was powerful, and he knew that she was not on the same side as Chrysate. The Greek witch had told him so herself. That was enough for Agrippa at present.

His men had carried Auðr up the hillside after the battle at the Circus Maximus, and since then, she had stayed in her rooms, coughing. The doctors had been unable to do anything for her. Agrippa prayed that she had enough strength and will to help him now. He was shocked when he saw her, as limp as a rag, slumped in her chair, her cheeks sunken and her lips pale blue.

Still, she looked up at him with her fierce silver eyes and nodded. She picked up her distaff from the corner. It should have been taken from her after the battle, and Agrippa wondered how she had gained possession, why no one had reported it. She turned her distaff sideways, and looked at his arm, splinted since the battle. His ribs still pained him as well, bruised and cracked, no doubt, but nothing to be done about that. Agrippa had fought in many battles over the years, and pain followed him wherever he went.

Auðr shook her head, touched his arm, and spun the distaff briefly, and with that, the pains in his arm and chest were gone. Agrippa tried not to be amazed, but he was. He thought for a moment about what it would be like to go into battle with such a sorceress, but then he snorted. This was not the Roman way, and he would not start being something else now.

"Thank you," he said, and that was all.

With Auðr, the general descended to the prisons.

Many of his former men cried his name as he passed, amazed that he still lived after what they'd seen in the arena. He walked past the traitors destined for execution, the soldiers who'd risen to Antony's commands and fought against Agrippa's men. All of them seemed to have lost their minds, in any case. At last, Agrippa discovered the Damascene huddled in the corner of his cell, trying to conceal himself in a shadow.

"You are a servant to Cleopatra," Agrippa said, and Nicolaus shook his head.

"No longer."

"You smuggled her into the city. Do you know how to kill her?"

Nicolaus was startled.

"Is she escaped? Where is she? What has she done?"

"She is still caged, or so the priestess swears," said Agrippa. "But I have looked into her eyes. I know what she is capable of."

"I have only an idea of what to do," Nicolaus said. "And that idea is a myth, not a certainty."

From behind Agrippa stepped Auðr. Nicolaus backed farther into the corner of his cell, convinced that she was a death bringer. He'd seen her working in the arena, her hands spinning, the light of her power surrounding her. His legs had grown spindly, and he doubted he could run when his cell door opened, but he planned to try.

She peered through the bars at Nicolaus.

Agrippa watched her fingers tracing complicated patterns in the air, winding them about that wooden spindle. He opened the door of Nicolaus's cell for her to enter.

Somehow, Nicolaus found that he could not move. Her eyes were strangely hypnotic. He felt himself tilting, and she put the flat of her palm against his forehead. Her brow furrowed, and she cocked her head as though listening.

His mind sped unwillingly through the events of his life, from his childhood to the present, dwelling on Alexandria. He felt it happening but could not control it. He watched as he paged through scrolls, filling in gaps in the text with his own inventions. He watched as he taught the summoning spell to Cleopatra and as he discovered her in the hold of the ship, the child in her hands, the dead slaves at her feet. At last, she came to his revelation. The Hydra.

He lurched backward, jerking himself away from her touch, but she'd seen enough to condemn him or save him. He did not know which she planned.

She nodded to Agrippa, and the man took the scholar roughly by the shoulder and steered him from the cell, up endless passages and finally into the light of afternoon.

"You will tell us what you know, myth or not," Agrippa said. "You will be of use to Rome."

"There is a temple of Apollo, located at Krimissa," Nicolaus stammered. "There we may find what we need to defeat an immortal."

"May?" asked Agrippa.

"We will," Nicolaus corrected. "Or so the legends say. What we need will be guarded, but it is there."

Auðr nodded, satisfied. This was her doing, or some of it. Something to destroy Sekhmet, something to wound her and make her retreat back to Egypt, and beyond. Back into the vault of the sky. She had not known what the historian knew, and now that she did, she directed all her strength to accomplishing it. If there was a weapon, it would be found. The fates of Agrippa and Nicolaus wrapped around her distaff, and she directed them to Krimissa.

9

Usem did not bother to ask for admission to Augustus's chambers. The wind had returned to him for the first time in days, bringing an ice storm to his chamber, and news that the plague had traveled still farther, that Sekhmet gloried at the edge of the sky, and now his mind was filled with his own responsibilities. He threw open Augustus's door and found the emperor dozing in his chair, clearly drunk. Augustus sat up, startled but not on guard, and Usem snorted with disgust. The man was no warrior. He was scarcely a man. Even as Usem looked at him, Augustus drank another draft of his potion, the theriac. The smell of the potion put the Psylli off. It smelled like witchcraft, like Chrysate's influence.

"There is a plague," Usem said. "It has broken out in the villages surrounding Rome, from one end of the country to the other, even to Sicily."

"I have no help for plague," Augustus scoffed. "You are the sorcerer, not I, and to cure a plague requires magic. It must run its course and kill whom it will. The countryside has always been vulnerable."

"The plague is traveling," said Usem. "It is not merely a summer sickness but something of the spirit world."

Augustus suddenly looked more alert. "Cleopatra?"

"Cleopatra may be captured, but the Old One is not. My wife has seen the goddess, and she has seen the plague traveling around the world at Sekhmet's pleasure. You might see it yourself if you went outdoors and looked at the sky. Have you not seen the flashes of light at the edge of the world? The stars streaking across the heavens? Surely, even the Romans do not think such things meaningless. I ask leave to go, assemble my people, and fight. The queen should have been destroyed when we captured her. Now it will be harder. I thought Rome shared my goals, but perhaps you do not. You keep the queen imprisoned, but the goddess she serves is more dangerous than she. What do you plan to do with her?"

"That is not for you to know," Augustus said, though he himself wondered the same thing. What was Chrysate doing in her room? "You will stay in Rome. If I travel, you will travel with me. You will be my general if Agrippa will not. You said that you would defend Rome, and I hold you to your word."

"I came here willingly," Usem said. "Do not waste my goodwill."

"I am the emperor," Augustus replied, his jaw tensing. "Do not waste my time."

"You waste your own time," Usem said. "And there is little of it left. If we do not go out in force to fight this, it will be too late. You bought a warrior when you agreed to hire me. Let me do my work."

He stalked from the room, and Augustus sat for a moment, uncertain, frustrated, before he rose to his feet and went in search of Chrysate. At least, she could reassure him that Cleopatra was still safe in her box.

The priestess's room was empty, the windows open, and the bed unrumpled. Augustus felt suddenly as though he had lost months since the battle. The hearth was lit, and a large bronze cauldron was upon it. Augustus did not recall ever having seen it there before.

He took a step toward it.

The room was very still, and Augustus suddenly felt terrified. There was nothing to fear. She was not here. Then he looked down at the floor. His slippers were soaked with blood.

There was something inside the cauldron. Something large.

Something moving.

Augustus could not find his voice. He had given her Selene. What had she done?

"No," he whispered.

With a screaming gasp, something rose from the cauldron, pale and streaming with dark water, naked, and with her hair plastered to her back.

Augustus fell backward onto the floor as Chrysate emerged from the boiling liquid, her skin clear and perfect as a statue's, her eyes startled at his presence.

He turned and sprinted from the room, his mind spinning, his heart racing. Witchcraft. Blood. A boiled corpse, or at least, that was what he was sure he'd seen, and then—

Perfect and young, Chrysate coming out of the fire. How had he forgotten her powers? She was not human, and he'd been sharing his bed with her. He nearly convulsed with horror.

"Agrippa!" Augustus shouted, running through the corridor. "Marcus Agrippa!"

This was Agrippa's fault. He had brought the witch to Rome, and now—

What had he seen? He didn't know. He should never have used witches. He should never have trusted witches. He bolted theriac directly from its bottle, desperate for calm. His heart was beating too quickly, his breath coming too fast.

"What is it?" The general arrived more quickly than Augustus had expected. "I was on my way to you," Agrippa said. "I have news of a weapon, a way to destroy Cleopatra—"

"Chrysate has done something, killed someone. I saw her, at the fire, in the fire—"

"What do you mean?"

"The silver box is gone," Augustus stammered. His mind felt tangled and drunk, and suddenly he was dizzy. Was she working a spell on him?

"It is not gone. I have just seen it. The guards watch it all night and all day. My own men."

"Then perhaps Cleopatra is escaped from it—"

"The queen is captured." Agrippa's face was suspicious, but for a moment, Augustus saw terror flash across it. "Or so I believed. Tell me I am not wrong."

"Usem told me that there is a plague," Augustus interrupted. "All over Italy. Everywhere but Rome."

"There are always plagues," Agrippa replied. "It's summer."

"The plague comes from Cleopatra's vengeance. She's missing," Augustus insisted. "And Chrysate has done something monstrous—" But even as he said it, Chrysate appeared behind him, opening the curtains of his bed.

"She does not seem to be missing," Agrippa said. "Did you forget who shared your bed?"

Augustus was terrified. She had not been there. Had she? Had he gone mad? She was wearing only a flimsy silk gown, and he could see everything through it. Her hair was still wet from the cauldron.

"I am here," Chrysate said. "I have been with you all night, as you should certainly know. If Cleopatra is missing, you are the one who has charge of her. Your guards guard her."

Augustus nearly screamed. He could not understand what was happening. He felt dizzy, and his slippers were still soaked in blood. He held one out to show Agrippa, and for a moment, the general looked startled.

"The kitchen slaughtered a chicken and made a soup for me," Chrysate said. "He tread in the blood. Do you not remember, Augustus? You are not well. If I were you, I would summon a physician."

She spun on her heel, leaving the room.

The general's lip curled in disgust.

"If you're looking for a creature who might cause a plague, I suggest you look into your own bed. You might look to your witch."

"I *am* looking to her! You must go out and fight this plague!" Augustus insisted.

Agrippa slammed his fists on Augustus's desk, tipping the theriac over.

"I AM A SOLDIER!" he shouted. "I wage war against men, not gods! Not Fates! Not witches! Not curses invented by drunkards! You sit here in your study, drinking your potion and wallowing in your fears. Your uncle would be ashamed of you. You do not rule. You rave!"

Augustus sputtered, stunned. Agrippa had never spoken so to him.

"How dare you?" he managed. "I will have you crucified!"

"I speak as your friend. There are threats out there. There are threats *in here*! Real threats. I will fight them for you, but you cannot ask me to fight the invisible. There are rumors in the streets that you've gone mad, and prophecies that Rome is cursed and doomed. I delivered them to you a week ago, and have you read them? You have not. What have you done? You stay here all day and all night with your witch and your drug. Your power grows weaker every day."

Agrippa paused, breathing heavily.

"I am done," he said. "Do what you will with me, but do *something*!"

"Get out of my sight," Augustus screamed. "I am governing Rome! You have no idea what I do!"

"With pleasure. I have a city to defend." Agrippa smacked his hand against the theriac, and the bottle sprayed across the room. "If you care anything for that city, I suggest you stop drinking this poison. It makes you blind."

He slammed the door as he left.

Augustus's heart raced, his brain straining at the base of his skull. A blazing light began to flash and rotate before him, like a sun newborn in the confines of his room. His eyes rolled backward, and the lioness approached him in the crimson darkness, her golden eyes slitted, her breasts bared, and her fingers placed on a bowstring. She looked at him with such knowing. Such understanding. She was the only one who knew what he had been through.

He should give himself to her, that was it. He should give Rome to her— He heard himself shout, and his eyes flew open. He dunked his head in a basin of cool water, raising his face from the liquid only when it felt that he might drown. In the polished glass above the basin, he saw his pallor, and a thin thread of blood trickling from his nose onto his lips.

He was losing himself.

Augustus sat down carefully, his legs shaking. Was Agrippa right? And the Psylli? He'd said the same thing.

He stood and went to the sword that hung above his mantel. He took it from the wall and swung it experimentally. It had been years since he'd fought. He was not sure he remembered how to do it. He looked at the pool of theriac on the floor. Had he hallucinated what he saw in Chrysate's chamber?

He looked at his bloodied slippers. No. He had not.

Agrippa was wrong about the theriac, a simple medicine, but still, he'd become too used to its effects. He needed all his strength now, all his intellect. He would significantly lessen his dose, wean himself from it.

He swung the sword again, his arms shaking. He buckled on his armor. It was heavy and clammy against his skin.

Augustus peered out the window, squinting in the sunlight. Where would he go? Who would go with him?

⇒10⇐

A ferocious howling began, the sound of thousands of dogs left out in a freezing wind or of wolves high in the hills, making their way into a city full of children. All around, there were ghostly sounds of snapping jaws and crunching bones. The wandering dead covered their ears and fled from the region.

Hades was an echoing vault, and each sound was magnified, bouncing over and across the river and back to Cleopatra and Antony.

"Where are we?" Cleopatra asked.

"Hecate is near," Antony said. "Those are her hounds."

Cleopatra turned her head slowly in the direction of the noise and saw a sight that chilled her. A tremendous form, her skin veined with the darkness of a stormy sea, lay on her side nearly covered with brambles and vines, a few hundred lengths away from them. A thick chain was wrapped about her ankle. As Cleopatra looked, the goddess's eyes opened slightly, a flickering. All around her, ghostly dogs leapt and snapped their jaws.

Cleopatra felt repulsed, but also something else.

"Who jails her?"

"The gods," Antony said. "She interfered."

"*I was a queen, too,*" a soft voice said, the sound echoing around them, rattling and hungry. "*Do not be so proud.*"

"Don't look at her," Antony told her. Cleopatra could not help herself.

She shuddered, but Antony strode on past the apparition, Cleopatra's hand in his.

"The witch who imprisoned me serves that goddess. She sought to use you and Sekhmet to bring Hecate up from the Underworld," Antony said. "To release her and upturn Hades."

"How would she do that?"

"She would sacrifice you," Antony said. "The longer we stay here, the more likely it is she will get her way. She still has your body. It is only luck that she does not know how to kill you."

"No one knows how to kill me," Cleopatra said. "I do not. Do you?"

"I don't *want* to kill you," Antony said. "I am the only one who feels that way."

At last, before them, crouching in the darkness at the mouth of a cave, was an enormous black dog with three heads, its throat wreathed with a tangle of hooded serpents.

The dog's eyes glowed red, and its fur shone with a dark and oily iridescence. Each of its teeth was as long as a ritual dagger, and it tossed its heads, rotating each one to look upon Cleopatra. The creature was as tall as an elephant, and its tremendous body filled the entrance to the cavern. It snorted and slavered, and its fur rippled with muscle and sharp bones. Its eyes were as bright as flames.

Cleopatra felt her body flexing, twisting, and preparing itself for battle.

"She does not live," Antony informed Cerberus. "And we will pass. You will clear the way for us."

Growling, the dog inhaled the air about Cleopatra's face.

Cleopatra felt her own jaws stretching into a hiss, whether serpent or feline, she was uncertain. Antony looked at her, clearly startled.

She gazed into the eyes of the snakes twined about the dog's throat and spoke with them in a language she did not know. She felt the empty chamber where her heart had been, filling with a rippling endless-tongued chant.

A version of the song that had flung her own body into the dust at the arena poured from her mouth. She was mistress of this new language, as easily as she'd always understood foreign tongues. The words were hers now.

"Give me your everything," the song went. *"You belong to me. We are one thing, and we have the same longings. We are one thing, and we have the same desires. Sing with me, serpent children, dance with me. We are one."*

The dog bared its teeth as the serpents about his throat tightened their grip on him, twisting and constricting his movements.

"Kill him," she told the serpents, for this was a creature in opposition to herself.

Antony gripped her arm, distracting her from her task.

"Persephone and Hades will not take kindly to that," he told her. "We should not anger them before we ask for their benevolence."

The tremendous dog slipped to the floor of the cavern, a high whine coming from its mouths, his six eyes closing as the snakes twisted about him.

"Let him sleep," she told the snakes. *"Let him dream. Do not let him die."*

The serpents reluctantly loosened their hold, and she sang the last notes of their song as she and Antony climbed over the sleeping beast, feeling its rattling breath and sighs.

"That was well done," Antony said, but Cleopatra still felt the violence that had nearly overtaken her. It receded only with effort. And the sight of the goddess, chained, had reminded her too much of herself. Her own chain was long now, and she could not feel Sekhmet, but how much time did she have before her mistress called again?

The sound of babies crying for their mothers stopped Cleopatra in the center of the passageway, brutally reminded of her children.

"Where have you taken me?" she asked.

"We must pass through the Cavern of Infants to reach the rest of Hades," Antony said. "There is nothing to be done. For some, this is more frightening than anything else they see here, but you have seen many things. This is not the worst of them. Take my hand."

They were surrounded by shades of newborns who'd been taken outdoors and left exposed on the rubbish heaps of Rome, ready forage for wild dogs. This was the fate of infants unacknowledged by patriarchs, even those of noble families. It was perfectly legal. The fortunate were plucked up from the street and sold into the slave trade. The less fortunate died unmourned and were sent here, to a nation of dead babies, an endless nursery of weeping infants as far as the queen could see.

Cleopatra felt her chest contract. The shades were nearly all daughters.

Antony pushed her along, but she looked back, aching in the places that remained her own, mourning the dead. Their tiny hands stretched up, grasping nothing. Their lips moved, suckling at nothing. There were no nursemaids in the Cavern of Infants, no caressing arms, no tiny carved lions, no language tutors. These ghost babies would never walk, nor talk.

"We must continue," Antony told her. "There is nothing to be done. The Underworld has its own ways."

"Wrong ways," Cleopatra informed him, furious.

"It grants you the favor of passage."

"They are in Rome. Do you think of them?" she asked Antony. "Alexander and Ptolemy, Selene? They are with Augustus."

"There is nothing to be done. They live, and we are shadows," he said.

"They do *not* live, not all of them," she said. "Some of them may be here. Caesarion died after you did. The Romans cut my son down in the square."

"I miss them as much as you do," he said. "Both the living and the dead. But now all we can do is save you."

Cleopatra's sorrow grew at the thought of Caesarion wandering alone through this Roman Underworld. Perhaps this was wrong, she thought with a flash of hopefulness. Perhaps he was in the Duat. He had died in Egypt. His mother was Egyptian. Perhaps it had worked the way it should have. Perhaps his pure heart had been weighed. Perhaps he was in the Beautiful West, safe there.

And so they went from the infants, and through the nameless suicides, through the court of Minos, where innocents executed on the testimony of liars were tried and tried again by juries of their dead fellows.

After days and nights of walking, Cleopatra and Antony passed into the fields of mourning, arranged like beautiful gardens with paths paved in tiny fragments of bone and blooming black roses and myrtle trees. Those who had died of love wandered here, brokenhearted and betrayed still, drowning in tears and inflamed by lust despite the blankness on their faces.

"Is this where you live?" Cleopatra asked Antony, and he shook his head, though his eyes, when she looked into them, seemed to slant away from her.

"We must go farther," he said.

Cleopatra wondered how long they had been walking through the Underworld, and how long her body had been caged in the silver box above. She wondered what would happen to them when all this was finished. She could think of no happy ending.

He brushed his ghostly fingers over her skin.

"When the dead are called from Hades," he said, "the living pound their hands on the earth so that we may hear them grieving us. When the dead are called from Hades, the living pour blood into the soil, so that we may drink of life. We thirst. We hunger. We are too far from the living in this place. The longer we stay, the more I fade, and the less I am Antony."

He brushed his lips over her hand, and she felt a chill.

"You are still Cleopatra," he said. "Still my wife, but I am of Hades now."

Cleopatra looked at him, feeling her universe collapsing all over again. The gods of the dead held their citizens tightly. His skin, which had been brown with sun, was paler the longer she looked on him. She could see the trees through his breastplate.

"Then we must leave here together," she told him. "Hurry. We must travel to the chamber where the gods dwell, is that not what you told me?"

"To Persephone," he said, and his voice wavered. "We are running out of time."

Cleopatra took his hand in hers and held it as best she could.

Together they ran through the ghostly battlefields of the improperly buried dead, where some men saluted him and other men cursed him.

Together they ran across roads of bone, and all around them, the world was winter, though in Rome the sun beat down on the city, and outside Rome, the countryside sweltered, the Slaughterer traveling from village to village, from temple to temple, killing and sending endless shades down from the summer and into the snow.

⇒11⇐

Agrippa and his small band of men rode south to Krimissa and to the temple of Apollo, dedicated in the time of Troy by the warrior Philoctetes. All of Italy was founded on myth, and when Nicolaus had told him the tale of what this place concealed, he'd nodded in recognition. He knew the story. It was part of the living and proud history of Rome, like the hut of Romulus.

Nicolaus was not with Agrippa's group. With a sword, the historian would be a danger to no one but himself. Instead, Agrippa had left him to watch over Augustus, enlisting the seiðkona as well. All that was necessary was that Augustus stay in the residence. The emperor was weakened by the potion he insisted on consuming. It would take little effort, even for a scholar and an ancient, to keep him stationary.

Agrippa held out little hope that anyone could keep Chrysate away from Augustus, but he hoped that Augustus might be tantalized by the historian introduced as a new biographer. The emperor fancied himself a writer of some skill, though he typically wrote only rhymes. Agrippa smiled in spite of himself, thinking of it as they rode around a promontory. He felt better, now that he was out of Rome. He was doing something about the problem. Never mind that he was the only one who was. At least Cleopatra was no longer under Chrysate's control. The room she was jailed in was lined at every seam with silver, and the box she was inside was wrapped in silver chain. Agrippa's most trusted men guarded it.

The Psylli had come to him before he left, and asked to go with him to Krimissa, but even after the battle at the Circus Maximus, he was no Roman soldier. Usem could not possibly be as well trained as Agrippa's own men, and he did not seem likely to follow orders. Agrippa had left him, instead, guarding the silver room. If Chrysate tried to use magic, Usem would know it.

At last, the temple was in view, and Agrippa's smile faded.

From below, the building shone in the late-afternoon sun, placed at the top of a spiraling cliff and nearly inaccessible by road. Agrippa looked up at it, nervous.

It was what he wanted, though, he could not deny that. He'd prayed for a solution, and the historian had given it to him.

Agrippa directed his company to wait for nightfall, and when it was fully dark, they rode hooded up the hillside, approaching the temple from the rear. The horses had to place their muffled hooves carefully, and a journey that under better conditions should have taken but a few minutes took well over an hour. The darkness was well used, however. Agrippa did not wish the temple's inhabitants to have advance warning of the soldiers' approach.

He hoped to do things peacefully, but he did not expect this would be the case.

The temple guarded a prize, or so Nicolaus swore. Weapons that would kill an immortal, that would fight against magic. They would be fatal to Cleopatra as well as to Chrysate. Chaos to fight chaos.

Agrippa adjusted his armor and ran his hand over his shaven head, smoothing nonexistent hairs. The horses crept onward up the hillside path, and the warriors of Rome sat tall in their saddles, the shine of their armor covered by dark cloaks. This was by no means the worst thing they had done in service to their leader.

Agrippa signaled, and his men dismounted to approach the gate. They ran their fingers across the stone wall, feeling for cracks in the mortar. One legionary began to climb, fitting his fingers into the stone.

A hoof slipped on a rock, and a ringing note sounded in the silence. Agrippa froze, directing his men to draw their blades.

After a few moments, a man opened the door slowly. This priest was not a problem, a crippled ancient with clouded blue eyes, but he was flanked by a younger companion, a dark-skinned man with a piercing gaze.

"I am Marcus Agrippa, and these are my men," Agrippa announced. "We travel on behalf of the emperor." They did not, of course. The emperor was in no condition to know anything about this journey.

"Greetings," the younger priest said. "We've been watching you come up the hill since sunset. You do not travel as discreetly as you imagine."

Agrippa straightened his shoulders. He was not as skilled as he had once been, or these priests were privileged with unearthly information.

"Your emperor calls on you," Agrippa informed him. "He asks that you provide him a service."

"We are simple men," the priest replied. "We can set you a table with what little food and drink we possess. You are welcome to bed here."

"It is not food and drink we require," Agrippa said. "It is not sleep."

The man looked steadily at him, a half smile on his face.

Agrippa began to wonder if he would need to kill him before entering the temple. He had no way of knowing how many were behind the walls, however. Such a killing might be less than advisable. He also had no idea of the whereabouts of the item he sought. It would be an unfortunate errand should all the priests become indisposed, leaving their treasure still hidden.

"No," the man said at last. "Warriors of Rome, I see that you call for more than a meal. I see that you call for the impossible. Is that not what your emperor does? He plays with fire, does he not?" The expression on the priest's face was unreadable. Was he mocking the empire?

Agrippa was uncertain, but at last the priest opened the gate of the temple and beckoned them in.

"Welcome to our fire, then, meager though it be. Sheathe your swords. This is a sacred place, and there is no use for them here."

Agrippa glanced up reflexively as he passed through the gates, and saw the arrows nudging out of windows and cracks in the rock. Bows aimed at him and his men. It was good that he hadn't acted in haste. They guarded their treasure. Agrippa felt oddly cheered.

He noted the muscles rippling in the arms of even the stable boy. He assessed the elder priest who'd first opened the gate and decided that perhaps the man was not as decrepit as he had initially appeared. The priest's walking stick seemed to conceal a blade, and the hunched posture he'd affected when opening the gate had evolved into a loose-limbed stride.

Agrippa pretended that he neither saw nor minded the villains aiming at him. He signaled silently to his men, and they rode into the temple grounds quiet, calm, and in absolute peace. They would act when Agrippa directed them and no sooner. These men were seasoned warriors, and they trusted their commander.

A marble statue of the warrior Philoctetes, grimacing in pain, the bow of Hercules in his hands, stretched over the entrance to the temple. The statue's leg was wrapped in bandages, and his wounded foot was raised off the ground. There was an inscription, which stoked Agrippa's heart into a secret, joyful fire.

> *Here lies Philoctetes, Hero of Troy,*
> *and inheritor of the poisoned arrows of Hercules, envenomed with the poison of the conquered Hydra.*
> *Warrior, fall down and weep for the death of Chiron, the immortal, killed by these same arrows.*
> *Fall down and weep for Hercules, killed by this venom.*
> *Sing hymns to the bravery of Philoctetes, who suffered ten years, wounded by Hercules' gift.*
> *Let these arrows never again be released from their bow,*
> *but guard them with your own mortal lives.*

Another statue was placed just inside the doorway, this one depicting the tremendous centaur Chiron, pierced in the leg with an arrow, his agonized face lifelike enough to startle the men as they passed by it in the near darkness. The centaur's blue glass eyes dripped marble tears as he tried to pull the arrow from his body. Agrippa shuddered as he passed beside it, feeling the unpleasant cool of the statue brushing against his bare arm.

The priests led the soldiers down a tight passageway and out into an inner courtyard where a table was already laid.

Agrippa smiled. His adversaries were charming. They seated themselves and beckoned for the small group of soldiers to join them. They took the first bites of the food, knowing that the soldiers would suspect poison.

Agrippa ate heartily. It was rare to be away from his commander. He found that he preferred it. Augustus had altered tremendously in the past months, and Agrippa mistrusted his friend's instincts. The food here was simple but good, and it reminded him of better days. He sat back from the table when he had taken his fill.

"You will give us what we came for," he said, and moved his hand to signal his soldiers. He heard the sound of arrows being fitted, of bowstrings being drawn.

He then heard the rushing noise of an arrow flying. It embedded itself in the table, directly before his plate. It had not been shot to kill but to warn.

"Why should we surrender our holding to you?" the elder priest asked. His eyes were no longer clouded but bright.

"And why should I not kill you?" Agrippa asked the priest, pulling a concealed dagger from its sheathe against his thigh and swiftly drawing it beneath the old man's chin, not to cut his throat but to warn the other priests. Why did Agrippa's men not move? What delayed their hands?

A thin trickle of blood made its way down from the blade. A scratch.

It was then that Agrippa felt his own throat begin to constrict.

O utside the temple walls, three men in homespun cloaks watched the gate. The smallest of the three fit his gloved fingers into the spaces in the stone. He hauled himself carefully up the wall, his muscles wobbling with exertion.

His companions, a younger man with ink-stained fingers and saddle-weary thighs after three days' hard riding from Rome, and a tall man, his dark skin nearly invisible in the shadows, hesitated for a moment and then, breathing deeply, followed the emperor into the temple.

⇒12⇐

Chrysate crouched on her haunches, nursing a flame and pinching a lump of beeswax in her fingers. Now that Augustus was finally gone, she was at liberty to cast the final portions of her love spell. Selene would relent. She'd already cast the rudiments, with the birds and flowers who sang for the child a nonstop melody, a trance-inducing chant, but Selene had managed to resist most of them. She would not resist this, and now that Chrysate had renewed herself, she was strong enough to perform it. She shuddered. It was exceedingly unpleasant that Augustus had seen her coming out of the cauldron, but she'd dealt with that well enough, throwing herself through the shadows and into his bedchamber, concealing herself there. The theriac had made the emperor uncertain. She'd merely emphasized it, and it had yielded a happy outcome. Augustus had left Rome shortly thereafter, no doubt because of his concern over his sanity.

Already tonight, Chrysate had slipped into the silver room, past the guards. The Psylli had been the only true barrier. Had he been guarding the room, she might have had more trouble, but he'd departed with Augustus. Now she had the silver box containing Cleopatra. She felt more confident by the moment. Why had she been so afraid? All she needed was Selene. It would work. It had to. For a moment, only a moment, but it was enough, she'd been able to see Hecate in the scry, chained still but stronger than she had been.

Chrysate sculpted the wax into the form of a young girl, her bosom and waist newly curving but her limbs still childlike. She entwined a long black hair into the figure's flesh, twisting the strand about the figure's wrists, and binding them behind the girl's back. She sang as she did this, a wordless incantation in a voice by turns rough and silken.

When the figure and spell were nearly complete, Chrysate pulled a golden pin from her braids and stabbed the doll through the heart. It opened its waxen mouth and gasped. It stretched out its waxen arms and writhed on the floor, pinned like a butterfly.

"*No love but mine,*" Chrysate said in Greek, stroking the figure with her fingertips. "*No heart but mine. No mother, no father, no husband, no lover.*"

She caressed the doll, and the figure arched like a cat under her touch.

"*None but I will have you,*" Chrysate told the figure.

The witch stabbed it through the heart once more, and the figure curled about the pin, clutching the metal to her breast. Chrysate smiled. Spells such as this one had many purposes, all of them sweet.

C leopatra's daughter woke suddenly from dreams of flower-strewn fields. The flowers had been the color of smoke, and the grass like sharp reeds. She'd walked barefoot up a long cliffside path, her eyes on the dark entrance to a cave high above her. On her right, the ocean had crashed against the rock wall, splashing her feet with foam.

The curtains blew in a breeze that came drifting, warm and scented with perfume. There was a pain in Selene's heart, and she lifted her fingers to touch her chest. There was nothing to be felt on the skin, but deep inside her was a hot, searing feeling, as though her heart were being torn in two. The pain faded even as she touched it. A dream, then. Just a dream.

She turned her head, hearing a sound. A chanting close by in Greek. "*No heart but mine.*" The whisper made her skin prickle.

"*None but I will have you.*"

Someone was in her chamber.

She sat up in bed, but even as she did so, she knew she had been mistaken. Her eyes were fully open now, and she could see the corners of her room.

She lay back, strangely uneasy, and gazed at the bouquet on her bedside table, the most glorious flowers she had ever seen. They had never wilted but seemed as fresh as the day she had received them, the first day she met the priestess.

She'd been apprenticing with Chrysate now for weeks, chanting songs of Hecate in the priestess's chambers, and all the time wondering where her parents were, what Chrysate had done with them. Her escape into Rome after the events at the Circus Maximus had not been successful. By the time the centurion had found her, she was hungry and scared and ready to return to the Palatine. She knew the priestess had captured her parents, knew that Augustus had tried to kill her mother, and yet she could not bring herself to sorrow. Selene, daughter of a queen who'd taken power not so much older than she was now, found herself wanting to turn back into a child. Chrysate daily took her hand, taught her new language, sat opposite her, peering into her face, smiling.

The flowers turned back into birds as Selene looked at them, and the birds fluttered about her chamber, singing a sweet, lulling song.

She could almost understand the words they sang. Almost.

"*It is time,*" she heard. "*Come.*" Then it became a simple melody again, but she was already out of bed, making her way down the corridor in her nightgown. The birds accompanied her, a singing cloud rising toward the arched ceiling of the corridor, then swooping to the floor.

She raised her hand to tap on Chrysate's door and found it already open. There were candles lit, and she could smell the priestess's perfume.

Selene pulled aside the curtains of the priestess's bed and saw only the silken coverlet. She touched the soft impression where her friend's body had been. The place was still warm. She turned back to the table, where the birds were congregating.

There was a silver box on it. Selene recognized it from her home. Isis and Dionysus together, the gods of her parents. She took a step toward the table. Then another.

She ran her fingers across its embossed surface, feeling her parents' faces in the silver. She'd seen Chrysate capture her mother within this box, and her father come from inside it, bowing to Rome. Her parents, she thought, dizzy. She was no one's daughter.

Selene fit her fingernails beneath the lid and began to pry at it.

"Princess," said an amused voice from behind her.

Selene turned, hiding the box behind her back as quickly as she could.

"I couldn't sleep," she lied. "They sang to me all night."

She gestured at the birds, but as she moved her hand, they transformed into flowers again, hundreds of them dropping from the ceiling and onto the carpet. Selene caught a soft pink petal in her hand and crushed it in her fingers. She could smell the scent of roses everywhere now. The petals continued to fall, until they covered her bare feet.

"You should not touch things that belong to others," the priestess said.

"I only wanted to see it," said Selene.

"Give it to me," said Chrysate.

Selene kept it behind her back, holding it tightly in her hand. She could not let go of it, even as she walked toward Chrysate, basking in the glow of the woman, her heart pounding as she came closer to her.

Chrysate's eyes shone with love, like Cleopatra's should have, like Antony's should have, and Selene felt herself pulled. Still, she held the silver box.

"You must undress now for the ceremony," Chrysate told her, and Selene did so. She undid even the band of linen about her chest, spinning as the priestess took the end of the fabric.

She unclasped the pin that tied her robe about her shoulder, and was left naked.

Her parents should have protected her from all of this, she thought with some deep part of her mind, and yet here she stood with the box that contained them in her hand. She could throw it into the fire. They could die. They were supposed to be dead already.

She thought of her mother, spinning in the arena, on fire. She thought of her father, wavering, half visible, calling her mother's name.

Somewhere the birds were singing, and if there was a strange pain in

Selene's heart, a tearing feeling, a piercing feeling, she could forget that and inhale the incense that burned and the perfume that Chrysate was anointing her with. She could smell the flowers, and something darker. The petals reached up to her thighs now, drifting softly around her.

They burned slightly on her skin, but she was grateful for that as well. She felt as though she might sink beneath them. Chrysate removed her opal ring, and placed it on Selene's left hand. It flashed a thousand colors, shining in the lamplight.

The knife the priestess brought from her robes shone as well, a lovely thing, tooled metal with a handle in the shape of a hound. The blade was long and very sharp, and Selene appreciated that as she gazed upon it.

It was a perfect thing.

⇒13⇐

At long last, Antony and Cleopatra came to a crossroad, where the path divided between the domains of the blessed dead of Elysium and the screaming laborers of Tartarus. At the crossroads, there stood an iron tower rising as high as the sky. Cleopatra looked to her husband.

"Are you certain?" he asked.

"We are here," she said.

"Yes. Ready yourself." He hesitated for a moment before putting his hand on the door and opening it.

Then, the only sound in the world was the sound of a creature unspeakably enormous, hissing and spitting in the darkness.

"We must not stop here!" yelled Antony, grabbing her by the hand, nearly snatching her off her feet, but the creature had already sensed them. Cleopatra felt something pass behind her ankles, and suddenly she knew. It was all around them. Antony drew his sword.

"Run when I tell you to run. The door to the throne room is on the other side of this."

She could hear its coils rattling across the stone, endless looping lengths.

"A serpent," she whispered.

"No longer," said Antony. "A shade."

It whipped toward her face and Antony shouted and slashed at it, but his sword went through its body. All Cleopatra could see were eyes, hundreds of them, glittering in the dark.

"Cut off one head, and two grow in its place," she murmured. "The Hydra."

"It has died a thousand times," said Antony. "Each time one of its heads was cut off, it went to Hades. Now all of its dead selves are here, guarding the doorway to the gods. Only one of the heads is immortal, still living."

He lashed out, slicing at another striking head. Cleopatra readied herself to run, but then something changed.

The monster was no serpent.

"Stop!" Cleopatra screamed.

It was Selene's face, appearing out of the dark, her eyes shining, her cheeks rosy. Her child.

Cleopatra took a step forward, and as she did so, Antony's sword slashed forward across Selene's face, leaving a long wound.

Cleopatra tore Antony's sword from his hands and, in moments, had him on his knees.

"How dare you—"

Selene's mouth opened, wide and shocked, and Cleopatra reached for her.

Selene hissed.

Antony looked up at her, his eyes sad. His skin was nearly transparent now. She could see the wall through his heart.

"We have to go through the beast," Antony said, and stood, reaching out his hand for his sword. Cleopatra found that she could not let go of it.

Hissing and spitting came from the dark behind her. Cleopatra's head spun to the side to track the Hydra's location, and when she turned back again, there were two Antonys.

"Don't trust him," Antony said.

"No," Antony said. "Don't trust *him*."

She still held the sword. The coils of the Hydra slipped past her calves. The invisible areas behind the serpent sparked with intelligence, with evil, and she heard the shifting of the monster's bones. Her two husbands looked pleadingly at her. One of them stood.

"Follow me," he said, but she would not. "You know me. I am yours."

"What are the words?" she asked, her voice scarcely loud enough to be heard. She took a step toward him. He was her husband, surely. His face filled with love for her.

"*Te teneo,*" said the other Antony.

The false Antony before her hissed, darting forward, venom dripping from his jaws, his mouth open for Antony's throat. Cleopatra lunged forward and threw herself upon the serpent. A scalding drop of something landed on her arm, and she gasped at the sensation, a blistering fire that did not go out but spread, and lit her fingers like torches.

She screamed in agony, and her husband grabbed her and pulled her from the serpent's clutches, heaving open the door that led to the lords of Hades, a door gilded with dark metal, glowing with moonstones and black diamonds.

Silence closed around them, a sense of tremendous space, as though they had stepped behind a waterfall and into a cavern. Cleopatra put her hand out and felt Antony beside her.

Only then did she open her eyes.

Their thrones were as tall as buildings, and their robes held the night sky in their folds. In the apex of the chamber's ceiling, a crescent moon glowed feebly. Cleopatra looked up, shuddering with the pain of the Hydra's venom.

Persephone's stony features danced with shadows. She was lit with the cold light of a phosphorescent sea, but her lips were those of a young and beautiful girl, and her eyes shone like the oil the Romans had poured over Cleopatra. Stars hung in her long, twisting hair.

Antony pushed Cleopatra forward.

"I bring you a queen of Egypt," Antony said.

Cleopatra hesitated for a moment, and then bowed her head.

The goddess bent forward, slowly, and scooped Cleopatra and Antony up in her hand.

"We greet you, queen of Egypt," Persephone said. She moved her fingers so that her husband could view the two small figures on her palm. "We greet you, though you do not belong in this place. You are not living. You are not dead. We have not seen one such as you here before. The way is hard, and it is not a place most choose to enter."

"And you? Are you not a king?" The Lord of Hades had a face carved in granite. His voice shook the walls of the chamber, and boulders fell from the ceiling and rolled across the floor.

"No," said Antony. "I am a soldier." He stopped, stammering. "I *was* a soldier."

Persephone smiled. In her other hand, she held a piece of gleaming black fruit. She put the fruit to her lips and bit into it. Her teeth were pearl white and shone in the dim light of Hades. The fruit dripped crimson juice.

Cleopatra felt a pang of sudden hunger, the first since she'd arrived in the Underworld.

"Well, soldier. Citizen of Hades. What is it you wish? Do you petition for your release? We cannot send you back to the land of the living with your companion. She no longer dwells there."

Antony looked at Persephone.

"I offer myself," he said. "Her soul is tied to an Old God. She cannot die, and she does not live. You may use me however you choose. I was a soldier, and many of my former men dwell here. I would organize an army in Hades. Or send me to Tartarus for your amusement. Do with me what you wish. I only ask that you help her regain her soul."

Cleopatra was horrified. "He is not an offering," she cried. "That is not what I want!"

"That is true," said the god. "He is ours already. He is only a shade. You are something else. What do *you* offer us?"

The god turned his gaze on Cleopatra. His eyes glittered and she was reminded of the Hydra. Could this god be trusted? Could anyone?

"I am a mortal," she began. "Yet my soul is shared by Sekhmet. I bargained with her, but now I would be free of the bargain."

Persephone laughed a bitter laugh.

"The gods do not release their prizes easily," she said, and her husband glanced at her, his eyes flashing. She extended her free hand and placed it upon his thigh. He took her fingers in his and touched them, a strange look of amusement on his face.

He turned to Cleopatra.

"Your goddess is not one of us. I cannot do anything about your soul."

"Then I wish to stay here with Antony," Cleopatra said.

"A love story," said Hades. "And I thought you brought us something new. Do you think all lovers do not ask the same boon?"

Cleopatra felt desperate. Was there nothing for her, then? Would she return to earth and wander, homeless and hopeless? She might take vengeance on Rome, but when that was finished, what would she do? Augustus would die, whether at her hands or simply through the passage of time. Her children would die.

Sekhmet would live and grow stronger. Cleopatra would be a slave to the goddess, feeding her, killing for her. She would never be free.

"Let me die!" she begged. "I have lost my country, my family—"

"As have many. Why are you different?" said Hades, impatient.

"You are dead already," Persephone informed her, and her voice was gentle. "But you are not for the peace of the grave."

"The goddess you woke grows stronger," Hades said. "The banks of Acheron are crowded with the unmourned. Whole villages have died, and none are left to bury the dead. Your goddess is insatiable. She has sent one of her children to hunt on her behalf."

He motioned over his goblet, and Persephone held Cleopatra and Antony up to look into the liquid therein.

A shooting star fired across the dark surface of the Underlord's wine and landed, igniting a hillside somewhere on earth. The creature that was left when the fire went cold was something Cleopatra had never seen before, a slicing thing, a sleek and deathly thing, like a cat but also like a shark, like a flame, and also molten metal. It smiled a terrible smile and bounded down the hillside and into a small village, its feet scarcely touching the ground.

In the town the creature entered, a pale inferno consumed each it looked upon. Cleopatra could easily see the flames surrounding each victim, though the victims did not notice them until they began to writhe with pain. They collapsed in the streets, in their doorways, in their beds, and they burned until they were dead.

"This creature aboveground, and the things it has wrought? They are your doing," the Lord of the Dead told Cleopatra. "You brought them to my country." She knew he was right.

"You must repair it," said Persephone.

"She cannot repair it," her husband said. "It is done. Her goddess will do as she wishes. We do as we wish, do we not?"

"Not always," said Persephone, and bit into her fruit again, the crimson juice flooding out over her hands. "We do not always do as we wish."

Hades gazed on his wife for a moment, as though thinking of an old argument.

"I would give everything I have to undo what I have done. I would be free," Cleopatra said.

Antony looked at Cleopatra. His face was grief-stricken.

"Give her what is left of my strength. I would have her take it."

Persephone looked at her, glanced at her husband, who nodded, and then she reached down and gave Antony a droplet of the juice she drank. A change came over him. His body became more solid, and his skin flushed.

He turned to Cleopatra, and he was her Antony again, completely, a solid, living man.

He kissed her, and she felt all that he had been in that kiss, all that he had wanted, all that he had dreamed. She felt his strength flowing into her and tried to pull away. It was as though she drank his blood.

Then it was done and she was alone again, in the hand of Persephone. Antony had disappeared. Cleopatra could not keep from crying out.

"Do not fear for him. He has gone back to the Fields of Mourning," said Persephone.

Cleopatra was startled. "What do you mean? Why isn't he where the heroes are?"

Hades looked at her. "He did not go to Elysium. He killed himself."

"For love of you," Persephone said. "He made Hades ring with crying your name."

Cleopatra held herself tightly. She would have died of love for Antony, and now their love had kept him from his heaven.

"And I?" Cleopatra managed.

"You go back into the world, dreamer," said Hades. "You waken."

"I would ask a favor, then," said Cleopatra.

The god of the Underworld leaned forward, his eyebrows raised.

"There are no favors here. If I do something, I do it because something has been done for me."

His lady stood up, shaking her head slightly, her face unreadable, and drifted from the throne room.

"You are a strange woman to seek to gamble again with a god after losing so much. A brave woman. Or a fool, perhaps," said Hades.

"I know what I ask," said Cleopatra. "And I ask it anyway."

Hades nodded. "What are your terms?" he asked.

"I will give you Sekhmet's Slaughterer," Cleopatra said.

"What use have I for such a creature?" said the god. "It fills my realm with unmourned souls. Death comes for all mortals."

"Mortals will outwit death," Cleopatra told him. "You will have need of a servant to bring you citizens. Hades will empty as time passes. The dead will go elsewhere. They will cease to sacrifice to this realm. It is happening in my country. It happened to Sekhmet. I visited her temple, and it was falling to dust. The other temples cannot be far behind. Once, the rituals of mourning were greater, were they not? Blood and honey poured into the earth to feed the dead. Now the shades here languish, starving. Your realm is shrunken. The gods of Egypt are fading because of you and your kind, and the gods of Rome will fade for some other. The Slaughterer will bring you souls when that time comes. It will be a useful servant for you."

"And if you bring me the Slaughterer, what do you desire in return?" asked Hades, his mouth curling up at the corner. "I cannot imagine it will be a small bargain."

"My love will go to the Duat. My children, if any of my children have died in this country, if any of my children are already in Hades, will go with him."

"That is a large request," Hades replied. "I hold no sway over Egypt's Underworld."

"You must bargain, then," she said. "I desire Antony to go to his place in the Beautiful West. I desire him to go to my heaven, and our children with him."

"Do you seek to meet him there, queen?" Hades asked. "You cannot.

You will not be welcomed in the Duat. The goddess who owns your soul was banished from there, and you will not pass the gates. You do not offer me enough."

"I am not finished," Cleopatra said. "I will bring you another. An enemy of your own."

Hades laughed.

"What enemy?" he asked.

"There is a priestess on earth who brings power to the goddess Hecate. They mean to overthrow you."

"Hecate," the god said, smirking. "Hecate has no power. She is a servant to her betters, punished for meddling in affairs that did not concern her. She's a dog now, chained at the gates. They will not succeed."

"They will try," Cleopatra told him. "If I am bested, they will use Sekhmet. My goddess is older than you. Hecate is older as well. Perhaps together, they are stronger."

Hades sat up in his throne. "They are not stronger."

"I will bring you the priestess who assists Hecate. I will deliver her to the gates. It is no small task. I ask another boon for it."

"What is your price?" the god asked.

"I desire the soul of Augustus, emperor of Rome, and I desire it for eternity. He will not go to Elysium. He is no hero. He will travel with me, no matter the mourners, no matter the sacrifices, no matter the prophecies."

The god of the Dead looked at Cleopatra, his eyes endless depths, and he smiled.

"Will you accept my bargain?" Cleopatra asked.

"I will," he said. "It is a good bargain."

Suddenly, there was a quaking, a groaning at the very base of Hades, and a sound of chains dragging across the ground.

⇒14⇐

Dark magic traveled through the corridors while Auðr worked at the fates of those in Krimissa. She looked up, distracted by the sounds coming from Chrysate's chamber. She had thought the Greek witch was merely working a love spell on the emperor, but now she could hear screaming from her room. The sound had been, at first listen, disguised as the song of nightingales and larks, but Auðr suddenly heard it for what it truly was.

A murder of crows, screeching over a victory.

Auðr moved as quickly as she could toward Chrysate's chambers, hobbling into the witch's rooms through the half-open door.

The floor of the chamber was covered with black petals, like ashes left behind after a tremendous fire. Dozens of crows clung to the bed frame, their dark wings unfurling as they looked down into the bed. The curtains were drawn, but the seiðkona could see movement behind them. A shadow shifting in the candlelight, bending over something stretched on the mattress.

The witch's hand moved. Auðr watched it in silhouette, drawing a line from one end of the figure on the bed and downward.

"You will love me," Chrysate said.

"Yes," said the girl.

"You will love only me," said the witch.

"Yes," said Selene. There were tears in her voice. A ragged sound in her breath, but her voice was certain and pure.

"None but I will have you," said the witch, and her voice changed in that moment into something ancient and murderous, the voice of earth-quake and landslide, the voice of dead rivers and poisoned flowers. The vicious and brokenhearted hounds of Hades howled beneath her tone.

The crows began to scream their song.

The wind rose up and tore away the curtains, and Auðr saw what they had been hiding, the creature crouched atop Cleopatra's daughter, and the girl, her skin pale with loss of blood, stretched upon the bed like something already dead. Auðr saw Chrysate's snarling face, the ravaged skin, the single, glowing green eye, the knotted hanks of hair, the bloodred lips stretched over sharp teeth.

"I sacrifice this child to Hecate!" Chrysate cried. "I take her body for my own, in service to Hecate!"

The priestess had torn open the girl's chest and climbed inside, though the girl still lived. The witch's claws tore still deeper into the girl's breast, and she began to twist her body into the space beneath Selene's skin.

Auðr raised her distaff, the fate like a thorny vine wrapping around it. She could feel Hecate in this room. So foolish. She'd been thinking only of Sekhmet and had not noticed what was growing only a few doors away.

"Hecate," Chrysate whispered, and the girl repeated it. Their voices twisted into spell, pulling at the gates of Hades, pulling at the chain that bound Hecate below the earth, even as Auðr pulled in the opposite direction.

Blackened petals flew and the crows shrieked.

Selene turned her tearstained face toward Auðr and reached out her hand.

"Tell my mother I did not mean to leave her for Rome," she whispered, her voice ragged.

Clutched in Selene's hand was the silver box containing Cleopatra.

She threw it, and as it spun through the air, time slowed. The corners of the room flashed with light, the birds on the canopy rose as the wind shook them, and the witch of Thessaly howled with wrath as she leapt for the box.

Cleopatra's prison tumbled through the open window and clattered onto the stones of the courtyard two stories below.

"NO!" screamed Chrysate, and threw herself out the window after the box, but it was too late. The box was open. Auðr ran to the window and looked out.

There was a moment of stillness, of nothing. It was empty, Auðr thought in terror, and its contents missing. Someone else had stolen them. Had Cleopatra been given to Hecate? If so, there was nothing more to be done. She'd made a terrible mistake, fumbling with the fates of mortals when she should have been spending all the time she had left on binding Cleopatra below the earth. She had seen the possibility of disaster and ignored it. She'd believed Cleopatra might be mistress of her own fate, might split from this and change the future herself.

The ground of the courtyard trembled, and the wailing began, millions of lost souls crying to come to the surface. The air was suddenly scented with asphodel and with the waters of the rivers of Hades. Lethe, with its limitless, soothing black depths, and Styx, whose waters ran with the blood of slaughtered innocents. Acheron, made of salt tears; Cocytus, whose waters wailed like grieving widows; and Phlegethon, whose surface burned with eternal flames.

A moth whiter than starlight rose from the silver box and hung in the air for a moment. Then, her eyes blazing, her skin as bright as candles, shining with a web of molten metal, Cleopatra appeared in the courtyard below Chrysate's chambers.

Her roar of fury rattled the palace, causing the servants to spring panicked from their beds.

Chrysate crouched on the stones opposite Cleopatra, shouting words in her ancient language, but Cleopatra's body was filled with fire, as though lightning had struck it and stayed inside its veins. She reached out her hand and clawed the witch's face, and the witch shrieked and flung herself across the courtyard. Where Cleopatra had touched her, there were long scores ripped in her flesh.

"You are my creature," Chrysate cried. "You belong to Hecate!"

Cleopatra bared her teeth and leapt at her, tearing at her skin. The liquid that came from beneath it was not red but dark, and the witch's skin was tattered by fangs and claws.

Chrysate hesitated, overmatched, before leaping into the darkness and fleeing.

The queen looked up to the open window above her and saw Auðr standing there, frozen. The seiðkona lifted her distaff, but Cleopatra moved like one in a dream, her eyes wide and unseeing. She lifted from the ground the silver box that had imprisoned her, pressing the spilled ash back into it, and then she, too, flew from the Palatine, her every step shaking the ground, moving as fast as fire in a dry season.

Her light blazed over the hillside, and then she was gone.

In Chrysate's rooms, Auðr looked around, stunned.

She shouted at the top of her voice, raising the alarm, though she knew Chrysate would not be captured by any human. She would be moving amongst the spirits now, fleet as a demon, but she was terribly wounded. Creatures such as Chrysate did not travel quickly by land.

Auðr bent over Cleopatra's daughter. She could see her heart, a precious red fruit, exposed inside her rib cage, bright as a phoenix nearing its rebirth. It was not beating.

She made a motion with her fingers, twisting the distaff in a complicated pattern, her face tense. At last, the seiðkona leaned over the girl and exhaled a word, quietly, into her lips.

Selene shuddered and gasped, taking a breath. "Where is my mother?" she croaked, her eyes darting frantically about the room. "Where is my father? Where is Chrysate?"

Auðr stitched closed the wound in her chest with a golden thread unspooled from her seiðstafr. The thread was the girl's own fate. It seemed smooth and delicate, but it was as strong as wire. She found a tiny waxen doll stabbed with a pin, its wrists bound together with a long black hair. She tore the skein of hair from the doll's wrists and carefully, gently, removed the pin from her heart. The girl in the bed arched for a moment, gasped, and sighed, and then relaxed again.

Auðr laid her seiðstafr against the forehead of the queen's daughter. The girl moved. Tears ran from her eyes, and she opened them.

"I don't want to forget," Selene whispered. "I want to know what happened. Don't take it away from me. I was stupid to trust her."

Guards surged into the room, their weapons drawn, and Auðr showed them the thing that had been discarded beside the bed. Part of the beautiful, bloodless skin of the woman Chrysate had been was lying crumpled and torn on the floor, like a fine garment thrown off in the heat of passion. A breast, and an arm like an elegant glove, the skin perfect and creamy. A scrap of a throat and lovely face. One side of a curving waist and a portion of round hip. The rest had been torn away and taken by the witch as she fled.

The guards, their faces horrified, this image of the emperor's ward and her attacker worse than anything they had seen in battle, ran about the room in disarray. They would die for this, they knew. They would be executed, or condemned to fight animals. They had let Selene be attacked and Cleopatra escape under their very noses. All of them had been sitting at dinner, drinking and laughing for hours, as though under a spell. They had no idea where the emperor was, nor his historian and bodyguard. Agrippa was away as well. The guards were alone with this, and they knew they would be blamed.

She will live, the seiðkona said to them, in their own languages, and in their minds. *She will live. She contains powers of her own, and those of others as well.*

For the first time, Auðr noticed the ring on Selene's finger, a blazing opal engraved with the face of Hecate. The witch had won the hand of the queen's daughter, if not her heart, and her dark power remained there.

The war was not over. There was no hope of a peaceful end. Cleopatra was free, Chrysate lived, and Hecate's bonds had been loosened. Even the failed sacrifice had yielded blood, and Auðr could feel Hecate pulling at her chains. The Underworld shook.

It was only beginning.

The seiðkona looked at the threads, the fates spinning about Rome, the possibilities.

Gods walked the earth, and the sky shone with arrows. The Underworld was at war, and the upper world as well. Emperors and queens, daughters and sons, witches and sorcerers.

The seiðkona did not know what would happen. She had changed the fates, and yet the chaos remained, the rift in the tapestry, the darkness.

Someone still tried to end the world, and someone tried to save it.

Auðr could not tell the two lines apart. They seemed the same.

Chrysate ran, the streets of the city unfriendly and unfamiliar to her. She was buffeted by a strange wind, which pressed against her face, tearing at her torn skin, beating at her injured body, reminding her that she had lost the queen.

She stumbled, scraping her withered hands on the stones. She was not supposed to be this misshapen thing, this hag, half covered in sweet skin, half covered in scales and darkness. Hecate had been so close. She had felt her coming.

She turned her face, the part of it that still existed as human, toward the moonlight, moaning. The wind would not offer her a respite, though. It raged against her broken cheek, threw sand into her one, bloodied eye.

She snarled, clawing at the wind. Nothing she did eased it, though she could see, outside of her vicinity, still air. The trees stood calm in the darkness. Only about Chrysate was there this bitter thing.

She screamed with fury, chanting curses, chanting spells, tearing at the air itself, but nothing kept the wind from whistling around her, shrill and violent. Nothing kept the wind from spinning her in wrong directions. Nothing kept the wind from surging into her lungs, filling her with dusty air and her own spells, blown backward into her mouth.

She could hear horses in the streets, pursuing her, perhaps, but she could not tell where they were. She could hear howling dogs, but she could not find them. They would protect her. They were the creatures of her mistress. But they howled, and they howled, and finally, Chrysate realized that there were no dogs. The sound she heard was the wind mocking her.

As she raised her hand to fight off the tornado, she noticed her finger. Naked. Her ring was gone. She'd left it on the hand of the queen's daughter.

Chrysate concealed herself in a doorway, shielding herself from the wind. The moon was high in the sky now, a pointed crescent, each edge sharp and wounding. It did not heal her. A tear slid down her cheek, scalding as it went, and she tasted the sour salt of it.

She watched the wind pass by, and she waited until it had gone. She listened for the footsteps of legionaries patrolling for her, and waited until they had moved on. Then she began to move again, whispering spells of concealment and searching for a dark and secret place to hide herself more effectively.

She thought, muttering to herself frantically.

She could still accomplish what she had planned. It would be bloody, and it would be difficult, but it was still possible.

➤15⬅

Agrippa woke, bound in a bright room. It was full daylight, and the elderly priest was sitting opposite him.

"Water?" he asked, and Agrippa laughed. His throat was swollen and so sore that he could not imagine swallowing, let alone swallowing a drink provided by the very man who'd poisoned him.

"Where are my men?" he croaked.

"They live," the priest said. "We do not kill our guests, unlike the men of the emperor's armies."

"Why did you poison me? I did nothing to wound you."

"You did not?" the priest asked. He ran his finger over his throat. The scratch was already healing. "One does not steal from Apollo. We are guards, and this is our lifelong task. Perhaps you do not understand that there is a reason for our devotion. I would not have thought Augustus's general was a fool."

"You guard something precious," Agrippa said.

"We guard something lethal," the priest informed him. "It kills. It has always killed, and yet it still exists. We keep it safe from the world."

"It's true, then," Agrippa said. "The arrows are here."

"Everything is true," the priest informed him. "Once a story is told, it becomes true. Every unlikely tale, every tale of wonders, has something real at its core."

"I need them. There is an enemy greater than any Rome has known," said Agrippa, shifting painfully in his bonds. Though he'd fought for years, he'd never before been captured.

"So you say," said the priest. "Just as anyone would, to gain possession of the arrows. They are too dangerous to use."

"It is too dangerous *not* to use them," Agrippa countered. "We fight an immortal, and there is no other way to kill her. We fight to save the world from a monster."

The priest looked at Agrippa and grimaced.

"And what monster will you create in using them? No one has ever used Hercules' arrows without paying the price. Now we have them here, safe from fools."

"I am no fool," Agrippa said. "I act to save Rome."

"Perhaps Rome should not be saved, if you need such a weapon to save it. Only a true hero may wield the bow of Hercules, but heroes are fools, too. The venom on these arrows killed the greatest hero of the world. Hercules died screaming, begging his friends to light his funeral pyre while he still lived, and that was from only a droplet of blood mixed with the Hydra's venom and smeared on his tunic. Do you know what happened to Philoctetes, the patron of this temple?"

"I do not," Agrippa answered. He did not care.

"Philoctetes was the only one who dared light the pyre, and so Hercules willed the bow and quiver to him. He wounded himself in the foot with his new arrows, on a ship destined for the Trojan War. He was left on an island by his friends, and his wound festered for ten years, while he went mad with the pain. At last, his friends returned. There had been a prophecy that only those arrows could win the war. In some stories, it is said that Philoctetes was healed on the battlefield, that by the time he fired the shot that killed Paris and won the war, he was cured of his agonies. We know better. There is no cure for the Hydra's venom, and these wounds take a long time to kill. Hercules knew this much, and he should never have saved the Hydra's poison. I do not trust you to make a better choice than he did."

"Trust me, then," someone said. The voice was familiar. Agrippa turned his head, stunned, just as the priest made a strangled sound.

Blood splashed, speckling Agrippa's robes.

Augustus stood in the window, sweating and pale, his eyes furiously

threw his body against the emperor and heaved him clear.
e moment, he heard Nicolaus shout. The historian waved a
t Agrippa.
e yelled.
grabbed Augustus by the arm, half carrying him to the gate,
priests and swords. Usem was close behind them, defending
is bayonet slashing.
launched themselves through the gate and toward the horses
them outside the wall, the fireball arrived in the air above
rd.
glanced up and glimpsed something with thousands of teeth,
made of molten metal, something with maddened eyes, some-
ning a strange, ecstatic song. Then it was gone.
Usem shouted. "We cannot stay here!"
stumbled and fell against Nicolaus, who dropped the box
Hercules' arrows. Agrippa grabbed the arrows and bow in
nashing them back into their vessel.
ing Nicolaus onto his horse, using strength he did not know
d. He took Augustus in his arms and pushed him atop his
l.
started to mount. They must get away from here before the
ever it was, noticed them. None of them were strong enough

s eyes blurred suddenly, and he staggered.
ld went dark. Agrippa could hear shouting, feel hands pound-
lder, feel himself being dragged along the stones and heaved
k of a horse.
d see nothing. He could hear running feet, the clashing of
uting, and a searing heat overtook his body, beginning in
could smell metal. A naphtha firepot? The contents would
oldier's skin and ignite, not quenchable with water but only
ing. Agrippa had seen them in the Circus Maximus. He'd
une to obtain the fire that had failed to burn the queen, but
een touched by naphtha.

bright. With him stood Nicolaus, whose mythic hopes had sent Agrippa on this doomed mission, and Usem, whose face was lit with the fire of war. He wiped the priest's blood from his dagger. Usem looked at Agrippa and smiled.

"You should have let me join you," he said. "Did you think I was only a sorcerer?"

"I made them bring me here. I will not stay hidden in my study any longer," Augustus said. "I will not stay in Rome, waiting to die in my sleep."

He swayed, the skin beneath his eyes bluish. The hand that held the sword trembled, but he was resolved.

"You must leave here," Agrippa said. "You must not risk yourself!"

The emperor put his sword to Agrippa's bonds and slashed them. Agrippa stood, and rubbed his wrists.

"I climbed a wall," Augustus said, grinning suddenly, his crooked teeth lending a strangely youthful expression to his face. "I crept unde-tected into a fortified temple. You would not have thought I could do it, but I have! Cleopatra's scholar acquitted himself nicely, by the way. It was kind of you to leave him with me. He rode hard beside me, though he is a scribe and poet, not a warrior. I would imagine you would do as much for me as my historian has done, would you not? Nicolaus has trusted me to save my own country. Will you do the same?"

Agrippa bowed his head.

"I will do the same," he said, and took the priest's walking stick from the dead man's hand. He removed the covering that—yes—hid the suspected blade, and tested its sharpness on his finger. He tossed it to the scholar, who flinched slightly, but then gripped it. Agrippa turned the priest over and found his own knife tucked into the man's belt. He smiled.

The priest had feared his prisoner. They were not so secure here as they seemed.

He took the priestly robe from the man's body and threw it over him-self. Augustus and Nicolaus pulled their hoods up over their heads, and Usem slipped out the window, pulling himself up onto the roof of the temple, followed by Augustus, wavering but courageous, and Nicolaus, gulping. Usem held out his hand for Agrippa, and the general took it.

The Psylli led, creeping along the roofline, bending low. He looked down into the protected courtyard of the temple, regretting all of this. The emperor was in no condition to be with him, and Nicolaus was not a soldier. Only Agrippa was a warrior, and he was still suffering the aftereffects of the poisoning.

"Watch them," Augustus said, pointing into the courtyard. A guard walked a circle around the statue of Philoctetes. Another guard walked in the other direction, and they crossed each other. The priests were perfectly synchronized, perfectly prepared, though Usem could see only swords, not crossbows.

Agrippa nodded. He was meant to be unconscious in his room. The rest of his legionaries were similarly captive. The temple was not at the same level of readiness it had maintained the night before.

"The quiver will be in a box," Nicolaus said. "A metal box. The arrows are too dangerous to be left uncovered. The priests will have them secured."

Agrippa looked at Augustus and smiled. Long ago, in their youth, they'd fought and tricked, learning techniques for attack from a leader of the guard in Apollonia. The emperor smiled back at him. Still, he was not well. He'd lost weight over the past months, and he looked spindly and pale. It was a miracle he was on his feet. He seemed hardly to be drinking the theriac now, and that was a blessing, but Agrippa mistrusted the shaking of his hands.

They were barely concealed on a rooftop overlooking their quarry. It was time for action, not worry. There would be time enough, should they survive this.

Usem waited, counting. The rhythm of the guards marching regained its previous perfection.

"On my signal," Usem whispered, and he positioned his dagger over

his head, aiming carefully. He'd have dagger, watching it twirl through the a flying, winging thing.

The priest it was aimed at did not s hilt into his chest.

Agrippa was already leaping down f Augustus in his wake, gasping with ex

The remaining priest had instantly defending the statue behind him. His his hands were steady, and Usem coul moved that he'd been trained as a figh retrieved the bayonet from the schola heard in panting wheezes. The first fi him back, away from the fighting. He asset.

Followed by Usem, Agrippa began t tus more tentatively behind them. Ag to monitor the terrain. More priests co needed to hear them. He could hear priest clearly could as well, for he lunge fighters, his sword flashing in the air.

Augustus seemed to momentarily jaw tensing. He parried fiercely, in a wa their youth. Suddenly, he saw Augustu of their training days, how he'd fough small size and reach balanced by his de

Augustus edged forward, his blade ground. Behind him, Usem closed in,

The priest looked up over the emp raised a hand to shield his eyes.

A ploy, certainly.

"Out of the way!" Usem shouted, he'd see nothing, and instead saw a tre speeding across the sky.

Agripp At the san metal box "Run!" Agripp pursued by their rear, As they waiting fo the courty Agripp something thing hum "Ride!" Agripp containing his arms, s Usem f he possess horse as w Agripp beast, wha to fight it. Agripp The wo ing his sho onto the b He cou swords, sh his calf. H attach to a by smothe spent a fo he'd never bright. With him stood Nicolaus, whose mythic hopes had sent Agrippa on this doomed mission, and Usem, whose face was lit with the fire of war. He wiped the priest's blood from his dagger. Usem looked at Agrippa and smiled.

"You should have let me join you," he said. "Did you think I was only a sorcerer?"

"I made them bring me here. I will not stay hidden in my study any longer," Augustus said. "I will not stay in Rome, waiting to die in my sleep."

He swayed, the skin beneath his eyes bluish. The hand that held the sword trembled, but he was resolved.

"You must leave here," Agrippa said. "You must not risk yourself!"

The emperor put his sword to Agrippa's bonds and slashed them. Agrippa stood, and rubbed his wrists.

"I climbed a wall," Augustus said, grinning suddenly, his crooked teeth lending a strangely youthful expression to his face. "I crept undetected into a fortified temple. You would not have thought I could do it, but I have! Cleopatra's scholar acquitted himself nicely, by the way. It was kind of you to leave him with me. He rode hard beside me, though he is a scribe and poet, not a warrior. I would imagine you would do as much for me as my historian has done, would you not? Nicolaus has trusted me to save my own country. Will you do the same?"

Agrippa bowed his head.

"I will do the same," he said, and took the priest's walking stick from the dead man's hand. He removed the covering that—yes—hid the suspected blade, and tested its sharpness on his finger. He tossed it to the scholar, who flinched slightly, but then gripped it. Agrippa turned the priest over and found his own knife tucked into the man's belt. He smiled.

The priest had feared his prisoner. They were not so secure here as they seemed.

He took the priestly robe from the man's body and threw it over himself. Augustus and Nicolaus pulled their hoods up over their heads, and Usem slipped out the window, pulling himself up onto the roof of the temple, followed by Augustus, wavering but courageous, and Nicolaus, gulping. Usem held out his hand for Agrippa, and the general took it.

The Psylli led, creeping along the roofline, bending low. He looked down into the protected courtyard of the temple, regretting all of this. The emperor was in no condition to be with him, and Nicolaus was not a soldier. Only Agrippa was a warrior, and he was still suffering the aftereffects of the poisoning.

"Watch them," Augustus said, pointing into the courtyard. A guard walked a circle around the statue of Philoctetes. Another guard walked in the other direction, and they crossed each other. The priests were perfectly synchronized, perfectly prepared, though Usem could see only swords, not crossbows.

Agrippa nodded. He was meant to be unconscious in his room. The rest of his legionaries were similarly captive. The temple was not at the same level of readiness it had maintained the night before.

"The quiver will be in a box," Nicolaus said. "A metal box. The arrows are too dangerous to be left uncovered. The priests will have them secured."

Agrippa looked at Augustus and smiled. Long ago, in their youth, they'd fought and tricked, learning techniques for attack from a leader of the guard in Apollonia. The emperor smiled back at him. Still, he was not well. He'd lost weight over the past months, and he looked spindly and pale. It was a miracle he was on his feet. He seemed hardly to be drinking the theriac now, and that was a blessing, but Agrippa mistrusted the shaking of his hands.

They were barely concealed on a rooftop overlooking their quarry. It was time for action, not worry. There would be time enough, should they survive this.

Usem waited, counting. The rhythm of the guards marching regained its previous perfection.

"On my signal," Usem whispered, and he positioned his dagger over his head, aiming carefully. He'd have only one chance. He threw the dagger, watching it twirl through the air, end over end, like a metal bird, a flying, winging thing.

The priest it was aimed at did not see it coming until it slid up to the hilt into his chest.

Agrippa was already leaping down from the rooftop, his sword drawn, Augustus in his wake, gasping with exertion.

The remaining priest had instantly drawn his blade, and he crouched, defending the statue behind him. His eyes were wide and startled, but his hands were steady, and Usem could see by the graceful way the man moved that he'd been trained as a fighter. He motioned to Nicolaus and retrieved the bayonet from the scholar, whose breath could already be heard in panting wheezes. The first fight was never easy. He motioned him back, away from the fighting. He'd be more of a liability than an asset.

Followed by Usem, Agrippa began to circle around the guard, Augustus more tentatively behind them. Agrippa's focus was divided in order to monitor the terrain. More priests could arrive at any moment, and he needed to hear them. He could hear Augustus's heart pounding. The priest clearly could as well, for he lunged toward the weakest of the three fighters, his sword flashing in the air.

Augustus seemed to momentarily rally, his back straightening, his jaw tensing. He parried fiercely, in a way that Agrippa remembered from their youth. Suddenly, he saw Augustus as he had been, the wiry fighter of their training days, how he'd fought up and down the hillsides, his small size and reach balanced by his determination to win.

Augustus edged forward, his blade meeting his opponent's, gaining ground. Behind him, Usem closed in, jabbing with the bayonet.

The priest looked up over the emperor's shoulder, and squinted. He raised a hand to shield his eyes.

A ploy, certainly.

"Out of the way!" Usem shouted, and Agrippa glanced up, certain he'd see nothing, and instead saw a tremendous blaze of light, a fireball, speeding across the sky.

Agrippa threw his body against the emperor and heaved him clear. At the same moment, he heard Nicolaus shout. The historian waved a metal box at Agrippa.

"Run!" he yelled.

Agrippa grabbed Augustus by the arm, half carrying him to the gate, pursued by priests and swords. Usem was close behind them, defending their rear, his bayonet slashing.

As they launched themselves through the gate and toward the horses waiting for them outside the wall, the fireball arrived in the air above the courtyard.

Agrippa glanced up and glimpsed something with thousands of teeth, something made of molten metal, something with maddened eyes, something humming a strange, ecstatic song. Then it was gone.

"Ride!" Usem shouted. "We cannot stay here!"

Agrippa stumbled and fell against Nicolaus, who dropped the box containing Hercules' arrows. Agrippa grabbed the arrows and bow in his arms, smashing them back into their vessel.

Usem flung Nicolaus onto his horse, using strength he did not know he possessed. He took Augustus in his arms and pushed him atop his horse as well.

Agrippa started to mount. They must get away from here before the beast, whatever it was, noticed them. None of them were strong enough to fight it.

Agrippa's eyes blurred suddenly, and he staggered.

The world went dark. Agrippa could hear shouting, feel hands pounding his shoulder, feel himself being dragged along the stones and heaved onto the back of a horse.

He could see nothing. He could hear running feet, the clashing of swords, shouting, and a searing heat overtook his body, beginning in his calf. He could smell metal. A naphtha firepot? The contents would attach to a soldier's skin and ignite, not quenchable with water but only by smothering. Agrippa had seen them in the Circus Maximus. He'd spent a fortune to obtain the fire that had failed to burn the queen, but he'd never been touched by naphtha.

He prepared himself for the end, whispering what prayers he could remember, wishing only that he had been able to save Augustus. He felt himself beginning to detach from everything he'd been.

In Agrippa's mind, the world was white and covered in snow.

Then the world was black and covered in raining ash.

Hades would take him. It was an honorable death for a soldier, to die protecting his commander. He tasted his own blood filling his mouth. He inhaled the scent of burning. A pyre, he thought. The rites were being performed for him. He would not wander the shores of Acheron, improperly buried.

Suddenly, though, the smell of burning was replaced by that of sea.

He opened his eyes and found himself tied to a saddle, seated, the ground bouncing beneath him. He thought in a flash of the many captives he had carried over his own saddle. He'd been captured by some invading, fire-wielding army. Were they Parthians? Warriors from Babylonia? He strained his ears for their language, flexed his muscles for any give in the ropes.

Agrippa gritted his teeth and began to twist in the saddle. Before him, he saw a dark, muscled arm, decked in war ornaments.

He became aware of a pain in his calf. It felt as though a red-hot ember had lodged beneath his muscles, as though he were caught in a million-toothed trap. He moaned.

"He wakes," a voice said in Latin. The horse slowed, and Agrippa found himself looking into the gray eyes of his oldest friend. Augustus's face showed deep concern.

"My leg," Agrippa managed.

"You fell on one of the arrows," Usem said grimly, from in front of Agrippa. The general discovered that he was riding on the Psylli's horse.

"The temple," Agrippa managed.

"Sekhmet's Slaughterer hit it, just as we got you on the horse," Nicolaus said.

Slaughterer? Agrippa felt himself writhe, his leg cramping and contracting. There was a piece of fabric tied tightly about his thigh. He looked down, expecting his leg to be grievously injured, but it was not.

There was a tiny wound on his calf, its edges bright and swollen with inflammation. A clean wound made by a sharp arrow, but pain radiated out from it like lava from the mouth of an erupting volcano. He felt himself, shamefully, screaming in agony. A vial was pressed to his lips, and a caustic, sickly sweet liquid dripped into his mouth.

He knew nothing more.

➤16➤

The queen sprinted through the city, her bare feet scarcely touching the street. She fed on the first meat she saw, a fuller stumbling from a doorway, his robes reeking of his profession, his blood hot and sweet as she bit into his throat and drank of him. Feeding would make Sekhmet stronger, but it was necessary. Cleopatra could not function without it. She left the man, pale and withered, in another doorway, and felt the now familiar rushing of love, of power, of satisfaction. Somewhere in her mind was the sound of singing, ancient temple songs, and priestesses worshipping her.

Worshipping Sekhmet. She could become the ruler of everything—

Cleopatra shook her head frantically, trying to clear it of the visions.

What had happened? How had she come to be here? Her body had been dragged suddenly up from Hades and Persephone's throne room, and still she did not know who'd opened the box that had contained her. She'd woken in the air, returned to her body, sensing her daughter in the house somewhere, and witches, but who had released her? In the chaos, she'd been unable to tell what was happening. The smell of blood was everywhere, but she ran from it. No time.

Her bargain weighed on her, and it was her first focus. She sought the Slaughterer first. The Slaughterer, she understood. She and Sekhmet's child had things in common. The priestess of Thessaly was a different sort of creature.

The wound her dreaming self had sustained in the Underworld burned her, though it was not visible here. Her body was perfect, unscarred, unbroken, no matter the pain she felt. The silver box she clutched in her fingers burned her, too, but it was a distraction from her arm. It was also a distraction from the pain in the place her heart had been. She'd done the right thing. She knew she had, but Antony was gone.

She shook off the pain and ran on. She had to accomplish the task or she would fail Antony, fail her children, fail everyone she loved.

The voice of the goddess was instantly back in her head. She ignored it as she ran, trying to keep it from understanding her purpose.

Kill, Sekhmet told her.

The Slaughterer had served the goddess well in the queen's absence, Cleopatra could feel. It had sacrificed so many that Sekhmet felt nearly blissful. Nearly happy.

Blood ran through the streets of villages. Corpses rotted. Now Plague traveled, hungering always, and Cleopatra could feel its work as it moved through the country, through the world, from island to island, from mountain to mountain.

The temples, Sekhmet directed the queen.

Cleopatra considered. Surely, Plague was traveling with the same directions.

Cleopatra imagined she could see Ra's boat traveling through the caverns of the Duat. Imagined she could see the Island of Fire. Imagined she could see Ra himself, the brilliance of his skin, the light of his face, the place on his forehead where Sekhmet had once lived.

She felt Sekhmet, her strength and her weaknesses. It took a great deal of bloodshed to release the Slaughterers. Six Arrows still waited in her quiver: Famine, Earthquake, Flood, Drought, Madness, and Violence. They hummed their deathly songs, desiring, wanting, while the seventh traveled the earth.

Cleopatra killed another man near the imperial residence. The taste of the blood flowed through the goddess, and the queen felt the blood placate her mistress.

Cleopatra killed others, several more in quick succession, and then she ran faster through the city, trying to avoid the populated areas, the smell of people, the hunger that would destroy her resistance. She was traveling nearly as quickly as Sekhmet herself, and the goddess roared, her voice echoing through the heavens as thunder, jolting Romans from their sleep and making them shake in their beds.

"What was that?" they asked one another.

None of them had an answer. They sat quietly in their beds, wide-eyed in the darkness, waiting, without knowing that they were waiting, for the queen to come for them.

Cleopatra knew that she would not kill them, but Sekhmet did not.

Sekhmet was convinced that her slave hungered for the citizens of Rome. She did not know that Cleopatra had set herself on killing one of Sekhmet's children.

Cleopatra lifted her chin and scented the air, the pungent, bloody odor of the killing arrow. The Slaughterer. She looked up, her throat vibrating like that of a cat stalking a bird.

High above her, she could see what seemed to be a tremendous star crossing the heavens, and she followed it, bounding over the land, out of the city and into the countryside.

In an untended orchard, far from where Cleopatra ran, a beady, black eye flickered. An ivory horn, its tip lethally sharpened, its protective cap of cork long since disappeared, shone slightly in the moonlight. The dark and scaly creature turned its armored head quickly and lumbered to its feet. Horses whinnied around it, bewildered by their companion.

The rhinoceros stood, and pushed its way through a gap in the fencing.

Three crocodiles slipped into the Tiber, fitting their reptilian forms through the gutters and into the river.

The snakes of Rome slithered into their tunnels, their burrows, their underground passages.

A tiger crouched and leapt, silently, to the top of the Temple of Apollo, on the Palatine, where a peacock was roosting.

A wild-eyed gazelle looked frantically about her, hearing something, hearing everything, before there was a swift flurry of wind, and her breast was pierced by an arrow. She was slung over a set of broad shoulders and brought home by an ambitious hunter for dinner.

Feathers fell from the sky, and blood pooled in the street, and the rhinoceros trotted through the darkness of the city, far from his home, shaking the dreams of every house he passed.

He followed behind his queen.

As night fell, Cleopatra arrived in Krimissa at the Temple of Apollo, following the trail of the Slaughterer. In twilight, she examined the fallen bodies of Romans from the Praetorian Guard and of priests from the temple's order.

For a moment, she was sure she smelled the scent of the emperor. Surely, that was impossible, though. He could not have been here. It was shadowed with something else, an herbal scent, and that with horseflesh and metal.

Upon the statue of a centaur, an inscription informed the reader that Chiron had died accidentally, pricked by a Hydra arrow when Hercules fired it in a display of prowess, and that, though he was a master of medicines, Chiron had not been able to cure himself.

The centaur had been an immortal, and the pain of the wound had caused him so much suffering that he had given up his immortality in order to die.

Hail Prometheus, said the inscription engraved below the wounded centaur's hooves, *who took willingly the gift of Chiron's immortal life, and who then suffered the endless punishment of Zeus. Hail Prometheus, who gave mankind fire and offended the gods.*

The chained man's liver was plucked out nightly in Hades. Cleopatra knew the story. Immortality sometimes had a steep and awful price.

She had known that already.

After a time, she moved on from the scarred place and back into the night, following behind the Slaughterer.

➤17➤

The road back to Rome was long and hard. On the rear of the emperor's horse, the bundle containing the poisoned arrows was tied, dangerously shifting and jolting, even within its metal case. Augustus feared it, irrationally. It was not as though the arrows could strike him without being fired from a bow. He had seen them only for a moment, when the case had spilled, but the knowledge of what the venom had done to Agrippa scared him.

Poisoned arrows were not the Roman way, or, at least, not a way of honor. There had been tales of poison since the beginning of Rome, however. Augustus knew it as well as anyone. He did not desire to be a poisoner, known in the annals as a man who employed such methods.

Still, the arrows tempted him.

With a poison such as they contained, a man might be the master of all he saw.

The effects of the poison were so great that Agrippa, famously stoic, moaned in his sleeping and waking, his face flushed with suffering. The last of Augustus's theriac had been given to Agrippa to take away his pain, but once it was gone, the pain dispensed with any hunger. At last, on the third day, Augustus was able to put food into his friend's mouth, and Agrippa looked at him with clear eyes.

"What happened?" he asked. "Where are we?"

"He is improving," Augustus said. He hoped this was true.

Augustus was convinced that the world was coming to an end. They'd not seen the fireball again, but he expected they would. It was not the sort of thing that disappeared. It was not the sort of thing that was quickly vanquished. Surely, it was Cleopatra's doing.

He'd looked back at the temple as they'd ridden away, and seen a priest running down the hillside, his skin smoking. The man had thrown himself off the cliff and into the waters below.

They rode past dying villages. They saw few people on the road, and he could not help but wonder where his citizens were.

Still, he found himself in oddly good cheer.

On the sixth day of their journey back to Rome without theriac, however, conditions quickly changed. Augustus began to wobble in his saddle, his legs feeling too short for the horse, and his mind feeling once again broken and useless.

When at last, under cover of darkness, they arrived in Rome and reached the Palatine, Augustus was scarcely himself. He thirsted for his tonic so gravely that his tongue was swollen in his mouth, and he could not speak. Usem helped him from his horse and half carried him indoors. Agrippa limped behind, carrying the bundle they had risked their lives to obtain.

"We must open the box together and stab Cleopatra with the arrow as soon as she emerges," Usem told Agrippa, and Agrippa nodded tightly.

"Physician!" Nicolaus cried, entering the residence. "Physician!"

It was not physicians who came forth to meet them but the seiðkona and the household guards, all with grave faces.

"Cleopatra is escaped," the leader of the guard said. "And Chrysate is gone as well."

"Together?" Augustus cried. He had misjudged everything. He had been a fool to leave for Krimissa, imagining himself a warrior.

"Not together, no," said the guard.

Moments later, Augustus stood over Selene, gasping in horror. Her eyes opened slightly, and she looked at him. The wound stretched over her breast and up to the hollow at the base of her throat. She had been cut open like a sheep for augury.

"Where is my mother?" Selene asked deliriously.

"You should not speak," Augustus said.

"I should not have come here," she said. "I should not have trusted you. You said that you would protect me if I helped you. You did not protect me."

What did the witch want with Cleopatra's daughter? He'd left Rome, and hell had broken free from its boundaries. This was all his fault.

Augustus staggered away from Selene, and ran through the house until he reached the room where he'd arranged for Cleopatra's sons to be held in his absence. It had seemed the safest course of action to cage them in the same room where the queen herself was caged. The silver box had been kept in a separate case, safe from the children's hands, but if Chrysate had gotten to Cleopatra, she surely would have gotten to the children as well. He fumbled with the key, and then threw open the gleaming door to the silver-lined chamber.

Amazingly, the two children were there, Alexander Helios and Ptolemy Philadelphus, their small faces blinking in the sudden light. He had that, at least. He still had her children.

Augustus swayed. If he gave them up, she might leave him alone. She might cease attacking him. Another thought occurred to him. If he killed them, he might avenge all the pain Cleopatra had caused him, all the strife and chaos. He'd nearly lost control of Rome, and the sons of his enemy would only grow into new enemies.

And yet—

It was not Cleopatra who had attacked Selene. It was his own witch, Chrysate. He'd brought the creature into the house. He had done this.

Augustus closed the door to the princes' prison. He slid to the floor, his back against it. What was he doing? What had he become?

"I failed," Augustus moaned. "I thought to fight monsters, and I became one."

Agrippa came upon Augustus and looked at him with infinite concern.

"We have a weapon against Cleopatra now," he said. "We will fight her, and we will fight the witch, too." But Augustus could not hear him. Augustus could not understand the words the man was speaking. Were they in another language? Agrippa picked the emperor up like a child and, limping with his own wound, carried him from the corridor and into his own bedchamber.

"Where is she?" Usem asked the wind, and a wisp of air fluttered past him.

The Psylli's face shifted as he walked down the corridor, the arrows of Hercules in his arms. He would not wait much longer, but for his wife, he would stay his hand.

⇒18⇐

Cleopatra waited for Sekhmet's arrow. She'd seen it crossing the sky hours before, arcing downward into a mountain village and eventually returning to the heavens. She'd draped herself in her cloak and hidden herself in the mouth of a cave in the area known as Cumæ. The sun still burned her skin slightly as she gazed out over the landscape. She did not care.

Her task would be accomplished tonight.

She sheltered in the ancient lair of the Sibyl of Cumæ, who had once called out prophecies to loyal citizens, her voice echoing from the crater walls. She'd asked for an extended life but had forgotten to ask for eternal youth, and as a thousand years passed, as many years as the grains of sand she'd foolishly demanded equal her days, she'd grown smaller and smaller, older and older, until all that was left of her was a voice, and a body so tiny that it had to be kept inside a bottle to avoid being lost. At last, even those things had gone. She was long absent from here now.

Cleopatra had listened for her when she arrived and heard nothing, only the whispers of bats roosting in the dark cave corners.

She closed her eyes and felt the Slaughterer journeying. She felt Sekhmet, her back stretched against the sky, catlike, taking the light of the sun as succor while she awaited sacrifices by Cleopatra and by her arrow.

Cleopatra had sacrificed more to her on the journey here. A shepherd calling to his sheep, his blood tasting of an old grudge against a scholarly brother. A prostitute painting her face for evening, her blood tasting of the time she fell down a flight of stairs and was picked up and bandaged by a man who turned out not to love her. A slave drawing water for an evening meal, his blood tasting of a spice market, of a wooden cage shared with a dying friend. A fisherman reeling in his nets, his blood tasting of a mistress in another port, mother to several bastard children. An old widowed man left outdoors to see the stars, who looked up at Cleopatra with dazzled eyes, smiling in the face of his death. He had no secrets left.

Each one of her killings weighed on her.

She'd never thought of these things when she was in power, when she was mortal. Thousands had died in battle, acting on her orders or killed by her soldiers. She'd ordered killings of the families of traitors, of opponents. She had been a queen, and as queen she had done what she thought necessary, regardless of the human cost.

She'd never thought about where their souls went.

Now, since Hades, it was all she could think of. As she drank of their blood, she knew all of their hidden things, all of their failures and glories, and she tried to send their souls to wherever they should go. There was no time for ritual. She left their bodies in the open so that they might be found and buried, so that they might not wait on the shores of Acheron, unmourned. Having seen that place, she could not doom souls to it knowingly.

A light appeared in the sky, brighter than the dying sun, brighter than the rising moon, moving toward the Cumæan temple as she watched.

Cleopatra leapt from her hiding place and bounded out into the daylight, her skin searing, her eyes blurring as she ran at the murderous grandchild of the sun god.

"You will not kill here!" she shouted.

It hissed at her, and its mouth was infinite, deep and black as the heavens and filled with uncountable fangs. Cleopatra knew, horribly, that her soul was bonded with this creature as well as with its mother.

What was she giving up to kill it? Her soul weighed heavier, heavier yet.

The Slaughterer shifted its face toward her, and she saw its mindless eyes. It did not care what she said. Once it had hissed, it did not bother to truly acknowledge her again.

She threw herself upon it as it turned its back to fly toward the temple and to its killing task there.

Cleopatra clutched its pulsating throat, its burning body, feeling its knife-sharp feathers cutting into her palms. She gasped as it twisted and bit her hand—and this was true pain, unlike the echo of pain her blood-less body had experienced since her transformation—but she held it still tighter, straining all of her muscle and bone against its escape. Its feathers sliced into her as it struggled, and its slender, arrow body twisted in her grasp.

"You will not kill," she told it, and for the first time, she heard its voice, faint, strangely musical.

And what of you? Will you not kill?

She screamed with rage, feeling a tearing pain as she broke the Slaughterer's back, snapping its spine.

Her fury was replaced with devastating agony as she held the broken arrow up to the light, Sekhmet's roar of sorrow rattling her own bones.

"I dedicate this soul to Hades," Cleopatra shouted, and then she hurled the body of the Slaughterer down, into the dark waters of Avernus, as she'd promised the god of the Underworld she would.

Cleopatra waited for the sky to open and strike her down, but nothing happened.

The waters steamed and boiled as Plague sank into them.

Her skin blistered, her body smoking, her hands burning, and healing cruelly even as they burned, Cleopatra limped back into the cave of the sibyl, sobbing at the loss of the thing she had killed. She did not love it, no, *she* did not, but Sekhmet did, and what Sekhmet felt, Cleopatra felt. The loss of a child. A dear one.

And what was she? A betrayer. A child killer. Was she not the same as the creature she had murdered? Was she not herself a murderer? At the same time, she had torn herself from Sekhmet. She had done something on her own, something in opposition to the goddess. She had delivered the first portion of her bargain. One more act, the sacrifice of Chrysate, and she would win Antony's soul and those of her children as well. They would go to the Duat. If that was all she could do, it would be enough. She might be a slave to a goddess, but they would be in heaven.

She stretched herself on the cold stones of the sibyl's cave. The bats looked down upon her, their faces curious. Their high-pitched song filled her ears and gave her no comfort.

At last, she slept, dreamless.

As she slept, snakes slithered into the cave. Cats twined their sleek forms against the rock walls. In the valley beyond the crater, a bear trundled down a hillside, and a tiger traveled silently across the field. The rhinoceros immersed itself in the lake of Avernus, washing the dust of the road from its rough skin. A small splash, and a crocodile surfaced in the lake, having traveled by water through underground caverns and along coastlines for days.

An elderly lion, toothless and mangy, padded across the mouth of the cave, lashing its tail, and guarding the queen who slept within.

⇒19⇐

Sekhmet reeled on her hilltop, gasping and shaking. The quiver of Slaughterers hummed with confusion. Only six were left, and one had gone into the dark, where she could not see it. Where she could not feel it. Where she could not find it.

Her youngest child had been taken from her, by the human she had made into a god.

Night fell, and still she was broken. Ra did not come to comfort her. He traveled senselessly, silently, his boat traversing the Duat. He cared nothing for his daughter. He'd abandoned her, and she was alone.

The wind spun about her head, blowing and singing, and Sekhmet shook with sudden cold.

The earth rattled with the grief and fury of the sun god's forgotten daughter, but she could not smite Cleopatra without smiting herself.

⇝ 20 ⇜

The seiðkona sat in Selene's room, her back straight in her chair, her seiðstafr spinning in her hands. The floor still quaked beneath the Palatine, and high above the house, there had been a long and woeful scream. A hungry star had died, and the seiðkona had heard it. A goddess grieved her child. The seiðkona stretched her fingers, paying close attention to the alterations in the tapestry. Sekhmet's fate had shifted. An immortal's child had been killed. Auðr searched for the thread of the killer and discovered that she already held it in her hand.

Cleopatra.

She looked up, feeling the movement of dark magic somewhere on the grounds. She twisted her distaff just slightly, and the sharp thread of the witch coiled about it. Chrysate would not enter this chamber. She felt the creature stop, change course, depart to another place. Soon, Auðr could no longer feel her.

She shifted her attentions to Selene. The girl's fate had been dark, and now it was brighter. She had taken her from death and brought her back. A queen. Selene would have a long life, be married by the emperor of Rome to an African king. A happy marriage. Recompense for her pain. Her heart would be further broken in the days to come, and Auðr had taken mercy on her.

Selene had no great acts left to perform. The seiðkona had shifted them away.

The witch's ring sat on a table in the seiðkona's chambers. Auðr did not know how to destroy it, but she had gotten it free of Selene's finger, and surely now it was a mere bauble.

In her tapestry, the seiðkona saw lives ending, and lives beginning. She saw a battle, and many dead. She saw the moon rotating in its orbit, gleaming like a tooth in a demon's smile, and she saw lightning slashing the sky. She saw herself walking the battlefield. She did not know which side she fought on, if she fought on a side at all.

Things looked dark ahead, things looked broken, but there might still be change.

Cleopatra had surprised her. She'd fought her fate. She had not given in.

The seiðkona would not either. She curled herself about her tightening lungs, willing herself to survive just a little longer. She had a part to play.

She knew she did, even if she did not know what it was.

I n his chamber, the emperor's skin prickled with constant terror, and nothing gave him ease. A string of rough, scarlet blotches ran from his throat to his thigh. He turned his head and vomited into the basin that waited beside his cot.

His mind was blotted with visions, Sibylline prophecies of his own manufacture. He saw Cleopatra and Chrysate wherever he looked, in every corner, beneath every veil, in shadows and in light. Kidnappers surged at him when he left his house to attend to his business, and then disappeared without touching him, their dark cloaks slipping into the cracks in the stones. Every flash of sun revealed a sword, half concealed, threatening his throat. Every flutter of wings told him that she was waiting somewhere nearby. He thought of the moth she had been when last he'd seen her. The bloodred body and the wings white as death.

His organs twisted in his body, reminding him of all the ceremonies he'd overseen, the augurs pawing through animal organs, announcing omens.

Slice yourself open, said his mind. *Read your own entrails. See if they tell you what to do. See if they tell you of the fall of Rome. See if they tell you how you invited a witch into your bed.*

He would die if he did not sleep. He knew this much.

Nicolaus sat in the corner, waiting to take down changes to the emperor's will.

Augustus fretted. Who would he leave Rome to if he died?

He could not leave the empire to Julia, to a daughter, but she was all he had. He thrashed in his covers, chilled and then boiling, frozen and then sweating. He summoned the seiðkona, leaving the will for later when he might have a moment of clarity. Perhaps she might take his thoughts and make him sleep. She hobbled into the room, older than she had been. Augustus felt as ancient as he ever had. Perhaps this was what happened when one fought immortals. Life passed in an instant.

"Will I live?" he asked Auðr, hearing his childhood self asking the same question of Cleopatra.

She placed her hands on his face, touched the air around him, spun her fingers.

You will live a long life, she said in his mind. He felt, suddenly, that he had not asked the right question.

He walked from his bedchamber on thin and fragile legs, and out into the sunlight of the courtyard, where Agrippa was standing, one leg bandaged, his armor already tightened.

A messenger from Cleopatra awaited him. He had known it was coming.

Cleopatra had sent a child she'd plucked from the village near her hiding place. It was fitting. Augustus had sent a message to Antony that way, the message that had led to Antony's death.

All who saw the messenger pass, in the towns that had been scarred by disease, in the towns that had been touched by the rumors of strange goings-on in Rome, of monsters, of a dying emperor, looked to the heavens and tried to interpret the signs.

Surely, they imagined the child they saw riding on the back of a running tiger, his tiny form jouncing as he held tight to the cat's fur. Surely, it had not been a tiger but some other sort of animal.

The boy stood before Agrippa and Augustus, offering them a message addressed to "Octavian, Augustus, Emperor, Fool."

Augustus took it, aggrieved, and read it aloud. The writing was elegant.

"Surrender my children and yourself, and I will leave your country and your people. I will not return here."

Agrippa looked at Augustus.

"The rest?" Agrippa asked.

"If you choose not to surrender, know that I will lay waste to Italy. I will kill everyone you love, and I will destroy your country as you destroyed mine."

"Rome will not surrender," Augustus informed the messenger. "Rome does not surrender. Its emperor is not a coward. We will fight."

"Midnight, then," the boy trilled, excited. "Seven nights from tonight. At Avernus. She will meet you there, and in fair battle."

"Avernus?" asked Augustus, appalled.

It was to the south of Rome, a crater where Aeneas had descended into Hades, according to the legends. There the rivers of the Underworld came aboveground in bitter springs and a poisoned lake, and caves housed creatures Augustus did not want to encounter. There was one cave in particular, at the ancient Greek settlement of Cumæ, which he remembered all too well from his fight against the pirate Sextus Pompeius, twenty years before. It had a chill about it, and a depth that was beyond sounding. It was an ideal hiding place for a monster, meandering, as it did, deep into the hillside.

Augustus did not want to go to Avernus. Nor did he want to stay in Rome. He could not fight her here, in a city filled with people. He thought of the plague springing from village to village. Too many would die, and the streets and buildings offered ample hiding places for a thing such as the queen. Better the wide, open expanses surrounding the crater. Better, he knew, but it made him uneasy nonetheless.

"Will she fight alone?" Augustus asked the boy.

The boy shrugged.

"It will not matter," said Agrippa. "We are Romans. Have we not fought on plains and in mountains? Have we not fought our way through the cities of Babylonia and the forests of Germany? We have fought at Cumæ and at Avernus."

"Not well," Augustus pointed out. The fumes of the crater lake had sickened the men. Birds were said to die midair above the place.

"My men are prepared, and we have our weapon now."

Augustus returned to the messenger, outside the doors of the study, and handed him a coin.

"Tell your mistress we will meet her."

He wondered if he imagined what he saw next. The striped, shining fur, the boy mounting the beast's back as though he were mounting a horse, the liquid stalking motion of the thing, and moments later, the lashing tail disappearing around the corner of the courtyard wall.

Shaking his head to dispel the vision, he returned to his study, where Agrippa had taken the bow from its box. Wincing at the pain in his still festering calf, Agrippa attempted to draw the bow, straining at its string.

"We need not use Hercules' bow," Augustus pointed out. "The poison is in the arrows."

Agrippa was still weak, Augustus knew, and moreover, the bow was meant to be drawn only by a hero, which Agrippa clearly was not.

Augustus had no doubts about himself in this regard. He would draw the bow when the time came. He would fire the arrows. He would kill the queen. It was his fated task, and he was the only one who would perform it.

Agrippa looked nervously at the arrows.

"I prefer the sword," he said.

"As do I," said Augustus. "We do not have that luxury. One arrow, and this will be done. One arrow, and she will be gone. Think of that. Do not worry. I will take charge of the bow."

"I must prepare my men to march," said Agrippa. He wanted the Hydra arrows returned to their grave, far from here. His calf blistered and seeped. It was wrapped in layers of bandages, and still it did not heal. He'd die of this wound, if not soon, then eventually. He knew it in his bones. He tightened the bandage about the leg and limped from Augustus's study.

Augustus deliberated about the princes of Egypt. At last, he decided to leave them in Rome, safely caged in their silver room. They were children, and he would not bring them into battle. He could not bring himself to kill them. He could not bring himself to let their mother kill them, either, as he was certain she would.

He would win this battle with the arrows of Hercules, and she would be conquered, completely this time. He had the seiðkona and the Psylli. He had the powers of the Western Wind and of memory. He had Agrippa's armies. What did she have?

No matter what Cleopatra and Sekhmet were capable of, they could not beat back all the forces of Rome.

There would be no more of this. When it was done, he'd return to Rome and to his daughter. He would return to these sons of Egypt. They showed promise, particularly the smallest one. He remembered the little boy's strength in the Circus Maximus, his determination as he ran into the arena. They would forget their parents, as their sister had. He felt a pang as he thought of Selene, still half conscious in her room. He pushed the thoughts away.

He would be their hero. Sons.

Augustus went to his chamber and called his servants. They bathed him, anointed him. He put the gilded laurel crown atop his head. They strapped his armor onto his chest.

He brought Cleopatra Selene with him, ensconced in a padded litter with the seiðkona beside her. The legionaries that had gone in pursuit of the Greek witch had not found Chrysate, and he no longer trusted the guards to keep the girl safe. It would not matter. Selene would not remember this. She was still not herself, sleeping her wound away, waking only occasionally, mutely.

His skin pricked with righteous rage, thinking of the witch. She would be next, after Cleopatra. He would find her, if he had to go to Thessaly himself.

He made his way outside and ascended the steps of the platform that had been erected for his speech. Before him, a legion waited, armed, their faces still and watchful. Beside him, Usem and Agrippa stood, strong and loyal. The emperor of Rome was ready to fight, and he rallied his warriors.

"We march toward an enemy we have not seen before, but we will prevail!" he shouted, flanked by Agrippa and Nicolaus. "We will return home to our wives and our children!"

He glanced at the Psylli and felt a pang of jealousy, comparing himself to the snake charmer's story. Augustus knew that he did not care enough about his family. He did not love them as much as he ought to. He loved Rome more. Was not Rome family enough? Was not Rome love enough?

It was.

"Though I cannot tell you what it is we will meet at Avernus, I can tell you that we are Romans. No enemy is as strong as we are. We've come from warriors, and we've been adopted by wolves. We have built Rome from out of the wild, and it will not return to chaos! We will fight and we will win, our swords bloodied, our arrows broken, and our voices carrying across the world. This is the empire of Augustus, and you serve beside me! I fight with you!"

He drove his sword into the air, listening to the cheers of his army as he rode from Rome, leading a legion of six thousand.

It was time.

The Palatine was nearly empty by the time the door of the silver room opened, and the princes looked up, startled by the light. They had been praying to the Egyptian gods, and praying for their mother, Alexander Helios leading Ptolemy. The elder held the younger in his arms on their pallet. The little one had been crying for days, and his brother did not know how to comfort him.

Since they had seen their mother captured in the arena, Alexander had lost hope. Still, they prayed for her. They prayed for their father. They had seen him, too. Somehow, their parents, who had been dead, were in Rome. Alexander promised Ptolemy that their parents would come for them. He promised Ptolemy that they would not die here.

He was not so sure of this himself. They were imprisoned. He could think of no reason for it, beyond that they had somehow become enemies of Rome. He spent his days and nights thinking of a means of escape. They could go back to Egypt. They could hide there, in Alexandria, until they were grown enough to do something. Then, he would try to make things right. He should never have trusted the emperor. Should never have marched in the triumph.

They heard the sound of footsteps in the corridor outside, and Alexander stiffened.

The door opened, and it was his mother, looking just as she always had. She put a finger to her lips to bid them be silent, but Ptolemy could not. He leapt up and ran into Cleopatra's arms, already crying her name.

Alexander Helios stayed on the pallet. There was something about her that made him suspicious. He could not tell what it was.

"Who are you?" he asked, calling his brother back. "I don't know you."

"How can you say that?" the woman asked. "How can you not recognize your own mother?"

Alexander saw, in that moment, her eyes flash with a strange green glow. He saw her skin, shriveled. An impersonation. She clutched Ptolemy to her breast, and over the little boy's head she smiled viciously at Alexander.

He had no choice but to go with her. He stood, pretending he believed her to be his mother. He had no idea what else to do. All he could do was follow Chrysate as she made her way out of the silver room, his brother clenched in her arms.

"Where are you taking us?" he asked, trying to keep his voice natural.

"I am taking you home," Chrysate answered. "I am taking you to your family."

⇒21⇐

The earth shook with the marching of legions, all moving toward Avernus. Messengers flew, whispering to centurions, whispering to generals, passing written instructions along with well-embroidered rumors. Horses, frothing, fell at the roadsides, shying at the strange snakes that coursed over the roads even in daylight. Their riders leapt off and ran on. Men marched onward, sweating and burning in the heat of summer's end, their armor heavy, their swords sheathed and sharpened, their feet beating a deep track into the dust.

Usem rode unsaddled, his coral ornaments polished. His dagger gleamed, its metal darker and stranger than anything the Romans had seen before. All who looked on him felt uneasy. The man's skin shone in the sun, and nothing about him was Roman. He wore something about his shoulders that sometimes was a leopard skin and sometimes was the night sky, and beside him, around him, a tornado traveled, cooling nothing.

The legionaries watched Usem talking with the whirlwind, heard her talking back to him, whispers carried on the breeze, pouring into their ears and eyes. The snake sorcerer rode beside the emperor, protecting him from unknown enemies, and the Romans, in spite of themselves, feared him.

With Usem and Augustus rode the emperor's historian, his armor rattling and ill-fitting. The soldiers had expected Nicolaus to perform the role of a poet, reciting words of war at night, singing songs of courage by day. Instead, the Damascene was silent, and this made the Romans even more nervous than they already were.

Their commander, Marcus Agrippa, wore bandages around his calf, and his face showed pain as he rode. Those who served nearest him saw him unwinding his bandages and redressing his wound, and they reported that it festered, hot and red, unhealing. He would not let servants touch it.

Only Augustus seemed himself, though his eyes were bright with fever. He rode ferociously up and down the lines of marching men, shouting encouragements to the army, asserting that they would best an enemy they could not imagine.

At night, roaring could be heard, but it came from no clear location. The earth shook and then was stable again. The soldiers looked to the heavens, thinking of Zeus and wondering which side he was on, that of the emperor of Rome or that of the dead queen of Egypt.

The purses of old women and of augurs filled with coins as they interpreted omens for the marching armies. Overhead, eagles wheeled, and vultures, too, following the leavings of the army.

Agrippa and Augustus, Nicolaus riding beside them, arrived in Alba only to find that the legion that had been garrisoned there had already marched south. Augustus was delighted to see that the army had received their orders and traveled responsively, but Agrippa was uneasy. Perhaps it was the pain of his leg. Perhaps it was something more.

Their next station, Formiae, was similarly emptied of men. Agrippa had sent the orders ahead himself, had written the letters, and yet he mistrusted the quiet. The legion had traveled too quickly. Their dust should still be in sight. Augustus, on the other hand, was exuberant, sweating in the heat of the sun, singing in the cool of the night, reminded once more of his boyhood beside Agrippa, beside Julius Caesar, of the glorious times before he'd become truly Glorious.

At night, the sky filled with stars, and Augustus looked up at them, imagining himself stationed amongst the constellations. He imagined his own gods looking down upon his deeds, approving.

He would win this time. He would win. He had an army behind him and Hercules' bow upon his back. Who knew what Rome would be when this battle was over?

Who knew what worlds existed to be conquered once Rome had beaten such an enemy?

Selene, in her litter, rocked down the dusty Appian behind the army, her eyes closed, her skin chilled. The seiðkona traveled with her, trying to draw her own strength together. She had so little now. Her time was nearly done.

As the legions marched into Avernus, Cleopatra waited. It was sundown, and the moon rose in a yellow crescent. She could smell the armies coming toward her. She could feel their footsteps and hear their lust for battle. She could feel Augustus and Agrippa.

She had not been in battle since Actium.

She missed Antony, their planning together, the nights before the battle had taken place. She missed her lover, her general, her partner.

She knew, though, that she would have to do this alone. He was gone, and this was her fight, not his. She would fight to save her children and Antony. She would fight to avenge herself upon the man who had taken everything from her.

She thought of Augustus's heart, and of how it would feel in her hands. She could feel it beating, his excitement as he approached. She could feel Chrysate, too, traveling somewhere in the vicinity of the Romans.

She would finish her task. She would be damned after tonight, if she had not been before. Her *ka*, if she ever reclaimed it, would fall against Maat's feather, and the Eater of Souls would take it. She prayed to her own country's gods, to Isis, long-neglected goddess of mothers. To Thoth, for knowledge.

She prayed not for herself, but for her children, the one who was gone and the ones who still remained. Her hands, when she spread them before her, were tipped with the claws of the lioness. Her body rippled with muscles that were not human.

She could not feel Sekhmet, but she had become a version of her. She could feel herself forfeiting the parts that had been Cleopatra.

The whirlwind where her heart had been no longer disturbed her.

At last, the queen rose to her feet and began to climb the hill toward the crater's mouth.

The armies of Rome had arrived.

She would meet them.

Chrysate had found a beautiful abandoned cave, and though it smelled of felines, of bats, and of something else as well, it would do. It went deep into the side of the rocks. It was cool and ancient, and the cool soothed her skin, chapped and burnt after days of travel. It had taken no small magic to conceal herself and Cleopatra's children in the litter of a senator's mistress, a woman she'd throttled just south of Rome. The elder child had fought her, tearing her skin and wounding her delicate flesh. Finally, after he'd managed to push the younger from the litter, screaming at him to run, Chrysate had been obliged to drug him. It had taken her a great deal of energy to lay hands on the small one, who was well hidden in the bushes, and he had kicked her and screamed that she was not his mother.

She found the entire thing wearing.

They'd left the slow-moving litter after a few days and traveled in the bed of a wagon, Chrysate's skin parching beneath the cloth that covered her. By then her charges were heavy and dull-witted with potions and disguised with the witch's ebbing magic. It had been no small labor keeping them with her, no small labor keeping them hidden.

She ran her fingernails over Alexander and Ptolemy. She did not care for children, particularly male children. There was no point to them, none but this.

They were her only currency now, but it was not time. Not yet.

→ 22 ←

Usem loped across the hill to where Augustus and Agrippa sat on horseback, their armor and regalia shining. The lines of Roman soldiers spread around them, each man perfectly distanced from the next, each man still and resolved. Waiting.

"If she is here, the battle will begin soon," Usem said, looking at the position of the moon in the sky, and the emperor shuddered. "Do you remember my price?"

There was a light in the man's eyes, an amber glow, and his teeth seemed sharper than they had before. The Psylli's snakes twisted about his limbs, hissing at Augustus, their eyes, all of their eyes, directed at him. The wind twisted about him as well, passing over his sweating skin, and it chilled him.

"I do," Augustus said. Peace for the Roman Empire would not be too great a price for this, he knew now. To be free of Cleopatra. To be free of witches and sorcerers.

"Then my family is at the ready," Usem said, pointing to the horizon. "Remember. We must kill her. Not trap her." The clouds were massed there, dark and full of lightning. As the Psylli pointed, Augustus watched horns appear on a cloudy skull, a cloudy tail lashing, a cloudy maw open in a roar. *His* warriors.

Augustus looked appreciatively at the lines, so measured, so plotted. What could resist the Roman army? Nothing.

The men were silent, watchful. Overhead, Augustus saw a bird flit across the sky, and the wind began to rise, touching each section of the battlefield.

A faint sound of drumming began to echo over the crater, and Usem's head whipped around, searching the dark for the source. Nothing.

From far across the battlefield, there was a single sound, a roar, long and hoarse and primal. The legionaries shifted uneasily, looking blindly into the dark. Whatever it was, it was nearby.

Suddenly, though, all around the Romans, the night was alive with sparks of light. Augustus drew in his breath. What was happening? He felt surrounded, but he could not see what surrounded him. The light was cold and seemed unattached to any army. The sparks moved, slowly, encroaching.

On the crest of the hilltop, the darkness stretched into silhouettes, and the Romans gasped as one, disbelieving the shape of what they saw.

The moon came out from behind a cloud and revealed Cleopatra's army.

Augustus was speechless.

The sparks of light were thousands of eyes reflecting like jewels. Cleopatra shone at the center of the line and the sound Augustus had thought was drumming, was not.

It was footsteps.

The earth vibrated with their coming. The queen was flanked by an army of animals. They covered the hillside like a carpet, no space between them. There were as many of them as there were Romans. Tigers and leopards and lions. A bull elephant, its tusks long and yellow. A rhinoceros. Everything the Romans had ever seen in the arenas, in marketplaces, in dreams, and in nightmares. Animals who had been captured and pressed into service. Animals who'd danced at dinners, fought with gladiators, and hungered for revenge from deep beneath the streets of Rome. They walked with one rhythm, and Cleopatra's hands lay on the backs of two leopards, white beneath the moonlight, their coats spotted with darkness, their teeth bared. The ground swarmed, alive with rats and snakes.

"PREPARE FOR BATTLE!" Agrippa bellowed, and within moments, all the men were running, to their stations, running for their lives.

"You will give me my children!" Cleopatra shouted. "Give them to me, and I will spare Rome its army. Keep them, and you will all die."

Her voice echoed unnaturally, amplified. Augustus could see the details of his enemy from his position. Her bracelets. Her tight linen gown unspoiled by these months, this year since she had been buried. He could see her curving body beneath the sheer fabric. She was a demon, he knew. He knew.

He could see the accursed silver box she carried in her hands. He could feel her breathing across the battlefield. Not human. Nothing human about her.

Augustus suppressed a sound as he caught sight of a crocodile clambering out of the water. Another. And another after it. The water roiled with their tails. Above the crater, the animals continued to come, eerily silent. No roars, no singing. They came as though they were ghosts, but they were not. Augustus could smell their hunger, the rich scent of the cats and the musky scent of the snakes. The moonlit sky grew dark with birds and bats.

"My children," Cleopatra repeated. "You took my husband from me, and I will have my children back."

"I will not give them to you!" Augustus shouted, finding his voice at last. "You are not fit to have them. Who are you to demand sacrifices of Rome? What you lost, you lost in war!"

Augustus felt all his men beginning to panic. He looked to Agrippa, and saw him making frantic gestures, instructing the men to hold their positions.

She was still too far from him to touch him. He was grateful for that. Not afraid, no. She was only an enemy, and there had been many enemies. His head wore the crown, and he knew that it was desired by every man who had ever walked the earth. And every woman, too. There was no one alive who did not want to rule the world.

She tilted her head, noticing for the first time the man beside the emperor.

"Nicolaus," she said, and the emperor heard sorrow in her tone. Beside him, the historian moved uncomfortably closer to Agrippa. Augustus pushed him back into the shelter of the pavilion. He was derailing the negotiation.

"You lost your husband and your children when you lost your city, and you lost your city because you were not strong enough to keep it. You will surrender to me!" Augustus continued, looking into her dark eyes. He would kill her. He held the bow of Hercules behind his back, with its deathly poisoned arrow.

"Do you believe your own words?" Cleopatra asked him, her tone warning. "Do I look weak to you, Octavian? I am not the woman who lost a war in Alexandria. I am no longer Cleopatra."

Augustus stood his ground. "You are nothing!" Augustus shouted. "You are a slave to this empire!"

Agrippa shouted a command, and the men of the Roman army marched forward around the rim of the crater in perfect formation, though their feet slipped and dislodged boulders at the crater's edge. A man fell screaming into space, tumbling into the dark and sinking beneath the lake's waters, weighed down by his armor.

The others of his line maintained their spacing. Their shields were raised to form a wall of metal before them.

Cleopatra merely raised her hands, and the sounds of her animals, heretofore silenced, ripped through the air. There was no line, and this was no normal battle formation.

Instead, the Romans were faced with a mass of beasts, sleek and rough, fanged and tremendous. The lions and tigers roared, and gathered themselves into shining masses of violence, and the Romans felt their bodies liquefy in fear. What sort of war was this? They were not bestiarii. They had not been trained to fight animals, and their commander had not warned them that this would be the case. Still, they stayed in their lines. They looked neither to the left nor to the right. They kept their positions. They marched forward, their heads protected by their shields, hiding their fear. As long as they kept to their lines, nothing could touch them. They were warriors.

Several men whispered prayers.

The elephant, fled from an arena, trumpeted and reared onto its hind legs, silhouetted against the starry sky. A tremendous bear rose over the crest of the hill, looking into the midst of the army with dark, intelligent eyes. It tossed its head and bellowed, each fang as long as a finger.

A leopard, lean and bloodthirsty, lifted its lip and snarled as it came.

The queen marched toward the Roman line, her animals following her, their bodies moving as though powered by a single soul. Her eyes glowed with an unearthly light, and from his position, Augustus watched her, raging. What right had she to bring animals against him?

Augustus nodded at Agrippa.

"Archers!" shouted the general.

The archers, positioned behind the infantry, pulled their bows from their backs and fit the special silver-tipped arrows into them. Each man had been provided with a rich quiver full.

"Fool," said Cleopatra quietly, as if to herself.

"Fire!" shouted Agrippa.

The men moved to draw back their bowstrings, but then stared at them, bewildered at the lack of tension in the strings, some sort of sabotage of their weaponry.

A rat leapt out of a Roman arrow case. Another. Soon, a swarm of rats covered the ground, and each of the Roman archers stood appalled, their gnawed bowstrings in their fingers, their bows useless.

The rats seethed about Roman feet, climbing Roman bodies, biting and scratching, and the Romans were, for a moment, in total disarray, their archers incapacitated.

"Infantry!" Agrippa screamed, signaling the lines.

"Kill them," Cleopatra whispered, and every animal on the battlefield heard her command.

Her cats, leopards, lions, and tigers, drew back on their haunches and leapt over the shields and into the legionaries, claws shredding the unprepared men, teeth rending their flesh. No shield could save them. A tiger died, impaled on a short sword, and as it fell, its body crushed the astonished soldier who had slain it.

The world rang with screams, with shouting and moaning, with ululations in the face of foes, and Cleopatra pushed forward, the emperor still her focus. Augustus kept the precious bow behind his back. He felt a trickle of sweat run down his side. Agrippa stood beside him, shouting orders.

Surely the Romans must outnumber the beasts, Augustus thought. They would win. They had the advantage of order in the face of chaos. Chaos could not possibly prevail. A guard surrounded Agrippa and Augustus, tightly spaced, shields raised.

Lightning flashed in the sky, and thunder shook the earth. High above, the heavens echoed with the sound of something enormous, roaring. The hairs rose on Augustus's neck, and he felt the air charged with the presence of the divine.

Beside him, Auðr's hands twisted frantically in the air, her distaff spinning threads, trying to balance the dead with the living. The goddess and Cleopatra were both present, but the thread of the Slaughterer was a frayed end in the Underworld, and Sekhmet's strand, where it had been braided to her child's, was ragged.

Cleopatra had injured the goddess.

She had pulled a part of her soul away from Sekhmet, and yet she continued to war. Auðr still could not see the entire pattern. Her eyes flickered over the darkness, a swooning miasma. Her lungs were tight. She was not strong enough to hold the two fates, that of the queen and of the goddess, apart from each other for long, and she knew it.

Sekhmet is here, the seiðkona said, and Augustus heard it in his mind. *She hungers for Rome. I cannot keep her from you. She will have you.*

A bolt of lightning struck the earth just before Augustus's pavilion, and he leapt backward, his skin singed. Agrippa stayed firm, fearless, devoted. Augustus shook off the terror and shouted orders at his guard.

The men looked toward the sky and panicked, as bats swooped down from above, into their faces. Shields began to flail. Swords lashed out at the creatures, who came diving downward on their thin wings, blacking out the stars. With them came the birds of night, their claws outstretched for eyes, their wings flapping into faces, their beaks spearing, their shrieks deafening.

The lines began to break down.

Men gasped, slashing at their feet as serpents flooded the ground, twining about their ankles and up their thighs, biting and coiling, tripping and tangling. A viper's head, chopped off by a blade, rolled into the crater, staining the waters and leaving the serpent's body, writhing headless, still strangling a dying man on the battlefield above. A mass of crocodiles, their bodies nearly invisible in the darkness of the rocky ground, lumbered out of the water, snatching soldiers' legs and soldiers' arms, dragging men into Avernus.

Augustus watched, horrified. Could he be losing this battle? No. Certainly not. Where were the rest of the legions that had come before them? Agrippa had sworn they would be there. Thousands of men. Agrippa had sent the orders himself. Augustus felt frantic, seeing his own Romans tiring, watching them slain and battling, falling to the ground and being trampled, killing one another inadvertently.

Usem fought before Augustus, his own sword flashing in the moonlight, bloodied, guarding the emperor's position.

Cleopatra was still too far from him to shoot, but as he watched, the Romans gained slight traction. The lines were broken and men were fighting blindly, but the animals, though savage, were not strategists. He watched three men heave a screaming lion into the crater, watched his army clutching poisonous snakes and throwing them back at the other side. They were brave, even in the face of an unprecedented melee. Augustus felt a strange pride along with his terror at the monstrous scene before him. This was not Rome, nor was it empire. This was a battle from the lands of myth, a story.

Everything is true, the priest of Apollo had said. *Everything.*

This was a story told to him in darkness, a story to bring sleep, and at the end of stories like this, the Romans conquered the savages.

Yet it was here before him. Blood flew through the air, and the screams of the dying and the raging echoed over the water. Augustus moved his hand where it clutched the bow of Hercules, feeling the smoothness of the wood and metal, the place worn in the weapon where it had been held by heroes far greater than himself.

He was a hero. He swore it to himself. If he was not a hero, then what was he?

He would save Rome from this monstrous thing, from this woman. *Despoina*, the sibyls had called her, but she would not be mistress of the end of the world. Augustus would stop her.

Cleopatra kept moving toward him, her face calm and collected, her hands rising in the air and commanding her creatures.

The sound of marching was suddenly upon them, and with the marching, a chanting cry.

"Thank the gods," Augustus breathed, and Agrippa nodded tightly at him.

Augustus looked up to greet his relief armies cresting the hill and instead saw an army at odds with his own. They held a flag, and it was not emblazoned with Rome's eagle but with a snake.

A group of elderly senators, with their bald pates and white togas fresh from the fullers, marched onto the hilltop with their army and massed with Cleopatra and her army of wild animals. Augustus looked up and saw a senator across the battlefield, smiling directly, triumphantly into his face.

Augustus felt Agrippa seize with fury beside him.

"Romans!" he shouted. "I am Marcus Agrippa, your commander! I am he who summoned you here!"

Augustus straightened the laurels on his head and leapt atop a rock to address the crowd.

"I am your emperor!" he screamed. "You will serve Rome or you will be declared traitors!"

This was his empire, his world. The senators would not win against him, and he would have them killed when this was finished. He would save Rome from all these traitors. He would save his people.

"Surrender!" Cleopatra yelled back from across the battlefield. A loyal soldier ran at her, his sword poised to slice through her body.

Cleopatra grabbed the man by the throat and lifted him into the air, breaking his body in her hands. She dropped him like a discarded toy.

In the crowd before the boulder, Augustus watched an ivory horn tossing a legionary into the air, piercing his kidneys and heaving him up and into his fellows. A glittering black eye, and dark, scaled skin trickled with tarry blood.

Usem ran forward and slashed at the rhinoceros and it retreated, bellowing, even as Augustus's own Romans, his own soldiers, marched forward at their counterparts, the men still loyal to Rome. Augustus watched, his breath catching in his chest, as the soldiers just before him, the men guarding him, began to cave in.

Usem shouted, and the beasts of the Western Wind were released against the betraying Romans. They snarled, their bodies created of dust and light, of dark and chill, of tornado and hurricane, of lightning and thunder. Their bodies contained uprooted trees and boulders, ships and creatures. The betraying Romans and the senators who commanded them wavered.

"I would never give you your children!" Augustus shouted. "Why would I give them to such a mother?"

She need only come a little closer. Behind his back, he positioned the bow. The arrow was already placed in it. Only the string remained to be pulled taut, and it could be fired.

"You must kill her," Usem hissed. "That is the only way this will end. Wait for me. I will give you room."

➤ 23 ⬅

Cleopatra's vision blurred with blood and light. It was as it had been aboard the ship, her hunger, her fury. She lost moments and then found herself with blood on her hands. The waters below were red and the lake was dotted with Roman corpses. The ground was slick and the fallen lay in heaps, arms spread out, their gods nowhere to be seen.

She could feel Sekhmet's glory. She was Sekhmet's glory.

It was all going according to her plan. Her army of beasts and Romans spread across the field, fighting at her command. Her body surged with the violence, with the bloodshed, and she felt her strength growing with every kill. Sekhmet, high above, roared.

Nicolaus dashed across the battlefield, too near her, and she leapt at him.

"Betrayer," she hissed.

"I did not mean to be," the historian whispered, and she could see that he had not. Still. He would be punished.

She clawed him, only once, from his shoulder to his wrist, his writing hand. Then she left him on the field and moved on, closer, closer, to the emperor.

Suddenly, before her was an unexpected warrior. The snake charmer. She hissed at him, and he hissed back, his knife dancing from hand to hand. She clawed at him, spitting with fury as his blade nicked her arm, in the very place where the Hydra venom had wounded her. He danced faster than light, faster than air, and suddenly, it seemed as though he was flying.

What was she fighting?

The Psylli rose on the back of a beast, and the beast spat dust and bone in her face. It spat salt water, a tidal wave of ocean, and fish, gasping, plucked from the deep, and still Usem attacked her, his eyes blazing.

Vengeance. Reckoning. Augustus was standing behind the man, fumbling with something behind his back, but she couldn't get past Usem.

The warrior and the wind were stronger than she had expected, and it took all her power to fight them.

The elder boy struggled, drugged though he was, but the witch had him, a rope twisted about his neck. What was left of Chrysate's face contorted as she dragged the child up the hillside path, invisible to those battling above her. The other boy she had by the wrist, her fingernails digging into his flesh. Her scry had revealed strange things, changes in the fates. She'd consulted it just before the battle. What had happened? What had the Northern witch done?

The end of everything, but she saw nothing for herself. No Chrysate. No Hecate. No cave in Thessaly. Nothing.

Chrysate tripped on a soldier's body and fell, her fingers slipping in his blood. The children were wailing. She heard their high tones over the deeper ones of the battle. Music. The heavens bent to listen. The gods, even the gods of love, loved war.

Chrysate pushed herself back to her feet, dragging her prisoners with her. The small one kicked at her legs, and she shook him until he was limp. The larger flung himself at her, and she hit him in the brow with the hilt of her stolen sword. Easier now. She laid them, almost gently, on the grass. No one was watching her. Everyone fought, insensible to what was about to happen.

Across the battlefield, she could see the queen, hear her battle cries, and watch the legions falling before her strange army of beasts. She was wreaking havoc, and Sekhmet was within her, all around her. She battled the Psylli, and all her attention was on him.

QUEEN OF KINGS ←

Chrysate whispered, and the sky shifted at her urging. A star came closer to light her work, sending a glow down upon the witch of Thessaly and her charges.

The moon's pale surface turned red as Chrysate laced her spell about the moon's surface and drew it down from its orbit until it hung just above her hilltop. She'd placed herself purposefully. There was a price, of course, but she had planned for this. For all of this.

Alexander Helios and Ptolemy Philadelphus, sons of Egypt. Royal children. The girl would have been more powerful, but the boys would do.

Were they unwilling sacrifices? It no longer mattered. They were drugged, and Chrysate, priestess of Hecate, *psuchagôgoi* of Thessaly, supplemented her diminished strength with the borrowed power of the sky. The waters at the bottom of the crater opened for her, and the bitter lake of hatred shone in the moonlight.

She drew her dagger from her belt and slit the younger child's throat, the skin soft and yielding. The child's eyes widened as she cut him, but he did not protest. The drug had him quieted, and he was frozen, scarcely capable of movement. She laid Ptolemy back on the bank for the moon to take as her fee.

Chrysate held Alexander out over the waters, and slit his throat— dull-eyed, she thought, like a goat, and dull-spirited, no match for his royal title—letting his blood pour down into the crater. It splashed in the dark liquid, Hecate's gift.

"I summon you," she shouted, exultant. "Come to me!"

The world froze in a moment as Hades opened, frost riming the armor of the Romans.

From the darkness, snow began to fall.

Pale shapes surged up through the boundary. There was a wailing deep in the lake. Fingers breached the surface of the freezing water, and then thousands of shades, hundreds of thousands of shades, crying for the royal blood that had been spilled in their sacrifice. Suicides and heroes, warriors and women, infants and ancients, they came surging upward into the cruel red light of the moon, and behind them, the Underworld emptied.

"Hecate! Hear me!" Chrysate cried. "Take them, take these fighters, take these wounded, take these dying and these dead! I dedicate their sacrifice to you! Feast on them and join me!"

The earth shook, and from beneath the hillside, the hounds of Hecate began to howl. Chrysate could hear the great Cerberus growling with fury.

The shades drank of life, their mouths wide-open. The blood poured from the child into the dead.

Chrysate was listening to one more sound below all of them, the rattling of a tremendous chain, a song, twisting and ecstatic, the song of a goddess rising from her banishment, when the shade of Antony rose from the crevasse, his body whipping with anguish, moving faster than light.

The witch laughed as he emerged. He was too late.

Antony screamed, his wails echoing through Hades and across the upper world. He held his children in his dark arms, but the younger was gone already. The elder was dying. Antony cursed, a dead man holding his dead children.

Cleopatra, battling with Usem and his wife, heard Antony's screams, gathered her haunches beneath her and leapt over the Roman army, across the impossible distance at Chrysate, her teeth bared, her claws outstretched.

There was a shudder across the battlefield as Chrysate raised her hands into the air and pushed her long nails into the moon, holding it tightly. She hurled it across the crater, the crescent's points serving as spears. It spun in the air, bright, lighting the world, but Cleopatra raised her hand, heaved the moon aside and kept coming.

Cleopatra grew larger as she charged, swollen with chaos, swollen with war. Her body was lioness, and her arms were serpent. Her face was her own.

Screaming, she bared her teeth to sink them into Chrysate.

The moon careened across the battlefield, slaying those it touched, igniting the grass. The shades surged across the battlefield, an army of teeth and claws, their mouths open, and all the blood in the world not enough for them.

The lake was filled with souls, and beneath them, something else began to surge upward, a darkness streaming with all the waters of Lethe.

The moon, flying through the sky and bouncing against the crater walls, was one moment blinding and the next blackness, and in the crater, tremendous fingers began to be visible, dark and drowned hair streaming in the waters, the skin blue with cold, the eyes deeper than night, reflecting their own moons and stars.

"Hecate," Chrysate cried, rapturous. "HECATE!"

And then the daughter of the Western Wind, pushed too far by the sacrifice of still more children, by the rising of Hecate from beneath the earth, switched from fighting against Cleopatra to fighting against Chrysate.

→ 24 ←

The battle seemed to slow about Cleopatra as she spun, her arms flying, her hair twisting in a wind that had come from nowhere. Where was the Psylli? Augustus looked frantically around. The wind began to blow in the face of Augustus's forces, and dust blew up into their eyes.

Cleopatra hurled herself onto Chrysate as the beasts of the whirlwind surrounded her.

Standing beside Augustus, Auðr lost her hold on the strands of fate that kept the queen and the goddess apart, and they snapped back together again. She sagged, her body conquered by the Fates. What would be would be. She could not control it all. What happened to Sekhmet would happen to Cleopatra. What happened to Cleopatra would happen to the world.

The witch's body was everywhere, clawed and scaled, writhing and snarling, and Cleopatra wrestled her over the void that led to Hades. The witch bit at the queen, twisting in her grasp.

Usem shouted directions to the wind, but the wind had ceased to listen to him. The beasts came at the witch of Thessaly, and Cleopatra came at her as well, and Augustus, screaming in the storm, threw his fists into the air and came at his enemies from still another direction.

In his hands, the emperor bore the shining bow of Hercules, strung with a shining arrow.

He saw the thing rising in the crater. He knew, as he had known nothing before, that it could not be allowed to rise.

Behind Chrysate, Mark Antony got to his feet. He was strong now, with the blood that had been spilled and the spells that had been cast. His fingers could grasp and his feet could touch the ground. Rage propelled him toward the witch, and she saw him, incandescent with it.

Chrysate did not care. He could not hurt her. Her spells were working. She could feel Hecate coming from beneath the earth, filled with the sacrifices made in her name. She stood her ground, and the ghosts swarmed about her feet, killing the dying and drinking of the dead.

Cleopatra tore at Chrysate's throat, but it made no difference. She drank of darkness, endless darkness, and the witch was renewed. Her laughter flowed into the queen, drunken and rapturous, as the sky filled with monsters, and the world shook. Cleopatra dug her fingers into the witch's heart but felt nothing but night. On the ground, her children stared up at nothing. In the air above them, two bewildered ghosts, wisps of pain, fluttered.

Cleopatra screamed with agony and rage, and it did no good.

Augustus aimed the bow, first into the crater, then at Chrysate. Then at Cleopatra. Which was he meant to kill? He could not tell. Usem shouted at him from across the crater, but he could hear nothing. He could see Agrippa's mouth moving as well, signaling Augustus, but the emperor did not know what to do.

He aimed the bow at Chrysate's heart at last, the fiend he himself had summoned to Rome. She smiled at him, daring him to shoot, and that was what made his decision.

"You will die," he said, and pulled at Hercules' bowstring, but it did not move. How could this be? It was his bow. He had taken it from its hiding place. He, Augustus Caesar, the emperor of Rome. This was his destiny.

The witch looked into his eyes and laughed.

Augustus pulled with all his might, but the string did not move. Augustus, his heart despairing, his shame infinite, his fury unalloyed, recalled the words of the priest of Apollo.

The bow of Hercules could be drawn only by a hero.

Mark Antony looked at him, a shade, his enemy, the man he had painted as a coward, as slave to a woman. He held out his ghostly hands.

Augustus handed the bow to him without a word. There was no other choice.

Antony pulled back the string and drew the bow easily. He aimed, trying to find a clear shot at the witch, but it was impossible.

Cleopatra's mouth was covered in blood, and her hair flew in the wind. Her eyes were lit with golden wrath, and her body was nothing human any longer. She was a goddess, shining and tremendous. Her feet did not touch the ground as she grappled with the witch. She tore at the woman's throat and lifted her high into the air, their bodies entwined.

Antony squinted at the light that emanated from her. He could not see for brightness.

"Shoot!" Cleopatra screamed. "Shoot her now! Hecate is coming!"

Antony could not shoot the witch without risking his wife. His fingers hesitated on the bowstring, the arrow trembling. The witch gained the upper position, and he caught a glimpse of her gaping jaws, her claws tearing at Cleopatra's breast, her strength increased by Hecate's presence.

Antony looked down. On the grass at his feet, Ptolemy stared sightless at the moon. Alexander lay covered in blood, drained by ghosts. The shades of his children moaned, bent over their lost bodies. He did not know what had happened to Selene.

Antony felt himself falling, felt his fingers weakening. Cleopatra twisted, her body between Antony and the witch. She strained to hold Chrysate, looking at her husband.

"If you love me, you will do it!" Cleopatra screamed.

He looked at her. His love. His wife, her hair bloodied, her hands talons, and her eyes golden. He could see her inside all of the chaos. Cleopatra was there.

"I am yours," Cleopatra said, and then Antony shot her.

⇒ 25 ⇐

The arrow of Hercules pierced them both, stabbing into Cleopatra's back and passing through her into Chrysate's body.

The sounds ripped through the sky. The Earth herself roared. The Earth herself cried out, and Antony's cry mixed with Cleopatra's scream of agony and Chrysate's wailing howl of despair. Sekhmet, bonded to Cleopatra, sharer of her soul, screamed in unison with her, doubled over, holding the place where the Hydra's immortal venom had entered her body. Stars dropped and scattered.

Cleopatra pressed her hands to the wound, and, for the first time since she had summoned the goddess, there was blood.

The queen released Chrysate, and the witch fell, spinning and screaming.

"I dedicate this soul to Hades!" Cleopatra shouted, her voice strangled.

In the crater, Hecate's shine dimmed, the water taking her back into itself, the chain of the dead wrapping about her ankle and pulling her down. The crater awaited Chrysate, and in it, the millions of ghosts she had called from Hades.

The army of shades rose up and took her beneath the waters, and Chrysate, witch of Thessaly, was gone into the darkness with her goddess, swept under and fallen upon.

Holding her wound, tears running down her face, Cleopatra hung in the air over the abyss and turned her gaze to Augustus, who stood, stunned, looking up at her.

She smiled at him, and he shuddered, unable to move. Her gaze was the deep indigo of twilight, and darkness rose within it. Cleopatra shone upon him, tremendous, blinding, looking through him. A god.

We are not finished, she said, and her voice was only in his mind. She reached out her hand, and though she did not touch him, Augustus felt a chill invade him. He felt her touching his heart, clenching it in her talons, and then he felt her tear it from him. Was it his heart? Or something else? He could not tell what was happening.

He gasped, feeling a sudden absence at his center, a loss. A searing pain, like lightning striking, shot through the absence, and he felt a wind whirling inside his chest. Cleopatra smiled.

Augustus fell to his knees, limp, bewildered, curling around the missing place.

Cleopatra turned away from the emperor and looked down at her husband.

Antony stood at the edge of the crater, his skin already flickering and fading as the witch who had summoned him died.

"I will see you again," Antony said to his wife.

"*Te teneo*," said Cleopatra.

"As you are mine," said Antony. "I will wait for you."

Cleopatra's face clenched with pain as she pulled the arrow from her body and threw it into the crater.

"You may wait until the end of time," she said.

Antony smiled at her. "I will wait," he said. He gathered their dead children into his arms, and there was a flash in the west, as though the sun had appeared at the edge of the sky and looked over it, onto the battlefield.

Those who were looking in that direction, those who could bear to do so, glimpsed something in the brightness. A ship, perhaps, and its captain leaning out of the vessel with long, shining hair, eyes as blue as lapis, skin made of gold.

Then it was gone, and Antony was gone as well, with their children, and with him Hercules' arrows.

Cleopatra lay on the ground, her body pale, her wound mortal.

She was dying at last. Her lips curled up in a smile.

She took a final breath, looking into the night sky, and then she was still.

There was a last divine roar of sorrow, one that caused the ocean beyond Avernus to rise up and throw itself against the cliff, and then the battle was done.

⇌ 26 ⇌

Augustus, rigid with horror, stood and took a step toward his enemy's body. She did not move. Blood flowed from her side. She'd done something to him, something he did not understand. His hands fumbled. A coin to pay her passage. He had nothing.

He knelt beside Cleopatra, put out his shaking hand, brushed the snow from her face and closed her eyes.

In the darkness of the crater, Augustus saw a single ghostly spot of light, a shining, wavering thing rising to the surface for a moment, its thousands of teeth, its watery gleaming form, its razor-feathered body, before it, too, dove into the depths, descending back to its home in the Underworld. Something pulled at Augustus. Home. He wavered on the edge of the crater, uncertain, and then looked around the battlefield, at the devastation there.

He looked at the monsters that still walked the earth, the lions and tigers stalking their prey, eating the dead.

The Psylli eyed at him from across the battlefield.

"We have won," Usem said. "This is a victory. I will not see you again."

"No," Augustus said.

"Nor Rome," said Usem, and nodded at him, only once. "May you live in peace, Emperor."

The monsters of sand and wind surrounded him, shrinking as he moved. Usem held out his hands to them, and they converged into a single form. A woman, her hair flying behind her, suddenly stood before the snake sorcerer, and Augustus watched her kiss him. He watched as the Western Wind's daughter took her husband in her arms, watched as the air whirled around them, watched as they rose into the sky and disappeared together into the darkness beyond the hillside.

The morning was coming, gray and sickly at the horizon. Augustus swayed, looking at the legions of Romans who stood, awed and bleeding, mingled into a single dazzled pool of men. There were senators dead before him, and loyal soldiers, too. He saw Agrippa making his way among them, speaking to the wounded, dedicating their shades to Hades, and the seiðkona, her distaff in her hand, touching the men and taking their memories with her.

By the time Auðr arrived before Augustus, he no longer feared her. She lowered her distaff to his forehead, and when it touched him, he felt his mind laced with a filigree of frost. All the pain was gone for the moment, the memories of broken things, the guilt.

For a glorious moment, he did not know who he was, and he was grateful.

He did not want to know who he was. He did not want to know what he had lost.

Auðr walked onward, and Augustus knelt on the hilltop beside the dead woman, a woman he now only faintly recognized. He stayed there, bewildered and uncertain for he knew not how long. At last, Agrippa walked up the hillside behind him, bloodied, his face scored with new lines.

"I found her among the wounded," he said.

A small hand took Augustus's fingers. He looked down, startled. Selene, her face smeared with dirt, snow in her eyelashes. He recognized her in a rush of sorrow.

"Rome has won," she said, her voice wavering. "And I am a Roman. I will go with you."

And then, without looking at her mother's body, without looking down, she led Augustus down the hill and away from the battlefield.

"We have won," she said, and only then did Augustus realize that he was crying.

When they had gone, Auðr bent over Cleopatra's body, coughing as she knelt. Her own thread, tangled with all of these, was moments from completion. She could see its tattered end in the light of dawn, shorn and frayed.

She looked at the queen's face. Peaceful. Where did she travel? the seiðkona wondered. Which of her gods had taken her?

Auðr twisted her distaff, employing all her remaining strength to wrap the queen's thread about it. She groaned as she tore at the fates, unraveling, her powers withering even as she used them.

The universe shifted above her. A pattern in the sky, a ripple in the gray as the sky began to roll, a shifting of seasons, night to day and back again. The last stars peeled back to reveal sun, and the last sun peeled back to reveal emptiness, and still the seiðkona labored, weaving the pattern, the warp and weft of the future, the edges of the universe in her hands.

At last, she rose and walked toward the historian.

It was nearly finished. All of it.

Nicolaus could not move, even as he watched Auðr approach him. Blood coursed from the ragged tear that ran from his shoulder to his wrist. He was going to die, he knew, but he could not bring himself to run.

He wanted to die.

The battlefield was covered in bodies, and the waters ran red. Vultures wheeled high in the sky, and soon they would land.

The seiðkona's hair had come unbound, and it twined in the air, a white nebula. Her lips curled as she assessed him. She put out a hand and touched his mouth with icy, bluish fingers. Her other hand gripped the distaff.

Nicolaus braced himself for its touch. He discovered that he was crying.

His tears froze on his face, and one fell to the ground, shattering as it hit the earth. He bowed his head toward her, giving himself over.

Let her touch him. Let her take away the things he'd seen and done. Let her take his mind and thoughts. Let her take him and all the words he'd clung to.

No, she said, her lips unmoving. *You will remember this.*

He looked up and was caught, pinned by her silver gaze.

You will remember all of this. You will tell this story. You will write it.

The seiðkona lifted her distaff over her head, and Nicolaus watched it move toward his brow.

As it touched him, his mind broke open, making room for everything it must encompass. He felt his own memories splinter and spin like marbles, rolling to the edges of his consciousness, to be lost there.

The distaff touched him for only an instant, and yet he was no longer only Nicolaus.

He *knew*. Everything. His mind swelled with it, agonizing, horrifying, filled beyond its capacity, and then filled more. Love and sorrow. Death and despair. Hunger. Bloodshed. Armor being donned and swords being sharpened, children waking from dreams, mothers holding their babies, lionesses hunting for prey. All the stories of the dead. All the stories of the living. All the memories she had taken from them were his to keep. He cried out, pressing his hands to his forehead, feeling his skull splitting open with the contents of the world. There could not be enough room in him for all of this. But there was.

Now his history was the history of millions. He knew everything, and there was no forgetting. He was the one who would remember.

He ran from the battlefield, holding his injured arm, tears running down his face. The skin began to heal as he ran, and he knew she had twined his fate with something else. He knew that he would not die tonight.

He had a purpose yet.

He was the keeper of the history of this day, and of the days before it. He would tell the stories of the serpents and the soldiers, of the gods and of the goddesses. He would tell the story of the queen and of her love, of their children, and of the shades who had come from below the earth.

All of it, all of everything and of everyone, was within him.

He was a historian at last, wholly and utterly.

He would tell the world.

Epilogue

The emperor hobbled through an orchard at the foot of Vesuvius, the wind pressing against his robes, chilling his thin skin, ruffling his sparse hair. Something was familiar to him here. The pattern of the stars against the sky, perhaps, was like a tattoo he'd seen once on a woman's back. Augustus searched his memory for the details, but it was no use. It was only a fleeting recognition, maybe something he'd dreamt long ago. He laughed quietly, a rasping cough of dark amusement. His mind had become like Oceanus, and all the places he'd once known were drowned in salt sea, peopled with ghosts. He could no longer tell truth from fiction, nor his own recollections from things he'd invented.

Augustus was seventy-six years old. He'd reigned over Rome, over his empire, for nearly forty-four years. It was the nineteenth of August, the month he'd named after himself. Other Augusts crowded his memory, one spent in Alexandria. He thought suddenly of Antony. Augustus had long outlived his old enemy, his old friend, his old idol, but he did not know why he thought of him now. He remembered walking into the cool depths of a mausoleum and—

No, no. He would not think of that.

A flash of memory, another August, this one on a battlefield. Tigers roaring and an emptiness where his heart had been, snow falling down upon him from the heavens. A god screaming from the sky, and his enemy, his beautiful enemy, bleeding in the snow. What had she done with his heart? What was the strangeness he felt? His soul—

He did not know.

He remembered an ancient woman with silver eyes, tapping him on the forehead with her distaff, emptying his history and replacing it with unknowns.

He had run back to Rome, served the empire, served the people. Dazed, he'd closed the Gates of Janus and brought peace to his realm. A price owed to a warrior, a price he knew he must pay, but his own life had not been peaceful.

Rome was his only daughter now. Julia, his sole blood heir, had betrayed him, conducting an affair with the last surviving son of Mark Antony, sacrificing to old religions, dancing naked in the city's temples, offering herself to anyone who desired the emperor's daughter. On her finger, she'd worn a ring engraved with Hecate's face, something she claimed she'd found in Augustus's own house.

Augustus had banished her from Rome and ordered her lover killed, but these punishments did not ease his pain. Just hours before arriving at this orchard, he'd given the order for the execution of his final grandson, the youngest son of Julia. The boy was a child of an unknown father, and the emperor could not take the chance of Rome being inherited by a descendant of his old enemy. No. He must pass Rome to Tiberius, his stepson, a man he disliked and distrusted. There was no other option. All his other heirs were dead, and his line was broken.

The emperor felt a grasping seizure in his chest, where his heart should have been.

He'd banished his friends as well. Nicolaus of Damascus, his biographer, he'd sent away when he'd given the emperor a copy of his history of the universe. It rankled. Even the sections pertaining to Augustus, which he'd dictated himself, seemed strange, filled with untruths. Had he talked in his sleep? He could not say.

He had Ovid sent to the Black Sea because something in his stories, in those *Metamorphoses*, those women transforming into beasts, those beasts transforming into women, those gods walking amongst men, reminded Augustus of—

What?

Something in them made Augustus believe that someone had gotten to the poet, whispered in his ear, told him all the secret things, initiated him into mysteries the emperor himself did not recollect.

And so he burned the plays, burned the verses, burned the histories, burned the biographies. He stood on the steps of the Palatine, a torch in his hand, and set the pages afire. He did not know what he was hiding. He burned everything, even his own writings.

He left the Sibylline prophecies, but he censored them, cutting offensive words from them with his own knife. Whole sentences and passages. Augustus remembered one of them, shivering with the memory.

"And thou shalt be no more a widow, but thou shalt cohabit with a man-eating lion, terrible, a furious warrior. And then shalt thou be happy, and among all men known; And thee, the stately, shall the encircling tomb receive, for he, the Roman king, shall place thee there, though thee be still amongst the living. Though thy life is gone, there will be something immortal living within thee. Though thy soul is gone, thy anger will remain, and thy vengeance will rise and destroy the cities of the Roman king."

He slashed away at that section, bewildered by it, making additions and subtractions, changing what it said. It was all familiar, and yet he couldn't grasp exactly what it was that so angered him. At last, he walked away from the tablet, his skin flushing with mad wrath. He had not understood why he felt so. He still did not.

Augustus fretted now. He suddenly remembered only the horrible things.

He thought of Marcus Agrippa, dead at fifty-five of blood poisoning, the legacy of a long-ago wound. He'd been on a campaign, and soaked his leg in vinegar in an attempt to relieve the pain of his old injury. By the time Augustus arrived, he was dead of it.

Augustus could almost remember the getting of that wound. Something about an arrow, something about a poison, something about a mistake, something about a flash of light.

The emperor's teeth felt loose in his mouth. He ran his tongue over the space where, long ago, he'd lost a tooth on a ship journey. He'd thrown it into the sea between Egypt and Italy. Now it might be a pearl. He was so old that his bones might by now be golden. His hair lapis. His teeth pearls. Somewhere in his memory, there was a god whose body was made of precious stones. A god who crossed the sky in a boat.

Augustus thought longingly of that. He himself was cold in the heat of the sun, and now, in the moonlight, he froze.

He turned his face toward the heavens, squinting to see more clearly. His spine protested as he moved his head, but still, there was beauty here, this night, this orchard, the trees hanging heavy with ripe figs, the smell of the grass, the perfection of the place. His father's orchard. He had not been here in years. His father had died in this very place, long ago, when the emperor was only a child. It was all so familiar, and yet, when he tried to grasp it, it flew.

He raised his hand and plucked a fig from the tree. A soft thing, the fig, perfectly ripe. He preferred them green. There was danger in enjoyment.

A beautiful woman stepped from behind the fig tree and smiled at him. He felt himself smiling back, toothless and old. His hand, when he lifted it to his mouth, was spotted with age.

She was young and lovely. A servant, but too beautiful for a servant. A guest? A dignitary?

He should know her. Something in the back of his mind cried out like a child.

Augustus thought, but he could not place her. Her eyes were rimmed in kohl, and her arms were decked with coiled bracelets in the shape of serpents. Her body was curving and tightly wrapped in a white linen gown. Her mouth was plump and painted with something red.

He bit into the fig—honey sweet and seeded, nearly overripe—and it came to him. He had been her lover once, long ago. Or he had loved her.

"Do I know you?" he asked her.

"Octavian," she said. She held her hand to her side, tightly pressing it against her waist.

"Are you injured?" he asked.

"I was," she said. "I was injured once, and gravely. I've been a long time healing, and you have had a long life. I did not intend that, but I do not regret it. You suffered."

Augustus felt indignant.

"I did not suffer," he began, but even as he spoke the words, he remembered nights sleepless, insomniac, haunted. At the same time, he wondered at himself. He was not dressed for night, nor for company. He was nearly naked. He felt his skin prickling as he looked at her.

"Do you not know me, Octavian?" the woman before him asked.

"I do not," he insisted. He felt his throat beginning to swell. The fig was scratching at his tongue. He coughed unhappily. He was chilled here in the night air. He wanted to go in, to his bed, to his sleep. He wanted to wake in the morning and watch the sun rise.

"I made a bargain once," the woman told him. "With a powerful king, in a country not far from here."

"A gamble?" Augustus asked. He thought of games played with bones and rocks, games played with coins. He thought, horribly, of placing a coin in Agrippa's mouth, to pay the boatman of Hades. The cold of the tongue as it touched his fingers. The rotten hardness of the teeth. The damp of the tomb he'd placed his friend inside, with all the proper ceremony, with all the proper ritual.

A sudden memory of another tomb, and an empty slab therein. A silver box engraved with Isis. A serpent, a serpent. He cringed involuntarily.

"A gamble," she agreed.

He coughed, and sat heavily on the dew-covered grass. A servant should bring him a cloak. He should not be out at night.

"It was a gamble over a soul," she said.

Augustus lay carefully back, anticipating a story and fearing it at the same time. In his life, he'd hired many tellers, heard many tales, and he had slept little. He found himself nearly looking forward to it. Sleep. Rest.

The woman looked steadily at him.

He thought suddenly of two little boys, lost long ago on a battlefield. He'd brought the last of the Egyptian children, Selene, back to Rome and married her to the king of Mauretania, giving her a dowry of gold as though she were his own daughter. He owed her something, though even then he could not remember why. Selene was dead eight years past. He'd commissioned a Greek poet to eulogize her. A good daughter. The only good daughter he'd had, and she was not even his own.

"*The moon herself grew dark, rising at sunset,*" Augustus whispered. It was a lovely epitaph, the eulogy, and somehow it reminded him of the woman before him. Selene had looked like her, perhaps that was it. "*Covering her suffering in the night, because she saw her beautiful namesake, Selene, breathless, descending to Hades. With her, she'd had the beauty of her light in common, and mingled her own darkness with her death.*"

The woman before him smiled. He thought he saw her eyes shining with tears, though it might have been the moonlight.

He regretted everything on earth.

"A soul?" he asked. "Whose soul? Yours?"

"Not my own," she said. "I had already sold my own soul when I made this bargain. No, Octavian. I did not act to save my soul but that of my love. Your soul has been with me all these years, since the battle at Avernus. You've lived without it, as I have lived without mine. Did you never notice its absence? Tell me, Octavian, was it a glorious life? Did you love? Did you find joy?"

Augustus looked at her miserably. She was so beautiful. Her lips were bright, even in the darkness.

She seemed taller now, somehow, and her skin paler, as though she had absorbed the moonlight. She smiled indulgently upon him.

Her teeth were pointed.

His throat was closing. He could scarcely breathe. A name drifted up from out of his past, a name he should never have forgotten. He did not understand how he had.

"Cleopatra," he said.

"*Te teneo,*" she told Augustus. "*You are mine.*"

She bent toward him, taking his body in her strong hands. She came closer, brushing her cold lips over his cold lips, and the emperor looked up into her eyes, seeing fires, seeing volcanoes, seeing destruction.

He watched Rome fall in a moment, watched the sky fill with metal wings, watched all he had built crumble.

He felt Cleopatra biting into his throat, and he struggled weakly. Her hand pressed down upon him, heavy as a coverlet, and he relaxed under her weight. It was a kiss.

Yes. They had once been lovers, he was sure. They were lovers again, it seemed. The kiss was sweet.

Cleopatra, queen of Egypt. Queen of Kings.

"You will live," her voice said to him, and he was, in his last moments, a boy again, fevered in his bed. "You will live a long life."

Then it was over.

Cleopatra stood, leaving the husk that had been the emperor of Rome on the ground, and walked away from the country that had been her unwilling home all these years.

Dying on the battlefield at Avernus, so many years before, she'd felt Sekhmet leave her heart, felt the hollow spaces fill again with her own *ka*. In memory, she glimpsed her death, the snowflakes falling upon her skin, her blood flowing slowly, cold and endless.

She'd found herself lying on a mossy bank beside a silver lake. The world was night, the pearl-round moon high in the sky, and yet it was also sunrise, the horizon all rose, gold, and coral. As far as she could see, there were rolling hills and valleys, the dewy green grasses and blooming wildflowers of midsummer, but this was not earth.

There were stars in the heavens, and she gazed up at them, the constellations showing familiar shapes, shapes she'd known in every land she'd lived in. On the grass about her, and on the smooth, silver water, she could see the shadows of the stars, and she was comforted by this, the tracery of her former life in the wildness of the waking world.

"You are in Elysium," a voice said. "You died at my gates."

"Where is Antony?" she asked, turning to see the god of the Dead before her. "I must go to where he is."

Hades nodded his head ruefully.

"As you wish. You have done me a large favor. I owe you recompense."

A flash of light, and she found herself transported again.

She saw the Island of Fire, with its scales for the weighing of her heart, the gleaming feather of Maat upon them. Antony and her sons stood before her, all of her beloved dead, Caesarion, Alexander Helios, and Ptolemy.

She walked toward them, overcome with joy, but then, without warning, she was torn from the Duat and pressed into her own broken body again.

The fate spinner had brought Cleopatra back from the death she'd longed for. Helpless, paralyzed on the battlefield, the queen felt Sekhmet reenter her heart.

I can see it all now, the seiðkona rasped, then, her hands on Cleopatra's face. *I can see everything.*

Cleopatra walked on into her future. Her love was in the Duat, waiting for her, and she was on earth, dreaming of him. She would not see him yet.

It is your destiny to destroy the world, the seiðkona had whispered to her, all those years before. *But you must also save it. They are the same fate.*

Cleopatra walked into the darkness, the stars overhead glittering, the moon a pointed crescent, her body filled with blood, her mind filled with night. Sekhmet would rise again now that Cleopatra had finished her healing. The queen could feel her hunger. Sekhmet had been wounded, too, with the Hydra venom, but she still had six Slaughterers in her quiver: Famine, Earthquake, Flood, Drought, Madness, and Violence.

Though this was finished, Cleopatra was not done. She did not know when she would be. It was not her decision.

The emperor of Rome was dead.

Long live the queen.

ACTA EST FABULA.

Historical Note

Lots of the things that happen in this book really occurred. Lots of the characters portrayed in this book really existed. Lots of their deeds and misdeeds, and many of their wildly unlikely actions—including some of the things you're no doubt sure I invented—actually happened.

Let me clarify that. Lots of the things that happen in this book really *are* historically based. However, much of the history we rely on to tell us the truth of what happened to Antony, Cleopatra, Octavian, Agrippa, and the rest of these characters in the early days of the Roman Empire is as much enhanced by fiction, imagination, and mythology as this book is.

History is written by and for the conquering heroes—in this case, the Romans—and so the classical sources that deal with Cleopatra and Antony are fascinatingly skewed documents, full of hyperbole, humor, hysteria, and contradiction. Much like today's political climate, persons on both sides of the events had a great deal to say about the players, some of it true (maybe), and some of it invention.

None of the major primary sources were contemporary with the historic events portrayed herein—Plutarch was writing nearly a hundred years after the death of Cleopatra, who committed suicide (or perhaps not) in 30 B.C.E. They relied on earlier sources, rumor, poetic license, and a hefty dose of subservience to the Roman Empire. Therefore, works of contemporary scholarship on these topics—as the authors themselves agree—have a limited pool to draw from when it comes to factual accounts of what did and did not happen in Alexandria and thereafter.

As a priest of Apollo states in this book, speaking of the mythic arrows of Hercules, *"Everything is true. Once a story is told, it becomes true. Every unlikely tale, every tale of wonders, has something real at its core."*

That is absolutely true of the history that inspired and informs this particular tale.

That said, I'm tremendously indebted to a variety of volumes dealing in fact and "fact," most notably Suetonius's *The Twelve Caesars*, Plutarsch's *Lives of Noble Grecians and Romans*, Joyce Tyldesley's *Cleopatra: Last Queen of Egypt*, and Anthony Everitt's *Augustus: The Life of Rome's First Emperor*. For a fantastic fictional biography—and a completely different take on many of the characters I portray here—I recommend John Williams's National Book Award–winning novel, *Augustus*. As well, I consulted Ovid, Virgil, Horace, Dio, Strabo, Shakespeare, and many more, some poetic, some historic.

One of the great pleasures of writing *Queen of Kings* was that I was able to use the biographical details of Antony, Cleopatra, Augustus, and more to a new effect, braiding history with my own imagined possibilities. The death of Cleopatra, for example, is portrayed in Plutarch as a locked-room mystery—the queen and her maids discovered dead, with the only mark visible on Cleopatra a couple of pinpricks. No suicide-assisting asp was ever discovered, and Plutarch himself seems suspicious that this was what happened. As time passed, death by asp became the accepted version. It was a small leap of imagination to imagine a different prelude to Cleopatra's "death," and a different explanation for the fang marks on her body.

In terms of ancient sorcery, religion, augury, and mythology, I drew inspiration and information from Apuleius's *The Golden Ass* (sometimes known as Apuleius's *Metamorphoses*), Ovid's *Metamorphoses*, *Naming the Witch* by Kimberley Stratton, and for some great thoughts on the creepiness and creativity of ancient world warfare, and on the Hydra's venom, *Greek Fire, Poison Arrows, and Scorpion Bombs: Biological and Chemical Warfare in the Ancient World* by Adrienne Mayor.

In regard to Greek witchcraft, Hades, and shades, I consulted a variety of sources and inspirations both classical and contemporary, including *The Aeneid* (which readers will recognize as the inspiration for the geography of Hades), the *Odyssey*, *Medea* (the character found both in Euripides' play and in Ovid's *Metamorphoses*). The classically accepted process for summoning shades is very similar to what I've outlined here. They really do require a blood sacrifice, which brings their consciousness and memory back from the faded world of Hades. Cleopatra's brief experience of Elysium in the epilogue is inspired by James Agee's beautiful poem "Description of Elysium."

I have the extraordinary good fortune of counting among my friends a scholar in classical and early Christian magic, so I used the work and words, some published, some not, of Dayna S. Kalleres as guides in the research process.

In regard to Egyptian history, magic, religion, folklore, and hieroglyphic evidence, I consulted a variety of documents, both ancient and contemporary, including *The Egyptian Book of the Dead* (more properly known as *The Book of Going Forth by Day*). Sekhmet is a real goddess, and her history as laid out in this book is, for the most part, supported by Egyptian lore. A particularly good account of the relationship between Sekhmet and Ra and the attempted destruction of humanity by Sekhmet may be found in Geraldine Pinch's *Magic in Ancient Egypt*. Discussion of Sekhmet's Seven Slaughterers may also be found in this excellent book, though Plague, as depicted in *Queen of Kings*, is inspired by the Irish legend of the Boyhood of Finn and Birgha, the spear he uses to defeat the lovely voiced giant, Aillen. Sekhmet's more contemporary incarnation, post-Isis, had placed her as a "women's goddess"—meaning that she presided over childbeds and menstruation—a definite demotion from her earlier responsibilities, which were waging war and destroying enemies of both Ra and the Egyptian pharaohs. It is no wonder, in my opinion, that in this book, she is ready for something a bit more interesting.

Chapter 4 of Book of Divinations is inspired by my favorite section of Bram Stoker's *Dracula*. The notion of a ghost ship whose passengers and crew have (all but the captain) been slaughtered by the monster they've unwittingly brought aboard has always made my skin crawl, and when I saw the chance to create my own variation, I was delighted to do so. The ship in Stoker's novel is the *Demeter*.

The Sibylline Oracles are a complicated collection of documents created mainly in the second through fifth centuries A.D., but encompassing fragments dating back to the first century B.C.E. They are scholarly forgeries of earlier oracular texts—the Sibylline Books—which were mostly lost in a fire in 83 B.C.E. In the time of Augustus, they began to be commissioned propaganda, and written by scholars on both sides. They'd be consulted and read aloud as the words of the gods. However, the scholars who wrote the Oracles came from all sides of the events—even from Alexandria—and so some of them predict Cleopatra's destruction of Rome, and others predict the glittering rise of Rome under Augustus. The quotations that begin Book of Divinations and Book of Lightning, and which are referenced throughout *Queen of Kings*, are from the oldest sections of the Sibylline Oracles, Books III–V. The quotations are taken unaltered from the 1899 translation of the Sibylline Oracles, and are generally agreed to be referencing Cleopatra and her dealings with Antony and Augustus.

As crazy as this may sound, given the Sibylline Oracles depiction of *"the widow,"* the *"cataract of fire"* and the cohabitation with a *"man-eating lion"* as well as the mutilated fragment involving Cleopatra being buried: *"thee the stately shall the encircling tomb receive . . . is gone . . . living within,"* this book was not inspired by them. I found these bits of awesomeness long after I conceived the book's plotline, as I was in the midst of writing the final battle. Needless to say, I screamed with joy when I discovered them. Augustus really did historically burn a vast quantity of books, and personally and specifically censored the Sibylline Oracles. I took a few wild, thoroughly enjoyable leaps in imagining the creation of the Sibylline fragments, and the literal nature of them.

The historian Nicolaus of Damascus is a real character, with the outlines of his actual biography roughly as Zelig-ish as they are portrayed here: philosopher to King Herod's court, tutor to Cleopatra's children, and at some point biographer of Augustus. I've reorganized his chronology somewhat. The 144-volume History of the Universe, mostly lost, is an accurate description of Nicolaus's work—though the secrets that might have been loosed in that 144-volume set are my invention. There are scraps of Nicolaus's work on Augustus still extant, mainly dealing with the boyhood of Octavian, and I consulted those when researching this book.

The outlines of the biography of Selene, Cleopatra and Antony's daughter, are depicted with significant poetic license here—but she did travel to Rome along with her two brothers after her parents' deaths. Alexander Helios and Ptolemy Philadelphus disappear without explanation from the historical record soon after, and most historians guess that they both died of childhood illness. I don't think it's a huge leap to imagine a sinister fate for the sons of Antony and Cleopatra in Augustus's Rome. Cleopatra Selene, on the other hand, remained loyal to Rome, and was eventually married, with a large dowry provided by Augustus, to the young African King, Juba II. Interestingly, Juba had, as a three-year-old child, walked in Julius Caesar's triumphal procession into Rome after Caesar's own Alexandrian idyll—the one that put Cleopatra on the throne. Selene reigned as queen of Mauretania (today's Algeria), loyal and subservient to Rome, and died in A.D. 6. The epitaph Augustus recites to Cleopatra in the epilogue is by Crinagoras of Mytilene, a famed Greek poet who lived in Rome as a court poet. So it's quite possible that said epitaph was indeed commissioned by Augustus to memorialize his one loyal "daughter."

Speaking of: A sidenote on daughters, and a storyline I couldn't manage to squeeze much of into this book, to my great sorrow. Julia, Augustus's only child, eventually fell in love with Mark Antony and Fulvia's orphaned eldest son, Iullus, sustaining a long affair with him (during her marriage to Marcus Agrippa, and later to Tiberius), which led to her banishment by her father, and to Iullus's execution. As well, there were rumors of her other activities, some of them involving illicit dancing and ritual in temples, and perhaps a plot against Augustus's life. Augustus died without blood inheritors, having banished not only Julia, but her daughter as well. One of his final acts was to order the execution of his last grandson, Julia's son. Personally, I suspect this might've had something to do with Augustus's suspicion that the bloodlines of his grandchildren had been tainted by his daughter's infidelity with Mark Antony's son. Regardless, Antony's line would eventually inherit the empire. The emperors Claudius and Nero were both descendants of Mark Antony and Fulvia's remaining Roman daughters.

Usem, the Psylli, is drawn from classical history. He belongs to a tribe referenced both in Plutarch (brought to examine Cleopatra after her death) and in Herodotus, and his tribe is famous both for their relationship with serpents, and for going to war against the Western Wind. In classical sources, the tribe loses the war, and is buried beneath sand dunes. However, their reappearance later, in Cleopatra's time, intrigued me, so . . .

Chrysate, the witch of Thessaly, is a creature drawn from my nightmare imagination as well as from a variety of classical sources (including Medea, who by tradition is from Thessaly, and certainly did some famous child-sacrifice. The ingredients and procedure for Chrysate's youth spell are taken from Ovid's Medea), as are many of her spells, though there is no historic link to Augustus. The price for drawing down the moon really is a sacrificed child, or one of the witch's own eyes.

Auðr, the seiðkona, is based in Norse history and mythology (see stories of Freya and the Norns, as well as many tales more historically based, about the *völva* and *seiðkona*—two words for the same kind of sorceress and seer) as are her distaff, and her powers over fate and memory. I was also inspired by the Germanic tribe of the Cimbri and their female seers, gray-haired women dressed in white, who accompanied the men into battle. The Cimbri were known to the Romans as early as the second century B.C. as a "piratical and warlike folk," and written about by Strabo. Though the lands north of England, in this book the birthplace of Auðr, were unknown to the Augustan-era Romans, and filed under "Oceanus," I couldn't resist bringing my seiðkona into the fray.

In A.D. 365, there was an undersea earthquake and major tsunami that caused many of the buildings in Alexandria, including Cleopatra's Palace, to slide deep beneath the harbor. By the eighth century, further earthquakes (though Alexandria is not on any known fault line) had destroyed much of the ancient city. At the time of this writing, the buildings of Cleopatra's Palace have been discovered, but archeologists (and other interested parties) have long been searching for Antony and Cleopatra's tomb, thus far without success.

One of the few confirmed images of Cleopatra extant today is in Egypt at the Temple of Dendera, commissioned by Cleopatra, but completed by Octavian after her death. On its facade, a life-size image of the queen exists. In it, she travels with her son, Caesarion, to deliver an offering to Isis. Her son is accompanied by a small figure representing his *ka*.

Cleopatra, on the other hand, travels alone, unaccompanied by her soul.

Really.

—MDH, November 2010
Seattle, Washington

Acknowledgments

Every writer has a Greek chorus of advisors, drinking partners, brainstormers, barnraisers, and ghosts, and mine may well be even larger than most. After my last book, someone published a review of my acknowledgments, claiming (I kid you not) that I was "too thankful" to too many people. Bullshit. When it comes to making a living off imaginary worlds, there is no such thing as being too thankful. Libations and sacrifices to:

THE FORUM

Michael Rudell, a great reader/matchmaker, just as much as he is a great lawyer. I'm lucky enough to be represented by that rare thing, an agency full of people who would all be fantastic desert island companions: David Gernert, whose raucous laughter, endless appetite for pages, and raconteur-ing rock the publishing world. Stephanie Cabot, with her dry wit, warmth, and excellent classics geekiness. Rebecca Gardner, for bright ideas and Greek food, along with Will Roberts for foreign rights. My editor, Erika Imranyi, for buying and editing this great big, wild monster of a book, along with Brian Tart and everyone at Dutton for supporting its journey from scribbles into actuality. John Power and Steve Twersky, ongoing believers *and* accountants, which is saying something. Lisa Bankoff, who out of pure goodness said nice things about *Queen of Kings* all over town. Simon Taylor, who got spectacularly giddy over this book and then bought it for the UK marketplace. All the other foreign editors, who *got* this book and bought it.

THE CHORUS

Let it be said publicly: Without all the friends who contributed willing ears, belief, and alcohol, this novel would not have gotten written. I'd been working for several years on another book, which I backburnered when I got the first tiny, mad kernel of the idea for *Queen of Kings*. I owe thanks to all the people who not only listened to me shriek about the travails of that other project for years but who encouraged me to write *this* one, after all the hours they'd spent patiently comforting me through something else.

Don't think you're done comforting me, friends, Romans, countrymen. This is a trilogy.

I couldn't be more fortunate if I had a magic lamp and a million wishes. Thanks to: Zay Amsbury, Mark Bemesderfer, Chris Bolin, Stesha Brandon, Ed Brubaker and Melanie Tomlin, Tom Bryant, Matt Cheney, Thea Cooper, Kate Czajkowski, Laura Dave, Caitlin DiMotta and Duffy Boudreau, Kelley Eskridge and Nicola Griffith, Lance Horne, Dayna S. Kalleres, Greg Kalleres, Hallie Deaktor Kapner, Doug Kearney, Jay Kirk, Park Krausen, Joe Knezevich, Josh Kilmer-Purcell, Thomas Kohnstamm and Tábata Silva, Erik Larson, Hana Lass, Ben McKenzie, Jenny Mercein, Michaela Murphy, Ruth McKee and Brian K. Vaughan, Samantha Temple Neukom, Leslie and Mark Olson, Rebecca Olson, Amanda Palmer, Matthew Power and Jessica Benko, Steven Rinella, Kim Scott, Sxip Shirey, Jennie Shortridge, Ed Skoog, Garth Stein, and Danielle Trussoni.

THE MUSEION

The extraordinary Martin Epstein (who should certainly also appear in the friend category), Deloss Brown, and Carol Rocamora at NYU all took my brain and filled it with classics, Shakespeare, and spectacular choruses, back when I was twenty years old. Things had to shake around for a while, but I'm quite sure this book is in part the result of their groundwork. As for my personal Library of Alexandria, many highlights are mentioned in the Historical Notes and Chorus sectors, but Jonathan Carroll, Angela Carter, Michael Chabon, Isak Dinesen, Rikki Ducornet, Neil Gaiman, Mark Helprin, Stephen King, Madeleine

L' Engle, Ursula K. Le Guin, George R. R. Martin, China Miéville, and Peter Straub deserve special mention for writing books that continue to blow my mind and remake it. All their (diverse) writing informs mine. Go read their books. You will not regret it. And: I must thank one band most especially for this book. I've never been a metal fan. Ever. But as I wrote *Queen of Kings*, I discovered Iron Maiden. This book was written to a soundtrack of equal parts The Mountain Goats, The National, Iron Maiden, and Stevie Nicks's "Gold Dust Woman." There it is.

TRIBE

My family have all been victimized by crazed midnight phone calls in which I recite speeches by Cicero and restructure a book they haven't yet read. Once again, I'm wildly lucky, both in the people I'm related to and in the people I married into. Huge love and gratitude to Adriane Headley, Mark Headley and Meghan Koch, Molly Headley and Idir Ben-kaci, the Lumpkin family, the Moulton family, and the Headley family, my son, Joshua Schenkkan, and my daughter, Sarah Schenkkan (Guys, you're upgraded. You're my stepkids, yeah, but you're my family, and I claim you), the Schenkkan/Rothgeb family. And the chorus of shades: my grandparents R. Dwayne and Marguerite Moulton, and my dad, Mark Bryan Headley. I miss you. I wish you could each have a copy of this book.

Gratitude as well to my two house-leopards. They don't care if they are thanked, but I wrote this book with their particular cat assistance, and the lions and tigers are based on them.

Finally, most important, gratitude and adoration to Robert Schenkkan, my favorite person in the universe, my beloved, my dearest one. You read this book at least seven times, lent me your bookshelves, picked me up when I was yowling, fed me dinner, poured me bourbon, kissed me, cheered me on, discussed and discussed, gave me your whole stunning heart, and every day made me so proud to be yours. People ask me all the time how I manage to be married to another writer, and the answer is that the other writer is you. You are so brilliant, so giving, and so the perfect man for me. This book, with all its magic, monsters, treasures, and eternal love affairs, is dedicated to you for a damn good reason, just as I am. *Te teneo.*

MARIA DAHVANA HEADLEY is a MacDowell Colony Fellow whose writing has appeared in *The New York Times*, *Elle*, *The Washington Post*, and other publications. She is the author of the memoir *The Year of Yes* (2007), which has been translated into nine languages. She lives in Seattle. Learn more at www.mariadahvanaheadley.com or www.cleopatraqueenofkings.com.